# 59 Memory Lane

Celia Anderson lives with her husband and one handsome but antisocial cat in land-locked Derbyshire, but visits her daughters in Brighton as often as possible for a seaside fix. She now writes full-time, having been a teacher and assistant head in her previous life. Other jobs have included packing curtain fittings with mental health patients, sticking ISBN codes on books in a library and finding reasonably safe activities for adolescent boys with severe behaviour problems. Her finest hour was getting a post as a cycling proficiency tutor without mentioning that she couldn't ride a bike. Celia loves cake, wine, the Eurostar and reading, preferably all at the same time. Her other hobbies all involve food or walking it off.

An enthusiastic member of the Romantic Novelists' Association, Celia currently organises the judging for the Romantic Novel of the Year Awards. She spends far too much time on Facebook and Instagram and dreams of one day being strong-minded enough to leave the house without her iPhone.

🐦 @CeliaAnderson1
📘 www.facebook.com/CeliaJAndersonAuthor
📷 www.instagram.com/cejanderson

# 59 Memory Lane

## CELIA ANDERSON

HarperCollins*Publishers*

HarperCollins*Publishers*
The News Building,
1 London Bridge Street,
London SE1 9GF

A Paperback Original 2019
3

www.harpercollins.co.uk

A catalogue record for this book
is available from the British Library

ISBN: 9780008305413

This novel is entirely a work of fiction.
The names, characters and incidents portrayed in it are
the work of the author's imagination. Any resemblance to
actual persons, living or dead, events or localities is
entirely coincidental.

Set in Birka by Palimpsest Book Production Ltd, Falkirk, Stirlingshire

Printed and bound in Great Britain by
CPI Group (UK) Ltd, Croydon CR0 4YY

**MIX**
Paper from
responsible sources
FSC® C007454

This book is produced from independently certified FSC™ paper
to ensure responsible forest management.

For more information visit: www.harpercollins.co.uk/green

For Ray, my memory maker

O thrilling sweet, my joy, when life was free
And all the paths led on from hawthorn-time
Across the carolling meadows into June.

'Memory' – Siegfried Sassoon

Love is knowing that even when you are alone, you will never be lonely again. And great happiness of life is the conviction that we are loved. Loved for ourselves. And even loved in spite of ourselves.

*Les Misérables* – Victor Hugo

# Chapter One

May Rosevere sits on the sun-warmed decking, watching the tide creep in. She does this most days if it's convenient, but the trouble with tide times is that they will keep on changing. If it's cold, May wraps herself in an ancient baby shawl to sit in her swing seat. The memories have faded from the wool, and the baby who wore it must be thirty by now, but it still makes her feel cosseted. She doesn't need the shawl today. Summer is in the air and the garden around her granite cottage is looking green and lush.

A man with a neat grey beard wanders along the beach. Tristram, thinks May, waving her handkerchief. He doesn't see her – his hat is pulled down over his ears and he's too busy throwing a bright red ball into the sea to look up towards May's place. The man's black Labrador looks at him in disgust and ignores the ball. His smaller, biscuit-coloured dog isn't any more enthusiastic, too busy digging in the sand. The sound of Tristram's booming laugh carries through the still air and he plods on towards the stone jetty that marks the western edge of Pengelly Cove. May reaches for the diary she keeps by her side, turns to the page for 1 June and makes a note. That ball will probably be washed up later. It must have a whole lot of good memories buried inside it. Then reality hits, as it does several times a day. Her beach-combing days are over. Even if she happens to see it float in, she can't get to it.

It's only a couple of hundred yards from May's back porch to the tideline, but the beach might as well be on the moon. Being a hundred and ten years old tends to limit your orbit. May's shoulders slump. This is a crisis. For weeks she's been feeling less and less lively, and she knows the reason why. Her memory supplies have completely dried up.

May looks down at the elderly cat curled up by her feet. 'Well, Fossil, I'm just going to have to come up with a plan,' she tells him.

The cat blinks its yellow eyes and says nothing. May doesn't really expect a reply. Although she has certain abilities, talking to animals isn't one of them.

'I need a new source of memories,' she continues. Fossil yawns, and sticks out the tip of his tongue. 'There's no need to be rude,' May says. 'This is serious. If I don't find a way to . . . acquire more of my treasures, I'm stuffed, as Andy would say.'

Andy is May's neighbour. His terraced house abuts her new home. May's solid granite single-storey cottage at 59 Memory Lane was built to last. It was a tea shop up until last year and in its time has been extended to have five rooms plus a bathroom and a long conservatory with a stunning view of the bay. It's too big for May really, but it's private, and suits her well. There are any number of basking places for the days when it's warm enough to sun-worship, a lawn around the house where the wooden benches and tables used to stand, and even a small car park that goes right up to the sea wall.

May rents the parking spaces out to a few selected villagers. She doesn't need the money – the sale of her house up on The Level has left her very comfortably off – but she likes the comings and goings and the friendly chit-chat when people drop off their cars at the end of the day. Loneliness has rather taken her by surprise since she moved, and the car park activity is a welcome distraction. Living alone has its benefits but she sometimes tires of talking to the cat. When she lived in the heart of the village, May knew everything that was going on, and kept a close eye on her neighbours' affairs by dint of popping in and out of their houses on a variety of pretexts and by getting involved in the social life of the local Methodist Church. You don't have to believe in God to make salmon sandwiches and dispense weak tea.

May's new home has weathered well, and looks as though it's been there for ever, the newer sections blending in seamlessly, with ivy and wisteria covering the joins and close-growing shrubs hugging the walls. There is yellow lichen on the roof tiles and the door is painted almost the same colour. She has huge earthenware pots of succulents either side of the front step that take no looking after, and a quirky blue and yellow ceramic sign that spells out the name of the cottage in swirly letters – Shangri-La.

Andy gardens for May whenever he has time, and does

a few hours' routine office work for a local garden centre when his landscaping business allows or the weather is awful. His six-year-old daughter, Tamsin, lives next door with him. May stirs, and groans slightly as she hears the pounding of small footsteps approaching on the wooden floor of the deck.

'Hello, May,' says Tamsin in a loud stage whisper. 'Have you finished your nap?'

'I wasn't asleep.' May lets her glasses slide to the end of her nose so that she can peer at the child. She looks angelic. Dark curls frame a round, rosy-cheeked face and her eyes are huge and brown with long lashes. Anyone might think butter wouldn't melt in her mouth, as May's mum used to say. They'd be wrong.

Tamsin reaches the garden chair and slips her arm through May's, head butting her shoulder. 'I've done with school,' she says.

'For today,' answers May, trying to look stern.

'For ever and ever. It sucks,' says Tamsin.

'That's not a very nice thing for a little girl to say.'

'What, that school sucks, you mean? Summer says it.'

She sits down on the boards and leans against May's legs. The pressure is comforting at first, but is soon painful. May grits her dentures. 'Summer says quite a lot of things that you shouldn't copy, it seems to me. Anyway, you can't just stop going to school, Tam. You've only done a year so far. It goes on for a lot longer than that, as a rule.'

'Dad can't make me go,' says the little girl, sticking out

her bottom lip. Tamsin's eyes are even darker than Andy's, and she's inherited the shaggy curls from him too. May knows there's a regular morning battle to get a ponytail in place. She's heard the screams. Tamsin's already ditched her scrunchy for the day and her blue cardigan with the crest has disappeared as well, probably under a bush somewhere.

'Why don't you like school? Has something happened today? You were fine yesterday when you came round.' May often keeps an eye on Tamsin until Andy comes home, if he's not expecting to be long. She's never been keen on children but this one is different. This one has a mind of her own.

'It's just boys,' says Tamsin. 'Why do we have to have boys?'

'Well . . .'

'They're stinky, and they push in front of us when we line up.'

'Hmm. But some girls push too, and boys often grow up to be grand men like your dad and Tristram, don't they?'

'S'pose so.'

The cat stands up, stretches, and makes his way over to Tamsin. His black fur is slightly dusty due to his habit of rolling in the flowerbeds. Tamsin looks at him doubtfully.

'Dad said I mustn't touch Fossil any more,' she says.

'Did he? When was that?'

'Yesterday. I kept sneezing, and he said it was either hay fever or cats. Like my mum used to get, he said. But

I love Fossil. He doesn't even smell that bad today, does he? Not like boys do.'

May thinks Tamsin might be going to cry. Tears are May's least favourite thing. An idea strikes her as she sees a red dot appear on the shoreline. 'Would you do a little job for me, my bird?' she says, in what she hopes is a winning tone.

Tamsin frowns even harder. 'What do I get?'

'Get? You don't *get* anything. Young people are supposed to help older ones. Don't they teach you anything at school?'

Tamsin shrugs.

'Would you just pop down to the beach and pick up that ball over there?'

'But it'll be all wet and slimy. Why do you want a ball, May? You haven't got a dog and Fossil doesn't play with stuff any more.'

'Well . . . I . . .' May tries to think of a plausible answer but her mind has gone blank. There's no easy way to say that the reason she's managed to live to a hundred and ten is that she has been appropriating her neighbours' memories for years. She's always told herself it's a form of borrowing, but that's not true, because once she's got them, she's never quite worked out how to give them back.

Now that she's living at the bottom of Memory Lane and can't visit people in the village any more, May has no way of collecting their treasured objects so that she can do what she terms her *thought harvesting*. But she couldn't stay in that rambling old family house once her legs started to get creaky. She was lucky to be able to keep it going for so long. Leaving Seagulls was hard, but this cottage is so much easier to live in, apart from the sad lack of new memory sources. The vibrations from her collecting missions have fed her mentally for a long time now, but she's bled them all dry.

Tamsin prods May gently, still waiting for an answer. She's right, in a way. A soggy toy won't do much good. But at least it'll have something inside it – some scrap of love and dog-type warmth buried in its depths. And May is desperate.

'Just for me, poppet, please?' she says, putting her head on one side and smiling in what she hopes is a sweet old lady way.

Tamsin shrugs again then potters off down the path, over the last of the cobblestones and onto the shingle at the top of the beach. When she reaches the sand, she slips off her shoes and socks and begins to twirl and bounce towards the lapping waves. Her solid little body is transformed when she dances, making her almost fairy-like. May watches. The child knows the beach completely and she wouldn't stray far from sight anyway. There's no need to worry, even if May was the worrying kind. She never has been until now. But unless she can find a new bank of memories, May won't reach the fabulous age of one hundred and eleven. It's been her dream to reach that milestone ever since childhood. All those lovely ones in a row, like a strong gate: 111. Her father, gazing at a particularly wonderful sunset over the bay, once exclaimed, 'If I live until I'm a hundred and eleven I'll never see anything as splendid as that sight.' Why that number? May thought, but the idea stuck, like a lucky charm.

After a few minutes, Tamsin hops back into the garden and drops the ball on May's knee.

'It's yucky,' she says, pulling a face. 'Told you it would be. Have you got any cake?'

May gestures towards the open kitchen door, and as Tamsin skips away (does that child ever walk anywhere?) she conquers her revulsion and clutches the ball tightly to her chest. But even squeezing it hard with both hands and her eyes tight shut doesn't release more than a tiny buzz of memory, and that seems to be mainly a dog's woolly thoughts about his dinner.

It's no good. I'm done for, thinks May, throwing the ball as hard as she can towards the shrubbery.

'May, why did you go and do that? I fetched it specially.' Tamsin appears with a large plate containing four slabs of angel cake and a bag of Maltesers.

'You were right, dear. It *was* very slimy,' says May, sadly.

Tamsin looks up as she hears the click of the latch on the front gate next door. 'Dad's home,' she says. 'I'll go and get him to make us a nice hot drink, shall I?'

She's back in five minutes or so, followed by a long, lean man with a serious expression. May wishes he'd smile more, but she supposes he's had a lot to make him melancholy since his wife died. Andy is an out-in-all-weathers kind of person, pure Cornish from head to toe. Tanned and healthy-looking, he's wearing faded denim shorts, heavy boots and a checked shirt with the sleeves rolled up – his usual gardener's uniform. He's very grubby. May looks at his well-muscled legs and forearms approvingly. Even at one hundred and ten she can still appreciate a vision like this.

Andy puts a mug down next to May and hands Tamsin a glass of warm blackcurrant juice.

'Oh, bless you, love. Aren't you having one with us?'

'No time. Tam needs to get ready for a birthday party. It starts in half an hour but she looks as if she needs a good wash first.'

Tamsin moans to herself and slurps her drink, spilling some of it down her front, then lies down again next to May, adding some soil to the stains on her school skirt.

'Where have you been today?' May asks. 'You look as if you've been working hard.'

'Just across the road at number sixty, trying to get Julia's place straight,' he says. 'It's gone wild since Don died.'

'It was bound to, really. Julia doesn't like gardening, does she? Probably hasn't got the right clothes,' May sniffs. She has no time for Julia Lovell, even though she's known her for many years and often shared the church kitchen with her when they were drafted in to cater for village events. Keeps herself to herself, that one, May thinks. Pretty much everybody knows what it's like to lose somebody but we don't all turn reclusive, do we? Drama queen. And why does she always have to be so dressed up? Her hair can't be natural. There's not a single grey hair amongst all that black. And straight as a die. Never bothers with curlers. Well, I suppose there's not enough of it to curl.

'Maybe not. I used to go round every few weeks and

give Don a hand when he got past doing the rough digging and so on,' says Andy, 'but she hasn't felt like bothering with it lately.'

'No. She wouldn't.'

'What have you got against the poor woman? She always asks after you.'

'Oh, you don't want to hear me harping on about old grudges. Water under the bridge. I just wish she wouldn't pretend to like me, that's all.'

'I don't think Julia's got anything against you, May.'

'Ha! Why does she give me those frosty looks then?'

'You're imagining it.'

'Whatever,' says May. She's learned that one from Tamsin and it comes in handy.

Andy laughs. 'Anyway, you'll never guess what Julia's found today.'

May looks at her neighbour without much interest and raises her eyebrows. He carries on. 'When she was clearing out Don's den . . .'

'His old shed, you mean?'

'Well, yes, OK – his shed . . . she found a massive sack of letters.'

Tamsin rolls over onto her back and stares at her dad. 'Why did the man over the road have a sack of lettuce?' she mumbles, through the last of the cake.

'Don't talk with your mouth full, sweetheart,' Andy says, 'and I said *letters*.'

'Oh.' Tamsin doesn't much care for things you have to read so she crawls under a nearby bush to make a hide-out, but May is all ears.

'Letters to whom?' she says. No need to let the grammar slip.

'Not *to* whom, more like *from* whom. He hoarded every single thing his family in the Midlands ever wrote to the two of them. They're incredible. Julia showed me a few.'

May digests this information in silence. Her heart is fluttering now. She hopes she isn't going to have some sort of seizure and pop her clogs just when hope is at hand.

'May? What's the matter? You look a bit wobbly today,' Andy says.

May stares out to sea, as the tide turns and the gulls wheel and cry. A sackful of memories, there for the taking. But however is she going to get her hands on them?

# Chapter Two

*. . . so the opal ring's definitely missing. I don't know what to do, Don. Mother's blaming each of us in turn and we've turned the house upside down looking for it. Nothing.*

Putting down the letter in her hand for a moment, Julia gazes out of the window, past the trailing clematis that climbs over the remains of an oak tree, and the wisteria taking over the shed roof, trailing its feathery lilac fronds so low every summer that Don had to stoop under it every time he retreated there.

What possessed Don to keep all these letters, and what in heaven's name is she meant to do with them now he's gone? If she hadn't finally made herself go into his den she'd have still been in blissful ignorance of the contents of the wooden chest.

She remembers the day he rediscovered the disgusting old chest. She was mystified as to why anyone would want to keep such a thing.

'You do know that piece of junk's riddled with woodworm?' she said, as he dragged it across the yard from the garage. 'I was going to put it out ready for Andy to take to the tip, or to sling on his next bonfire.'

'Not infested any more, love,' Don said, straightening up and rubbing his back. 'Didn't you see me out here yesterday with that can of stuff I found in the cupboard under the stairs? I've zapped the little devils. Those worms are history!' He laughed joyfully and patted the oak chest as if it were a faithful dog.

'But what are you going to do with it?' Julia asked. 'It smells disgusting.' She wrinkled her nose at the eye-watering chemical fumes still coming from the wood.

'It'll cancel out the stink of my pipe tobacco then. I'm having a sort out in the den. The drawers in my desk are stuffed. I can't even open them properly. This'll be perfect to store everything in.'

'Wouldn't it be better to throw something away?' Julia knew she was wasting her breath as she said this. Don didn't believe in getting rid of anything unless he had absolutely no choice.

Julia's eyes prickle again as she conjures up the smile he gave her as he struggled on towards the shed with his prize. The oak chest left deep scuff marks on the path. She can still see them if she looks closely. As he heaved it through the door, he cheered and gave her a victory salute.

If only she'd taken a photograph of that moment. Such a charmer, was that man, but somehow so innocent with it. Their granddaughter, Emily, has the same wide blue eyes and twinkly smile.

With a pang, Julia wishes Emily were here, and not working abroad. New York is much too far away. These thoughts of Don are unbearably sad to cope with on her own. How is she going to get through the rest of her days without him?

Sighing, Julia forces herself to pick up the letter again. Don kept every bit of correspondence they ever received, it seems, and never bothered to sort them into any kind of order. This one is from the younger of his two sisters, Elsie. Like most of the family, Elsie adored the Cornish village where Don and Julia made their home, and visited it regularly. Ever since Julia married Don back in the spring of 1959, when he was fresh from the air force and so handsome he could have had his pick of any girl around, her summers were spoken for. She spent them changing beds, washing sheets, planning menus and thinking up suggestions for trips so the guests might take themselves off to give her a few hours of the solitude that she craved.

She didn't mind the visitors coming. Well, not much. Don was so hospitable she'd have felt mean to say she needed a break. Anyway, in those days they had their old caravan down the coast to escape to when the season was over. And boy, they certainly enjoyed being alone again. Julia blushes at the memories. She reads on, rubbing her tired eyes as Elsie's voice speaks to her down the years.

Anyway, other than the crisis with the ring, my most important news is that I've managed to change my holiday week, and so has Kathryn. Will can't come with us this time but he sends his love. He's been a bit peaky lately, moping around like a dog that's lost its bone. I wish he'd get himself a girlfriend. Mother thinks he's just waiting for the right one to come along.

Never in a month of Sundays, thinks Julia. Don's younger brother, Will, wasn't remotely interested in finding a girl, and now he's a retired priest in the wilds of County Kerry. The baby of the family, Will has an ethereal charm, but a large part of his charisma is his fun-loving impulsiveness. Moping around sounds unlike him, although he sometimes was annoyingly moody. Julia casts her mind back. The ancient ink, almost invisible in places, brings that summer vividly to mind.

Elsie and Kathryn tottered off the train as dawn broke, crumpled and sticky but wildly excited at the thought of their week in Cornwall. Julia, heavily pregnant with Felix, plastered on her best welcoming smile. Oh God, here we go again, she thought. Sometimes she felt like the owner of a rather cramped B&B instead of a woman with a new and very large extended family who all loved the seaside. The big double bed had only just been changed after her mother- and father-in-law's visit. It was good that Don's sisters never minded sharing a bed – it meant less laundry, and they'd only be in and out of each other's rooms half the night if not. They never seemed to stop talking, those two. The whole family was the same. What did they find to say? Julia wonders. Did they never just simply run out of words?

She rereads the last line. What was it that was bothering Will that time? Julia vaguely remembers the youngest of the family being paler than usual on his next visit, but nothing was ever said. To be fair, Julia's thoughts were preoccupied with her own exhaustion and how she was going to cope with a newborn when she'd never even changed a nappy before. Will was almost fragile in looks – a beautiful blond boy, with high cheekbones and such narrow hips that he always had to wear braces to stop his trousers ending up around his ankles. Kathryn and Elsie were much tougher cookies.

She drops the letter and picks up another one. Elsie again, rattling on from earlier the same year, that January so long ago. Julia just began to suspect she was having a baby around then. She was twenty-six by that time, but so ridiculously naïve that she had to ask her neighbour to reassure her that the signs she noticed weren't the beginnings of some horrible disease. She longed for her mother, or some other homely body to run to, but her parents had decided to settle in India after her father's retirement from the army. Don had just started his new job, and they scraped together enough cash for the deposit on 60 Memory Lane. It was a shabby place – borderline derelict in parts – but they fell in love with it. The pregnancy wasn't expected. Neither of them had much idea about family planning.

Elsie's letter is starting to put together a picture in Julia's mind. She reads on.

Well, you'll be pleased to hear that Mother has finally come around to your way of thinking, and her precious opal engagement ring is going to be passed to Julia. I expect you're right and I hope it brings her luck, as it has for Mother and Grandma, or so they insist. I'd have loved to have it, of course I would, and so would Kathryn, but with two sisters, I guess there had to be a fair way. Even Will has had his eye on it but I don't know who he's planning to give it to! Still no girl on the scene.

Reading about that ring has stirred up feelings she would rather have left buried. Don, usually the least cynical of men, was very suspicious about its disappearance, just when it was about to be delivered to him for his new wife.

Ruffled, Julia shakes herself and flexes stiff shoulders. She's been sitting still too long. It's time for a cup of tea and maybe a piece of the fruitcake she's made from her mother's favourite recipe. She doesn't bake much nowadays because she has to go by instinct. She's had to ever since the old cookery book, handwritten and full of the neat, sloping writing Julia loved, disappeared a couple of years ago. She's searched high and low but it's never turned up. Good job she's still got her marbles at eighty-five, and can remember a handful of the best recipes, although the sticky lemon cake has never turned out quite the same without the book to guide her.

The door knocker clatters, followed almost immediately by the bell ringing. Julia mutters under her breath, words her mother definitely wouldn't have approved of. She gets to her feet and makes her way to the front door, still grumbling. It's no good pretending she isn't at home.

The trademark knock and ring tells her that the woman out there won't give up easily.

'Hello, Julia,' says Ida, as Julia opens the door. 'I hope I'm not interrupting your tea?'

Julia forces her mouth into something resembling a smile. Ida Carnell, standing sturdily on the step, has an in-built radar for the moment when the kettle is going to be switched on and the cake tin's about to appear.

'No, of course not, Ida,' she says. 'Come in and join me for a cuppa.'

'Oh, well, so long as I'm not being a bother.'

Ida follows Julia to the kitchen, talking all the way. Really, thinks Julia wearily, this woman is almost as bad as Elsie and Kathryn in their heyday. Granted, Ida's a pillar of the local Methodist Church and has got a heart of . . . well, if not pure gold, something fairly close, but does she ever shut up?

'. . . and so I didn't think you'd mind me calling on you. It's very important. I've got a favour to ask. It's about my new plan.'

Oh, no. The last time Ida had a plan, Julia had been roped into making scones for a hundred and fifty people. Not another fund-raising tea . . . oh, please not? But Ida is still talking.

'Have you heard of the Adopt-a-Granny scheme? A lot of local churches are trialling it, since we had a memo from Age UK reminding us how many old people are lonely and housebound.'

A cold feeling creeps up Julia's spine. She's got a hunch she won't like this, whatever it is.

'No? I thought you might have seen my article in the parish magazine? Anyway, I've made a list.' Ida gets out a large ring-bound notepad and a pen. 'Can I put you down for May?'

'Why? What happened in May? It's June already; I think last month passed me by.'

'No, I didn't mean that. Your neighbour, May. At number fifty-nine? Shangri-La? I'm really worried about her.'

'You want me to adopt *May*? As my granny?'

Ida laughs. 'Not exactly. She's only about twenty years older than you, isn't she?'

'Twenty-five, actually,' snaps Julia. This is ridiculous. Is the woman insane? Why would Julia need a granny? And if she did, how could May ever be a likely candidate for the job?

'Well, age is only a number, as they say, and I know Andy's been worried that May can't get out of the house now. Julia, the thing that really bothered me – well, it doesn't sound much when you say it out loud, I suppose – it's just that when I came down to fetch my car yesterday, she was just staring out to sea.'

'Ida, lots of people like looking at the sea. I do myself. It's very relaxing watching the waves. That doesn't mean she needs adopting.'

Ida frowns. 'I knew it was going to sound silly. I don't use my car all that often but the other day when I called to get it to go to Truro she was doing exactly the same thing. Sitting on the decking just . . . staring . . . with such a sad look on her face.'

'I still don't think—'

'And then as soon as she saw me both times, she started to chat about the weather, as if she'd been dying for somebody to talk to. May's never been one for small talk. You know that as well as I do.'

'But . . .'

Ida holds up a hand. 'Yes, yes, I know you two have got history, as they say. An even better reason for you to get together over a nice cup of tea and let bygones be bygones.'

'You think so?'

'I do wish you wouldn't purse your lips like that, Julia. You remind me of my mother, and she could be quite terrifying at times. It's for a good cause. The scheme's going well so far.'

'Is it really?'

'Oh, yes. You'd be surprised how many people in the village need a bit of company, but will they ask? No, they won't. Too proud, or something . . . So, the story so far is that Vera from the shop's adopted that nice old lady from Tamerisk Avenue. You know – Marigold – the one with the mobility scooter and the smelly Pekinese that rides in the basket?'

'But Marigold's got six children and any number of grandchildren.'

'And when was the last time you saw any of them in the village? They only turn up when they want to cadge money off her. She barely sees a soul from one week to the next.'

'I don't think—'

'And George and Cliff have really come up trumps.

They've taken two for me. Joyce Chippendale, the retired teacher who's registered blind, and the old boy from the last fisherman's cottage on the harbour?'

'Old boy? You surely don't mean Tom King? He's younger than *me*. He must only be in his late seventies.'

'Well, yes, but he doesn't get out much since he retired. Being a psychiatrist all those years took all his time up so he hasn't really got any hobbies, *and* he looks as if he could do with a square meal. George is going to bring them both over for lunch or dinner at their restaurant a couple of times a week.'

'How kind.' Julia shivers. She knows this cannot end well.

'I want to get other villages involved if this takes off. It's a huge problem, Julia.'

'What is?'

'Loneliness, dear. But listen to me being tactless; I don't need to tell *you* that, do I?'

Julia gives Ida one of her special looks, the kind she used to use to quell unruly Sunday school children years ago. 'And what's that supposed to mean?'

'Well, with you losing Don, and everything. You must be lonely nowadays . . . with your family so far away . . .' Ida's voice trails off as she finally senses Julia's icy disapproval.

'Missing somebody isn't the same thing as being lonely, Ida,' says Julia, making a valiant attempt not to punch the interfering old busybody. Violence isn't her thing, but she's never felt more like doing somebody a damage. The cheek of the woman! Ida's only about sixty and she's still got a perfectly healthy husband, even if he is a bit dull. Who is Ida to make judgements about Julia's needs?

Ida falls silent for a moment and then rallies. 'Yes, you're probably right. No offence meant, and none taken, I hope?'

'Perish the thought.'

'Oh, good. I'm going to ask Tristram to join the scheme next. If George and Cliff are doing it, he'll not be able to resist. The two main fish cateries round here – Cockleshell Bay and Tris's Shellfish Shack – both giving away meals for charity? It's a great story. I'll get the local paper onto it as soon as it's really up and running. But first I'm going to call a meeting for us all.'

Julia waits, holding her breath. Sure enough, here comes the blow.

'So, anyway, I thought Andy could bring May over tomorrow? About tea time?'

The words 'Resistance is useless' spring to mind. Whatever Julia says, Ida will steamroller over her. She squares her shoulders. No, she mustn't be browbeaten. Ida can't make her invite May over to visit, can she? It's Julia's house and she just won't allow it.

'I can't have visitors at the moment,' she says. 'It's completely out of the question. I'm sorry, but you'll have to find someone else.'

Ida leans forward and looks into Julia's eyes earnestly. Her chins are quivering with emotion. 'But, Julia, don't you think it's our duty to do what we can for one another?'

'Well, yes, but—'

'That's settled then. I'll go and see May as soon as I

leave here and let her know. She'll be thrilled to bits, I'm sure. Tomorrow it is!'

Julia opens her mouth to argue again and then decides it's pointless.

'Are you rushing off to see May immediately?' she asks.

'Not when you've gone to the trouble of putting the kettle on for me. And isn't that your famous fruitcake I see there? May will enjoy a slice of that tomorrow, too.'

'If she comes.'

'But why wouldn't she? I'm sure May will be delighted to get out of the house and have a lovely chat with you.'

Julia says nothing. There are one or two excellent reasons why May might avoid visiting 60 Memory Lane, but she's not about to share them with Ida.

# Chapter Three

Across the road half an hour later, May glares at Ida as her visitor takes the last chocolate biscuit from the plate that Tamsin fetched from the larder. Andy has taken his daughter home now – he escaped as soon as he made the two ladies a fresh pot of tea.

'I really shouldn't,' says Ida, munching happily, 'because I've just started going to that slimming group in the village hall and it was all going so well until I had to eat some of your lovely neighbour's fruitcake.'

'Lovely neighbour? Which one's that then?'

'Now, now. You know very well who I mean. Julia sends her love.'

'Really?' May frowns. It doesn't sound likely. Sending love to May wouldn't be on that one's priority list. After the incident with the missing soup spoons, they've never been more than civil. The very cheek of the woman, insinuating that May had pinched a whole bunch of tatty cutlery. She'd had enough trouble pocketing the sugar tongs. Of course, the real damage was done while Charles was still alive. Julia never liked May's husband. Not many people did, come to think of it.

Ida's eyes are shining with goodwill. She's always had

this annoying habit of thinking everyone should be fond of each other just because they live in the same village, thinks May. Most of them do get on, but May prefers to choose her friends for herself.

'Yes, of course she sent her love – why wouldn't she? Julia speaks very highly of you.'

'She does?'

'Not only that, but she's asked me to see if you'd like to pop over there for a visit tomorrow.'

'Are you pulling my leg, Ida? Why would Julia suddenly want me to go and see her? We haven't spoken a word to each other since Don's funeral, and that was only in passing. Anyway, I don't get out of the house on my own these days. I'd end up flat on my face on the cobblestones.'

Ida smiles. There's something of the shark about her when she's got an idea in her head. 'That won't be a problem. I'm sure Andy will take you across the road when he finishes work.'

'But—'

'Now, there's no need to worry. He's working in my own garden tomorrow, as luck would have it, so I can make sure he gets home in good time. Julia's expecting you at half-past five. And if you're lucky, she might show you some of her treasure trove. I've never seen so many old letters in my life.'

May is silent. Of course! Why hadn't she thought of this before? She should have snapped Ida's hand off straight away. Those letters. All the memories just waiting for her. Can it be that her prayers have been answered? She's never been sure about God, but it doesn't hurt to hedge your bets, and she always likes to send up a few requests while she's listening to the Sunday morning hymns on the radio.

Some of the words to the hymns are quite poetic, and she sings along with gusto. Her favourite is the wedding one. She likes the lines:

Grant them the joy which brightens earthly sorrow,
Grant them the peace which calms all earthly strife.

It paints such a lovely picture of marriage. Hers wasn't at all like that, especially after May found Charles in bed in the middle of the morning with the baker's delivery boy, if you could call a strapping nineteen-year-old a boy, but there's no need to be cynical about the institution in general.

She rustles up a big smile for Ida. 'Well, it sounds as if you've got it all sewn up,' she says. 'But I still can't see why Julia would choose to invite me over? In truth, Andy told me he was anxious because she wasn't seeing *anyone* at the moment. She's turned into a bit of a hermit.'

'I know, and it's been a worry to us all. She hasn't been to the morning service for months. She's taken Don's death very hard. They were true soul mates, weren't they?'

May presses her lips together. She's always hated that expression. As if souls could talk. If that was the case, there'd be a lot fewer arguments and misunderstandings in the world. Her own husband wasn't so much of a soul mate as a pain in the backside, especially in the later days, when he had dark suspicions about his health issues. If only he'd had the sense to see the doctor. After Charles died she began to appreciate his finer points again, but while he was with her the temptation to smother him was sometimes almost irresistible, the awkward sod. Pedantic, waspish and far too fond of flower arranging.

Ida's peering around the room now. Nosy old bat. 'You've got some lovely ornaments and pictures,' she says. 'It's hard to imagine how anything can be around so long and yet still be so perfect.'

'Like me,' says May, with a cackle.

Ida smiles. 'You're absolutely right. Everyone always says how young you look, May. How do you do it? What's your secret? Do you use some sort of fancy face cream?'

'You must be joking,' says May. 'I wouldn't spend good money on that muck. No, my looks are down to a small daily dose of port and brandy, plenty of heathy food and clean living, that's all.'

May has trotted this mantra out so often that she might almost believe it if she didn't know the truth. When she first realised that it was possible to pick up vibrations from certain objects, or whatever she liked to call the effect that she got, May was young enough to think that all children got a sparkly feeling of wellbeing when they touched things that had an interesting past. It took quite a while to match her magical moments to the treasures she sometimes managed to collect by trawling the local jumble sales and junk shops with her mother.

Pocket money didn't go far when you were an avid collector, but her father seemed to understand her needs better than her mother, and if he took her out shopping he would indulge her by slipping a bit of extra cash into her pocket at vital moments. And when May realised how many people in the village had memories hidden away in their possessions, the harvesting really began to move into gear. A special, secret sort of magic, that's what it is, and it needs to stay that way.

She remembers the first time she was overcome by the feeling that she must have something precious that didn't belong to her, even though, at ten years old, she knew very well it was wrong. May's mother took her to their nearest neighbour's house for tea, and while the two ladies were busy in the kitchen May spied a tiny enamelled box with a tightly fitting lid. She picked it up and cradled it in the palm of her hand. Patterned with purple violets, the box seemed to hum to itself, as if it had secrets that only May could hear.

May prised off the lid with a fingernail, all the while listening in case the grown-ups came back. Inside was a curl of hair, soft and blond. May held her breath and put her finger into the middle of the hair. The warmth and energy that flowed from it was so dramatic that she withdrew her hand with a gasp. After a moment, she tried again, preparing herself this time. Bliss. Glancing over her shoulder, May slid the curl into her pocket, then closed the lid and returned the box just as her mother reappeared carrying a plate of fairy cakes.

Since that day, there have been many other chances to find what she needs, but May has had to be careful. Now and again she's come very close to being caught.

Unaware of the unsettling thoughts racing through

May's mind, Ida checks her watch and gets to her feet, accidentally treading on Fossil, who hisses his disapproval and runs for the cat flap. 'Whoops! Sorry, cat. So that's settled then. Andy can fetch you as soon as he's finished at mine. I'm very excited about this new scheme, May. It's going to benefit so many people. Poor Julia is so lost nowadays, and you'll get a lot out of it, too.'

'Oh, yes, I do hope so,' says May.

A tiny bubble of excitement shivers inside her. She'd better take her largest handbag when she goes across the road tomorrow.

# Chapter Four

Andy calls for May the next afternoon on the dot of half-past five. She is wearing her best dress, which is cornflower-blue, and a pair of low-heeled court shoes in honour of the occasion. She's not about to let Julia think she's gone to seed while she's been stuck in the house. The dress is sprigged with tiny buttercups and daisies. It makes May think of the rolling meadow behind her old home up the hill. She sighs. Oh, well, no point in looking over her shoulder – a beach on your doorstep is worth a dozen grassy fields and woods, after all. You couldn't see the sea properly from the big house even though it was high up on The Level because the trees in between blocked the view.

Andy gives an impressive wolf whistle when he sees her. 'Blimey, May. You still scrub up well. You don't look a day over seventy.'

She bats him with her handbag and turns to the hall mirror to tidy her already immaculate hair. She's always been glad that when the rich auburn of her hair eventually began to fade, it turned a beautiful snowy white. May misses being a foxy redhead sometimes, but her hairdresser thinks she's very glamorous and calls every

Monday to wash and set May's curls in the usual bouffant waves. No blow-drying for May – she sticks to her faithful sponge rollers. A hefty squirt of hairspray and she's ready for the week. The style hasn't changed for years – why should it?

'Pass me my lipstick, please, Andy. It's on the side there. And the perfume. You can't go wrong with Je Reviens, I always say. Thank you. Don't want to let the side down, do I?'

He laughs, and offers May his arm as they head out of the door and down the uneven steps. She holds on tightly to Andy as they go over the cobbles, wobbling on the unfamiliar heels, and breathes a sigh of relief when they're safely on the other side of the narrow lane. The breeze is fresher today, and May can see several small boats bobbing around near the harbour over to the right of the beach. There's a strong smell of salt and seaweed in the air, and her heart lifts. It's good to be outside and going somewhere for a change. The garden's all well and good, but May misses being in the thick of things.

'Come on then, May,' says Andy. 'We'd better not keep Julia waiting any longer. I usually go around the back and let myself in, but we'll do it the proper way today as this is a special occasion.'

May rolls her eyes but makes no comment. Julia opens the door almost before they've rung the bell.

'Hello, May. It's good to see you,' she says, but her smile doesn't reach her eyes, and May isn't fooled.

Andy helps May inside and Julia pushes a high-backed chair forward so that May can lower herself to a sitting position using the chair's arms to support her. As May glances up, cursing herself for this new sign of weakness, she sees a look of pity on Julia's carefully made-up face. May seethes inside but puts on her best party expression. There's a lot to play for here.

Julia's wearing an elegant grey shift dress, beautifully cut but rather grim, with a single string of pearls to finish the look. Well, her neighbour's gone to the trouble of smartening herself up as usual, thinks May, but her blood boils at the realisation that Julia is feeling sorry for her. She's filled with an even stronger resolve to get hold of at least one of Julia's letters today. If she can soak up even a few memories, she'll begin to feel better again. It's been too long.

'I'll get going then, girls,' says Andy. 'Tamsin's at Rainbows up at the church hall and I need to pick her up soon and get her home for tea. See you later.'

'Bye, love,' says May, taking the opportunity to look round the room as her neighbour sees him out. There are a few heaps of letters on the table. She must have interrupted Julia in her sorting. Good.

'So, a cup of tea, May? I've made some scones for us,' says Julia, coming back in. It's a spacious, light room, with a dining table at one end and French windows opening onto a view of the other end of the cove. May can't see this part of the world from her windows, and it's a refreshing change to look out towards Tristram's long, low bungalow and restaurant on the headland. It's a while since she's had the chance to eat at The Shellfish Shack.

Tristram's an old friend and an attentive host, and the food there is sublime. May wonders how much a return trip in a taxi would be. It doesn't seem long since she was able to walk there from her old home. But as soon as she gets hold of some new memories, her energy will come flooding back. There's no time to lose. The alternative doesn't bear thinking about.

Julia pushes the letters out of the way to make room on the table for their afternoon tea before she bustles off to the kitchen. 'Jam and cream on your scone, May?' she calls.

'Yes, please. Jam first, obviously. Is it your own?'

'Oh, yes. The last of the blackberry jelly from last year. Don loved it.'

There's a silence as May remembers Don's boyish glee whenever he was offered anything sweet to eat. Julia isn't clattering around the kitchen any more, although May can hear the kettle boiling. Maybe she's blubbing in there. May wonders if she should go in and offer some sort of comfort but she's never been very good at hugging and so forth, and anyway, Julia would probably dig her in the ribs or poke her in the eye if she attempted anything like that. While she's trying to decide what to do, Julia comes back in with a loaded tray. Her eyes are a bit pink but there's no sign of tears. May heaves a sigh of relief.

They sit and eat their scones in silence for a few moments. 'You haven't lost your touch, dear,' says May, reaching for a paper napkin to wipe away the last crumbs.

'I haven't made much cake of any sort since . . . well, you know. It's no fun baking for yourself, is it?'

'Haven't you had your family over to see you, then?' May doesn't really need to ask this as she knows Felix and Emily haven't visited lately. She's more than aware of any comings and goings around her new neighbours' houses. There's nothing else to do these days but people-watch, so she's sure Julia's son and granddaughter haven't been near the place since Don's funeral last November.

Julia sits up straighter. She drinks her tea and seems to be searching for the right words. 'They're very busy,' she says, 'and of course Emily's still working in New York, so she doesn't get over here very often. Her mother has settled somewhere beyond Munich, out in the sticks, you know. She was always banging on about going back to her homeland, so Emily has to put visiting Gabriella at the top of her list when she gets time off. They booked tickets for me to fly over to Germany for Christmas but I had to cry off at the last moment . . . sadly.'

'What a shame.' May heard this news from Andy at the time and remembers that Julia was ill, although Andy wasn't convinced that a slight chill should have made her miss all the festivities. May suspects that Julia's feelings about family Christmases are as lukewarm as her own.

'And Felix?' May probes. She's been wondering if the old feud is still simmering. Felix's wife managed to cause quite a rift between her husband and his parents, before she upped and left with the owner of a Bavarian *Biergarten*, and even the mention of Gabriella's name has put a chill in the air.

Julia shrugs. 'He's still based in Boston but he travels all over the world. Business is booming, as they say. I expect he'll be here soon. It's my birthday at the end of next month.'

Julia's eyes fill with tears and May's heart sinks. She

remembers the loneliness of birthdays after Charles died. He wasn't very good at presents and fuss, but at least he always took her out for a decent pub lunch at the Eel and Lobster on the green. Charles loved a nice plate of scampi and chips, and May always went for a home-made pasty with heaps of buttery mashed potato. It's well over fifty years since May's husband went voyaging and didn't come back. There were whispers of suicide amongst the villagers but the official view was accidental death, due to the storm that suddenly whipped up. Eventually, the remains of Charles's boat were found near to the harbour and his body was washed up on the next tide after that.

Charles was much too experienced a sailor to make such an obvious error of judgement; everyone who knew him must have been aware of that fact. He was many things, but reckless wasn't one of them. Although May was surprised at the verdict, she held her tongue. It was easier that way.

May let the dust settle after the inquest and kept a low profile for a while. Life without Charles seemed strange, but soon became the norm. They didn't marry until they were in their forties, soon after May's parents died. At the time May felt unusually lost, cut adrift from her comfortable routine, and moving Charles in seemed like a logical step for them both. They had been together for only eleven years when the tragedy happened so May's used to being alone now, but she can see that Julia has got a long way to go before she reaches that sort of self-sufficiency.

'Come on, don't cry,' says May, patting Julia's hand

awkwardly. 'You had a good life with Don. Nothing lasts for ever in this world.' Or does it? she thinks. Maybe if I can get more memories, it might.

Julia is looking at May with deep loathing now and she realises she's said the wrong thing.

'That's not the point,' Julia mutters.

'Well, it is really, dear,' says May, pulling a face and reaching for her teacup, 'but with hindsight I can see why today might not be a good day to say it.'

Julia's mouth twitches, and then she laughs long and hard – a great guffaw that's most unlike her. 'Oh, May – you're a real one-off,' she says, wiping her eyes.

The sudden connection between them doesn't last for more than a few seconds but after that, the time passes quickly. They talk about their neighbours' foibles and the arguments at the stark grey Methodist Church about the new minister's penchant for long sermons and soppy new hymns, and it's not until Andy knocks on the back door to announce his arrival that May realises she hasn't even tried to smuggle a letter into her handbag.

Julia goes to the kitchen to meet Andy, and May stands up, swaying slightly. If she leans over, she can reach the pile on the table. She holds onto her chair back with one hand and takes an envelope at random, slipping it into her handbag. It feels like a good one – quite thick, and there's a buzz just from holding it. Her heart flutters. She thinks about taking a second letter but the voices are coming closer. She zips up her bag just in time, as Julia and Andy come in, followed by Tamsin, still wearing her Rainbow uniform.

'All talked out, ladies?' Andy asks. 'Ready for the off, May? Tamsin needs her bath; they've been clay modelling tonight, and she's a bit grimy. And she's wearing most of her tea. It was spaghetti. I think I overdid the sauce.'

'I don't need a bath. Clay doesn't smell bad,' says Tamsin, but Julia takes her by the shoulders gently and guides her in front of a long mirror. Tamsin giggles. She has a streak of clay all down one cheek and a lump of it buried in her curls, plus a hefty blob of tomato mush on her chin and around her mouth.

'You'll need your hair washing tonight, my pet,' says Julia, and Andy throws her an agonised look. May's heard the noise from the bathroom on shampoo nights. It's even worse than the ponytail protests.

May is ready now. She doesn't meet Julia's gaze as she leaves the room. The brief burst of warmth between the two of them has dissipated, and the tantalising letter is tucked snugly inside May's bag. She can't wait to tap into its memories.

It doesn't take long for Andy to get May home and settled in her favourite chair, with Fossil rubbing around her ankles.

'Shall I make you a sandwich?' Tamsin says. It's her latest skill. She can only do ham or jam so far but she's building up to cheese. It's the cutting that's tricky. 'I'm getting better at the buttering bit now,' she adds hopefully. 'There's not so many holes.'

'No, you get back home and get into bed when you've had that bath. I'm full of Julia's scones, thanks.'

May hears them go, with Fossil following just in case

there's any fish going spare at Andy's. Her bag is on her knee before they've even had time to cross the gap and go through the gate between Shangri-La and their terraced house. She fumbles for the letter, fingers made clumsy by urgency. As she pulls the faded blue sheets from their envelope, the familiar buzzing begins and she sighs with relief. It's happening. She hasn't lost the knack of tapping into the precious memories.

For a little while, it's enough just to hold the pages in her hand and feel a warmth spreading through her body. It builds slowly: a tingling, effervescent shimmer of hope, cascading into ripples of delight. May wriggles blissfully. This is what she's been missing so desperately. On one level, she's still in her cosy living room hearing the cry of the gulls and the faint sound of Tamsin pushing the cat back in through the flap in the kitchen door and telling him it's nearly bedtime. On the other hand, she's floating above the room, high on a wave of wellbeing and happiness.

It's the lifeblood, flowing into her veins. The power to stay young, or at least to slow the march of time. One hundred and eleven is surely going to be possible now. Eventually, May feels the intensity of the memories ebbing, and reaches for her glasses as Fossil jumps up to settle on her lap. Pulling out the closely written sheets, she sees Kathryn's name on the final page.

As she begins to read, cascades of tiny bubbles dance through her narrow frame and she has to stop every few sentences to catch her breath.

We've just had a newspaper cutting from our Nottingham family telling us of Pauline's engagement! Quick work, what? I bet her engagement ring isn't as good as Mother's. Opals take some beating, especially three such beautiful stones – and the tiny diamonds around them are so pretty too. If only we could find it. Mother's heartbroken. She's started behaving very oddly, accusing each one of us in turn of hiding it. As if we would. We all know how much she wants Julia to have the ring. Will's very upset about it all. Has he written to you lately? That boy gets more and more secretive the older he gets, it seems to me.

May leans back in her chair. After months of memory-deprivation this is almost too much.

She recalls the large, noisy family and their visits very well. Charles was quite chummy with Don's relatives for a while. He used to take them out in his boat.

It's time to put the letter away for the night, even though the mystery of the ring is intriguing. Perhaps there will be more clues in the later ones. May's sure Julia has never had a ring like the one Kathryn describes.

May is lost in echoes of the past now, and thinking of Kathryn puts her in mind of another girl from long ago, with the same name but spelled differently. She reaches over to fetch a dusty book from a low shelf, and sniffs the musty fragrance happily as the pages fall open at her favourite entry.

May's old school friend Catherine was what they used

to call 'a card'. She loved making up silly rhymes, usually about their teachers, leaving them around for people to find at the most inopportune moments. Catherine really came into her own during a fad for collecting autographs that swept the girls' grammar school. These weren't in the modern trend of finding famous people to write in your autograph book, but merely a way of proving how many friends you had by letting them fill the pages with trite, jokey and sometimes rather rude messages.

When May passed Catherine her own precious leather-bound book, she hoped that the other girl wouldn't write anything that her parents shouldn't see. She was relieved to read a poem that was more thoughtful than Catherine's usual doggerel and reminded her of her father's words about living to the ripe old age of one hundred and eleven when he'd gazed at that beautiful sunset so long ago. Coincidence? May has never believed in them. This was surely a sign. The poem was entitled 'My Years With You', and read:

> The Bible always tells us
> That in the eyes of men,
> The time that we might hope for
> Is three score years and ten.
>
> But when I view our friendship
> Those years seem far too few,
> And I will always hanker
> To spend more time with you.

So let us aim for five score
Plus ten before we're done.
And when we reach that milestone
We'll add another one.

May was enormously flattered to read this, but came back down to earth with a bang when she found out that Catherine had written the same ditty in at least half the class's books. Even so, the thought of living to the grand old age of one hundred and eleven strongly appealed to May, and over the years the magical number has become her Holy Grail. She's so nearly there now.

More letters are needed, and quickly. Julia's got so many she'll hardly miss a few, will she? And May's need is so much greater than Julia's. Her birthday is on the horizon – only three months away – and she *has* to get there. She simply has to.

# Chapter Five

The next day at around noon, Julia looks out of the kitchen window and sees Andy perched on an upturned crate eating his lunchtime sandwiches. He's been weeding the rows of broad beans and courgettes he planted in the spring. It's Saturday, so Tamsin is with him, sitting cross-legged on the grass with a lunch box open in front of her.

Tamsin waves as Julia approaches them with a loaded tray, carefully avoiding the ruts in the path.

'Have you got my tea things, Aunty Jules?' she asks, jumping up.

'Absolutely. I wouldn't forget you, my love,' says Julia. She puts the tray down on a nearby garden table in the shade of the oak tree and spreads out the contents – a brown teapot with a multi-coloured knitted cosy, Andy's oversize mug, a blue and white jug of milk, a tin of biscuits and last of all a miniature tea set for Tamsin.

'Thank you,' says the little girl, eyes sparkling. 'Tea is my best drink ever.'

'You told me Vimto was your favourite this morning,' says Andy, 'and yesterday you said you'd never again drink anything but strawberry milkshake.'

'Yes, but tea's my favouritest favourite,' says Tamsin, then begins humming to herself as she rearranges the teacups more to her liking. Julia remembers her son taking the same pleasure in the tiny cups and saucers, milk jug and teapot with their blue Cornish stripes. His own daughter, in turn, loved them as much as Felix had. Julia sighs. She misses Emily more than she misses her son. Felix isn't an easy person to get on with – he's often a bit too fond of the sound of his own voice – but Emily is a delight.

Julia presses her lips together to stop them wobbling. Now's not the time to get all emotional over a few little teacups. Perhaps she should write and ask Emily to visit at a specific time rather than hoping she'll make the decision herself? The fear of seeming pathetic catches at Julia's heart, but she *so* wants to see her granddaughter.

'You sad today then?' asks Tamsin, busy adding milk and a sugar lump to her tea.

Andy frowns at his daughter, but Julia takes a deep breath and smiles. 'Not especially, sweetheart, it's just that I've been reading these old letters and thinking about the old days.'

'Oldays, oldays, oldie oldie oldays,' sings Tamsin to herself as she hands Julia one of the little cups brimming with sweet, milky liquid. Julia takes it, braces herself, and knocks it back in one.

'Careful. You'll get the burps,' warns Tamsin, 'Daddy gets the burps sometimes. And sometimes he—'

'Anything interesting in the letters you've sorted so far, Julia?' Andy says hastily, helping himself to a couple of digestives.

'I . . . er . . .'

'Oh, sorry, I didn't mean to pry. They're probably full of personal stuff.'

Julia rubs her eyes to ease the gritty lack-of-sleep feeling that's built up in them over the months since Don's death. 'No, I wasn't being cagey, it's just that for a minute I couldn't remember which one I was reading last. I'm sure it was from Don's younger sister. She was talking about . . .'

There's a friendly sort of silence as Julia racks her brain to think of the gist of that letter. She's been sorting the letters into decades and is drawn to the fifties and sixties for many reasons. Her own recollections of that time keep mixing themselves up with Don's family's news. But as hard as she tries, she just can't remember what the main point of the letter was. Something about a ring . . .

'I'll just pop inside and fetch the one I was reading last to show you,' she says.

Five minutes later, Julia's back outside, and Andy looks up from retying Tamsin's shoelaces. 'What's up?' he asks, taking in her flushed cheeks.

'I can't find the letter I was telling you about.'

Andy laughs. 'Well, I'm not surprised. Talk about needle in a haystack – there must be hundreds of them.'

'Yes, but it was only yesterday, and I remember putting it on top of the pile. It isn't there now.'

'I'm always losing things,' says Tamsin helpfully. 'I lost my best spider last week. I left it in a jam jar in the kitchen, and when I went back, it had gone away.'

Andy doesn't meet his daughter's clear gaze and

changes the subject quickly. 'How did you get on with May? You haven't said much about the visit.'

'It was fine,' says Julia absently. 'She's coming over every Friday, if you can bring her.'

'Course I will. Did you find plenty to talk about?'

'Hmm? Oh . . . yes . . . it was quite painless.'

'Does May give you a pain then?' asks Tamsin. 'She doesn't make me have a pain. I love May. Don't you love May?'

'You bet she does, sweetheart,' says Andy, still watching Julia's face. 'We all do. Why are you so anxious, Julia? Did you two argue or something?'

'Oh, no, it's not that. I'm just bothered that I can't put my hands on that envelope.'

'Who did you say it was from?'

'I didn't, but it was from . . . one of Don's sisters, I think.' She bites her lip.

'Which one? There were two, weren't there?'

Julia doesn't answer.

Tamsin waits for a moment and then counts on her fingers as she recites the names. Sisters fascinate her. She has asked Andy for one of her own several times but he says it's a bit difficult when there isn't a mummy around. 'Kathryn and Elsie,' she says, in a singsong voice. 'And then there were the three boys. Uncle Don told me about them.'

'I thought there were only two brothers, Julia?'

'No, there was—'

Tamsin butts in. 'There was Will. He was the littlest, and then another little boy called Peter but he went to live in heaven when he was a baby. I bet he knows my mum, doesn't he, Dad? She probably cuddles him when she's missing me.'

Julia and Andy are silent, and Tamsin, bored, wanders off to dig a hole in the newly turned soil near the greenhouse. Sometimes she gets to make mud pies in this garden if she asks nicely. Andy turns to Julia again.

'Is reading about all these times in the past getting a bit too much for you, do you think?' he says. 'Only you secm distracted, somehow. Maybe you should put them away for a little while? Have a break. Write to Emily, or something. See if she fancies a visit.'

'What are you getting at? I'm not going gaga. I don't need a break.'

'No, I wasn't saying—'

'You think I'm losing my marbles, don't you? Well, it's possible. It happened to my mother at about this age.'

There are tears in Julia's eyes as she marches back into the house, and she wipes them away with the back of her hand, slamming the kitchen door behind her. Andy frowns. Now he's done it. Why did he have to be so tactless?

His mind returns to their conversation over and over throughout the day, and by evening he's decided to take action. If Julia won't get in touch with her granddaughter, he'll do it himself. Emily gave him her email address and phone number after the funeral, just in case he needed her for anything to do with Julia, and now he does. This is serious.

Andy has seen Emily off and on over the years when she's visited Pengelly and sometimes actually plucked up the courage to talk to her, but she always seemed rather aloof, even when she joined the rest of the local gang on the beach for impromptu barbecues and illicit cider binges. Her gothic phase was quite scary but she's left that far behind her now.

It was a chilly day when they said the final goodbye to Don. Emily was wrapped up warmly in a soft black coat so long it almost swept the floor, and she'd added a cherry-red cashmere scarf and lipstick to match. He remembers her telling him that her grandfather posted the scarf the winter before, when Emily wasn't able to get to Cornwall in time for Christmas. Don was always good at presents. Emily's hair was out of sight for most of the day, tucked up inside a fur hat. She looked like a Russian princess, Andy recalls, pale and delicate, but stunning.

Afterwards, when they gathered at the local pub with all the available villagers for Don's send-off drinks, hefty sandwiches and chunks of pork pie, Andy watched breathlessly as Emily pulled off her hat, and corkscrews of golden hair tumbled down her back. It was cross between a shampoo commercial and a Pre-Raphaelite painting come to life.

Andy needed a large whisky to take his mind off the sight. But later, when he tried to talk to Emily, she was so sad that he had not the heart to tell her how lovely she looked. And anyway, he hasn't been interested in serious relationships with women since Allie died. You couldn't really count Candice, could you?

He opens his laptop and starts a new email before the unsettling thoughts have a chance to get a grip.

'Hi Emily,' he writes. 'I'm just dropping you a line to say . . .'

What *is* he actually going to tell her? Your grandma's acting strangely? I'm worried she's not even beginning to deal with Don's death? She hardly ever leaves the house? He tries again.

. . . to say that Julia isn't acting quite like herself, and I wondered if you could give me a call, or I could phone you for a bit of a team talk? I'm really concerned about her state of mind, and the way she's forgetting things that have only just happened. I know it's hard for her being alone in the house after all those years with your grandpa, and grief can affect people in different ways, but I'm afraid it's more serious than just missing him and feeling sad. I won't tell her I've written to you – don't want her to think I'm interfering.

Love, Andy

He frowns at the screen, deletes 'Love' and adds 'Regards', then changes it to 'Best wishes', and presses Send. At least he'll have tried. Whether she gets back to him is another matter. Flying around the world doing glitzy book deals and hobnobbing with top authors must be very time-consuming. Writing to a mere gardener will be way down her list of priorities. She probably won't even bother to reply.

# Chapter Six

'Well, of course I'm OK, darling,' Julia says. 'Why wouldn't I be? I miss Gramps – I'm bound to, aren't I? But I'm keeping very busy sorting his things.'

Emily imagines her grandmother, short dark hair as smooth and neat as ever, sitting next to the telephone table with her elegant legs up on a footstool, dressed in one of her daytime outfits – a print frock, maybe, or a soft sweater with a knee-length skirt. She can hear Radio Three playing in the background. It's the sort of tinkling piano concerto that Gramps hated. He'd have switched it over to something more upbeat.

'So what have you been doing with yourself? Are you getting out and about much?'

There's a pause. 'There's a lot to do at home at the moment. And I've got to tell you about the letters, Em.'

Emily listens, fascinated, as Julia fills her in on the chest full of family treasures.

'You're kidding? Family memories going right back to the fifties? How cool is that?'

'I know! But it's not just that. I've found another couple of letters this morning, ones I'd not read before, or I can't remember having seen them, anyway. I'm getting the strangest hints here and there about something that's been missing for a very long time and has never been found, as far as I'm aware.'

'Really? What is it?'

'A rather unusual opal ring. I remember Don telling me about it. He wanted me to have it when we got engaged but I think his sisters or maybe his brother had other ideas. It belonged to their mother, and then it was lost just before she was going to give it to me.'

'Wow. Was the ring valuable?'

'Yes. But also hugely important to the family. It was supposed to bring luck to the wearer. Three perfect opals in an antique setting with little diamonds. I read somewhere that opals are meant to enhance memory and decrease confusion.'

'Really? I don't think a few stones could do that, do you?'

There's a short silence. Emily can hear her grandmother breathing rather heavily. Is she crying? 'Gran? Are you OK?'

Julia heaves a huge sigh. 'Yes, dear, I'm fine. I so wish I'd got the ring now, though. I could certainly do with it. I'm sure I'd cope better if it was on my finger. It'd give me strength, I know it would. Opals are so pretty. They catch the light, and almost seem to glow.'

'It sounds beautiful. So can *I* read the letters?'

'Oh, I don't think I dare risk any of them to the postal system. They're too precious.'

'No, you mustn't. That'd be mad. Shall I come and see you? I'm way overdue a visit.'

'Emily! That would be lovely! When can you come?'

The sheer excitement in her grandmother's voice adds to the heap of guilt Emily's been carrying around for the last few weeks. She knows she should have been back to Pengelly long before this, but there's been Max to think about. And having Max on the brain has taken up way too much of her time lately.

'I'll talk to my boss. I'm owed quite a bit of annual leave but I've been too busy to take it this year. I can probably be with you by next weekend, hopefully on Sunday? Only a week to wait. Is that OK? I've got some meetings I can't get out of in the next few days, but after that it should be fine.'

'So long as I'm not putting you out.'

There's a slight chill in Julia's voice, and Emily feels her shoulders slump. She could have phrased it better, but work's so full on at the moment and it's not going to be easy to get away at short notice.

'It's no problem, honestly, Gran. I can't wait to see you. Will you make a lemon drizzle cake?'

Another silence. Then Julia clears her throat. 'How about chocolate fudge, for a change?'

'Mmm, that sounds yummy. You know I love anything you bake. Right, well, I'll get going and make the arrangements then. Love you.'

'You too, darling. See you soon!'

Emily's heart twists at the joy in her grandmother's voice as they end the call. She gets up from the huge sofa where she's been lying in her usual position: flat on her back with her legs up on one of its arms, her head on a heap of cushions at the other end. This is a rare day off for her, and she's still in her dressing gown. It's a black and gold silk kimono that Max bought her back from a trip to Japan. Emily had been so touched at the time until she'd found out accidentally through his secretary that he'd bought his wife exactly the same one in blue and green.

She reaches for her laptop and makes short work of booking a flight to Heathrow and then sorting out car hire. It'll be best to present Colin, her boss, with a ready-made plan to stall any arguments. He owes her several favours, after all, with the extra hours she's been putting in lately. Then she texts Max to tell him of her trip. He's working on his latest crime novel at his family home in Cape Cod this week. Emily knows hopping on a plane or heading out in his top-of-the-range sports car at a moment's notice won't bother him. But will he want to see her enough to make the effort?

Max cares about her – she's sure of that – but the trouble is he doesn't care enough. They met at the glittering publishing party when his latest mind-blowing psychological thriller was launched. Emily wasn't looking for a relationship, preferring to be a free agent and keep men at arm's length as much as possible, but Max has seriously tempted her to change her mind, for a little while at least.

She remembers the impact of seeing Max for the first time. It really was the old cliché about eyes meeting across a crowded room. She spotted the man in the shabby cord jacket and jeans as soon as she came in after talking to the caterers, but he was deep in conversation with his agent, Ned, a bumptious character whom Emily usually tries to avoid. As she picked up a glass, he turned and looked straight at her. He murmured something to Ned and leaned in to hear the reply. Then he patted the other man on the back and strolled across to stand in front of Emily, one hand in his pocket, the other holding a flute of prosecco.

In her high-heeled silver sandals, Emily was exactly the same height as Max. His green eyes fixed on her blue ones, and she felt her stomach flip and her heart start to pound.

'Ned tells me you're the lady responsible for this affair,' he said. 'How come we haven't met before?' He sounded like a smoker, which was one of Emily's pet hates, and his hair was receding – another black mark in her book. But his smouldering eyes more than made up for these deficiencies.

Emily was at that moment very glad she'd bothered to put on the new crimson dress that clung to her curves. It was a bit too short with these heels but it showed off her well-toned arms and shoulders. She had even been to a very swanky hairdresser's that afternoon in honour of the occasion, and her hair was artfully tousled, her blond curls just how she liked them but didn't manage to achieve very often. In the morning she'd look like a haystack, but for now . . . yes, she was feeling pretty good.

'I'm fairly new to this branch,' she said. 'I came over from the London office three months ago.'

'Their loss. I'm very pleased you did. What time can we leave?'

'I'm sorry? Aren't you enjoying the party? It's taken me ages to organise.'

Emily heard the plaintive note in her voice and cursed herself for sounding needy, but Max just laughed. 'It's great, but there's one problem.'

'Is there? I thought I'd covered everything. The canapés will be coming round soon, and there's proper champagne for the toast . . .'

'Stop panicking, honey. The problem is that there are too many people. Two is the ideal number. You . . .' he touched the tip of her nose, '. . . and me.'

Much later, as they lay in his hotel bed listening to the subdued roar of the night-time city, Emily was horrified at herself for falling for such a cheesy chat-up line, but her whole body was tingling and her lips were swollen from so much kissing. It wasn't until the end of a week of passion that she discovered Max had a wife and three children in Massachusetts, and that he had absolutely no intention of leaving them.

That was the time to call it quits, but the dangerous thing about Max is that he knows how to have fun, and even boring activities become sparkling in his company. He turns everyday events into adventures. Now, in the tiny open-plan studio that goes with her job, Emily pushes thoughts of this addictive lover out of her head and sits down at her desk to email back to the man who's poked her conscience with a sharp stick.

Dear Andy,

It's very good of you to be so concerned about my grandmother.

Does that sound sarcastic? Oh well, if he wants to take it that way, he's welcome to.

I think it's best if I come over and see for myself how she is. Work has been crazy since the funeral or I'd have been before.

Emily bites her lip. She shouldn't have to apologise to some hick gardener who's sticking his nose into her business, should she? But then she remembers how happy Gran had been to hear from her, and carries on. The man means well. Probably.

I'll be in Pengelly next Sunday (11 June) sometime, depending on traffic. I expect we'll bump into each other, like we always have.

She deletes the last sentence. It's only manners to ask to see him properly, not just hope to find him in the potting shed.

I'll give you a call when I get there. Maybe we can meet up? Thanks again for your care.
Emily

There. That's done. Emily presses Send before she can waste any more time altering the message. She glances at her phone. Still no reply from Max, but that's no surprise. He'll be in the garden room at the back of that dream of a house on the coast. When he first showed her photographs of his home, soon after she let slip she knew he was married, Emily thought he was joking. 'THIS is yours? It's enormous,' she gasped, looking at the pool with its Swiss chalet-style changing room and the lawns sloping down towards the bay. 'What on earth did you do before you were an author?'

Max looked a bit shamefaced at this. 'Oh, I was a struggling writer for years before Ned took me on. We've always lived in Marcia's family home.'

'Right. Well, I can see why it's worth staying with her then.'

He flinched at her tone. 'Ouch. I guess I deserved that. I know it must look like I'm some sort of gold-digger to you, honey, but honestly, I stay because of the kids and because . . . well, Marcia's kind of . . . unbalanced.'

'Is she really? That must be awkward for you.'

'Now don't be catty, babe – it doesn't suit you. I need to be there for my kids. I'm the only stable thing in their lives.' Max's eyes misted over and his voice trembled. Emily was fooled at the time. It took her a while to realise that not only was Max a fine writer, he was also an excellent actor.

Her phone pings with an incoming message. Hmm. Sooner than she thought.

Hey, babe, missing you too. No chance of me getting over before next weekend though. Marcia's on the skids again, and I'm in charge here. Catch up when you're back? Love you Honeybunch xxxxxxxxxx

Honeybunch? When has he ever called her that? He must be getting his nicknames mixed up. That one most likely belongs to Marcia. Emily hesitates, but not for long. It's time to make a decision. She'll miss Max in so many ways, but the thought of being alone again is suddenly tempting. The relief of not having to feel guilty about Marcia will almost make up for losing her capricious, charming lover. She taps out the words that will set her free.

Max, let's leave it here, shall we? It's been good, but it's over. I should have done this weeks ago. I'm sure we'll end up at the same parties from time to time when I get back from England, and I hope we can stay friends. Take care, Emily

She sends the text and then turns her phone off. It's done, and she doesn't feel nearly as depressed as she'd expected. A long, hot soak in the tub is what's needed now, followed by an evening of crappy TV and several bowls of Ben & Jerry's. And before she goes to bed, she'll write herself a reminder to stay clear of men, especially the kind with super-sized egos, and wives back home. It's the only way to stay sane.

# Chapter Seven

Ida Carnell's lounge is the sort of room that Julia usually tries to avoid. For one thing it's so stuffy in here, with all the windows firmly closed. Then there's the overload of occasional tables, footstools and pouffes just waiting to be tripped over, and the heavy abundance of knick-knacks on every available surface is enough to bring on a migraine in someone who hates clutter.

It's the first time Julia's been to a social event of any kind since Don's death, and she's feeling strangely dis-orientated and vulnerable, as if her skin's too thin. She'd tried to get out of it, but nobody manages to go against the flow for long when Ida has her heart set on something.

'Here's the last one of us. I'm so glad you could all come at such short notice, especially on a Tuesday night when some of you should really be at choir practice,' says Ida, ushering in George Kennedy. 'Cliff sends his apolo-gies – he's minding the restaurant. Have a seat, George, and I'll get us all a drink. Coffee, tea or something stronger?'

The other members of the Adopt-a-Granny scheme glance at each other furtively. Julia can tell they all want to go for the more exciting option but nobody wants to look like a lush. She takes pity on them.

'I'd love some white wine, Ida, if that's not putting you out?' she says.

There's a collective sigh of relief, and everyone else puts in their orders quickly. Soon George and Tristram are each nursing a large gin and tonic, Dominic Featherstone, who lives in May's old house, has lager, and Ida, Julia and Gladys Mountbatten from the garden centre are clutching huge glasses of chardonnay. Only Vera from the village shop is looking disapproving, virtuously sipping an orange juice. Ida's a generous hostess – she's provided top-quality Kettle Chips and little bowls of olives and nuts for her guests – and soon the atmosphere is nearly as warm as the room.

'Right, I'll get on with the business in hand,' says Ida. 'Tristram, would you mind taking the minutes?'

'Ooh, very official,' Vera says. 'I thought this was just a friendly chat to see how the scheme was going, Ida?'

'Yes, but I always like to have something in writing. It saves trouble if we forget what's said. Agreed?'

The others all nod. Julia thinks it would take a brave person to disagree.

'So, the first item on the agenda is to say a huge thank you to you all for letting me involve you in my project.'

'An agenda as well? This is turning into a parish council meeting,' sniffs Vera.

Tristram exchanges glances with Julia and grimaces; her heart gives an unexpected little flutter. He's very handsome, in a twinkly, slightly rakish way. His beard looks newly trimmed and he's wearing a tweed suit with a waistcoat over a collarless black shirt. He looks like a model for an upmarket country gentleman's catalogue, but with attitude. Then she blushes, filled with shame that she's caught herself looking admiringly at another man with her own dear chap hardly cold in his grave, as the gruesome saying goes.

'An agenda is a fabulous idea, Ida,' he says, smiling at their hostess reassuringly. She beams back, and Julia reflects that Tristram has been married four times and his charm is legendary. He's also very kind, though, and she's sure he can't be flirting with Ida . . . can he? Anyway, his reply has the desired effect and the meeting bowls along quite comfortably after this.

'And so you've all got your allocated grannies or grandpas,' says Ida, after reminding them how the system will work. 'I just want to tell you that you're all superstars for agreeing to take part. There's too much loneliness around us these days. When I was growing up, one granny and granddad lived two doors away and the others were only in Truro. Nowadays, families are spread all over the place. We'll have another meeting in six weeks to see how it's going. Are there any problems so far?'

There's a brief silence. Then Vera clears her throat importantly. 'There's that pesky Peke,' she says. 'I hadn't bargained for the hairs. And it yaps.'

'Oh dear. I know Marigold's very protective of her little dog,' says Ida. 'Perhaps I could have a tactful word and ask her to leave it at home when she visits you?'

Vera snorts. 'Good luck with that one,' she says. 'I've

been trying to keep it out of my shop for years. Oh, well, it's quite decrepit now. Shouldn't last much longer. Smelly old thing.'

There's an appalled silence as the assembled group digests this acidic remark. Tristram in particular looks disgusted. He's always been a dog lover, and his two are never far from his side. Having said that, he probably wouldn't take them where he knows they're not wanted, and it *is* a food shop. Ida rallies.

'Anyway, other than that, are there any other issues we need to discuss?'

'We've had our first visit from Tom King and Joyce Carpenter,' says George, 'and they both seemed to enjoy themselves. Actually Tom was giving Joyce the eye all through lunch.'

'Well, that wouldn't get him far, would it?' says Vera. 'The poor woman's virtually blind.'

Julia picks up her glass and tries to stop her lips twitching. It isn't in the least bit funny to lose your sight, after all. But then she catches Tristram's wicked glance again and nearly chokes on her wine.

'I'm more than happy to take Bob Farmer swimming every week,' says Tristram, as Julia tries to recover her equilibrium. 'He loved it this morning. He did more lengths than I did. Maybe he should adopt me instead? He's only eighty-five, and I'll be eighty soon.'

'You both look super fit,' says Gladys, 'and it's not about that, it's giving him a chance to do what he's always liked doing. He can't drive now, and the bus is only every two hours. It doesn't go as far as the leisure centre either.'

'How about you, Gladys? Is it going well with Lucy?'

'I had a great time with her. Lucy's a poppet,' says Gladys. 'I fetched her over to the garden centre this morning and she helped me pot out some seedlings. She loved it. She's had to move into a flat and she hasn't got a garden now. She's always welcome at Chestnuts. I'm glad of an extra pair of hands.'

'And Julia? How are you getting on?'

Julia's back in control now. She takes another tentative sip of her wine while she thinks how to answer. Tristram watches her. How much does he remember about what happened years ago between Julia and Charles? Even May doesn't know the full story, as far as Julia's aware. Maybe it has been wrong of her to let herself continue to resent May so much over the years when it was May's husband who'd caused most of the problems, but surely the woman had known what he was like and the damage he was doing? Couldn't she have stopped him? And then was the incident with the spoons . . . She feels the pounding of her heart as tension, never far from the surface since Don's death, threatens to swamp her.

Julia takes a few deep, calming breaths. 'We had a good chat,' she says, when the silence begins to feel awkward, 'and we'll meet up again very soon, if Andy can bring her over to me.'

'I've got to say this is a fabulous idea of yours, Ida,' says Dominic. He's been quiet up to now. Julia hasn't had a chance to get to know him yet. He and his wife, Cassie, haven't lived in May's old house for long.

'Thank you, Dominic. I almost didn't ask you and

Cassie to join us in the project,' says Ida, 'because you've hardly had time to get your breath back since you arrived. But then I bumped into her in the shop when I was explaining the scheme to Vera and she said she'd love to be involved.'

'Cass wanted to be here tonight instead of me, but both of our youngest twins have got colds and they like their mum around when they're grizzly. We've talked to our allocated granny on the phone and we're fetching her round tomorrow. Luckily she likes kids. Our oldest pair of lads is . . . loud, is the best word to describe the little monsters, I think.'

'Who have you been paired up with, Dominic?' Julia asks, racking her brain to think of someone in the village who fits the bill. Female, old enough to be classed as a granny, likes children . . . No, she can't imagine who it could be.

'Her name's Angelina.'

This time it's Tristram who spits his drink out, and there's a general outcry as Dominic speaks.

'Oh, no, you're joking, aren't you? Ida, really? Why would you do that to Dominic and his poor unsuspecting wife?' says George, wide-eyed.

Ida has the grace to look slightly shamefaced. 'Angelina's lovely,' she protests. 'She's just eccentric, that's all. And she's very lonely.'

'Lonely? I bet she is.' Vera's laugh is humourless.

'What's the problem, guys?' asks Dominic. 'She sounded OK on the phone. A little . . . excitable maybe?'

'That's a good word for Angelina,' says Gladys. 'She

has a tendency to scamper through the streets semi-naked when the muse takes her. She's very arty. If she runs out of Bacardi when she's in the middle of painting one of her mad seascapes she just leaves the house and runs up to the pub in whatever she happens to be wearing. Not much, usually. She likes to be unfettered when she paints.'

'There's no harm in her,' says Tristram. 'I nearly married her once.'

'You nearly married everyone once,' Julia says, 'except me,' and then regrets her outburst as everyone turns to look at her.

'Yes, however did I miss you out?' Tristram puts on a mystified expression. 'Maybe you were always spoken for. But as for Angelina, you'll have a great time with her, Dominic. She likes a laugh and she really does love child-ren.'

He gazes into the distance as if remembering something amusing. Julia feels ruffled. What's Angelina got to make a man like Tristram go all googly-eyed over her? She must be ninety if she's a day. Her hair is cropped short and dyed a fearsome orange, as it's always been since she found her first grey hair. She wears a bizarre collection of shapeless linen garments and multi-coloured scarves, when she bothers with clothes at all.

Tristram catches Julia staring at him and grins. 'What's the problem? I like older women, always have done. And Angelina was gorgeous in her day. Still is, come to that. As are all you ladies present.'

Vera snorts and mutters something about men who need their eyes testing. After this, Ida seems to think it's time to draw the meeting to a close. She tops up everyone's glass and they end by having a good old gossip. Even Vera accepts a small sherry and begins to soften.

'Don't be fooled, that smile's probably just wind,' murmurs Tristram, catching Julia watching the doyenne of the shop in amazement as she stuffs crisps into her mouth and titters at something George is saying.

'She should be given sherry on prescription,' says Julia. 'It'd make the village a much happier place.'

'Thank you so much for giving up your time tonight,' says Ida as they all file out half an hour later, slightly flushed. 'I can't believe how quickly you've all taken this on board. Some people think Pengelly is just a little backwater at the end of the world but to me it's so much more.' Her cheeks are glowing. 'And you won't forget the farmers' market, will you? A week on Saturday.'

'I don't know anything about that,' says Dominic. 'Should I?'

Ida pats his arm. 'Oh, I must have forgotten to mention it when I was talking to Cassie. The market's a monthly event, mainly on the green but with a few other stalls dotted here and there, and a bouncy castle and so on for the littlies. This time I'm having an information station right outside the pub to tell everyone about Adopt-a-Granny.'

'Sounds great.'

'And I'm hoping you'll all drop by at some time during the day in case anyone wants to ask questions. You're the experts now.' She hiccups slightly and hugs Dominic as he leaves.

'I think Ida's been hitting the sherry bottle too,' whispers Tristram to Julia. Vera wobbles on the step and catches hold of him as he speaks.

'Do you want to come back with me for a nightcap, Tris?' she says, wriggling her shoulders. 'I've got sloe gin.'

Tristram's look of alarm sets Julia off giggling helplessly. She walks ahead and takes deep breaths. It wouldn't do for Vera to see her laughing. But the sherry has done its work well, and Vera yawns hugely, giving Tristram the chance to escape with an excuse of an early morning booking for ten breakfasts tomorrow.

'I'd love to be sociable but you understand what it is to be responsible for a business, Vera. We both need to be on the ball,' he says. 'Gina and Vince do so much already so I can't ask them to get up at the crack of dawn just because I've stupidly agreed to host the local twitchers' annual beano, can I?'

Julia returns his grin as he says a polite good night to Vera at the shop door and offers Julia his arm to walk her home. For a few moments, the whirlpool of her mind steadies and she relaxes into the luxurious sensation of being cared for. The ever-present sadness and the spasmodic, terrifying confusion ebb, and warmth flows through her body. They walk down the lane in silence, completely in accord.

# Chapter Eight

The second letter is even easier to appropriate. May is left on her own for nearly ten minutes while Julia gasses on the phone to her granddaughter. She can hear Julia babbling like a schoolgirl as she chats to Emily about what she'd like to eat when she flies in from the States.

May has no idea what she's getting when she plunges her hand into the heap of envelopes on the table.

She pushes the letter right to the bottom of her bag as Julia ends the call and comes back in, still chuckling.

'That girl. She never changes, thank goodness,' Julia says, pouring May a third cup of tea without asking.

May purses her lips. She doesn't normally have more than two cups of tea at this time of day. It's hard enough sleeping through the night without having to get up for a widdle every hour. But Julia is passing her the dainty china cup and saucer now, and handing over a plate of shortbread.

'Have you been baking again?' asks May. 'Is this your mother's recipe? She was a grand cook, wasn't she?'

'She was, but I've somehow managed to lose her cook-book,' says Julia, 'so I've gone back to the tried and trusted

Be-Ro recipes. I think she copied most of those into her own book anyway, and just pretended they were family secrets, to be honest. The lemon cake's never been the same since, though. I can't seem to get it right any more.'

May pretends to be searching in her bag for a hankie. The recipe book, written in Julia's mother's elegant copperplate, is at this moment nestling in her bedside cabinet. It was lying around in the church kitchen one day when she and Julia had both been roped into helping at a charity tea. She's used up all the memories out of it now, and a very gluttonous sort they were too. Gave her raging indigestion. She supposes she should sneak the book back now. It's no use to May.

'I'd have thought you'd have made all those cakes so often you'd not need a book?' she says.

Julia flushes. 'Well, that's the thing. I'm having a few . . . issues . . . with my memory. Are you ever forgetful these days, May?'

'Of course not! Just because I'm older than you doesn't mean I'm going barmy, does it?' May has always believed attack is the best form of defence.

'No, I wasn't suggesting anything of the kind. There's no need to be so touchy. It's not all about you. It's me that has the problem.'

There, it's out. May bites her lip. 'What sort of things are you forgetting?' she asks.

'All sorts. I can't even remember where I met Don. I was awake half the night thinking about it.'

'Oh, bereavement can do that to you,' says May soothingly. 'I wouldn't worry, dear.'

'Really? Did you find that after you lost Charles?'

There's an awkward silence. 'Yes, I believe I did,' says May, eventually. 'But everything passes. Just be patient, that's my advice.'

May helps herself to another finger of shortbread. Julia looks slightly soothed.

'So how's your Emily doing?' May says, when the tricky moment's passed. 'She must be past thirty by now. Any wedding plans?'

'She's thirty-three actually, but you know how these young ones are. They think marriage is out-dated. I don't think Em's even got a boyfriend.' Julia heaves a sigh. 'The years go by so fast, don't they? She's so busy with her high-flying job. The publisher she works for has got offices in London, New York, Paris and goodness knows where else now. Em's never in one place long enough to find a husband.'

'Like her dad. He's still a bit of a jet-setter, isn't he?'

'Well, he thinks he is. I wish Felix would retire. He's well past retirement age, for goodness' sake. If he stopped flying around the world I might get to see him occasionally.'

She reddens, and busies herself collecting the teacups and plates. May mentally files the information away. That's the first time Julia's ever let slip anything to suggest she's even slightly unhappy with her family's neglect.

'I've always had a soft spot for young Emily,' May says. 'She's a sweet girl. She often used to pop in and see me when she was staying with you. Did you know that? It was when I lived up on The Level, of course.'

'Did she?'

There's frost in the air. May smiles to herself. Julia's very possessive about her family, and it's time she loosened up. 'Oh, yes. She hasn't seen Shangri-La yet. I hope she visits again soon.'

There's a pause. 'But *you* never felt the need to have children, did you, May?' says Julia.

May winces and shakes her head. Julia's fighting back. No need to mention the fact that Charles wasn't much of a one for procreation. In fact, until she found him in a compromising position with the baker's 'boy', she'd assumed it was her fault for not being attractive enough. Sex wasn't a big deal for him even at the start of their marriage. More experienced in bed than Charles at the time – unusual for those days – May was never one to follow the rules. Even so, she didn't mind much when the occasional fumbles stopped and she and Charles settled into a quiet life of companionship.

Things weren't quite the same between them after that seedy incident, but at least they stopped going through the motions of pretending they wanted to sleep in the same bed. Oh, the bliss when he moved into the spare room. She largely ignored her husband's occasional flings, and she felt he was always very discreet. May even managed to have a few brief affairs herself, which livened up her life considerably. But as for children, that's a whole other story, and not one for Julia's ears.

Andy knocks loudly and bursts in through the open back door at this point, breaking the unsettling train of thought. 'You ready for home yet, May?' he says.

'Yes, anytime you are.' May struggles to her feet, clutching her handbag close to her chest. She can hardly wait to get home and see what nuggets the precious envelope holds.

'Don't rush off. Can't I get you a drink, Andy?' Julia asks. Noooo, thinks May, I want to go home. Say no, Andy.

'It's OK, I need to get back to Tamsin,' he says. 'She's next door with Violet, and I think she'll outstay her welcome if I don't hurry up back. I don't want to push my luck.'

'You're lucky having Vi to help out, aren't you?' says Julia. 'She's got her hands full with all her grandchildren these days. She must be a glutton for punishment, as my mother used to say.'

'*I'd* have Tamsin more if you needed me to, you know that,' says May. 'I'm not in my dotage yet, you know.' She sniffs. Sometimes she thinks Vi takes liberties, almost as if she and Andy are related.

May takes Andy's arm and lets herself be escorted over the road, after thanking Julia politely for her tea. It's been a surprisingly pleasant hour or two, even with the under-lying spikiness, but she's rather alarmed at the speed with which Julia's memories are flowing away. She bites her lip, guilt rearing its head. Her father always told her not to take too much from one person. A few memories here and there can always be spared, was his motto. Still, May's need is greater than Julia's at the moment, if she's ever to reach that magical birthday.

Tamsin hears them approaching and jumps back over the fence from Vi's on the other side, into her own garden.

'Bye, Vi,' she yells. 'Hey, that rhymes, did you see what I did there, Dad? I said, "Bye, Vi"!'

'Very clever,' says Andy, yawning.

'Bye Vi, have a pie, bet you wish that you could fly,' sings Tamsin, skipping into the house ahead of her father.

'I can't wait till she's in bed tonight,' Andy mumbles, making sure May's safely inside her own house before he leaves her. As he gives May a quick hug, Andy's phone begins to ring and he pauses to answer it, raising his eyebrows in apology.

The conversation is frustratingly one-sided but May knows who's on the other end. It's the woman she thinks of as That Candice.

'I can't tonight,' mutters Andy. 'No, Vi's already done more than enough for me this week. I'm not prepared to ask her to sit for a whole evening. No . . . I know it's been ages . . . Well, maybe next week . . . We could take the kids swimming after school. Look, I'm sorry, OK? Bye.'

He disconnects, a deep frown line between his eyes.

'It must be hard work bringing Tamsin up on your own, love.' May looks at Andy with her head on one side. 'Did you never think of . . .?' She stops, not wanting to offend him, and he half turns back, his mind already on Tamsin's welfare.

'Marrying again? It's fine, don't look so worried, you're not saying anything I haven't thought myself lately. But how could I put someone else in Allie's place?'

'That's one way of looking at it.'

Andy grins at May. 'Anyway, whatever happens, it won't be Candice, if that's what's bothering you.'

'Good. You can do better. I'd watch your step, though. That one's got other ideas.'

He laughs. 'Maybe. Got to go, or Tamsin will decide to run her own bath and flood the landing again. The carpet's only just drying out from last time.'

May waves him off and sits down in her favourite easy chair, ready to unveil the new letter. This one's from Will. May remembers him as rather an egotistical young man, beautiful but sulky. He writes:

*That blasted ring, they go on and on and on about it. If I'd seen it, I'd tell them, wouldn't I? You know I'd never take what's yours, and I believe Julia should have it, to save arguments between the girls. Mother says it's our family's lucky charm, and it has to be passed down to the right person at the right time or we'll be doomed. What a load of twaddle. Anyway, how are things with you? Have you seen anything of Charles? Has he asked after me? I might see if I can get a few sailing lessons from him next time I'm down. You could mention it, if you run into him?*

May reads on, letting the delicious tingle spread from her fingers right through her body, warm and sensuous, like melted chocolate. It's a sensory overload. Better than champagne. Better than caviar. And a lot better than sex, in most of May's experiences, at least. Not all, but most. One exception stands out, but it's best not to think about him.

The phone on the sideboard rings, shocking May out of her blissful reverie. She gets up unsteadily and goes over to answer it.

'Hello, May, it's Julia. Just checking you're home safely.'

'Well, of course I am,' says May rather too sharply, irritated beyond measure at this foolishness. What could have happened to her between Julia's house and her own, supported by Andy? Then she relents. She's enjoyed her time across the road, and if she upsets Julia, she won't be asked back. 'I'm sorry, you startled me. I think I might have been nodding off.'

Julia clears her throat. 'Well, I'm glad you're relaxing. Erm . . . I don't suppose you noticed a letter when you were over with me earlier, did you?'

'I noticed heaps of them, dear,' says May, chuckling. 'Why?'

'I seem to have lost one I was looking at earlier.'

May hears a sob, quickly stifled. 'Are you feeling quite well, Julia?' she asks.

'No . . . no, I'm not. May, I can't remember which letter I was reading last, or who it was from, and I can't find it, and . . .' Julia tails off, gulping for breath.

'Now, calm down and get yourself a nice mug of hot chocolate, or something similar,' says May. 'I think you might have been overdoing it, delving into old times so soon after losing poor Don.'

'Not just Don. I'm losing my mind too, May. This is the beginning of the end. What am I going to do?'

May chews on her knuckle. How should she deal with this? She seems to recall something along the same lines happening before once or twice with people from the village soon after she'd taken their mementoes, although it could have been more common than she realised, because why would the villagers bother to tell her if they'd forgotten random things about their past lives? She'd only found out by accident a couple of times over the years, three at the most. It's as if her harvesting sometimes leaves them with gaping holes in their memories. Holes they're never able to fill.

'I don't understand,' she hedges.

'Neither do I, May. My mind seems to have gone blank when I try to think about what I was reading. I can't even recall who the letter was from. I wondered if you'd . . . you'd maybe seen me put it anywhere?'

This is a tricky situation, but not disastrous. Julia's noticed there's a letter missing, but she seems more jittery about her own memory than suspicious of May's involvement. What's the best way to handle it? It seems to May that how she tackles this problem will affect her life . . . and eventual death. She needs Julia to be calm and unsuspecting so that she can have access to the letters in the coming months. She's so nearly one hundred and eleven. Come on, May, she tells herself, don't mess this one up.

Fossil bursts through the cat flap and into the living room where May sits pondering. He leaps onto her knee and begins to knead the boniest bits of her thighs with his needle-sharp claws.

'Ouch!' shouts May, more loudly than she intended.

'What's the matter? May? Are you hurt?'

May doesn't answer. She tucks the letter well out of sight under her chair cushion, and waits.

'May? Have you fallen? Hang on, I'm coming over . . .'

The line goes dead, and May smiles. *Result*, as Andy might say.

Two minutes later, May hears Julia rattling the handle of the back door. There's no need for that – it's open. Some of the older residents of Pengelly still can't be doing with locked doors. Never have done, hopefully never will.

'May?' Her neighbour comes into the room and sees her with Fossil on her knee. She clutches her chest, like a character in a bad sitcom. 'Oh, thank goodness. I expected to find you slumped on the floor. Why did you stop talking to me?'

Irritation is creeping into Julia's voice now, and May needs to act fast. She passes a shaking hand over her face. Oh, yes, she can ham it up too when she needs to. Those years with the village Amateur Dramatic Society weren't wasted after all. 'I . . . I . . . everything went black for a minute or two . . .'

Julia springs into action. 'How about I make us a nice cup of tea?' she asks, bustling into the kitchen without waiting for a reply. 'You just sit still and get your breath back.'

Listening to the comforting clatter of cups and saucers, May breathes a sigh of relief. Julia will have ignored the serviceable mugs on their hooks. She's got style. 'And maybe a fig roll, dear?' May calls. 'They're in the tin on the dresser. Next to the teabags.'

Julia's soon back, and settles the tray on a low table. She pours their tea without asking if May wants her to be mum, and soon they're sipping away as if they do this at May's cottage every day. The first part of the mission is accomplished. Now for the next steps.

'I'm relieved you're feeling better. I wonder if your blood pressure needs checking?' says Julia, frowning. 'Sometimes if it drops suddenly, you can keel over. It happened to me once or twice when I was carrying Felix. I really thought I was going to find you flat on your back with a head wound, or something.'

'You've got a very lively imagination, dear,' says May. 'You should write a novel.'

'I often wish I could. I have to make do with reading them.'

'You should have a try. You'd need one of those USPs, though.'

'A what?'

May sighs. She'd thought Julia would be well up on publishing terms, with Emily being in the business. 'Unique Selling Point. I heard them talking about it on the radio when they were interviewing that lady who wrote a story about the girl looking out of a train window?'

'I haven't read that one. What's it called?'

May snorts. 'Er . . . *Girl on a Train?*' she suggests.

Julia shakes her head. 'No, never heard of it. What could I have for a UFO then?'

'USP, dear. I'm not sure.'

May thinks for a moment. 'How about your letters? They'd make the perfect starting point for a book,' she says, clapping her hands together.

'My letters? Why would anyone want to read a story

about Don's family? I mean, they were a friendly bunch, I'll give them that, but not very interesting.'

'Think about it, Julia. Those letters are what you might call an archive. Who else has a treasure trove like that to draw on?'

'I'm not sure if Don would like us to use his personal things like that. They belong to the family. They're private.'

'Oh, come on, dear. All the folk who wrote the letters are dead now, or pretty much, aren't they?'

Julia flinches, and May curses herself for being tactless. She pats Julia's hand. 'I'm sorry, I didn't mean to upset you. But I could help you to sort them and plan a story based around them. Andy could catalogue them properly. He might even type some of them out if you ask nicely. He does all sorts of useful clerical jobs at the garden centre – he's very organised.'

'Do you really think so? Andy's already read quite a few of them. He seems fascinated.'

'I do. It'd be a joint effort. We could make a start straight away. They need sorting, don't they? You and Andy could come here to do it and Tamsin could play outside where we can all see her. It'd be fun.'

Julia's looking interested now. 'I wonder . . .' she says.

# Chapter Nine

Emily sits at her desk on the fifteenth floor reading Andy's latest email and quietly panicking. It's a huge relief that Colin has been encouraging about her trip to England, when she explains the reason behind it. His own elderly uncle is beginning to have memory problems too, wandering around in the night in his dressing gown and slippers.

'Just do it, Em,' he says, when she's poured out her worries. 'But if you could clear your desk and sort those last few meetings this week, I'd be eternally grateful. Family first, though, always. Never forget that. And the West Country in June will be heaven. I'm deeply envious, darling.'

Emily hugs him and thanks her lucky stars for an understanding boss. She knows Devon-born Colin isn't like most New York City high flyers, with his taste for Scrabble, loud pullovers and flamboyant socks. He often claims to be pining for all things British, and never fails to have a tray of Earl Grey and Fortnum & Mason biscuits served on the dot of half-past three every day, whomever he happens to be with in the office.

The email is giving Emily a cold feeling in her heart, although it starts well.

'Hi Emily,' Andy writes.

I thought I'd fill you in on what's been happening. I expect your gran's told you about the huge stack of letters she's found? Well, May (you remember her, of course you do, what am I talking about, you'll have known her for years) has just suggested that I help catalogue them all. The letters are fantastic – they go right back to the fifties. And – get this – your gran wants to write a book based on them. I've got to say I don't reckon she's up to it at the moment but it'd be a bad idea to put her off at this stage. Anything that brings her out of herself a bit's got to be good. We can always rethink later.

Anyway, looking forward to seeing you to talk about Julia and how she's been – I've got a sitter for my little girl, Tamsin, because although she'd love to meet you, she doesn't miss a trick and would be sure to report back to May and Julia on what we discussed, probably word for word! Not that we'll be whispering secrets or anything, but I thought I could take you out for dinner, maybe? There's a great little seafood place along the coast, and Monday is their quiet night. Cockleshell Bay – have you been there? It's run by a lovely couple of guys, George and Cliff.

I'll be in touch when you're here. The formidable gang of two has already started sifting through the letters but that needed to be done anyway, so if you think I'm interfering and want me to mind my own business, I will. Julia's been muttering about family secrets, but I'm not sure what it's all about. Maybe she's filled you in already? I hate to tell you this but I'm getting more and more worried about her. I'm glad you'll soon be here. Yesterday I found her in tears because she couldn't remember Don's sisters' names and she'd forgotten whether she'd had breakfast or not. Am I wrong to encourage the crazy book idea?

See you soon, sorry to flap – I want to help but I don't know what to do for the best any more.

Andy

Emily rubs her eyes and yawns. If only she could transport herself to Pengelly right now, without the effort of getting through a mammoth workload, flying to England and driving all the way to Cornwall on a hot afternoon. To be sitting on the beach, listening to the sound of the waves and looking forward to scones and clotted cream for tea would be perfect.

Her incoming email alert pings and Emily's stomach lurches. Max hasn't been in touch again since her last text. She kind of hopes he'll just leave her alone now, but her bruised pride would like him to protest more at the sudden end to their affair. The message is only Colin, though, checking she's not forgotten yet another meeting this afternoon. Deep joy. Roll on Pengelly, and the smell of salt water and tar instead of over-sanitised office air, lightly scented with artificial citrus tones. The sooner the better.

# Chapter Ten

It's an ugly phrase, but May's mother would have described her as being 'as happy as a pig in muck' these last couple of days. She and Julia seem to have called a truce (although whatever old annoyance was ruffling Julia will have to be tackled at some point, May supposes) and made a proper plan to join forces in their quest to make it easier for Andy to catalogue the letters. May is still smarting at the way Julia seems to think that family life and motherhood are solely her own territory, but if May doesn't want to dig up the past in a big way, she's going to have to take it on the chin.

May's done a bit of gentle probing over the last day or two and now she knows for sure that Charles is the root of whatever is bugging Julia, but further than that she can't fathom, as yet. What can he possibly have done to make Julia so antagonistic, even after all these years and, whatever it was, why does Julia blame May for it? Charles was a law unto himself. May was never able to influence him.

The next day, as they've planned, Julia turns up with the first batch of letters in a shopping basket. She proceeds to potter back and forth all morning bringing more, while

May makes endless pots of tea and provides chocolate digestives and fig rolls every now and again.

'This is the last lot,' Julia gasps, as she puts the basket down on the dining table with a thump. 'I thought I was never going to get to the end of them.'

May sits back, deeply content. With the letters here, she has no need to worry about where her next memory fix is coming from, and she's got the prospect of a companion every day, if she wants one. The idea of Julia as a friend is growing on her, and now she's wondering why she's let the other woman get away with being so snooty over the years. Somehow, she has to get past this ancient burning resentment.

'Julia, can I ask you something?' she says.

'Fire away.'

'Even before the incident with the soup spoons, you didn't seem to like me much. I've been wondering what I did to annoy you?'

Julia's cheeks are pink as she meets May's gaze. 'Well, I wouldn't say I didn't like you . . . and I probably jumped to the wrong conclusion about those old spoons.'

'Come on, dear, spill the beans. I won't be offended. You've given me the cold shoulder for years. I just want to know why, that's all. Because you're not the sort of person to be stand-offish for no reason, I know that now.'

There's a long silence, but May can be patient when she needs to be. Eventually Julia clears her throat. 'I suppose it all goes back to Charles.'

'I thought as much.'

'But really, I don't see why we have to drag bad

memories up after all this time. Can't we just draw a veil over it?'

'Well, we could, if I had some idea what *it* is. And what's Charles got to do with you not liking me?'

Julia gets up and goes over to the window. With her back to May, she says, 'I told you, it's not about whether I like you or not. Look, I'm not ready for this sort of talk just now, May. It's hard enough to get through the days without Don. I can't tackle any more emotional memories. Can't we just get on with the letters?'

May sighs and gives in. They start to work their way through the heap, putting the photographs on one side. The rush of memories is potent, and May is soon over-whelmed. She realises she mustn't start reading the letters properly otherwise she'll be comatose before long, so she settles for just checking the dates. Even so, she can tell her face is giving her away. She can't stop smiling.

'We've done enough for now,' says Julia, after an hour of intense sorting. 'I'll just read you a bit of this one, though. It's from Elsie.'

She clears her throat.


Thanks for having us to stay again, Don. I know it wasn't one of our more successful visits. Blame Will and his weird moods for that. I can't believe he dashed off like that before the holiday was even over. I had to come home on the train alone, which wasn't much fun, and to think he hitch-hiked all that way in the middle of the night! I still haven't got to the bottom of it, and now he's jacked his job in and gone off to Ireland. It's that Catholic Church at the root of it. He's never been the same since he turned his back on the Methodist chapel and started going to Mass.

'What's all that about?' May asks. Something's tugging at her memory, and it's making her feel sick.

'I have no idea. The date's 15 March 1963. Does that mean anything to you?'

May closes her eyes, suddenly dizzy, and Julia leans forward.

'You look a bit . . . well, Emily would probably call it "spaced out". Are you OK to work a bit longer or shall we have a break?'

May really is feeling quite peculiar now. The thought of a little lie-down on the bed is very tempting. March 15 1963. Her eleventh wedding anniversary. And the day after Charles drowned.

# Chapter Eleven

The hire car smells vaguely fishy, and also as if someone's been smoking in it. Maybe it was previously lent to a kipper manufacturer? It's started making rather strange clunking and creaking noises after fifty or so miles, but Emily ignores them and eventually the sounds die away.

The last fifty miles are the worst. Even with the radio playing full blast, it's hard to stay awake. She passes the time thinking about holidays past. Long days by the sea, making sand castles when she was younger, shell-gathering later, hanging out with the local kids and visiting some of the more friendly villagers. May Rosevere has always been Emily's favourite. May has an endless supply of slightly scandalous stories about her neighbours and a wicked sense of humour. Not only that, she let Emily rootle through her jewellery box and try everything on. Better still, her biscuit tin seemed to be bottomless.

At last she reaches Pengelly after more than five hours' driving with only one short break. As she coasts down the main street, she remembers how her grandfather always met her by the pub on the green, and jumped into the car to travel the last couple of hundred yards with her. She was never able to give him an exact time of arrival, so he waited on a bench outside. He never minded how long he sat there.

The awful realisation hits her, once again, that Gramps is gone for good. There are so many things to miss about him: the way he hugged her as if she was the most important person in the world; the happiness in his voice as he said, 'You're home, Little Em!'; the sparkle of those blue eyes so like her own – all gone.

Blinking hard, she sees a tall figure sitting on the rickety seat outside the Eel and Lobster. Gramps' bench. Her heart skips several beats and she slams the brakes on, causing the Range Rover behind her to toot madly. The man in it gives her a V sign as he screeches past, but the figure on the bench is on his feet now and giving one back.

It's not Gramps – of course it's not. Emily never thought it was, really. She winds her window down.

'Hello, Andy,' she says, rubbing her eyes.

'Oh, hello, Emily. I was afraid I'd miss you going past.'

'No chance of that with the noises this car's been making. But it got me here eventually.'

'I wasn't expecting you just yet. I've only just started my pint. Fancy joining me for one?'

He holds up his glass, beaded with moisture. It's true, he's not made much headway into it yet. Emily's taste buds spring back to life after the long, fetid drive. It's been ages since she's drunk anything but tonic water with a mean-spirited splash of vodka and a lot of ice and lemon to bulk it out. Even at the most lavish publishing parties she's gone easy on the prosecco in case she misses vital undercurrents or starts to babble to an important client.

'What about the car?' she says, rather feebly. 'I'm driving. I know it's only down the road, but I'd hate to fall at the last fence. It's been a long day.'

'Geoff at the pub says it's best if you park it up here anyway, because May's car park's full. Your grandpa's old banger's taking up all the space on the drive at number sixty, and the battery's flat so we haven't got around to moving it yet. The garage is full of all sorts of junk . . . I mean, things being stored.'

Emily laughs. 'Junk is about right. OK, I'll park in the corner under the oak tree – then if it's hot tomorrow I won't singe my legs getting in.'

She drives into the car park and tucks the car away as neatly as she can. Her bag isn't heavy – she was determined to travel light this time – but Andy's already reaching an arm out to take it from her.

'You look shattered,' he says. 'Why don't you go and sit round the back so we can see the harbour and you can have a slurp of my beer while I go and get you one of your own. Or would you rather have some wine? They do quite a good sauvignon blanc.'

'Beer would be brilliant,' says Emily, doing as she's told.

The view is spectacular. Stretching out to one side she can see the curve of the sandy beach, and to her right are the harbour walls, encircling a row of little boats. She can hear the mournful cry of the gulls and the hammering noises of someone making repairs to a wooden dinghy dragged far up onto the pebbles.

Pengelly in early June. Emily can't remember ever arriving at this time of year. Christmas breaks, school holidays and snatched weekends here and there during her working years haven't prepared her for the freshness in the air and the timeless magic of a Cornish village without too many visitors, although as tourist spots go, this place has always been a bit off the beaten track. It's cloudy now but the breeze is warm on Emily's face and a sense of peace steals over her. Soothed, she reaches for the glass and has downed more than half Andy's beer before she realises how fast she's drinking.

Andy comes back out with a tin tray holding two more pints and a couple of bags of nuts. 'Don't look so guilty,' he says, grinning. 'I thought that might happen. Here's another. Finish that one first, though. You've earned it after coming all this way.'

'Won't Gran mind if I'm late?'

'It's fine. I told her I'd meet you here first. Sorry the drinks took so long. I got talking to an old guy sitting at the bar. Tom King, do you know him?'

Emily shakes her head. 'Don't think so. Should I?'

'Probably not. He'd have been working when you were around. He's retired now. It seems sad.'

'What does? Being retired?'

'No, seeing him in there just propping up the bar and staring into his pint. He always seemed so busy – dashing here and there. I don't think he knows how to fill his time now.'

'I guess that's how Gran's feeling. Everything's changed so much.' Emily sighs. 'It was lovely of you to come and get me. Just like . . .'

'I know. She said he always did that. I didn't want you to feel worse than you already do about missing him.'

Emily swallows the painful lump in her throat that's threatening to choke her, noting as she glances down at her phone that there's still nothing from Max. Heartless git. Her head's throbbing now.

She reaches for the end of her plait and takes the bobble off it, then gently eases her hair free with the hand that isn't holding the glass, shaking it loose with a sigh of relief. Andy makes a strangled noise in his throat and she looks up, startled.

'Did you say something?'

'N-no. Just . . . erm . . . clearing my throat. Hay fever, probably.'

'Oh, do you get it badly?'

'No, not really. Not at all, usually. Allie used to get it. I don't know why I told you that, sorry.'

Emily searches for a way to change the subject to something more neutral. 'I can see there have been a few changes in Pengelly since I was last here,' she says, peering up the road. 'Has the shop had a face-lift?'

Andy grimaces. 'Yes, Vera's moved upmarket, or so she thinks. She's got a deli counter and she stocks posh designer gins and marinated tofu and locally sourced wonky veg.'

'Hasn't the village hall been painted too?'

'We had a work party for that. George and Cliff at the

fish restaurant sponsored it and we raised money for new curtains.'

Emily sighs. 'It must be great to live in a village. I don't know any of my neighbours. We're all working silly hours.'

'It's OK most of the time, so long as you don't mind them knowing your business almost before you know it yourself. Have you heard about Ida Carnell's Adopt-a-Granny scheme?'

'No, but tell me now!'

'It was Ida who bullied your gran into taking May under her wing. That's going well so far but some of the pairings have been a bit . . . volatile, you might say. Tom, the one who I just saw in there –' he gestures to the pub – 'well, Ida's noticed he seems a bit lost too, and he's been teamed up with George and Cliff, but he's taken a fancy to their other protégée, Joyce Chippendale. He likes older women, he says.'

'Oh, so it's not confined to ladies, then?'

'Never let it be said that Ida isn't inclusive. Apparently Tom propositioned Joyce the very first time they all met up at the restaurant for lunch. And then Marigold – she's being adopted by Vera – allowed her Pekinese to relieve itself in a big way on Vera's gravel drive. It all got a bit messy after that, in more ways than one.'

'Right.' Emily's giggling now.

'So don't think that just because we live in a sleepy backwater, nothing ever happens here.'

'Absolutely not. I wouldn't dream of assuming such a thing.'

Even though they've reached the end of their conversation,

the silence following it is friendly. Emily concentrates on her drink and Andy watches a small tabby cat walking down the road towards them. When it gets nearer, it stops and washes its face.

'Where have you come from, you pretty little thing?' Emily asks the cat, reaching down to stroke it.

'Be careful, it's a stray. It's tried to follow me home several times. I made the mistake of giving it some tuna once because Tamsin was worried about it, and now it wants to move in.'

'Aren't you a cat lover then?'

'Well, yes, I like them well enough. We never had one before because Allie was allergic to cats and dogs in a big way, so I thought Tamsin might be, too. She already gets asthma.'

'It doesn't follow that cats will make her wheeze, though.'

The cat is purring now, winding herself around Emily's legs and bashing her head against the outstretched hand. 'He's probably got fleas,' warns Andy.

'He's a she. Look at her belly. She's pregnant.'

'Is she?'

'Yes, I know she's skinny but her tummy's all swollen, look.'

The cat lies down and rolls over on her back obligingly. Andy stares, fascinated. 'You can actually see the kittens moving,' he says.

'Yup. She'll be having them any day now, I think.' Just then a silver Jeep comes careering down the road towards the pub. It slows down, horn beeping, and Emily sees an arm waving madly and a shock of white-blond hair. The woman in the car is wearing oversized sunglasses and her lipstick is red and glossy.

'Hi, Andy,' she yells.

Emily thinks she's going to stop but a tractor is approaching from behind her and there's a van coming the other way.

'Laters, hun,' the woman screeches, pulling away with a squeal of tyres.

'Who was that?' Emily asks. 'She looked kind of familiar.'

Andy looks at his feet, suddenly red in the face. 'Candice. Just Tamsin's friend's mum. We sometimes take turns with the school run.'

'Oh, yes. I remember her. The hair's a different colour but the voice is the same. She never liked me when you were at school together and I used to come to the beach with you all.'

'You're imagining it. Candice is OK. Just a bit . . . well, loud . . .'

'If you say so.'

They've nearly finished their drinks now, and Andy yawns and stretches his arms above his head, rotating his shoulders. 'That was a great way to start the evening, but I'd better go and rescue Julia and May. They're looking after Tamsin at May's cottage, and she should be having her bath and supper around now. I've got a babysitter all lined up for tomorrow night, though, if you're still up for dinner along the coast? We can watch the sun set over the bay and eat the best seafood in Cornwall.'

Emily nods, almost too weary to speak. They finish their drinks and the last few nuts, and Andy picks up Emily's bag. As they turn the corner down the steep cobbles of Memory Lane, Emily looks back. 'The cat's coming with us.'

Sure enough, the little animal is trailing along behind them, not too close, but she clearly means business. Andy sighs. 'Don't look at me like that,' he says. 'I'll give her some more tinned fish and let her in for a little while. But if there's even the slightest sign of Tamsin's breathing suffering, that cat's on her way, OK?'

Emily grins up at him. She's glad she wore her flat sandals – it's a change to have to crane her neck to look at a man. Then, just when the warm glow from the beer and the relief of being here safely are making her relax at last, she has to go and spoil it.

'Don't you think you might be being a bit overprotective of Tamsin?' she says.

# Chapter Twelve

Julia looks across at her granddaughter's white face and wonders if it's exhaustion that's making her look so grim or if there's more to it than that.

'Have some more salad, darling?' she says.

Emily shakes her head. 'This is lovely, Gran. I've eaten loads already. A proper old-fashioned tea. It's years since I've had sliced cucumber and onion in vinegar.'

Julia frowns. She's not sure if she likes being called old-fashioned. It's almost as bad as fuddy-duddy, isn't it? What's wrong with traditional food anyway? Emily looks up, seeming to realise she's said the wrong thing.

'I didn't mean it wasn't perfect,' she says. 'Oh, I can't say anything right tonight. I've already managed to upset Andy. Why are men so touchy?'

'He isn't usually like that. What did you say, exactly?'

Emily repeats the last part of the conversation. 'And then he asked me how come I knew so much about bringing up kids. I never said I did! He left me at the door without saying anything else. Rude, wasn't it?'

'Well . . .'

'Don't say you're going to stick up for him, Gran? I was just making a point. You can't mollycoddle children. If he never lets Tamsin have a pet, how will he know if she's allergic to animals? It's not fair on the poor girl.'

'Being a parent isn't that straightforward, sweetheart. He's already lost his wife. I expect he spends a lot of time being terrified that he'll lose Tamsin too. I know it's not rational, but then love isn't, is it?'

Emily shrugs, reminding Julia of the teenager who used to want to come and stay with her grandparents in the holidays, but then spent most of her time moodily stomping up and down the beach or shut in her room writing reams of poetry. She begins to clear the table, with what Julia considers to be an unnecessary amount of clattering.

When they've loaded the dishwasher, Emily follows Julia outside to sit on the swinging seat overlooking the bay. The evening sun is still warm, and the tide is coming in.

'Who's that man with the dogs? He looks familiar,' says Emily, bad mood forgotten as she relaxes into the cushions and gazes out across the bay.

'Oh, that's Tristram. You remember, Em, he was a great friend of your grandfather's. I've known him for years – ever since we came to Pengelly when we married. Tris was still a teenager then. After Gramps retired a group of the older men used to play bowls together on the park. They're very competitive, and Tristram often won. I'm sure you must have met him.'

'Oh, yes, I can see his face properly now he's taken his hat off. He's the guy with the fish restaurant over on the headland. I thought that was where Andy was taking me tomorrow, but we're going to the other one. That's if he's still speaking to me after tonight.'

'Yes, that's Tris. He's had The Shellfish Shack for years but when his daughter came home for good they decided to branch out and move to the beach place. They specialise in freshly caught fish and seafood. Gina runs it and his son-in-law's the chef, but Tris is the one who's in charge. Everybody knows that.'

'Isn't he a bit too . . .?'

'Old? Yes, he's nearly eighty, I guess, but he's full of beans.'

'Talking of which, you're looking a lot better than I expected, Gran. I thought you'd be sort of . . . well . . . droopy, somehow.'

Julia laughs. 'I was feeling that way, darling, but the last few days have livened me up no end. Although . . . anyway, I've been working with May to get the letters sorted, so Andy can catalogue them. That's if you approve of the idea,' she adds hastily, 'involving the other two, I mean.'

'Fine by me. I really like May, but I kind of got the impression you two didn't get on so well before? I didn't imagine that, did I?'

'A person can change their mind, can't they?'

'Don't *you* get huffy with me, Gran – I feel like I'm walking on eggshells around here tonight.'

'Sorry. I'm just finding that I like May a little bit more than I thought I did. She's cranky sometimes – we all are – but she's got her good points. I reckon I let my feelings about her husband get in the way. He was a horrible man. I . . . hated him.'

'Why? I thought May was single. I can't remember her ever being married.'

Julia ignores the question. 'It was a long time ago. Charles and May married late and he died before he was even sixty years old.'

'Oh, that's so sad – what happened?'

'He went out in his boat one night in a storm and never came back. It was days before his body was washed up. Nobody missed him for a while. Apparently May just thought he'd gone off on one of his jaunts around the coast. The boat turned up first . . . well, what was left of it. The rocks round here are pretty fierce.'

Emily shivers. 'How awful. Why would anyone go sailing in bad weather?'

'Who knows? He'd been making it known he thought he'd got something seriously wrong with him. There was talk of him doing away with himself at the time, but unofficially. It was all rather mysterious. The night was so wild and the sea so rough, you'd have had to be mad to go out in a boat just for fun.'

'The poor man. And poor May.'

'To be honest I don't think May was too sad. They had a very spiky relationship. Charles preferred men.'

'Ah. And May knew about that?'

'She pretended not to. I don't think she realised the village had guessed long ago, but Charles played away quite often, and he left a trail of destruction behind him. He wasn't the kindest of people. He was the sort who gives gay men a bad name. His cruel streak was nothing to do with whether he liked men or women best, but some of the older villagers judged him on that.'

'It happens.'

'Good job we've got George and Cliff to redress the balance now. They're just the opposite.'

'The couple from the other fish restaurant, you mean?'

'Yes. They'd do anything for anybody. They married last year and had a huge party. It was wonderful – everyone was there. But Charles . . . he was a bad lot through and through.'

There's a chill in the air now, and Julia wraps her cardigan around her more tightly and heaves a huge sigh.

'Sorry, Gran, I've made you depressed now. Tell me some of the things you've been reading about in the letters?' Emily says, reaching for Julia's hand. 'I can't wait to have a look for myself.'

Julia opens her mouth to speak, but no words come out. Emily waits. After a moment or two she says, 'Gran? What's the matter?'

'Oh, it's nothing. My memory isn't what it was, that's all. Must be my age catching up with me. It's better you see the letters for yourself.'

'If that's what you'd rather I do. I just thought . . .'

'It's hard to remember specific points, darling, there are so many. Elsie was always writing, and so were the others.'

'Is May enjoying it too, this research?'

'Yes, she loves it. I think she's been as lonely as me just lately. When she lived in the middle of the village she was always in and out of her neighbours' houses, but she's not so good on her legs now. Mind you, for someone who's a hundred and ten, she's doing pretty well.'

Julia breathes a sigh of relief, hoping that the tricky moment has passed.

'Look, here's Tristram and his boys – Buster and Bruno. I hoped you'd get to meet the dogs,' she says, wanting Emily to be diverted enough to drop the subject of the letters for now. The ploy works.

'That little one's so cute. Even from a distance I can see it's got a really worried face. Look at its tail, all curled up like a question mark.'

'That's Buster. He's a puggle.'

'Pardon?'

'A cross between a pug and a beagle. I hadn't heard of it either. He's so naughty.'

'In what way?'

'He steals food,' says Julia, pulling a face.

'Oh, come on. Don't all dogs try to do that?'

'You haven't met Buster. He's a master thief. Bruno wouldn't lower himself to such antics. Although he *is* partial to eating blackberries straight from the bramble bush.'

Tristram's coming towards them now. Buster is having one last splash in the waves, joyfully biting the breakers as they come in. The more dignified Labrador is avoiding getting wet, plodding along sniffing at the seaweed and other tempting smells. Tristram whistles, and after a moment of indecision, both dogs gallop up the beach and over the ridge of slippery rocks and pebbles near the road.

'Hello there! Have you got time to say hello to my lovely granddaughter?' shouts Julia, waving madly. If Tristram doesn't take Emily's mind off asking awkward questions, she doesn't know what will.

'Good evening, ladies,' Tristram says as soon as he gets near enough. He stops in front of them, doffing his battered hat and bowing. 'A chat would be most acceptable. Dogs are all well and good but their conversation is uninspiring on the whole.'

He shakes hands with Emily and sits down in the seat opposite them. Julia has the bizarre feeling that she's seeing Tristram as if for the first time. His neat grey beard and matching hair indicate that he's not in the first flush of youth, to say the least, but nothing else about him seems elderly in any way, and his smile is like sunshine. There's a look of Gandalf after a trip to the barber's shop about him. Wise, but probably a bit of a maverick. Really, she thinks, this debonair gentleman with the mischievous eyes is a pleasure to behold.

'It's good to see you again, Emily,' he says, 'and looking more stunning than ever. New York must suit you. Not working too hard? Or is that a silly question?'

Emily smiles back. 'It's great to be having a break. What gorgeous dogs,' she comments, as Buster, barking madly, starts to bound up and down Julia's small garden, and Bruno flops down with his head on Julia's shoe, drooling slightly in a friendly way. 'The small one seems a bit distracted, though.'

'I bet he's seen a cat. He always reacts like this. Has Julia recently got one?'

'No, but . . .' Emily leans forward to peer across the road. Yes, there's the little tabby sitting on the pavement washing her whiskers. Andy comes out and glances across to see where the frenzied barking is coming from.

'Hello, my friend,' calls Tristram. 'Long time, no see. Is that your feline creature?'

Andy hesitates and then crosses the lane to shake Tristram's outstretched hand. 'Hi, Tris,' he says. 'I need to get back in two minutes because Tamsin's waiting for a story. She's watching out of the window to see if I've found the new member of the family.' He glares at Emily. 'Vi's with her. I suppose *some* people would call me over-protective, but she's only a little girl.'

'Of course you wouldn't go out and leave her without someone to watch her. I don't even do that with these boys. Though to be fair, Buster's a bit of a head case. He got into the oven and ate three hot chicken portions, bones and all, last week. It's a wonder he's still around to bark at your cat. He could've choked, stupid boy.'

'We both need to be on our guard in different ways, I guess. So anyway, how's your chip shop doing, mate?' Andy says. He half turns his back on Emily rather pointedly and sits down.

Tristram roars with laughter and Emily raises her eyebrows.

'Ignore him,' Tristram says. 'He's a Philistine. My fish emporium is famous throughout the West Country and beyond. You must come and eat with us before you go back to the big city. Maybe this young fella will bring you?'

There's a stony silence. Andy is suddenly very interested in making a fuss of Buster, who's finally calmed down and come to say hello, and Emily is looking out to sea, shading her eyes to watch a fishing boat chugging towards the harbour.

Julia sighs. 'You're very quiet tonight, Andy,' she says, deciding to bite the bullet. 'Did you say you'd got yourself a cat?'

'She got me really. We seem to have been adopted by her,' says Andy, still avoiding looking at Emily. 'Maybe it's another of Ida's fiendish plans. Not only that, it looks as if the poor little beast's about to have kittens. Can I tempt you to one, Julia? Tristram?'

Tristram guffaws again. 'Can you imagine the fun we'd have, between keeping a kitten out of Buster's jaws and stopping it eating all the best prawns? No, thanks. But, Julia, how about it? A kitten's fun, and it might grow into a good companion for you.'

'Companion? I'm not in need of that! And I'd probably seem even crazier if I started collecting cats,' says Julia, pulling a face.

'Crazy? Whoever called you that? Name the dog!'

Bruno looks up at the key word and wags his tail lazily, tongue lolling out of the side of his jaws. Julia bends to stroke him. 'Nobody yet, Tris, but it's only a matter of time. A widow living alone, not going out much? I'm fair game.'

'That's the daftest thing I've ever heard. You're the last person to be accused of being dotty. Isn't she?' Tristram appeals to Emily and Andy, and they both jump in quickly, strenuously denying that anyone could ever doubt Julia's sanity. Julia smiles. Nice try, folks, she thinks, but you're not fooling anybody, least of all me.

Emily yawns and stands up. 'Well, if nobody minds, I'm off to bed,' she says. 'Today seems to have gone on for ever. Night-night, everybody.'

Tristram and Andy both stand up as Emily goes into the house. Julia is pleased that they both know how to act like gentlemen, but can't help wanting to bang Emily and Andy's heads together. Why can't they just get along nicely with each other? She can't be bothered with all this hassle.

'That's a beautiful girl you've got there, Julia,' says Tristram, 'but she looks as if she's in need of a good rest. These young ones sometimes don't seem to know how to stop and smell the coffee. How long is she staying?'

'A fortnight, I think, but I might be able to persuade her to have a bit more time with me. I haven't seen her since the funeral and I'd love to keep her for longer.'

'Well, maybe Andy can help us out there?'

Andy stares at Tristram. 'How can I possibly do that?'

'Oh, the jungle drums have been busy, as usual.'

'I'm not with you.'

'I was having a pint with my old mate George last night. He tells me you've booked a table for two at Cockleshell Bay tomorrow night for yourself and the young lady.'

'Yes, I did, but I don't know if she'll be free now.' Andy's jaw is set and his face is thunderous.

'You made a good choice. Apart from my own fine

establishment, it's the best there is, and you must have remembered I'm closed on Mondays. George and Cliff have the best place to eat in the area. She'll love it. Emily won't ever want to leave when she's tasted Cliff's crab chowder.'

'And I'm sure she's not got anything else planned,' says Julia, making a mental note to stop at nothing to get Emily out of the house tomorrow night with Andy. She has a feeling it won't be easy.

# Chapter Thirteen

Lying in bed listening to birdsong and the distant roar of the waves, Emily feels more content than she's been for months. The thrushes and blackbirds in the garden are singing their hearts out and the cry of the gulls adds another layer to the clamour. She's had the window open all night and the curtains are moving slightly in the breeze, wafting the intoxicating scent of blossom into the room under the eaves.

Slipping quietly out of bed, she pads across the varnished boards to kneel on the window seat, leaning her elbows on the sill and breathing in the clean, fresh scents of the seaside. There's a hint of damp in the air but the clouds are moving quickly across the sky today and Emily hopes the sun will appear later. The sight of the empty stretch of sand takes her breath away. Without consciously making the decision to do so, she's wriggling into denim shorts and a T-shirt, her long-time uniform for Cornish days, and lacing up the ancient Converse she's found in the bottom of the wardrobe. It's not even five o'clock yet – plenty of time for an adventure before breakfast.

Tiptoeing down the stairs, Emily is reminded of all the

other times she's done this over the years, avoiding the creaking step third from the top, opening the squeaky back door inch by inch, running down the path to the bay, feeling . . . free. Gran and Gramps weren't early risers, and she was never able to wait for them to get up, even on rainy days. She always made sure she was back well before Gran started frying bacon and eggs, so nobody was any the wiser and Emily usually got the very best of the morning, before a single footprint marred the perfection of the sand.

With the sharp tang of salt and seaweed and the promise of sunshine later, Emily's spirits rise, just as they always do at the start of her holidays here. No two days are the same in Pengelly. She remembers May telling her something that an old boyfriend had said to her years ago.

'He reckoned I was like the Cornish weather,' May said, grinning. 'One minute sunshine, then storms and heavy rain that blotted everything else out. Black clouds, thick fog sometimes, bright flashes of lightning and long hot days when time seemed to stop.'

Emily was impressed. 'He must have been pretty besotted to say those things and to put up with your changing moods, if that's what you really were like?'

'Oh, yes, he was, dear, for a while. No doubt about that. And I think I loved him more than I've ever loved anyone.'

'So what happened?'

May didn't answer the question, changing the subject to something mundane. Maybe Emily will ask again when she sees her this time.

Distracted by the sheer joy of being on the beach again, she jogs down to the waterline and unties her laces, kicking off her shoes. Her hair's still in its night-time plait and she unravels it quickly, letting it flow around her shoulders as she wades into the sea.

The chill of the first waves lapping over her toes sends a shudder through her but she carries on until she's knee-deep, rolling up the frayed hems of her shorts until they can hardly be seen under her T-shirt. Her hair lifts in the sea breeze and she laughs with sheer joy. An exuberant breaker almost knocks her over but Emily stands firm, enjoying the power of the current around her calves and the itch of salt water on her skin.

After a few minutes, she paddles back to shore and picks up her shoes, tying the laces together so she can loop them around her neck. It's then she spots the flash of light in one of the upstairs windows of Andy's house. A torch? No, it's too bright to see something meant to be used in darkness. What, then? A reflection? Glass? Her mind leaps ahead. Binoculars or a telescope. He's spying on her. The weirdo.

Seething, Emily raises a hand and waves in Andy's general direction. Immediately, the glinting rays disappear. Ha. Got you, she thinks. But why would Andy be watching her? At this ungodly hour she'd have thought most of the village would be fast asleep.

Emily heads for the other end of the bay, feeling the gritty sand under her bare feet and trying to shake off the uneasy sense of being stalked. Maybe he's a closet birdwatcher? There are plenty of twitchers around here.

But how interesting can it be spotting gulls? Tedious, surely? She gives it a try. It'd be, oh, there's a gull. Yep, there's another two. And three more . . . Not very inspiring, you'd think?

Tonight's the night when she's supposed to be going out for dinner with this man. Last night he could barely bring himself to look at her and now he's spoiling her morning walk. How is she going to get through a whole evening with him? If he's going to take offence at every little thing she says, it's going to be hard work. At least Max had been fairly thick-skinned, unless you tried to dent his ego, of course. In any case, it's definitely time to have a break from men. Who needs them?

As she mooches along, stopping to pick up a shell now and again, Emily becomes aware of the sound of barking. Sure enough, two familiar shapes are getting bigger as they bob closer. Pale, bristly fur and a madly curling tail, an anxious face and a short-legged body bounce slightly ahead of a solid mass of blackness and a long-legged stride. Buster hurtles towards Emily like a damp heat-seeking missile, flinging himself against her legs and beside himself with joy while Bruno lopes along behind him, eager to join in the fun. Emily kneels down to make a fuss of them and waits for Tristram to catch his dogs up.

'I hope my hounds aren't making a nuisance of themselves?' he says, when he's near enough to be heard. 'They spotted you from the other end of the beach. I think you've made friends there.'

'But Bruno isn't wet,' she says, as Buster shakes himself enthusiastically, giving Emily a shower.

'No, he's terrified of water. I've never known a Lab before who doesn't love a swim. Very odd.'

Emily fondles Bruno's soft ears and scratches Buster under his chin. She wonders if a small dog would be allowed in her apartment, but it's a forlorn thought, because who would take it for walks and keep it company when she's travelling, or at work for so many hours a day? 'They're both lovely,' she says, standing up and stretching as Buster hurtles back towards the waves and leaps right into the biggest one he can find, 'I wish . . .' She falls silent.

'Didn't you have a puppy when you were growing up?'

'No, we moved to Munich when I was quite young, and before that we were in Bristol. My parents said a city was no place for dogs. I was allowed a fish tank.'

'Hmm. Difficult to take a fish for a walk.'

They fall into step and walk back up the beach. Emily's stomach rumbles, and she wonders if the pan will be sizzling when she gets back to the cottage. Her gran's breakfasts are stupendous – local sausages and oak-smoked bacon, fresh farm eggs with deep yellow yolks, grilled tomatoes, mushrooms from the farm shop . . . Emily's mouth waters.

'Have you got a young man in New York, Emily?' Tristram asks suddenly.

Emily stares at him, unsure whether to be offended by the intrusion. 'No,' she says eventually, 'not any more. And what about you? Are you married?'

'Same answer; not any more,' he says, pulling a face. 'My wives are all long gone.'

'Wives? You make yourself sound like Bluebeard.'

'Well, I tried several times. I'm aiming for Henry VIII's final total, that's what I tell my daughter. Not really, though. I think four wives is enough, don't you?'

'You've been married four times?'

'Yes, and all of them were lovely women – they just weren't the right ones for me, or more likely I wasn't the right one for them. I'm not very good at marriage. Too unpredictable, that was the main criticism. Oh, and also much too impulsive. Just don't seem to be able to make a woman happy, or not long-term anyway.' He grins at her. 'I do OK for a while, though. Short-term husband material, that's me.'

They've reached the bottom of Memory Lane now, and without discussion they sit down on one of the seats overlooking the bay with Bruno at their feet. All the benches have brass plaques dedicating them to the dear departed. This one is in memory of 'Arthur and Maud, who loved the view over Pengelly Sands'. Emily wonders how many times these two wandered along the beach, maybe hand in hand, in love, planning their future together or, later, sharing memories. Arthur and Maud would have been sure of each other's feelings. He wouldn't have had a wife and a gang of kids tucked away somewhere, and she probably never doubted his devotion.

Tristram sees Emily reading the inscription, and makes a disgusted face. 'I knew those two,' he says, 'and they couldn't stand each other most of the time. Don't be fooled. Their son put this bench here to make himself feel better for never coming to see them, but you couldn't blame him. They were grumpy as hell.'

The dream of the couple holding hands as they skip through the shallow waves on the waterline vanishes, and Emily is back in the land of cynicism. Is anybody really happy with their partner? Emily's mother and father dislike each other intensely; Tristram has never achieved a happy marriage, and she is now single by choice.

Tristram stands up and calls Buster, who comes running immediately, tail waving and ears flapping. At least a dog gives his whole heart. 'You're going out with Andy tonight,' he says.

'I was supposed to be. He doesn't seem so keen now, and neither am I.'

'It wasn't a question. You *are* going for dinner with my friend Andy. That man needs a night out with a beautiful woman. *You* deserve some fun. End of story.'

Tristram pats Emily's shoulder as if to take any sting out of his words, whistles to his dogs once more and they set off together down the beach. Emily watches them go and turns to head back home for breakfast. She can already smell the coffee brewing. And for now, that's enough.

# Chapter Fourteen

May wakes early, as usual, and is soon relaxing in her favourite cane lounger on the deck. She's slightly disorientated this morning, because she's been thinking about her parents and their shadowy figures seem very near this morning. May has been replaying one particular conversation in her mind. She remembers it almost word for word.

'May, has it ever occurred to you that you're . . . not quite like other folk?' her father asked as they walked across the beach one spring day.

'What do you mean, Pa?'

'I've seen you accumulating trinkets. I know how you feel about them. We're both different, you and I. My mother was the same.'

He paused there, running his hands through his ginger hair until it stood on end. May sat down on a rock and waited, eyes wide. She had the sense of standing on the edge of a cliff. It was a long way down.

'Go on,' she said.

'I first noticed how other people's possessions made me feel when I was in my teens. Not everything, but some had an unusual energy inside them . . .'

May held her breath.

'It was the feeling of euphoria they gave me. A sort of a buzz, you could say, and it sometimes lasted for several hours. I'd been having a bad patch, health-wise. A bout of whooping cough had laid me low, but when I paid proper attention to my collecting again, I began to feel stronger and healthier.'

'But, Pa, I get it too – the buzz.'

'I know you do.' He sighed deeply. 'I don't know if it's a good or bad thing.'

'What makes you say that?'

'Because I strongly suspect that you and I have the power to harvest memories from certain objects. I've noticed how you love collecting old things, and I've seen the look on your face when you first hold a new . . . acquisition, shall we call it? Will you show me now? Here's something a bit special.'

He handed her a coin from his pocket. May looked down at the gold sovereign nestling in her palm. Holding it more tightly, she focused her mind on its shiny surface and let her thoughts wander. The resulting flood of muddled memories made her gasp, and then the feeling settled into one of pure happiness.

'I wanted to see you in action,' said May's father, smiling at her rather sadly. 'It's just as I thought.'

'But what does it mean? And what happened to your mother?' May was on the verge of panic now. It was one thing having the sensations she experienced explained, but did she really want to know the answer to this question? What if the power she shared with her father was going to change her life, and not for the better? She gave him the coin back and held up her hands, palms outwards, as if she were pushing him away. 'Maybe you don't need to say any more.'

'No, I must. We have to understand as much as we possibly can about what happens to us when we soak up all those memories. As you know, Ma died in a flu epidemic, but she always looked incredibly young for her age. Everyone commented on it. And she was an avid collector of antique dolls. You look very like her.'

May had never even tried to put her talent into words. It had been part of her life for as long as she could remember. Right from her first proper memories of lying in her pram in the garden looking up at trees moving in the breeze, she'd been aware of the power of certain objects. The string of tiny wooden animals that was suspended across the front of her pram to amuse her was a constant source of happiness. Later when she was much older, May found out that the mobile had belonged to her grandmother as a baby. The echoes from it gave her a deep sense of wellbeing even years later.

The relief of hearing her father bringing their shared skill into the open was intense, if scary. May closed her eyes and counted to ten in the hope that she wouldn't cry. This was too important to be spoiled by bawling like a baby. Her father cleared his throat.

'May, how old were you when you really noticed the memories transferring themselves to you?'

May closed her eyes and thought back. The vague feelings and suspicions had become stronger over the years, but the crucial moments had been on her eighth birthday when her parents had taken her to London and they'd gone to the British Museum.

'Do you remember the London trip?' she asked her father. 'I was totally overwhelmed by the memories there.'

'Of course. That was why I persuaded your mother that you needed a bit of culture in your life. I thought it would be conclusive proof that you shared my talent, if you can call it that. I didn't expect it to have such a severe effect. You fainted clean away in the oriental ceramics section.'

'I was terrified. It was like being submerged in the past. I was drowning in it.'

'Do you remember how I tried to talk to you about all this at the time? You closed up and wouldn't discuss anything even slightly relating to your ability.'

She nodded. It had all seemed too daunting to mention. Her memory collecting was private, and much too precious to be put into words in case it disappeared. The vague feeling of being unusual had grown stronger as she got older, but there was always the fear that she'd suddenly lose her special talents if she spoke of them.

May's father talked to her more often about their shared skills after that, and as they discussed it, they gradually worked out what was happening every time they stole an echo from someone else's mind.

'Might we live for ever then, Pa?' May said, after one gruelling session.

'No, but I think it's entirely possible that we might last a very long time, love,' he replied. 'The saddest part about it is that I can't get your mother to accept it. She refuses to even speak about it.'

'But she's bound to feel like that if she can't do what we do. We'll both carry on living and living and living, and Mum will just die.' May's tears flowed then, and Pa held her tightly.

'The thing is, I'm not sure how this affects other people, May,' he said.

'How do you mean?'

'Well, I try very hard to ration myself. If the memories are flowing into my body, they must be leaving someone else's at the same time, surely? That's why museums must be a good source, if you're running low. Nobody owns the exhibits so I'm hoping nobody suffers.'

'What about the old things I buy? If a person's got rid of something already, they can't need those memories, can they?'

He sighed. 'I don't know. I hope not. Just be wary, May. Don't get greedy, that's all.'

May gazes out to sea. She *is* getting greedy with Julia's letters now. The poor woman's being drained of valuable thoughts that should only belong to her. Can May stop before more damage is done? She's not sure if she's able to do that now. If only her father were here to consult.

As it happened, he was wrong about living a long time, thinks May, as she looks back down the years from her seat on the decking. Hitler had other plans for her father. She's feeling a little chilly now, so she pushes herself to her feet and hobbles indoors, sinking into her sofa with a grunt of relief. The old sadness still washes over her, though. Pa went to London in the spring of 1941 in the hope of hearing his old university tutor speak to a group of fellow enthusiasts about the importance of ground-breaking new research in the field of genetics. The event was long awaited and he was brimming over with excitement, but May's mother begged him not to go.

'Are you crazy, Bernard?' she said. 'The Blitz isn't over yet. The newspapers say there's more to come. It's much too risky.'

'I've got to. It could be my last chance. Hardcastle hardly ever lectures nowadays. They say his health is failing. And anyway, I won't be in one of the dangerous areas. It's in the suburbs. I'll be fine.'

He wasn't. May's mother never got over the loss of her life partner, succumbing to pneumonia just after the war ended. May still misses them both today, as she always will. Dear people.

She hears a soft knock on the back door and a voice calls, 'May? Are you there? Can I come in?'

'Is that you, Emily?'

'Yes, I've come to see if I can talk to you about Gran. I told her I wanted to see your cottage. And it's true, I do.'

Emily breezes into the room like a breath of fresh air, dispelling May's sad thoughts. She even smells bright and clean. Her hair is flowing down her back, tangled and golden in the morning sunshine, and she's dressed for action in faded jeans and a checked shirt with the sleeves rolled up.

May considers Emily, her head on one side. Although she hasn't seen her often they have always had a connection; the sort that transcends the generations. There's something different about the girl this time.

'Well, you're a sight for sore eyes, dear,' says May, beaming. 'I was feeling a bit blue for some silly reason, but we can have a cup of tea . . . or coffee, if you'd rather? And then you can bring me up to date with all your news. You must lead a very hectic life these days, what with your exciting job . . . career, I should say.'

Emily's only half listening. She's gazing around May's living room, eyes sparkling.

'I love your new home, May. You've got so many interesting things to look at. You haven't brought everything from the big house, so it's easier to look at the things that are really precious.'

May glances around too, as if seeing her cosy living room with new eyes. It must seem very odd to a younger person. She's kept her favourite belongings, so the cottage is rather crowded, but as Emily says, a lot of the less important bits and bobs have gone. The dining table is covered with a maroon chenille cloth with deep fringes and there's a brass pot in the centre of it holding a fine aspidistra. The dining chairs are a mismatched collection, chosen for comfort rather than style, some with worn brocade seats and others of carved wood with ladder backs, and seat pads in bright colours.

There are bookshelves lining one wall and they're stuffed with all the books she couldn't bear to part with. Her parents were avid readers and May has read most of the novels over the years since their deaths. It's a way of keeping them close.

'I loved your other house,' says Emily, 'and you must have had to get rid of a whole heap of stuff when you came here, but you've still got your treasures. Have you always collected beautiful things?'

'Yes, I suppose I have. Even more so when I started to see the world.'

Emily makes encouraging noises. May knows she's loved to hear her tales of the past since she was old enough to ask the right questions. May begins to talk about her travels. Emily has heard most of this before over the years, but she settles back in her chair and listens happily.

It was the honeymoon trip to Venice with Charles that finally kick-started May's late-developing wanderlust. Charles was wholly unimpressed by the holiday – he didn't approve of 'abroad' – but May was enchanted with everything about the experience.

When they returned home and Charles moved into the family house – still much too big without her parents, somehow – May immediately began to plan her next expedition. Inexperienced in the social aspects of married life and reluctant to change his routine, Charles often gravitated to the pub to play backgammon with a few cronies, giving May ample time to pore over her collection of maps and atlases and make plans.

She was completely footloose, having moved to a new job in a bank two years previously and now been forced to leave, as were all married women in such positions.

Charles, although not a warm-hearted man, was generous with his money, of which he had a fair amount. He'd never been a big spender although he owned a lucrative art gallery in Penzance. May suspected that her husband was encouraging her growing passion for travel so that he could have time away from her, but she was undaunted.

Her first solo expedition was to Scotland by train. By the time May was on her fourth trip – now venturing overseas and tackling Brittany on a bicycle – Charles was well used to her long absences, and so were their neighbours in the village.

'Did you bring lots of treasures back from your expeditions?' asks Emily. 'I'm addicted to buying painted pottery dishes when I go anywhere. I've got so many I could open my own gift shop.'

May begins to tell Emily about some of the treasures she's accumulated, being careful not to go into details about how she came by them. 'But I like old mementoes best,' she says, 'Things with a history of their own.'

'Can I see some of them?'

'Of course. Stay there, I'll fetch a few.'

Emily's eyes open wide when she sees the array of objects that May spreads on the table five minutes later. She's gathered them in a wicker basket but now they're displayed on the tablecloth in all their glory.

'Here's something you'll like,' says May, picking up a shallow blue dish painted with pale yellow lemons. It's much more delicate that the chunky pottery she expects Emily favours.

'That looks very old. Did you buy it from a pottery or

a shop? I like to get mine directly from the maker if I can.'

May doesn't meet Emily's eyes. 'Oh . . . I can't remember. It was a long time ago in Sorrento. Look, here's another thing I picked up on the same trip to Italy.'

She holds out a small wooden figure and Emily recognises the familiar features of Pinocchio. He's slightly battered, and part of his long nose is missing.

'I think you were robbed if you bought this,' says Emily. 'It's a bit tatty.'

May has a sudden uncomfortable flashback to the moment when she realised that the little Italian girl she'd been idly chatting to on the next table had forgotten her toy. Pinocchio lay abandoned on the café table as the girl skipped away holding her father's hand. May guessed that there would be trouble later when the loss was noticed. She still had time to call them back. Instead, May picked up the little doll and held it tightly in her hand. The sweet rush of childish memories flowed over her like a spring tide, followed by older ones, right back in the workshop where the figure had been made. Breathless and shaken, she pushed Pinocchio to the bottom of her bag and hurried back to her guesthouse.

'And here's a beautiful bracelet,' says May quickly.

Emily holds the heavy silver bangle in one hand, running her fingers over its engravings. It's studded with gem stones, and they sparkle as Emily slips the bracelet onto her wrist, unable to resist trying it on. 'Wow. This must have cost a fortune,' she says. 'How much did you have to pay for it?'

'Oh, well, money's there to be spent. Let me tell you about the other bits and bobs.'

'And now you're settled in this snug little cottage,' Emily says, as May eventually runs out of breath. 'It's perfect, isn't it? Anyway, I've let myself get distracted, as usual. I really came to ask you how you're finding Gran these days. You've been seeing quite a lot of each other, haven't you?'

'Yes, we're getting on quite well, thank you,' answers May, wondering where this is heading. She has a sinking feeling and the room feels chilly all of a sudden.

'I'm really worried, May. It looks as if Gran's forgetting all sorts of things,' says Emily. 'It was Andy who let me know what was happening, and I'm glad he did. She seems fragile, although she insists she's loving sorting through the letters.'

'Oh dear.'

'I thought at first she seemed fairly lively and cheerful, but today she's so tired she's having a lie-down on the sofa, and it's not even lunchtime.'

'I see.'

Emily waits for May to expand on this remark, but there's nothing to say. May reaches for her tartan blanket and tucks it around her knees. The pleasant warmth of the day isn't penetrating her body any more. What is she going to do? She desperately needs the effervescent energy of the letters, but Julia is clearly suffering, and it will only get worse if she carries on.

Her father was right. May should never have let herself become so avaricious. Taking memories from the odd small belonging hasn't had much effect on her neighbours, or so she believes, but this is serious. And now she's stupidly allowed herself to grow fond of the woman who holds the key to her dream of reaching that magical birthday.

Emily gasps as a groan escapes May's pale lips.

'Are you feeling ill, May?' Emily asks, coming to kneel in front of her.

May shakes her head. Being ill would be simple compared to this.

# Chapter Fifteen

Andy gets ready for his night out with mixed feelings. He's checked with Julia that Emily *is* still coming with him – she was in the shower getting ready when he phoned so that's a good sign. It's a bit daunting to be going on what feels alarmingly like a date, especially when it's with someone who so obviously thinks he's a clucking father. If this evening's to be a success, he's going to have to put his feelings about what she said behind him and start from scratch. The important thing is to talk about Julia and decide if they need to do anything else at the moment other than keep a close eye on her.

Hearing Vi let herself in and halloo up the stairs, Andy takes one last look in the mirror and decides it's the best he can do. Grabbing his wallet, he heads for the front door, hugging Tamsin on the way out and threatening her with dire things if she doesn't go to bed and stay there when Vi tells her to. There's not much chance of that. Vi is totally unflappable, easily a match for Tamsin. Not for the first time, he thinks how lucky they are to have her next door.

'Hello, love,' Vi says as Andy comes into the kitchen.

'Wow, you look fabulous! You should pull the stops out more often.'

She comes over and brushes his lapels. Vi's a tiny dynamo of a woman, and she has to stand on tiptoe to reach when she ruffles his hair. 'I like the rugged but slightly dishevelled look,' she says. 'Very Aidan Turner.'

'Give over, more like Worzel Gummidge,' he answers, but is secretly pleased.

May's pottering in her garden as Andy leaves his house. She's very careful these days, he notices, always using her walking stick and taking her time on the rougher parts of the paths.

'Have a lovely time, dear,' she calls, waving her stick in the air.

Andy pulls a face. 'I hope we will,' he says, feeling a fresh shiver of apprehension.

May winks at him and watches as he heads round the side of Julia's house. Her expression is thoughtful.

Emily is standing in the kitchen talking to Julia. She smiles when she sees Andy, which he supposes is a good start.

'You look very spruce tonight, love,' says Julia, coming over to brush a piece of fluff from his lapel. What is it with these women and their addiction to grooming? 'You should dress up like this regularly.'

'That's what Vi said.'

'I bet she did.' Julia sniffs appreciatively. 'Ooh, you smell nice too. I do love a decent aftershave – something not too flowery or heavy. Don was fond of his cologne, too. I can't remember what his favourite brand was called. Something beginning with A, I think.' She frowns.

'I don't have much cause to be smart, as a rule. This is a red-letter day, and we've both made the effort, it seems,' Andy says, looking in admiration at Emily.

There's something almost medieval about her tonight. She's wearing an ankle-length dress in soft sage-green cotton patterned with tiny dragonflies. The neckline is scooped low enough to display a subtle hint of cleavage and her necklace is a startling combination of blue and green beads, twinkling in the evening sunshine that's pouring through Julia's spotless windows. Emily's golden hair is loose and flowing except for a thin plait each side of her face, looped back and fastened with a silver clip. In her flat sandals, she's smaller than Andy and somehow seems more defenceless than usual. She's even painted her toenails.

'You look amazing,' he says, unable to take his eyes off her, 'just like Galadriel.'

Julia grins. 'Well, it was obviously worth digging a frock out, Em, and Andy's going to enjoy having a pretty woman on his arm. Off you go, and have a wonderful evening. You've got your key, haven't you?'

'Yes, so there's no need to wait up. You need your sleep,' Emily says. She's pink in the face from the compliments. 'Thanks for the loan of the necklace, Gran.'

'Well, it'll be yours one day so you might as well get some wear out of it.'

'Don't say that – you'll need it yourself for ages yet.

I wish we still had the ring, though, so you could wear it.'

'What ring?'

'You know – you told me about the opal ring that's missing.'

'Did I?' Julia closes her eyes to think better.

Emily exchanges glances with Andy and grimaces. 'It doesn't matter, Gran. It'll come back to you. There's a lot on your mind at the moment, isn't there? See you later, don't wait up.'

Suddenly, as he helps Emily into the waiting taxi, Andy's nerves leave him and he's filled with a wild sense of freedom. His eyes stray to Emily's curves in the soft dress and he makes himself look away. She'll think he's a right pervert, peering down her front, like a randy schoolboy. But she's just so gorgeous.

'I'm really glad we're doing this,' he croaks. Oh bugger. Even his voice is giving him away.

Emily smiles. 'D'you know what? So am I,' she says. 'It's good to be out with a bloke with no strings attached. Just friends, yeah?'

'Oh, yeah. Absolutely,' says Andy, taking a deep breath and turning to look out of the window. Just friends. Remember that, mate, he tells himself.

They're at the restaurant already, and he pays the driver and escorts Emily inside, holding her elbow gently to guide her up the flight of stone steps into the dimly lit, fragrant warmth of Cockleshell Bay. It has small windows and a low ceiling, but the view from the terrace where French doors are wide open is breath-taking.

George welcomes them with open arms. He's a giant of a man, who likes to test everything on the menu thoroughly before it goes out to the punters. 'Andy, my friend. Good to see you. And you've brought a delightful lady to grace our little establishment. Have we met before, O ravishing creature? No, we can't have – I'd never forget that hair or those stunning sapphire-coloured eyes. An elven queen in our midst.'

Emily blushes. 'I haven't been here before,' she says, 'but if you carry on ladling out the soft soap like that, I'll definitely be back for more. I'm loving all this Galadriel stuff.'

'This is Don and Julia's granddaughter, Emily,' says Andy.

'Of course it is. Now I know why those eyes seemed familiar.'

George escorts them to the best table, overlooking the beach, and brings them ice-cold water in a carafe. The evening light is at its most perfect at this time, Andy thinks, seeing that they're going to have a fabulous view of the sunset very shortly. It's a romantic place. Is he wrong to be thinking like this? Emily doesn't seem to have any idea what she's doing to him. Surely Allie wouldn't mind him having designs on another woman after all this time? It's been over six years, for goodness' sake. Well, apart from that one night with Candice . . .

'It's so good to stop dashing around and relax for a little while,' says Emily, raising her water glass to Andy and gazing out over the bay.

'Yes, I guess your world's pretty frantic compared to the pace here, isn't it?'

'I'm very busy at work, it's true.'

'And . . . and in your private life? I don't want to sound nosy, but are you . . . involved with anyone at the moment?'

Emily opens her mouth to speak just as her phone buzzes to show a text coming in. She takes it from her bag and glances at it. 'Sorry, Andy, just making sure it's not Gran.'

He watches her mouth tighten as she reads the message. Probably not Julia then – if it was an emergency she'd have rung, wouldn't she, not written an essay? Andy waits, his heart sinking. Emily puts her phone back into her bag and stares out of the window, oblivious to the wonderful colours that are now starting to streak the sky.

'Emily?'

She sighs, and brings her attention back to him with an effort. 'I'm sorry, that was really rude of me. I just wondered if she was OK. But it wasn't Gran.'

'No, I didn't think it was.' George appears with menus and a complementary glass of prosecco for each of them, but Andy's lost interest in the food and wine for the moment. 'Was it a message from someone special, then?'

'Not any more. His name's Max. He's in the States at the moment but apparently he's coming here to see me. A surprise visit. He lands tomorrow.'

The evening rolls on as they eat an amazing paella and drink a very fine chablis. The sky continues to paint its stripes of gold, amber and deep blue, but the sunset's wasted on Andy tonight. So some guy called Max is coming. Terrific. Just when everything was starting to fall into place.

Back at Shangri-La, May is even more preoccupied than Andy. Seeing those two young people going off to enjoy themselves has stirred her up. She settles herself on the veranda to watch the sun perform its tricks with the colour palette and hopes fervently that Andy and Emily are on the brink of finding that they're interested in each other as more than friends. It's time that lovely man had some fun, and Emily seems like just the right sort of girl to jolly him out of his sadness. Her mind jumps forward to thoughts of weddings, and she laughs at herself when she realises she's planning the next fifty years for them.

Looking back on her own nuptials, May pulls a face. That day dawned mistily and there was a chill in the air, even though it was late July. May and Charles had decided on a mid-week, very small affair – they'd walk along the road to church together, and afterwards would eat fish and chips on the beach with Charles's close friend Cyril and May's elderly and utterly charming aunt Barbara, who was travelling from Exeter especially to see her niece 'properly wed'.

In the event, as she prepared for the day May was overtaken by a desperate longing for her parents, and for the much more extravagant celebrations they would have wanted. Her hands shook as she tried to make her hair look decent.

This isn't unusual, she told herself firmly as she took

deep breaths. Many brides and grooms must resort to artificial means to steady their nerves, but all of a sudden she knew she couldn't go through with it, unless . . . She certainly didn't want to have a shot of brandy and smell boozy when she faced the vicar, or fall up the church steps. There was only one way. Reaching into a drawer in her dressing table, she pulled out a roll of fabric. Aunt Barbara, worried at the lack of pomp, had insisted that even at a low-key wedding the bride must follow the tradition of 'something old, something new, something borrowed and something blue'. May's dress was new and also blue, her shoes were last year's summer sandals and the something borrowed lay deep inside the bundle now on her lap.

Unrolling it carefully, she lifted the necklace up to catch the light from the dim overhead bulb. It glittered quietly to itself, several rows of stunning amethysts strung on gold chains. As she placed it around her neck and fumbled with the clasp, May cried out loud, so overwhelming were the waves of joy emanating from the jewels. Effervescent bubbles of delight brought her to her feet, and she caught sight of herself in the mirror on the wall. Her eyes were shining now. Gone was the look of apprehension. Even her hair looked more alive, crackling with static electricity and curling in just the right way for once.

May's wedding day stands out in her mind as a snapshot of giddy happiness, thanks to Aunt Barbara's necklace. It's a pity the same can't be said for the rest of her marriage.

# Chapter Sixteen

The bad weather arrives a day earlier than forecast. May gazes out of the window at the dripping trees and wonders whether the rain will stop Julia coming across the road for their daily fix of letter sorting. They're getting on with the job quickly now, and they've got an efficient system going. Gusts of wind are battering the windows every few seconds, making her feel as if she's under siege, and the waves are crashing against the rocks and the harbour walls, sending up explosions of spray.

As she watches the road, May sees Andy come out of his house with Tamsin, both bundled up in waterproofs and wearing wellies. The rain water is pouring down the hill, making rivulets that are perfect for a little girl to jump in. Tamsin holds onto her dad's hand as she hops and skips her way up the lane, but Andy's shoulders are slumped. May heard him come home the evening before. It couldn't have been much after nine o'clock. Not a successful night by anyone's standards, she thinks. What a shame.

May feels restless today. Maybe it's the weather, or perhaps she needs a quick burst of energy. She picks up a letter at random from the next pile waiting for sorting and holds it gently in both hands. As she lets the tingling of the incoming memories enter her body, May feels herself begin to relax. At first she has no need to read the words – the images tumbling into her mind are enough. This one's from Kathryn, and that lively young woman is an ideal candidate for May's harvesting. Even at this distance in time, Kathryn's personality is strong enough to bridge the intervening years. After a while, soothed and happy, May begins to read Kathryn's news and is soon totally absorbed.

I'm sorry to tell you that Mother is frailer than ever. The ring has preyed on her mind more than I can say over these last months, and she seems to be blaming her ill health on its loss. She says she should never even have considered giving it to Julia, and I think she's right, to be honest. I would have loved it and would have taken good care of it. Joe and I are engaged now, and if I have a little daughter of my own in the future, she would be the perfect person to have the ring after me. You only have Felix, after all, and what will he want with an opal ring?

Elsie shows no signs of settling down, and Will, of course, is now in Ireland for good. A priest in the family – who'd have thought it, Don? Mother doesn't know whether to be proud he's become so devout or scandalised that he's been totally absorbed into Catholicism . . .

May takes a deep breath and stands up carefully. She's overdone it now. The buzz is taking over. To calm herself, she grabs her stick and walks over to the window, taking tiny steps so as not to overbalance. As her head stops spinning and her vision rights itself, May sees the front door opposite open. Julia emerges, looking up at the sky in disgust. She puts up her umbrella and sallies forth across the road, trying to avoid the worst of the little streams flowing down towards the beach.

'Come in, dear, and get warm,' shouts May, as Julia bursts in, shaking her umbrella under the porch before she drips all over the lino.

'Ugh. It's horrible out there. Shall I put the kettle on?'

'Good idea. I've got the electric fire going, so it's cosy in here. Let's have some of that new gingerbread Ida dropped round for me. She's not a bad soul, for all her gossiping.'

They settle down in front of the fake flickering flames, tea tray and cake tin between them, and Julia sighs contentedly. 'I'd have gone stir crazy if I'd stayed in the house a minute longer,' she says.

'Really? Is Emily not in a good mood this morning?'

'She most certainly is not. Apparently, she had a message from a friend last night. A gentleman friend, by all accounts, name of Max, and he's arriving today – from America, mind you – to see her.'

'No! But . . .'

'I know. There she was, having a lovely night out with Andy, and he has to go and spoil it all.'

'Did you know about this Max person, then?'

'I had my suspicions there had been somebody fairly recently but she was playing her cards very close to her chest so I guessed it was a situation I wouldn't approve of, if you get my drift, May?'

May purses her lips. 'Married?'

'As it turns out, yes – with three children and a very unstable wife, so Emily tells me.'

'Oh dear.'

They sit in silence for a while, drinking their tea. Eventually May says, 'So what about Andy?'

'I don't think Andy comes into it. Emily's got to go off to Newquay airport in hideous weather to fetch this . . . this person who's messed up her night out and now clicks his fingers and she jumps. I'd have told him where to get off. She says it's all over between them but it seems he has other ideas and she feels honour bound to at least talk to him when he's come all this way to see her.'

'Where will he stay?'

'He's booked a suite at the most expensive hotel in Penzance. You know the one I mean? With the chandeliers?'

'Not short of a bob or two then?'

'Just what I thought. Anyway, I feel so sorry for Andy. I think he had hopes of his own. He's not really looked at another woman since Allie died. Well, not one you'd class as a lady, anyway. It's time he had some fun.'

'I agree. So terribly sad for them both.'

Julia looks as if she's on the point of bursting into tears and May hastily takes steps to change the subject.

'Shall we do a bit more sorting?' she asks. 'If we can arrange a few more of the early letters into the right piles Andy could make a start on cataloguing them. He won't be able to work outside today.'

'Have you done some without me?'

'Only a few. This one was interesting. It's all about Don's mother regretting saying you could have the ring.'

'Let me see.'

Julia reads the letter in silence, becoming paler by the minute. Eventually she looks up.

'Is it true, do you think? Is the ring a lucky charm? Because if it is, I want to find it. I need that ring, May, and quickly.'

'Give me the letter back, Julia – I'll file it. You don't need to think about it now. Maybe we can solve the mystery if we carry on reading. I would love to get the ring back for you, wherever it's ended up. Don't worry yourself.'

Julia hesitates for a moment and then hands the envelope over. As May takes it, a rush of energy floods her body and mind. Julia blinks, as if she's just woken up from a deep sleep.

'Worry about what? You'll have to remind me what we were just talking about, May,' she asks, her voice fainter than usual. 'I don't know why, but my memory's like a sieve these days.'

May shivers, torn between delight at the rush of sparkly wellbeing from the letter and a painful stab of guilt that she's depriving Julia of something valuable. It's unexpectedly rewarding having a friend, and the more she sees Julia, the more she wants to get to know her even better. May can't understand why she didn't realise what she was missing by being so independent. Julia's sense of humour is surfacing now as she begins to really relax in

May's company, and giggling together over some of the crazier letters has been fun. But what if the other woman never gets her memories back? She gives herself a little shake. It doesn't matter, surely? When Julia has all the letters in her possession again she can dip into the stories of the past any old time. Hopefully this is only a temporary problem.

'Come on, love, we've got work to do,' she says, reaching for the next envelope.

They rummage through their respective heaps companionably for an hour or so, exchanging the odd comment when something particularly interesting comes to light. Mid-morning, the kitchen door opens and Andy comes in. His expression is grim.

'Emily's phoned to say her hire car's broken down on the way to the airport,' he says, 'so I'm going to rescue her.'

'Oh, no! Is she safe?' asks Julia. 'That's not a good road to break down on. Too many bad bends, and it's very narrow in places. Have you told her to get out of the car?'

'Yes, don't worry. She's near a pub so they've let her go inside to keep dry. She's on her second coffee already.'

'That's a relief. Poor girl,' says May.

'The car hire company is coming to fetch it and she'll get another one later. But she's worried that she's meant to be picking up this Max character, and she's very late now so I said I'd go, and then take her on to fetch him. I'll phone if there's anything to report.'

He raises a hand and sets off again, with the air of a man on his way to the gallows.

'Bother,' says May. 'That's really going to put the cat among the pigeons.'

Julia bites her lip. 'I know. It's so annoying. Why did the stupid American man have to turn up and ruin everything?'

May's picked up another one of the letters again by now and can already feel the tingling sensations back in her fingertips. She sits up straight in her chair, letting the energy flow through her veins. It's like an instant face-lift, but all over her body. She opens it and begins to skim read. A phrase catches her eye.

*I think Will knows more than he's letting on about the ring.*

Julia leans forward to look at her more closely.

'You look lovely today, May,' she says. 'Well, you always do, of course, but there's something extra . . .'

May smiles and thanks Julia graciously. She knows her silvery-white hair looks as near perfect as she can make it – the hairdresser came as usual this week and the waves are still smooth and glossy, thanks to a generous coating of hairspray every morning and night. She's wearing a cherry-red jumper over a tweed skirt – both close-fitting, showing her neat figure. She crosses her legs, displaying shapely ankles. May is proud of the way she looks. She's always been glad she 'pays for dressing', as Charles used to say, but this isn't anything like the face and body of someone who's aiming to be a hundred and eleven on her next birthday.

Julia puts her head on one side and observes her friend carefully. 'You're one of those people who ages gracefully, I guess.'

'I suppose I must be. Just lucky, that's all.'

'I've never known anyone look so good for their age, though.'

May's keen to carry on reading, but Julia's still talking. 'Don loved the way I looked, even up to the day he died. Marriage is a wonderful thing when it works, isn't it?'

'If you say so, dear. Julia, this letter from Kathryn. I think it's important . . .'

Julia isn't listening. She reaches into her shopping bag and brings out a package.

'I nearly didn't bring these over but maybe it's time to share them. They're from Don to me, written very early on. We were apart right at the end of the war while I was waiting to be demobbed from the WAAF and he was trying to find us a house here in the village, and then when he was staying with his family in the Midlands, retraining and so on.'

May's eyes light up and she stretches her hand out, then pulls it back sharply. 'But these are personal. I don't think you should give them to me to look at.'

'It's fine. Go ahead.'

Nervously, May picks a letter out at random and begins to read, marvelling at the tiny, ultra-neat handwriting; Don used every inch of space to express his longing for his love. The greeting at the top is 'My own darling,' and May can visualise the handsome young airman who swept Julia off her feet.

It was so good to see you again at the weekend. I'm sure I didn't say half of what I meant to. I was tired with work and almost overwhelmed at being with you again.

Julia leans forward. 'Keep going,' she says. 'I want you to know how it was for me and Don. Then you'll see why I look "fed up" all the time, as you put it. I miss him so much. I'm not just being grumpy.'

'Have I ever said that? I do understand why you're grieving. You were loved by your husband, Julia, very much, and you loved him back wholeheartedly. That's something I have no experience of. None at all.'

May carries on reading, her heart heavy. The buzz from the letters is being eroded by the pain she feels, and the growing regret that when it comes to having had a loving marriage, she's missed the boat completely.

# Chapter Seventeen

Andy knows his driving isn't up to his own high standard as he heads for the pub where Emily's waiting. The rain lashes against the windscreen, and even with the wipers going at double speed he can barely see the road ahead. At last, the huge roadside inn comes into view, its car park half full even on a day like this. A waft of chip fat meets Andy's nostrils as he pushes the door open and he pulls a face. Emily jumps to her feet the minute she spots him.

'I'm so sorry to drag you out in this filthy weather,' she says, her eyes on his sour expression.

'Oh, I wasn't being grumpy about fetching you, it was just the smell of grease,' he says hastily, but her look says she doesn't believe him. He sighs.

They hurry out to Andy's car. Emily's got a flimsy folding umbrella but the wind is getting up and she almost loses it before it turns itself inside out – a twisted mess of multi-coloured PVC. She hurls it into a skip at the side of the car park in disgust and climbs into the front seat as Andy takes off again, at a reasonable speed this time.

'So, how do you know this guy we're fetching?' he asks,

through gritted teeth, negotiating a reckless cyclist who's weaving all over the road after a gust of wind catches him and threatens to blow him under Andy's wheels.

'We met at a publishing party in New York,' says Emily, closing her eyes as the cyclist swerves in the opposite direction and just misses a tree. 'He's an author.'

'Will I have heard of him?'

'Maybe. He writes crime thrillers under the name of Damion Wintersmith. Psychological stuff. A bit weird, to be honest.'

'Ah. Yes, I've read one of his.'

'Only one?' She grins at him and Andy feels his tense shoulders relax slightly.

'It wasn't really my thing.'

'No?'

'I do like crime thrillers but there was a bit too much . . . um . . .'

'Sex?'

'No, just a bit too graphic – I was thinking more of the blood and gore side of it. Somebody fell out of a high building and landed on some spiky iron railings on the first page. The description was stomach churning. I'm not usually squeamish but it put me right off my dinner.'

Andy spots the first signs with pictures of planes on just up ahead and slows down. His heart sinks at the thought of seeing Emily greet this mystery man. 'I'll drop you at the entrance and go and park,' he says.

They coast into the airport and Emily leaps out and rushes towards the arrivals area as soon as the car stops. Andy hopes she won't be long. The more he thinks about meeting Max, the less he wants to. Why should the man assume he's got the right to just turn up here with no warning? It doesn't suggest much respect for Emily's plans. Is she supposed to drop everything and fit in with Max? What makes her even consider doing that if they're supposed to have broken up? His mood isn't improved by the lack of available car parking spaces and he cruises round for several minutes, cursing small airports everywhere.

At last, he sees the pair of them emerge from the main door. Andy tries to wipe the surly look from his face and jumps out of the car to meet them.

'Hello there,' he says, holding out a hand to shake Max's.

Max has both hands full with his luggage and grins apologetically. 'Sorry, can't do the proper British greeting at the moment, buddy,' he says, swinging his bags towards Andy as if he's a porter.

Andy opens the boot, takes the bags and throws them in unceremoniously. 'Welcome to Cornwall,' he says.

'Emily says you've been her knight in shining armour today,' Max replies, opening the front passenger door and leaving Emily to clamber into the back. 'I sure do appreciate your assistance.' Then, just as she fastens her seat belt, he changes his mind and gets into the back with her.

Feeling like the chauffeur as well as the porter now, Andy sets off to drive home, not surprised to see that the rain has stopped and a watery sun is trying to come out. Why wouldn't it, with Max here? Despite his instant dislike of the interloper, he can sense the man's charisma.

Rumpled from the flight, bleary and somewhat travel stained, Max still exudes a powerful charm. Emily seems to have a lot to say to him. They murmur to each other and he can't catch what they're talking about. Why didn't she get in the front with Andy when she realised Max was getting in the back? This is just plain rude. Andy seethes silently.

Max is looking all around now as they head for the coast road to Pengelly. 'Hey, this Cornwall of yours is kind of cute,' he says, 'but these roads! Jeez, why don't they widen them, or make some better ones? It must take for ever to get anywhere.'

'Cute? Well, yes, I suppose that's one word to describe us,' Andy says. 'And they don't widen the roads because they would have to knock down these ancient hedges and walls and take over fields that have been farmed for generations.'

'And that's so bad . . . exactly why?'

Emily begins to gush about the scenery and the joys of living in such a beautiful place but Andy isn't mollified. This man is a total knob, in his opinion. Why would Emily hook up with such a pompous idiot? Just being a famous author doesn't make you a worthwhile citizen. Max isn't listening to Emily anyway; he's too busy checking his phone and tapping out messages. Who could be so important that he can't pay proper attention to his beautiful ex-girlfriend? Emily seems to have come to the same conclusion.

'Who are you texting, Max?' she asks, a chill in her voice.

'Oh, just my agent, babe,' he says, shoving his phone into his pocket. 'No rest for the wicked; ain't that what you guys over here say, Adam?'

'My name's Andy.'

'Sorry, sport. I'm crap at names. Always have been,' says Max brightly.

'That's OK, Malcolm,' says Andy.

'But my . . . Oh, I get it. The British sense of humour. Very funny.'

'What does Ned want?' asks Emily. 'He should give you a break when you're on holiday.'

'Well, that's just it, kiddo – he's here too, on vacation with his family. He's staying in some place not far from here. They've got a cottage almost on the beach. His kids are surf crazy.'

'Ned's in England? Don't tell me: you already knew that when you decided to come over.'

Max is ignoring her now, texting again. They drive in silence for the next few miles, until the village comes into sight. Emily nudges Max with her elbow.

'This part's called The Level,' she says. 'It's the centre of Pengelly. There's a shop, two churches, a garden centre and the pub where my grandpa used to wait for me whenever I was expected home. Oh, look – someone's put a poster up for the farmers' market.'

'Life on the edge, babe. You guys sure know how to have fun.'

Emily's eyes meet Andy's as he glances into the rear-view mirror, and she blushes. He remembers the happiness he felt as they drank their beer outside the pub just a couple of days ago and inwardly curses Max for spoiling everything.

'But you can see why I love coming here now, can't you? Smell that sea breeze,' Emily says, winding her window down.

'It's pretty, sure enough,' says Max, dismissively, getting out his phone again as it buzzes.

'I suppose you'll be wanting to go to your hotel fairly soon?' says Andy.

'Oh, there's no rush. Emily says her grandmama wants to meet me first. I can call a cab when it's time to go, so there's no need for you to be waiting around for me.'

Andy blinks in amazement at the man's effrontery. As if he'd be spending his evening hanging about just in case Max needed a lift? Not likely.

Emily opens her door as soon as Andy's pulled up outside Julia's cottage, and hops out. 'Thank you so much,' she says, hovering near the driver's door as if she wants to say more. He stays in the car and nods in acknowledgement, as Max gets out and waits. Emily looks at him, frowning, and then seems to get what the problem is.

'Oh, could we just get Max's bags out of the boot, please?' she says.

Andy gets out of the car as slowly as he can and retrieves the case and holdall, both made of soft, pale brown leather and clearly very expensive. Max takes them without comment. Maybe he expects me to carry them into the house for him, thinks Andy, fighting the urge to punch the smug git.

'Right, well, I'll be off then,' says Andy, but Max is

already striding down the path, having spotted Julia standing in the open doorway.

'Hey, beautiful lady – surely you cannot be the grandmother around here? It's just not possible,' Max says, dropping his bags as if he can't waste a moment to be grasping Julia by the shoulders and kissing her on both cheeks. Andy thinks he might be sick. His phone bleeps in his pocket and he sees a text. Candice. Could this day get any worse?

# Chapter Eighteen

Emily wakes just before the dawn chorus starts. The events of the day before run through her mind like a bad home video. As the birds finally begin to sing, she gives up on sleep and slides out of bed, treading carefully on the polished boards so as not to wake her grandmother. Julia waited up for Emily last night and must be ready for a lie-in today – she looked exhausted. It's way too early to jolt her from her slumbers and the thought of bacon and eggs makes Emily's stomach lurch. She dresses quickly, putting on yesterday's denim shorts and T-shirt, adds a thick sweater against the morning chill and pushes her feet into flip-flops, the easier to kick off and paddle when she reaches the beach.

As Emily jogs barefoot down to the sea, she hears a familiar bark, and Buster barrels towards her, tongue hanging out of one side of his mouth in his happiness at seeing a friend. He's closely followed by Bruno, who woofs delightedly and licks Emily's knees.

'Hi, Tristram,' Emily shouts, waving.

Tristram is busy flipping stones into the waves further down the beach, expertly skimming them to skip three, four, sometimes five or six times. He turns away from the sea and joins his dogs at Emily's side. 'Hello there,' he says. 'You're up early again. Trouble sleeping, or just high on life?'

'High on life? I wish!'

'What's up, sweetheart? I heard you had a visitor from foreign shores yesterday. Didn't he live up to expectations?'

Emily gazes at Tristram. How can this man who doesn't know her at all put his finger on the problem so perfectly?

'My ex turned up out of the blue,' she says. 'And I agreed to have dinner with him. It was a mistake. It's left me feeling queasy and grumpy.'

Tristram grins. 'No need to say more,' he says. 'Sometimes that happens.'

'How do you mean?'

'Well, in my experience, something that seems pretty good in its own setting doesn't transfer to everyday life. It's like holiday romances, isn't it? You must have had that happen to you in your teens?'

'It was already over, but go on. This is like a masterclass in relationships from an expert.'

Tristram laughs heartily at this, making himself wheeze so much he has to bend double and clutch his knees to recover. 'Expert? You're looking at the man who keeps a small-town divorce lawyer in business.'

'OK, I get your point, but any advice you can give me will be gratefully received. I feel a total fool today. I've wasted so much time on a man who turns out to only be in love with himself. I should have been concentrating on my own career, not his.'

Buster has quickly become bored with the conversation.

They watch him leaping in and out of the shallows for a few moments, while Tristram ponders on this and Bruno settles down for a short nap. The sky is bright now, and the sunrise is spectacular, with cloud formations that seem to be made of spun gold, and pink and purple streaks spreading right across the bay. Even as they watch, the colours fade and the morning light settles into normality. Emily thinks that's probably a good thing. Too much of this sort of splendour would be hard to bear.

'How about coming back to the restaurant with me and the boys for coffee and a croissant or a nice sticky Danish? My lass will be up and have the kettle on by now,' Tristram says. 'I think you need to get a few things off your chest, young 'un.'

Emily's eyes smart. Her grandpa had often called her by that pet name. She nods, and follows the man and his dogs along the beach. They fall into step as if they've been walking together for years.

'Have you always been in the food industry?' she asks.

'That's a funny way of putting it. It's not so much an industry as a way of life. I love food, see? And I love watching folk enjoying it, knowing I made that happen for them. If I can make a living doing that, I'm happy.'

'And your daughter feels the same?'

'She does, luckily. I didn't push her into it. She's always been a good organiser. Then she married Vince, and together they made it all work better for me. They were living in York for years but they decided to come home because I . . . well, I wasn't feeling so good for a while.'

'Really? You look so fit and healthy.'

'Oh, I am.' He taps his chest. 'It was a problem with my old ticker, but the doctors fixed it good and proper. I had to have a triple bypass,' he says proudly, 'and I never even knew I was ill. They tried to make me retire afterwards but I told them no way – you're a long time dead. What would I do all day?'

Emily's having trouble keeping up with Tristram now as he strides across the beach. Is he trying to prove something? He certainly looks well, with the bronzed cheeks of a seasoned sun lover and plenty of laughter lines around his eyes. He carries on telling her about his business as he walks, and Emily ups her pace.

'So anyway, my place was a high-class chippy before that: Andy was spot on there. It was doing OK but it was never going to make the Michelin guide, if you know what I mean? Then Gina and Vince burst in and put us on the map. We found the new premises, and the view's as good as the grub. It's Rick Stein without the bank loan needed to get in. Jamie Oliver without the flannel.'

'I can't wait to see it.'

'You don't have to – we're here.'

Buster bounds round the back of the low building in front of them in search of snacks but Bruno flops down on the front step and Emily stops next to him to take it in properly. Set right on the headland at the far end of the bay, Tristram's restaurant has wide coastal views in both directions. It's almost all glass on the beach front, and the roof is covered with weather-worn green tiles.

'You must have done so much work on this,' Emily says, taking in the silvery grey paintwork and the floor-to-ceiling windows. Either side of the door is a flourishing olive tree in a dark green pot, and herb beds surround the walls: mint, thyme and rosemary rubbing shoulders with other more exotic plants that Emily doesn't recognise. The painted wooden sign has a picture of a plate of giant prawns decorated with black and green olives and slices of lemon, simple in design but striking, and the words 'The Shellfish Shack' are picked out in black, gold and silver. There's a covered terrace with rustic tables and chairs, where diners can eat and watch the waves at the same time.

Tristram stands with his hands on his hips, surveying his livelihood proudly. 'It's been a team effort,' he says. 'Come and meet the others. Round the back you go, Bruno-boy,' he encourages the dog. 'They're not allowed front of house, Emily. They'd have me shut down.'

Inside the restaurant, all is warm and cosy. The fragrant smell of coffee brewing and pastries baking makes Emily's stomach rumble loudly, and Tristram laughs. 'That's the effect we want,' he says. 'Gina, Vince, this is Emily – she's Julia's granddaughter, over from New York.'

The voluptuous woman by the sink turns and smiles. She exudes comfort, with her wild black curls and rosy cheeks. She's wearing a huge pinafore but there's quite a lot of cleavage on view too, and her lipstick is scarlet. Vince, the chef, is busy chopping vegetables, and beams at Emily. He reminds her of a friendly bear.

'We heard you were down here,' he says. 'It's great for Julia to have you around. She's told us all about you.'

'This place is fantastic,' Emily says, looking round admiringly at the half-boarded walls hung with delicate watercolour paintings of sea urchins and other sea life. 'Whose are the pictures?'

Tristram raises a hand and looks mildly embarrassed.

'He was going to bin them, would you believe it?' says Gina. 'We rescued them from the back of the car when he was doing a run to the tip.'

'People often ask to buy them, so it's time you did some more, Tris. We're not letting these go,' says Vince, pouring coffee for them all and getting a tray of crisp golden croissants out of the oven.

'I might well do that, but not until I've bought myself some new paints. The old lot are all dried up and my brushes have seen better days. It's my birthday soon, though,' Tristram says hopefully. 'I'll be eighty.'

Gina and Vince exchange glances and smile but Tristram doesn't notice. He's busy making sure everything they need is in front of them. They sit around one of the tables that have been set ready for the lunchtime rush and drink their coffee. Emily finally begins to relax as, famished now, she eats her second croissant, loaded with apricot jam.

'Can I ask you all something, guys?' Emily says, as she leans back and discreetly loosens the top button of her shorts.

'Ask away.' Vince is up and clearing the table now, and

Gina's already at the sink again but they both stand still, waiting for Emily's question.

'Have any of you noticed anything . . . different about my gran lately?'

'What sort of thing were you thinking of?' asks Tristram.

'Oh, anything at all really. She seems a bit more forgetful than usual, as if there are sort of holes in her memory. And yesterday when she came back from May's she was acting very strangely.'

'What was she doing?' Vince sounds intrigued rather than concerned. 'I haven't seen any changes in Julia, though, have you, love?'

Gina shakes her head, frowning. 'So, what *was* she doing yesterday?'

'Just wandering around with a vacant look on her face, as if she'd had a shock.'

'Maybe rereading those old letters is upsetting her?' suggests Tristram. 'It must be quite painful digging up all the memories that you've buried for years.'

'Yes, I guess that's what it must be,' says Emily, relieved. 'And if she was really different since Gramps died, you lot would have spotted it by now, surely?'

There's a short silence as the others carry on with their jobs, clearly still thinking about Emily's worries. Tristram is putting the day's newspapers out on a stand for the customers, and Gina has started preparing tiny vases of fresh flowers for the tables.

Eventually, Vince clears his throat. 'What does Andy think about this?'

'He was the one who brought it up in the first place,' says Emily. 'He wrote to me. That was why I came home. Well, obviously I was planning to come over anyway . . .'

'I tell you what, sweetheart, we'll all keep our eyes open. If we notice anything strange, we'll let you know. The more people looking out for Julia, the better. We all love your gran, don't we?' Tristram says.

The other two nod enthusiastically and Emily is so moved she can't speak.

Tristram carries on. 'I've always had a soft spot for Julia but she never had eyes for anyone but your grandpa. She's a beautiful woman.'

His voice tails off and Emily sees that he's blushing. Before she's had a chance to process this interesting fact, her phone vibrates. A message from Max. Oh, joy.

Hey babe, sorry you had to dash off last night. I had a great time in the end with the bar staff. They're all fans of my books, it turns out. Ned wants me to stay over at his holiday let tonight and maybe tomorrow so we can have a few drinks. I'll give you a call when I'm back. Love you, M xxx

Is this man for real? She ran out on him, leaving him high and dry in a strange hotel, making it obvious she couldn't stand him kissing and pawing her, and he still bounces back and expects life to go on as normal. What an ego. And why is he still telling her he loves her after all that's happened? What part of 'it's over' does he not understand?

She puts her phone away without answering, unsure how to express her feelings in a text. Tristram tops up her coffee cup.

'I'm guessing you're in need of this,' he says, handing her another croissant.

Emily accepts, comforted by Tristram's kindness, though what she really wants is for Max just to go away.

# Chapter Nineteen

Julia decides to allow herself a good long lie-in. She hears Emily go out at the crack of dawn so there's no point in getting up yet, and her bed feels like a sanctuary today. It was hard seeing Emily looking so miserable last night, and the long session digging up old memories at May's yesterday has tired her more than she likes to think. There's still a vague feeling of dizziness when she turns over, and a light-headedness that's rather alarming. She drifts off to sleep again eventually, and when she wakes it's past nine o'clock. She can hear Emily pottering round the kitchen. What a comforting sound that is.

She wishes Em would stay longer. She's clearly come all this way because she's worried. A fortnight isn't anywhere near long enough. Julia's heart aches at the thought of saying goodbye to her darling girl so soon. As she stretches herself in preparation for getting up, an idea pops into her head. Could she do it? It goes against her usual impeccable honesty and integrity. Just how much does she want Em to stay? Enough to play the batty old lady card? That shouldn't be difficult the way she's feeling. Enough to do some serious acting? Yes, indeed.

Easing herself out of bed, Julia wraps her dressing gown around her long nightie. It's not her custom to go downstairs in her nightclothes. She usually likes to be fully dressed and made up before she faces the world, but today she doesn't even run a brush through her hair.

Emily looks up and smiles as Julia enters the kitchen. As she notices what Julia's wearing, her expression alters.

'Aren't you feeling well today, Gran? I thought it was a mistake you staying up and making me a hot drink. You should have been tucked up in bed.'

Julia sits down at the table and leans her forehead on one hand.

'Gran? What's the matter?'

'Oh, nothing, darling. I'm just not quite . . . I think I'm . . . I wonder if you'd mind giving Allie a ring? She's got some special herbal tablets that always pep me up.'

Emily is very still now. 'Allie? Do you mean Andy's wife?'

'Yes, of course. There's nobody else of that name round here, is there? Just nip over there for me, would you? She'll probably be in the garden. There'll be lots to tidy up after all that rain we had yesterday. Allie loves her flowers and vegetables.'

Emily doesn't speak for a moment. Then she comes over and puts a hand on Julia's shoulder. 'Have you had a very deep sleep, Gran? You seem a bit . . . confused?'

'I'm not in the least confused. What do you mean?'

'Well, Allie died when Tamsin was born, didn't she? You remember?'

Julia hears the touch of desperation in Emily's voice

and isn't sure whether to be jubilant or ashamed, but she has to keep going with this charade now she's begun it. Em mustn't go home yet. It's not just for her own sake she wants to keep her. How is Andy going to woo the girl if she hops off back to America?

'Allie's died? What do you mean? Does Andy know? What's Tamsin going to do without a mother?' Julia lets her voice wobble and puts a hand to her mouth.

'Gran, why don't you go back to bed and I'll bring you some breakfast on a tray? A poached egg on toast? That was what you always gave me when I was poorly.'

'Am I poorly then? I must admit I do feel a bit peculiar this morning. Are you sure you don't mind?'

'Off you go. I'll be up as soon as I've rustled you up an egg and a pot of tea. I won't be long.'

Emily's got a hand under Julia's elbow now and is helping her to her feet. Julia lets herself be guided towards the stairs and then goes up very slowly, holding tight to the banisters, bringing one foot up to join the other like a small child. She looks back at Emily's pale face gazing up after her and feels a sharp pang of guilt but this has got to be done. And anyway, it's quite true that she's been forgetting things. This is only a slight exaggeration of the facts.

As she turns towards her bedroom Julia sees Emily dart back into the kitchen. She'll be going to find her phone. Andy will soon know what's happening, and he'll come over as soon as he finishes work, if not before. He's only up the road at Ida's again today – she's summoned him back to add an extra step to her new porch.

'Are you safely tucked up in bed yet, Gran?' Emily calls.

'Yes, dear,' Julia answers, wriggling under the covers and leaning back on her pillows. She lies very quietly, beating her conscience into submission.

Looking around the familiar bedroom, Julia is re-assured by the friendly pattern on her wallpaper of wild flowers in subtle colours climbing up trellises. The window is open and the birds are still singing away, happy that the rain is over for now. What she's doing can't be wrong if she's doing it for the right reasons, surely? Looking for a diversion from all this soul-searching, she reaches under her pillow and pulls out a letter, one of the small pile she kept back. She was halfway through reading it when she fell asleep the night before, having waded through a recipe for rock buns, an account of a church social and Elsie's moans about her mother. Now comes the interesting part.

*Could you do me a favour, Don? I've been trying to think of a suitable present for us to give Will for his twenty-first birthday next month and I've hit on a plan. How about if we ask Charles if we could pay him to give Will a few proper sailing lessons? Do you think you could sound him out for me? Will really likes Charles, and I reckon that would be a great gift.*

Julia pushes the letter back under the pillow as she hears Emily on the stairs. Mustn't blow her cover. She snuggles down and concentrates on looking wan. But sailing lessons? She hadn't known about those. No wonder Will and Charles became so close all of a sudden. Elsie played right into his hands there. Julia closes her eyes as a few unwelcome memories float back, patchy now but still painful. It's like trying to catch a cloud in her hands. Will she ever feel like herself again or is this the beginning of the end?

# Chapter Twenty

Andy finishes Ida's wooden step in record time and is knocking at Julia's kitchen door as the church clock strikes eleven. Emily is in there mechanically wiping down work surfaces and looks up as he comes in. He feels a sinking sensation when he sees the alarm in her eyes. Andy has never coped well with illness, especially since Allie first started to show signs of toxaemia in late pregnancy. He tends to panic and lose the ability to think sensibly.

'Oh, you made it sooner than you expected. Thanks so much for coming,' she whispers, opening the door wide.

'Is she asleep?' Andy's whispering, too.

'I think so. I crept in a few minutes ago and she was out. She looks completely shattered. Sit down, I'll make tea.'

Andy pulls a chair up to the table and absent-mindedly reaches for a biscuit. Julia always buys chocolate digestives especially for him and sure enough, the battered tin biscuit barrel is fully stocked. He eats two while Emily's pouring boiling water onto the tea leaves that Julia favours and then realises that this must have looked very rude.

'I'm sorry, I've walked in here and started munching digestives as if I own the place,' he says, reddening.

'Don't be silly, Gran enjoys you making yourself at home. She's very fond of you and Tamsin. Protective, too.'

'Well, we love *her*. Everybody loves Julia. Even May likes her now. Or at least they're talking.'

'I know, unbelievable after the years of cold-shouldering each other. I think they each needed a friend. Anyway, that's heart-warming to hear and you're not the first person to say it, but it should be me looking after her, particularly if . . .'

She hesitates for a moment as if trying to find the right words, and then spills out her worries about Julia's appearance and what she said about Allie this morning. Andy listens, his face grave.

'Maybe it's just tiredness,' he says hopefully. 'She's been spending an awful lot of time poring over those letters with May, and before that she's been sorting and getting rid of things ever since your grandpa passed away. It's got to have been hard for her.'

'But you've noticed this kind of thing before – that's why you wrote to me.'

He nods. 'It's been making me think about all sorts of things to do with getting old. My grandpa's completely confused now. That's mainly why my mum and dad went up to Yorkshire, to be near him.'

'Oh, I didn't realise. It's only when you start talking about dementia that you realise how many people are suffering.'

'I know. When I look back, I can see that he'd been having problems for a long time. He got very withdrawn, almost reclusive after my grandma died. He stopped going to play bowls and gave up his allotment. His friends were all about the same age and they were all suffering in different ways. They needed an Ida-type person to get them together.'

'Every village needs an Ida, I guess. Does your grandpa live with your parents?'

'No. He did to begin with but then he kept wandering off and getting lost. My mum agonised over what to do for ages. Nobody spotted how bad he was getting until the rot had really set in. We couldn't help thinking if we'd noticed sooner, he might have got some kind of treatment in time to make a difference.'

'So where is he now?'

'In a little private nursing home in Harrogate. They're brilliant. He does all sorts of activities to stimulate his memory. Some of them work, some don't.'

'But at least they're trying.'

'Yes, and that gives my folks some hope too. They don't feel so useless.'

'Andy, I don't want to look on the black side, but I'm really scared. If Gran gets like that, what am I going to do? I can't be here all the time.'

'Maybe we should get her to see her doctor before it gets any worse?'

Emily grimaces. 'I doubt she'd go, but we can try.'

They sit warming their hands on the mugs of tea, even though the kitchen isn't in the least chilly. Andy stirs himself and tries to make his next question sound light and unconcerned.

'Changing the subject, but where's your friend Max today? I thought you might have stopped over at the hotel last night. Did you come back early this morning?'

Emily shakes her head. 'I got home last night about ten.'

'Oh? Had he got an early start to see his *agent*?' Andy can't seem to keep the sarcasm out of his tone but Emily just shrugs.

'Not that I know of,' she says.

'And so . . . is he coming over here later?'

'No.'

The one-word answer and grim look that goes with it doesn't encourage further comment, but he presses on. 'So, are you free tonight?'

'I suppose so. If Gran picks up a bit. Why?'

'I thought maybe you could come over to mine for a drink after Tamsin's in bed? We can have a chat about what to do next to help Julia. I'll have a word with May too in a bit, see if she noticed anything strange yesterday.'

'Well . . . OK. That sounds like a good place to start. What time? I'll need to have dinner with Gran first.'

'Eight-ish? I usually start bath time about half-six but the stories seem to take longer and longer every night. She does love a good book.'

'Oh, me too. I could come a bit earlier and read a few to give you a break if you like?'

Andy considers this, touched that she wants to help. 'That's a lovely idea. The only thing is that if she knows

I've got a visitor, she takes for ever to settle down. She thinks she should be down with me to help entertain. Maybe when she knows you better and you're not such a novelty?'

'I don't suppose I'll ever be here long enough for that to happen, will I?'

They look at each other sadly. Andy can't think of anything to say that doesn't sound needy. Emily chews her lip.

'Mind you, if Gran carries on like this, I don't see how I can leave her, do you? I'm worried sick.'

'What about your job, though?' Andy feels like punching the air and shouting 'YES!' at the top of his voice, but manages to keep a lid on his glee.

'I'm still owed at least another week's leave even after I've taken this fortnight. I'll just need to sweet-talk Colin. He's my boss.'

Andy tries to keep from beaming but he can't. Emily grins back, eyes sparkling.

'Gran comes first,' she says, 'because my dad won't be free to help, I'm sure of that, and there's nobody else.'

'There's me,' says Andy. Oh, no, she's doing that thing with her hair again, unplaiting it and running her fingers through it to get the tangles out. He swallows hard and concentrates on the view of the garden.

'I must look a wreck,' Emily says, shaking her hair. 'I haven't even managed to have a shower this morning. I went out on the beach and bumped into Tristram and his dogs again. He took me to his restaurant for breakfast.'

'Cool. It's a great place. Did you meet Gina and Vince?'

She nods. 'If I'm here a bit longer, I'd like to get to know them properly.'

There's a noise in the hall and they both look towards the open door. Julia is standing there, pale but bright-eyed.

'What are you doing out of bed?' asks Emily. 'I was just thinking about making you some lunch.'

'I overheard you both talking. Did you say you might be staying a bit longer, darling?'

'There's nothing wrong with your hearing, is there?' says Emily. 'I was thinking aloud. It depends on Colin really. Why, would you like that?'

Julia blinks back happy tears and Andy gets up to leave. This is all too emotional for him. He needs to pay a visit to May.


Across the road, May is sitting with her feet up on a stool watching one of her favourite daytime programmes. The TV is turned down because she likes the subtitles. That way she can still hear what's going on outside.

'Hello, dear,' she says, smiling up at Andy. 'I thought it was Julia when I heard the door open.'

'And that's why I'm here.'

He brings her up to date on the morning's events. May clasps her hands in her lap and listens attentively. When Andy gets to the part about Emily making plans to see if she can stay longer, May smiles so broadly that Andy thinks she's going to lose her dentures.

'That's the best news I've had all year,' she says. 'And how's Julia today?'

'Emily packed her off back to bed. She's been asleep again. That's not like her, is it?'

May shakes her head, looking very thoughtful. Fossil comes running in and jumps onto her knee, his bony little head nudging May's hand to be stroked. Time seems to slow down as the clock on the mantelpiece ticks away and the electric fire flickers and ticks gently.

Andy leans back in May's rocking chair and lets his worries flow away for a little while. He's not been able to relax properly for a very long time, what with assuming sole responsibility for Tamsin and the dragging melancholy that's dogged him, but somehow today feels like a new beginning. If Emily stays, they'll be bound to have the chance to get to know each other.

'So what's *your* angle?' May's words come out of the blue, and Andy sees that she's watching him closely now, her head on one side like a curious little bird.

'How do you mean?'

'Well, how are *you* going to help Julia to get Emily to stay?'

'Me?'

'We can't do it all for you, Andy. You're not a bad-looking chap, you know, and you've got a kind heart, even if you are a bit gloomy. That Candice isn't the one. Teeth, hair and not much going on between the ears, if you ask me.'

Andy's hackles rise immediately. Who is May to criticise him? She didn't like her husband all that much, by all accounts, so she can't have been too devastated when he died, and she's never had children so how can she understand the pressures of being on your own with a small, demanding child?

'Gloomy? I've lost my wife and I've got a little girl to bring up who worries me a lot. I'm ever likely to look anxious.'

'It's six years since Allie died, and there's nothing wrong with Tamsin apart from the odd cold. You should lighten up, dear. A girl . . . well, a woman, I should say, like Emily, won't be attracted to a moaner.'

'You're out of order, May,' Andy snaps, standing up to go, but she reaches out a hand to stop him.

'I only want the best for you, my dear,' she says softly. 'I know you think I'm an interfering old lady but I've seen a few things in my time and I can tell when two people are made for each other. Sit down and we can talk it through. Let's not argue.'

Andy subsides into the chair again and lets it rock, the rhythm soothing his ruffled feelings. Is May right? He has a sneaking suspicion that there have been times when he could have snapped out of his despondency but it's often easier to just let it wash over him and feel sorry for himself. He's got used to being the grieving widower. The ladies of the village still bring him cakes and the odd casserole, for pity's sake. That should have stopped years ago.

'So, in my humble opinion you need to move fast,' says May. 'Get her round to your house and charm the pants off her.'

'May! It's a good job Julia can't hear you. And actually, I've already asked Emily round later for a drink, after Tamsin's asleep.'

'Good for you. At last you're . . . what did I hear someone say on the television last night? Oh yes, I remember, at last you're *growing a pair*.' She chuckles at his aghast expression. 'Life's for living, dear. Get a decent bottle of wine and some nice snacks – olives, breadsticks, nuts, that sort of thing. Put some soft music on your stereo machine. She'll be putty in your hands.'

Andy starts to laugh too, and soon they're both help-less, tears rolling down May's cheeks. Is she right? Andy hopes so. He gives May a hug and sets off up the steep cobbled street towards the village shop to pick up some supplies.

# Chapter Twenty-One

Emily rifles through the heap of clothes on her bed, and despairs. Most of them are only suitable for wandering about on the beach. It's going to have to be her faded Levi's and a silky blue shirt.

Get a grip, Em, she tells herself. It's just drinks with a friend. There's no need to stress about what to wear.

She gives her hair a final brush, feeling the static electricity arc through the curls, making them stand out in a halo, crackling. A squirt of perfume, something light and zingy that she bought in duty free, and a slick of lip gloss and Emily's ready. Her skin's still glowing from her early morning walk on the beach and there's no point in slapping on lots of make-up. She'll only look as if she's trying to impress Andy. Being single is the way forward now. It doesn't matter in the least what he thinks about her appearance.

Emily gazes at the finished product in the full-length mirror on the back of the bedroom door and is surprised at how happy and healthy she looks, considering her best beloved relative seems to be failing fast and the most promising relationship for years is dead in the water. She clatters downstairs to see if Gran's safe to be left on her own.

Julia is sitting in front of the fire with a blanket over her knees, knitting.

'I'm sure I don't need to be all wrapped up like this, darling,' she says, smiling up at Emily. 'Oh, you *do* look lovely.'

'Thank you, but I'm not going anywhere unless you promise to stay put and rest. I'm going to make you some Horlicks and put the cake tin handy. Do you need to go to the loo?'

'Emily, please – I'm not a toddler,' Julia says, but Emily's relieved to see she's still smiling and she's got some colour in her cheeks.

Ten minutes later, Emily's crossing the road to Andy's house. It feels odd to be arriving empty-handed. Should she have brought wine with her? No, he's asked her for a drink, not dinner, so it'd be silly to do that, wouldn't it? This dithering is unlike Emily, who considers herself fairly sophisticated, happy to mingle with all sorts of people without a trace of nerves. She tells herself not to be so ridiculous. This is just an evening in with a friend.

Andy opens the door before Emily's even had a chance to knock.

'I didn't want you to ring the bell and wake Tamsin,' he whispers. 'She's only just gone to sleep.'

They tiptoe into the kitchen and Emily looks around, pleasantly surprised at the tidiness. She'd assumed that a busy single dad's home would be a bit on the messy side. How sexist was that? Ashamed of her presumption, Emily takes it all in. This place is brightly painted in turquoise and white, with beautiful, gleaming blue and green glass-effect tiles around the cooker and all the units. There's a row of well-used cookery books on a shelf, and an ancient pine dresser loaded with an assortment of chunky pottery plates and dishes. The wooden fruit bowl in the centre of the table is generously filled with bananas, apples and a giant pineapple, and there are glass storage jars on the worktops containing every sort of pasta known to mankind.

Andy sees her looking at the jars. 'My girl loves pasta, as you might have guessed,' he says.

'This is a lovely room,' Emily says.

'Thanks, it's the only place I really changed after Allie died. We were about to have it renovated but Tamsin arrived early and then . . .'

'I'm so sorry you had to go through that awful time,' Emily says, wondering if she dare give him a hug, but Andy's opening a bottle of claret now, and changing the subject.

'Tonight's about the future, not the past,' he says, handing Emily her drink. She takes a sip and then realises she's forgotten to clink glasses and say 'cheers'. Hopefully it's not a bad omen. There's a piano concerto playing softly in the other room. She's not very well up on classical music, having been brought up on a diet of Dire Straits and Yes with a dash of Pink Floyd or Fleetwood Mac, but it's very easy on the ear.

They go through to the sitting room, which is dominated by a vast, squishy settee covered in cushions and throws. The other two chairs don't look very comfortable, but Andy's already turned the music down and settled in one corner of the sofa. Emily's not sure if cosying down next to him will seem too familiar. He sees her hesitating and pats the cushion beside him.

'Come on, there's room for at least six of us on here; you won't crowd me,' he says.

A deep peace settles on the room and they sip their wine in silence. Emily is soon warmed to the core as the music plays quietly in the background.

'You'd better eat some of these cocktail snacks,' Andy says, eventually, gesturing to the huge array of nibbles on a low table nearby. 'May will be checking. I was given my orders. I had to hide them until Tamsin was in bed.'

Emily adores olives, and Andy's bought dips too, and cheese straws and celery and all sorts of her other favourite things. She digs in happily. The CD ends and Andy replaces it with . . . yes, an old Dire Straits one. Emily feels even more at home now.

When they've made inroads into the food and talked about a whole host of random things, Andy reaches for a notebook and pen. 'Right, let's make a list of all the things we need to think about for Julia,' he says, 'and then we can plan how to get everything moving.'

As he speaks, Emily notices that the track just beginning is 'Romeo and Juliet'. It's her favourite of all the old songs her mum used to play over and over again, especially on long car journeys. The wistful guitar leads into the passionate, sensual lyrics. She remembers as a young girl wondering what 'making love' was and then later, when she'd worked that one out, being confused as to why it would make you cry.

Andy stops speaking as the music swirls around them. He turns to look at Emily properly for the first time, and she realises that he's been avoiding her eyes so far, sitting by her side and concentrating on eating although, thinking about it, Emily realises she has demolished most of the snacks single-handed and Andy's had most of the wine. She is acutely aware how close their hands are, his left hand almost touching her right. Hoping he won't notice, she leans a little bit closer, inhaling the lovely clean smell of him: lime shower gel and the now familiar light, spicy aftershave.

The song builds to a crescendo, Mark Knopfler pouring out all the aching hurt of rejection and bad timing. Andy moves slightly. They're touching now and Emily feels the warmth flowing from him. Completely forgetting her vow to give up on men, she slides her hand underneath his and their fingers link. They sit like that for a moment and then, as the music ends, turn to face each other properly. Andy's eyes are soft with longing, and he looks so kissable that Emily can't resist touching his face and leaning nearer. He bends forward and their lips meet, gently at first. Emily wraps her arms around him, head spinning, but just as Andy begins to respond in a very satisfactory way she hears another less pleasant sound.

'Bugger,' mutters Andy, disentangling himself abruptly. Emily pulls her shirt down and jumps to her feet as he leaves the room at a gallop. There's no mistaking the pitiful noise of a small child vomiting.

'Can I help?' she calls after him.

'No, I can deal with it.'

Deflated in more ways than one, Emily flops back onto the sofa and drains the last of her wine. She waits a few minutes and then plucks up her courage to go upstairs. She can't just abandon him to a pile of puke.

In Tamsin's room, a heap of stained bedding tells the story of what's happened. Andy's got his daughter in the bath, and Emily can hear him talking to her quietly, soothing her sobs.

'It doesn't matter, poppet,' he says, over the sound of splashing. 'You're all clean now. We'll soon get your bed made up and some nice clean 'jamas on.'

'I think I sicked on Stripey,' says the little girl sadly, gasping and hiccuping as she tries to stop crying.

'No, the cat came downstairs just after you went to sleep. She's fine. Now, out you come, here's a big fluffy towel to wrap you up.'

'Sorry, Daddy. I love you.'

'No need to be sorry, pigeon. You can't help it if your tummy explodes now and again.'

'What were you watching? Did I make you miss the telly?'

'Oh, no, I . . . wasn't doing anything important. Now, where are those clean 'jamas?'

Emily's heart sinks. She tiptoes away and quietly lets herself out of the house. Her face burns. She must have been crazy to kiss Andy. What was she thinking? It was only yesterday she was fighting off Max's wandering hands and vowing to go it alone in future. At least Max was open about being tied up with his responsibilities. Or was he? Not really, she supposes.

As she walks down the path, Emily turns, in the vain hope that Andy's heard her leaving and is going to call her back. Instead, she sees a madly waving hand in the front window next door. May is gesturing frantically for her to come in. Emily's heart sinks. This isn't the time for a heart-to-heart. She wants to shut herself in her bedroom and snuggle down under the duvet to lick her wounds.

May has the window open now. 'Emily. Come here, dear! I need you,' she shouts.

Emily resigns herself to the inevitable and heads for May's back door. The old lady doesn't sound panicky, so it's not a crisis. With luck she'll be able to escape fairly soon.

'Is everything OK?' Emily asks, slightly irritated that May is now back in her favourite armchair looking mightily pleased with herself.

'I'm so glad I caught you,' May says, 'although I hadn't expected to see you so soon, to be honest. I thought you'd be with Andy for much longer.' She shoots a coy look in Emily's direction.

'Well, so did I, but it didn't turn out that way,' snaps Emily.

May raises her eyebrows and waits. Before she can stop herself, Emily is pouring out the whole sorry tale of what went wrong. When she's finished, May nods thoughtfully.

'He's a poor mixed-up soul, that's for sure,' she says.

'Mixed up? He's still in love with his wife and he mollycoddles his daughter – that seems simple enough to me.'

'Well, there is that, but you're easily a match for a

memory, and Tamsin just needs a firm hand. Anyway, forget about those two for a minute. Let's talk about you, dear.'

'Me?'

'Yes. As far as I can see, you're an independent woman. Whatever man you decide to take up with in the end will be very lucky to have you. But what's the rush? Being alone can be a very good thing, at least for a while. I know I'm guilty of matchmaking in my head sometimes, but I can see now that you might not be ready for Andy yet.'

Emily is silent, pondering on this. Fossil startles her as he jumps onto May's knee and she realises that she has no idea why May called her in.

'Did you want me for anything in particular?' she asks, watching as May strokes her cat. It's very peaceful here, and she's glad she came, whatever the reason.

'I'd like to show you something,' May says, 'because you're like me – you've got an eye for nice things. Pass me that box, please. I don't want to disturb Fossil.'

Emily reaches for the wooden casket that May's pointing to. It's rather shabby but has beautiful inlay and has been well-polished.

'Now, have a look at this,' says May, opening the box and lifting out the prettiest necklace that Emily has ever seen.

'Oh, wow, that's gorgeous,' breathes Emily. 'Are they amethysts?'

'They are indeed. My Aunt Barbara left this to me when she died, many years ago. I've always loved it.'

'I'm not surprised. It's beautiful. She must have been very fond of you.'

May grins. 'Maybe. I guess it was more that she just didn't have anyone else to leave it to, but we always got on well. She lent this necklace to me when I got married. I haven't looked at it for a long time until recently but I just wanted you to see it.'

'Thank you, May. I love it.'

'Put it on then.' May laughs at Emily's puzzlement. 'I want to see it on a young person instead of round this wrinkly old neck.'

Obediently, Emily takes the necklace and fastens it in place. She stands up to look at herself in the oval mirror on the wall. May smiles, and carries on stroking Fossil. 'I knew it would suit you. You can borrow it anytime. Maybe for your own wedding one day? If you decide you do need a man after all.'

Later, warm and cosy under the downy duvet at last, Emily drifts off to sleep thinking of May and her wise words. For the moment, a wedding is the very last thing on her mind.

# Chapter Twenty-Two

Thursday morning starts hazily, with a heavy sea fret that gives the beach an eerie feel. Even the birds are subdued. Julia can't settle to anything. She's already tidied her cardigan drawer, eaten a pile of hot buttered toast and watched a particularly tedious medical drama. None of these distractions has helped and now she's managed to drip melted butter down her clean blouse.

Sighing, she trudges upstairs to get changed. Julia can't bear clothes that aren't pristine. There are plenty to choose from in her wardrobe. Don never minded how much money she spent on looking nice. The bed looks tempting and she almost gives in to this awful weakness and has another nap. Emily's instructed her to take it easy while she goes for a quick walk.

Julia thinks her granddaughter has probably gone out of the way because she wants to make a phone call to her boss back in New York. She still seems adamant that she's going to try to stay longer, although last night at Andy's was obviously not a roaring success. Julia was already in bed when Emily came back across the road from May's house, but the few words exchanged had been enough to cause alarm when Em came in to say good night.

'But why didn't you just go into the bedroom and start making the bed up?' she'd said, perplexed at Emily's air of defeat.

'I didn't want to get under his feet. Andy said beforehand that Tamsin wouldn't settle if he had visitors, and I didn't like to rummage around in his cupboards looking for clean sheets and stuff.'

'Oh, Em – I bet he'd have appreciated you lending a hand. It must be hard doing that sort of thing on your own.'

'I bet you wouldn't say that if he was a single woman with a child, would you? It wouldn't be such a big deal then, would it?'

'What do you mean?'

'Oh, nothing, I'm going to bed. I called to see May too, and I'm shattered. Get some sleep, Gran. You need all the rest you can get. We'll talk tomorrow.'

Julia lay awake for a long time pondering on what Emily said. Was she saying that Julia made extra allowances for Andy being a man alone? And was it true? If so, she didn't mean to give him preferential treatment. Julia has always considered herself something of a feminist, backed up heartily by her lovely husband, but if this is the case, she's let the side down badly and not helped Andy's recovery by mollycoddling him. But no, with hindsight, she hasn't done anything to hold him back, just supported him when she could. It's time to stop thinking of him as *that poor man looking after his child alone*, though – he's a sad soul who's lost someone dear, but then so is Julia.

Clean and tidy, Julia comes downstairs to find Andy at her door. She hugs him briefly and leads the way to the living room.

'Have you finished work early?' she asks.

'Yes, Vi's had Tamsin again today,' he says. 'You have to have forty-eight hours off school if you have a tummy bug. I'm sure it was all the ice cream she had at tea time yesterday but they don't make exceptions. I feel awful to keep asking poor Vi but she doesn't seem to mind. One of her grandchildren is at home with a cold today so they're doing jigsaws together and watching *Frozen* for the millionth time.'

'I'd have had her for you; there was no need to bother Vi.'

'But you're on strict instructions to take it easy. I don't want you having to be at my little monkey's beck and call when you should be putting your feet up.'

'Did you come over for anything in particular or are you just one of Emily's policemen, keeping an eye on the elderly and infirm of the parish?'

He laughs. 'She can be pretty fierce when it comes to you, can't she? That's love for you, though. You're very precious.'

'Hmm. Anyway, how did last night go?

'On a scale of one to ten? I'd say minus two. Take a potentially relaxing evening, add a vomiting child and what've you got? An extra load of washing and a guest who legs it at the first sign of sick.'

'Emily just didn't want to step on your toes, I expect. She seemed to think you wanted to sort things out yourself.'

'I handled it all wrong. I just didn't want to look as if I couldn't cope, and Tamsin's no good at night if she gets too excited about visitors. I was fed up because we were . . . anyway, I'd better apologise.'

'There's no harm done, love. You can always ask her to come over again.'

'Do you really think so?'

'Worth a try.'

'OK. Anyway, I have something else to ask you. May's been reading more of the letters. She rang me this morning to see if I was coming to see you because she wants to find out more about some argument or other that keeps being hinted at in the later ones.'

'But why phone *you*? Couldn't she have asked me herself? I've only just spoken to her, actually. She didn't mention the row.'

'I think Emily's been talking to May about how worried she is about your health. May was afraid of bothering you when you were feeling under the weather.'

'But there's nothing wrong with me.'

Andy looks hard at Julia. She pulls a face. 'Well, yes, I have been feeling a bit shaky . . . and I can't always seem to quite remember things I've only just done . . . but it's probably nothing. Go on then, tell me what May wants to know.'

Julia listens to Andy's deep voice bringing up that old family feud with a heavy heart. She shudders at the memory of all the fuss it caused at the time. She wanted to bang all their heads together.

'. . . and so I thought there must be some other letters

stashed away somewhere, with more details about it. May says they come to a sudden halt and then jump forward many years.'

'Why do you want to bother with all that? It was a stupid waste of time and energy, and it upset Don terribly.'

'I'm just being nosy, I guess. It's just the idea of a family at odds with each other that fascinates me. My parents and my sister have always been really boring. They never argue. They don't even bicker.'

'But you hardly ever see them since they moved up to Yorkshire. They could be fighting away like crazy and you'd never know.'

'Nah, they're much too easy-going to do anything like that. Lovely, but set in their ways. I was just thinking that if this book based on the letters ever gets written, a nice meaty feud might make a good focus.'

Julia thinks for a minute and then gets up, holding onto the arm of the garden bench to steady herself. She's still not feeling right after the experience with May. It's shaken her even more than she realised at the time.

'There's one place I haven't looked,' she says, 'and I've only just remembered about it. There's a drawer in the bottom of the wardrobe that's still full of old bank statements from way back and receipts for just about everything we ever bought. I suppose Don might have put any missing letters there. But it could be that we just haven't found that batch yet. Perhaps they're mixed up with all the others.'

'Were there many letters about the feud then?'

'Yes, the two girls wrote to him for weeks, wanting Don

to pull a magic solution to the problem out of his hat somehow. Will had taken himself off to Ireland by that time, so he was safely out of the firing line. I told Don to burn those letters. He read and reread them until they made him half crazy.'

'But what *was* the big problem?'

'Let me go and see if I can find the missing ones and then I'll explain. I'm sure they're not with the rest or I'd have found them by now. I won't be long.'

'OK, I'll just go and check Tam's still asleep and then be right back.'

Julia returns to the living room just as Andy comes in again. His eyes light up when he sees the large brown envelope in her hand. 'They were at the very back of the drawer,' she says. 'I reckon they're all here in this packet. And there's something else here, too.'

She pushes her hand into the envelope and brings out a small leather box. 'Oh, heavens! Andy, it's the ring . . . it must be.' Julia fumbles with the catch so much that she drops the box on the floor, and Andy picks it up, flicking it open for her. A wave of disappointment crashes over her. The box is empty. There's just a ridge where a ring must have once sat, nestled in red velvet.

Julia drops the box back into the envelope in disgust. 'You can give these to May,' she says, 'and tell her I don't want to read them.'

'But what was it all about? Can't you just give me an idea?'

She folds her hands in her lap and sighs. 'Very well, if you insist. It was when their mother died that everything got nasty. Will was in Ireland at the time, pretty much incommunicado, busy being holy in the depths of the countryside. Don had managed to get home to see the old lady just before she passed away, but it wasn't until the will was read that the trouble started.'

'Why? What was the problem?'

'Well, it seemed that their mother had been so disgusted with all the arguments about the ring that she left everything she owned to a cousin in Scotland, who'd always kept in touch by mail but was something of a recluse. The only thing mentioned separately was the opal ring itself. She'd stated that if it was ever found, it was to come to me.'

'Wow! Toxic stuff.'

'Yes, indeed. The sisters were livid. They tried to make the cousin refuse to accept the legacy but human nature being what it is, the man said the money was his, fair and square. They had to sell the family home, which left Elsie without a roof over her head and Kathryn with a huge chip on her shoulder because she'd hoped to buy a house with her new husband instead of renting a rather rundown flat with a view of the pipeworks.'

'Hmm. So how did that affect Don? Was he angry about not getting a share? And Will?'

Julia smiles. 'Don wasn't in the least bothered for himself. He'd have liked me to have a bit of spare cash, but otherwise he wanted them all to shut up and move on. Will was less forgiving but he couldn't really make a fuss in his situation. He already had a home and a house-keeper that came with the job, and very few expenses.'

'What happened next?'

'Oh, they contested the will but there was nothing they could do. We didn't see the sisters for a couple of years. They never really got back on speaking terms with each other and they eventually started coming down here at different times. All very sad and awkward.'

She picks up the box again. 'But you do see what this means, don't you? If this is its box, the ring must have been here too, at some point.'

'True.' Andy takes the package from Julia as the back door opens. 'Emily's here,' he says, jumping up.

'Don't you go sneaking out the front. Stay and talk to her,' says Julia. 'I'm going to make a salad.'

She passes Emily in the doorway and sees her grand-daughter's shoulders set as she notices Andy. Leave them to it, she says to herself, let them sort themselves out. They're grown-ups, for goodness' sake. Although to be fair, that theory hadn't worked with the sisters and Will.

Half listening to the mumble of voices, she sets about getting tea ready and hopes Emily is more flexible and open to apologies than her father, Felix. Julia's only son is the most unforgiving person you could imagine. Julia just hopes he stays out of the way until she can get Emily settled with Andy and Tamsin once and for all. She's got a feeling her social-climbing son would prefer the successful charmer Max rather than a jobbing gardener with a child in tow for his daughter.

# Chapter Twenty-Three

The little house is cosy when May's finished switching on table lamps and drawing the curtains. It's early yet, but tonight she's in the mood to be alone and undisturbed because Andy's dropped off the new packet of letters for her to read, with promises to come back as soon as he can to go through them with her. He's also shown her the ring box and told her how terribly sad Julia was to be so close to finding the opals and then to discover the ring was still missing.

Before she opens the bulging envelope, May pulls another letter from the small parcel entrusted to her by Julia. They are full of information about Don's preparations for Julia to come and be with him in Cornwall now they're safely married so they're not too dangerous to read, but every now and again, Don's desperate yearning for his young wife overwhelms him and May has to stop and catch her breath. How wonderful to be consumed with love like that. Regret for all she's never experienced floods her mind, combined with heady echoes of long-ago passion.

May is fearful now. As long as she can remember she's been able to control the effects of the treasures she's used to get her fix of memories but everything's changing and she doesn't know why. It's as if the break when she wasn't able to recharge her batteries at all has made her greedy and out of control. Even more terrifying is the thought that the new feelings might just be because she's getting older. Her father never had the chance to test the long-term effects of memory harvesting, and neither did her grandmother. Their premature deaths give no guidelines. May has nobody to reassure her about what might come next. Increasing forgetfulness? Bones riddled with arthritis? The future looms, making her painfully aware of her own mortality.

It's easy to sense when she's at risk of overdosing on the letters, but May can't seem to stop herself. She needs more and more memories all the time but how is this going to impact on Julia? If the other woman becomes weaker and weaker as May's energy grows, how can May justify the sacrifice of her new friend's health? Why should May's welfare come before Julia's? Round and round her thoughts go, with her conscience pricking more painfully each time she considers Julia's future happiness, or lack of it.

The more she thinks about the effects of her memory harvesting on Julia, the worse she feels. Whatever happened in the past to make Julia so resentful (and May hasn't given up on finding out about that business with Charles, oh no), the fact is that their friendship is now more important to May than she can explain. Although she was gregarious as a child and then a young woman growing up in the village, her years of solitary travels have made her self-sufficient. She can keep her own counsel – she's had to, on more than one occasion. Friends have been less and less necessary. But now, the thought of Julia's bewilderment at losing her sharp grasp of everything is disturbing.

Unfolding the delicate paper from long ago, May takes a few seconds to breathe deeply and stabilise. She makes a huge effort to steady herself and begins to read.

*Darling – today being my rest day, I've been over from Falmouth to see Mrs Peters and have fixed everything up for us. To make sure you get the following instructions, I'm going to send the letter by express post. Send me a telegram in reply please to the above address.*

So far, so good. The memories flowing in make her heart beat faster but they're not damaging, just full of pent-up excitement. She carries on.

*It's an eleven-roomed house and all the rooms I think can be classed as outsized. You'll fall in love with it, I'm sure, as I did straight away. We're to have our own sitting room and bedroom and the use of the dining room and kitchen and the 'usual offices' for thirty shillings per week. The bedroom is massive and even the bathroom is twice the size of ours at home, and there's a nice big garden and a grand view from our bedroom window. The bedroom will swallow our big carpet (I'm going to send for it). Unfortunately, the cooking is done on an oil stove.*

*Will you come either Friday or Saturday to please yourself best, darling? I can't wait to see those opals on your finger. I've waited a long time to see that ring where it belongs. Mother's happy for you to*

*have it. I just need to find out where the girls have put it for safety.*
*They've all being rather vague about the whole thing. Surely they can't*
*have lost it?*

This is fine. May's back in control. There's no reason to open the brown parcel from Andy tonight. She's brimming with memories and she needs to sit back and let them ebb from fizzing ecstasy to a warm glow.

She goes into the kitchen and makes a milky drink to take her mind off the other letters but there's no escape from the lure of the envelope. As far back as she can remember there has never been an object that has had the power to appeal to May at this distance. She tries going outside into the garden to get further away from it but the urge to touch the packet is just as fierce. She can almost hear its siren call and her heart is beating much too quickly in response.

Taking a deep breath, May comes back inside and begins to assemble a snack to distract herself, eventually flopping down in her chair in the living room. As she sips her cocoa, she ponders again what on earth could be in these particular letters to have such an extreme effect on her mind and body.

When she's eaten three crackers with some cheese and a pickled onion and tidied the kitchen, May finally gives in. It's no good, she can't resist whatever is inside that envelope. Returning to her favourite chair, she settles down with the package on her lap. Even through the thick paper she can tell she shouldn't be doing this. The vibrations from the old memories are dangerous in their intensity. Put it down, May, she tells herself firmly. But the temptation is too strong. Cursing her own weakness, she lifts the flap and draws out the letters.

Most of them are blue, written on Basildon Bond paper. The writing is similar on them all, but even at a glance, May can tell that the same person hasn't written these.

The first one is a single sheet. May's head begins to spin as she reads the opening paragraph.

I know the others will have written to you, but I want you to read this carefully, Don. The family is in turmoil. There's so much hate. I never thought we'd come to this, after all we've been to each other. The lies that have been told, and the bitterness and venom – you wouldn't believe it.

The other thing you need to know is something Will told me over the phone when we were talking about the will. It was about when that nasty little man Charles drowned. He hinted all wasn't as it seemed and that on the night he was lost at sea, Charles seemed really odd and unsteady. It's bothered Will ever since, he says. I think he panicked and just ran for home. I'll tell you more next time. I must go now, my head's pounding . . .

Horror engulfs May as she stares at the next letter in the stack. Is this it? Her nemesis at last? She doesn't even have time to open it before a crashing wave of emotion engulfs her. May clutches at her chest, trying to let the envelopes slide to the floor and out of her reach, but her other hand just won't seem to let go. Her knuckles whiten as she gasps for breath. Bitterness and anger from the past surge through her body and, helpless to resist, she falls forward.

Now May is swaying alarmingly, waves of nausea coming one after the other. She plummets forwards and her head hits the edge of the coffee table. Her eyes roll upwards as she slumps onto the carpet, face down in the swirling turquoise and gold patterns of the Wilton. The last thing she hears is the clock striking ten. Bed time. May closes her eyes and lets the pain take over.

# Chapter Twenty-Four

Andy is itching to get back to May's to have a look at the new letters but Tamsin can't go to her dancing class tonight because of the sickness ban, so he has to content himself with calling May to see if there's anything interesting to report. The phone rings for ages with no answer. Maybe she's gone to bed early? No, that's not likely, especially when she's got something to do that keeps her interested.

'Who are you ringing, Daddy? Is it Aunty Julia?' Tamsin says, looking up from her colouring book. She's got a streak of blue felt-tip pen down one cheek and her hair bobble has come out.

'No, I was just wondering how May is,' he replies, frowning.

'Why?'

'Well, erm . . . no reason really.'

He peers out of the side window. There's a light on in the kitchen. The second call brings no reply either.

'Tam, I just need to go round to May's very quickly to check she's OK. I'll be back so fast you won't even know I've gone,' he says.

'I can't stay here on my own. It's not allowed. You said so. You said—'

'Yes, I know I did, but this is only for a minute. She's not answering her phone.'

'Oh. Maybe she did a sick like me?'

'Maybe. So will you be all right just while I go and check?'

She thinks for a moment. 'No.'

'But—'

'Why don't I come too?'

Andy ponders this as his anxiety levels rise. May's most likely in the shower or something. But if she's not . . . if something's wrong . . .

'I'll be super-quick,' he says, ignoring Tamsin's wail. 'Just stay here, OK?'

As he goes across the short gap between the houses he looks back to see Tamsin's small pointed face, her eyes wide. He waves to her and she waves back but she's not smiling.

'I'll be as fast as . . . as Buster when he smells chicken, sweetheart,' he shouts, giving her a thumbs up signal. She turns her head away in disgust. The perpetual worry of all this child nurturing being solely down to Andy threatens to swamp him, and a wave of unreasonable anger at Allie for leaving them makes him breathless as he enters May's kitchen, shouting her name as he comes in. There's no answer and very soon Andy sees why.

May is lying on her side on the hearth rug, one of her slippers dangerously close to the electric fire. What he can see of her face is an alarming shade of putty and there's a livid red mark across her temple.

'Oh shit. Oh bugger,' Andy mutters, beads of sweat

appearing on his forehead. He drops to his knees by her side and reaches for her wrist to try to take her pulse but his first aid knowledge is ridiculously inadequate and he's not really sure where he should be pressing. His heart is pounding now and he fumbles in his pocket for his phone and then realises he's left it with Tamsin.

'Hang on, May, I'll get an ambulance,' he says to the prone figure, grabbing May's phone from the sideboard.

'Is she breathing?' asks the operator, when he's connected.

'I don't know!' Andy's voice comes out way too loud and he takes a deep breath. 'Can't you just send an ambulance without all these questions? We're wasting time. If she's not already dead she looks like she's dying.'

'An ambulance crew is already on its way.' The telephone lady's voice is soothing and Andy tries hard to get a grip. 'They'll be with you very soon. I just need you to sit by the patient and let me know what you see. Then I can talk you through anything that we can do before the team reaches you.'

'Oh. Right. Well, she's a horrible colour and I can't hear her breathing.'

'Is she bleeding at all?'

Andy checks. 'No, not that I can see.'

'Does the lady wear false teeth? If so, could you remove them for me in case they obstruct her airway?'

Andy looks down at the poor, crumpled figure of his friend. Can he put his hand in her mouth and pull her teeth out? What would she think of that? But there's no choice, so he steels himself and eases her jaw open, gently wiggling the dentures until they slide out into his other palm. Yuk. Slimy. But as her mouth closes again, May makes a little noise in her throat.

'She's alive! I heard her groan a bit.'

'Well done. And her teeth are out of the way? Good. Well, I think the team should be with you any second now.'

Right on cue, Andy hears the wail of the siren as the ambulance trundles down the steep street. He dashes into the kitchen, deposits the dentures in the sink and flings the back door open, wiping his hand on his jeans.

'Thank goodness. She's in here,' he shouts, as the man and woman head for May's garden gate, each carrying a huge holdall.

Andy can see Tamsin's face at the open window. She leans forward. 'Daddy? Is May deaded?'

'No, love. She's just fallen over. These people are going to go and look at her now to try and pick her up, OK?'

To his intense relief Andy sees Emily fling open Julia's front door. 'What's happened?' she calls, jogging across the road.

'I think May's had some sort of fall. She's slumped on the rug in front of the fire and she's banged her head. I thought I was too late but she made a little noise. Tam's on her own in there.' Andy's babbling now. He points to where Tamsin's leaning as far out of the kitchen window as possible to see what's going on.

Julia's at her front door now, pale and staring.

'Go back inside, Gran. May's had a fall of some sort but the ambulance people are with her,' Emily shouts. 'I'll stay with Andy and see if I can help.'

'Bring Tamsin over here, dear,' says Julia, her voice easily carrying across the narrow street. There's authority in it, and calm assurance. Julia's in charge again, any weakness forgotten for the moment. Andy breathes a huge sigh of relief that someone has seen his dilemma and is stepping in.

'Tam, we're going over the road to Julia's,' he shouts to the little girl. 'Go and get your school bag and put a couple of books in it for Julia to read to you.'

'OK, but I can read them to *her*,' she says. 'Shall I bring Stripey?'

'No, she needs to stay put in case she has her kittens. Hurry up, sweetheart.'

Emily's inside May's house now, and Andy thinks it must be getting pretty crowded in there so he takes Tamsin's hand and holds it tightly as they cross the road.

'You don't need to squeeze my fingers like that, Dad,' she says. 'I know how to do roads. Not the big one up the hill, but I've looked both ways already. Is May going to be better soon?'

'I hope so. The ambulance people are seeing to her. I'll go back to them now you're here and you can read Julia a story.'

Julia holds out a hand and Tamsin slips her own into it comfortably. 'We'll be fine, won't we, Tamsin?' she says. 'I've got some of those teacakes you like for supper.'

'Can we toast them on the fire?'

Andy can hear Julia chatting away to his daughter as they move into the house. 'Yes, I've got the long toasting fork out ready. I like a nice fire even in the summer. My house is always chilly in the evenings. Emily was planning to do the teacakes with me, just like she did when she was a little girl like you. We can save her one, though, and one for Daddy.'

He turns to go, feeling the weight of responsibility shift for a little while. Now all he needs to do is make sure May's being properly looked after.

Inside the living room, Emily's keeping well out of the way as the two paramedics work on the small figure on the floor.

'What's happening?' Andy whispers.

'They're giving her some oxygen, ready for putting her in the ambulance.'

'Have they said what they think's wrong?'

Emily shakes her head and they watch the team work in silence. May looks worse, if anything, and Andy's finding it hard to believe she can come out of this unscathed. 'She's a hundred and ten, you know,' he says to the man, when he stands up for a moment to get his bag.

'So I'm told,' he replies, 'but her blood pressure's fine and she's breathing on her own. We're just topping her up with oxygen to be on the safe side. We'll be taking her to hospital very shortly. Does either of you want to come with us or is there a family member to contact?'

Andy and Emily look at each other. 'There's nobody but us. I should go with May,' he says, 'but what about Tam?'

'Don't worry, I'll go,' Emily says patting his arm. 'You're needed here. I'll pop over and get my bag and tell Gran what's happening, OK? Back in five minutes. But I'd better take the new hire car rather than go in the ambulance so I can get home again. It's still parked up at the pub.'

'I don't mind coming to fetch you.'

'But there's Tamsin. You'd have to ask Vi again and it might be hours before I can come back.'

Andy nods, deeply grateful that she's doing all this without a fuss. Feeling a stab of disloyalty, he finds himself imagining how Allie would have reacted to this crisis. Not as calmly as Emily, he has to admit. She was always caring and loving, but in an emergency she tended to hyperventilate. He drags his mind away from Allie. This is about May.

The old lady is wrapped snugly in a blanket and on a stretcher by now. Andy thinks her face is a little less grey and clammy but it's hard to tell with the oxygen mask obscuring most of it. Her beautiful white hair is in disarray. She won't like that, he thinks. But Emily will deal with it. He's sure she'll have a brush or comb with her. He imagines her checking her bag's contents now. What will she think is essential kit? Phone, charger, water bottle, notebook, pen, Kindle, make-up, emergency packet of Polos, chewing gum.

Andy's seen Emily's handbag – it's made of tapestry and is the size of a small backpack with lots of pockets. It reminds him of the one Mary Poppins used in the old film. She'd let it fall open the night they were out for a meal and he'd been amazed at the number of belongings she considers it necessary to carry around.

The team is ready to move now, and Emily comes back in, with the bulging bag over her shoulder.

'Tamsin's fine,' she says to Andy, 'she's on her second currant bun already.' Emily steps to one side as the stretcher is manoeuvred through the narrow doorways and out towards the waiting ambulance. May's eyes are tightly closed. At least she's breathing. 'But will you be fine, too?' Emily asks, giving Andy an impulsive hug.

Andy holds onto her for as long as he can get away with, breathing in the lemony scent of her hair and suddenly wishing he could stay here with his arms around Emily for ever.

She pulls away from him and heads for the lane. 'I'll ring you as soon as I know something. Or even if I don't. Try not to worry. May's a tough cookie. I'm sure she'll come through this and be as good as new by tomorrow.'

Five minutes later Andy watches the ambulance pull away from the kerb and imagines Emily waiting in her little car at the top of the hill, ready to follow it, and prepared to be there at the hospital for as long as it takes. He wishes he could go with her. Waiting around in a hospital is a lonely business; he knows that from experience.

The ambulance crew doesn't put the flashing light or siren on this time. Is that a good or bad thing, he wonders. A few of the neighbours are out on the street, concern on their faces. They're a bit of a nosy lot down here, but they mean well and they really do care. He goes towards the nearest group and gives them a brief update, leaving them to spread the word up the lane. It's time to go and rescue Julia.

# Chapter Twenty-Five

The next few hours seem like the longest Emily's ever known. Still comatose and looking very frail and ill, May is thoroughly examined and there are frequent checks on all her vital signs, but she doesn't wake, not even for a moment.

Emily sits by May's bed when she isn't in the way of the action and talks quietly to her, in between reading chapters of the thriller she brought with her. It's a chilling story of love, death and regret. Emily wishes she'd chosen more carefully. One of Julia's old romances from the bookshelf in her bedroom would have been much more comforting. A gentle D. E. Stevenson, taking her away to the Scottish border country, or maybe an Elizabeth Goudge with all the ins and outs of family life.

'I don't think you'd like this story, May,' she says. 'It's scary, and most of the characters hate each other and themselves. I could do better than this. Maybe I will, one day. I'm hoping for a happy ending but there's not much chance of that at the moment.'

There's no response from May. A nurse points Emily towards the drinks station at the end of the ward and she fortifies herself with some very sweet hot chocolate.

All around her, in cubicles that line each side of the long ward, are patients in various states of distress and sickness. Anxious relatives pace the floor, look for doctors to interrogate, drinking weak tea and sending furtive text messages, hiding their phones as best they can so as not to disturb anyone or get told off by the doctors.

'May, I'm just going to go outside for a minute and ring Andy,' Emily says, when she's got down to the nasty powdery bit at the bottom of her plastic cup.

She slips out of a side door, shivering in the cool evening air. Andy answers on the first ring. 'Hello? Emily? What's happening?'

'Nothing much to report, but I thought I'd just keep you up to date. They aren't sure why May collapsed but they're doing all sorts of tests. She hasn't woken up yet but she's peaceful. I'm sure she isn't in any pain.'

'Well, that's something. I wish I was with you. It's not fair for you to be doing this on your own.'

'I'm fine. I'm going to have a Mars bar out of the machine next. I haven't had one of those for years. Maybe if I wave it under May's nose she'll wake up. Does she like chocolate?'

He laughs, and Emily's heart warms at the sound. Andy's got a lovely deep chuckle. He should try that laugh out more often, she thinks. 'Is the Pope a Catholic?' he says. 'She *loves* anything with chocolate on it or in it. That might just do the trick.'

'Right, I'm going back, if I can find someone to let me in. I'll ring again in a little while.'

'Thanks for this, Emily. You've come all this way to

look after one old lady and you've ended up with another. I'm . . . I'm really glad you came home, though.'

'Me, too. I just wish I'd brought a more cheerful book with me. Hey-ho, I'll see if I can find an old copy of *Hello!* magazine. Hospitals always seem to have those. More soon.'

Emily rings off and catches the eye of a nurse inside the emergency unit, who presses the buzzer to let her in. The machine in the waiting area's out of Mars bars so Emily treats herself to a KitKat and gets a packet of chocolate buttons for May, just in case she wakes. May's in the same state as she was when Emily left her but a different nurse is taking her blood pressure and smiles encouragingly.

'Is this your grandma?' she asks. 'I've only just come on duty and I'm not up to speed yet.'

'No, she's . . . just a friend, really.'

'Oh. Well, it's good of you to take the time to come in with her. We get a lot of old people stuck in here on their own for hours with nobody to speak up for them and if they're like this, we can't get any answers at all.'

'Is she any better, do you think?' Emily realises this is probably a silly question when May's spark out in bed with a face the colour of porridge, but she has to ask.

'She's holding her own at the moment. Her blood pressure's steady and she's breathing normally. The doctor'll be along soon with the results of the first tests. Are you going to be here for a while?'

'I'm staying.' Emily can't bear the thought of May waking up to find herself abandoned, and anyway, Andy needs her here to give him any news. It's good to feel useful and appreciated. Her life in New York is busy and her job's usually fascinating, but nobody depends on her or minds that much if she's not around, it seems, least of all Max.

The nurse bustles off and Emily sits down next to May again. 'I've brought us some chocolate to keep us going,' she tells her, unwrapping the KitKat and biting off half of the first finger. She wafts the rest of it under May's nose. Did her nostrils twitch? A flake of chocolate drops onto the pristine white sheet and Emily brushes it off, glancing over her shoulder as the doctor comes in, a slim, dark-haired beauty with a serious expression.

'Hey, I just came at the right time,' the doctor says, her face breaking into a smile. 'If I was fast asleep, that's the thing that'd get me going. Are you a relative of Mrs Rosevere?'

'No, I don't think she's got any of those left, nor many friends either,' says Emily. 'May's a hundred and ten. She's outlived most people. She's my grandmother's neighbour. I just happened to be around.'

'OK. Well, the news is as good as you can expect for someone who's unconscious. I . . .'

The doctor breaks off talking as May raises a shaking hand a couple of inches off the bedcover. 'Do I smell chocolate?' she croaks.

# Chapter Twenty-Six

The next morning, May is propped up in her hospital bed sipping a weak cup of tea and feeling every one of her hundred and ten years. She's been moved to a ward that seems to be where people come to die. Although the five other patients in the beds surrounding her are probably what the staff term 'elderly', they all look young enough to be her children, May estimates. Two of them have moaned and cried out all night and another keeps trying to break out of the ward.

As May watches, the escapee, Albert, is led back to his bed.

'But I need to meet Bill at the pub,' he says to his nurse, tugging on her sleeve. 'He'll be mad as anything if I'm late. It's my round.'

'I'll give Bill a ring,' she says soothingly, 'and maybe you can see him tomorrow.'

In your dreams, mate, May thinks. She knows for a fact Albert has been here for a week already and the only place he's heading for is back to the care home, if he's lucky. Dorothy in the next bed, the most compos mentis of the other five, has given May a potted history of the ward's inmates in the night when they were kept awake by Albert singing 'I Get a Kick Out of You' at top volume. By four a.m. May was ready to do the kicking for him.

'How are you feeling today, May?' asks the rather fetching male nurse who's been taking care of her since the early hours of this morning.

'I'll be better when I'm home,' she says, then regrets her words when she remembers how kind he's been, helping her to the toilet, bringing water and squash and generally making her feel less alone. 'Not that I don't like it here, you understand. Well, I don't actually *enjoy* it, but you're all doing a wonderful job,' she adds hastily.

He laughs. 'I know what you're saying. Let's hope you get back where you belong as soon as possible.'

'Today?'

'I'm not sure. The doctors'll be doing their rounds at about ten o'clock.'

'I'd best have a wash then and get someone to do my hair. Don't want them to decide I'm ill and feeble.'

'No chance of them thinking that, May. Give me half an hour and I'll come back and get you sorted. See you soon. Oh, I nearly forgot. Your bestie rang.'

'What did you say? My beastie?' May wonders if the world has gone mad. Fossil's a bright cat, but to be able to use the phone . . .

'No, *bestie*! Best buddy? Said her name was Julia, and she's missing you. Wanted me to give you her love and to see how you were doing.'

May ponders on this while she waits to be released. Fancy Julia bothering to check up on her and even more strange, to send her love. They haven't been on those sort of terms, have they? May finds herself almost moved to tears. Their friendship must have slid forward into some new stage while she wasn't looking. It's rather wonderful to think she's been missed.

When the doctors appear on the dot of ten o'clock, May's looking as good as she possibly can on three hours' sleep and with a livid bruise down one side of her face.

'Mrs Rosevere, isn't it?' the senior one says, picking up the clipboard that holds May's notes. He's got a long, solemn face and sideburns that wouldn't look out of place at a seventies revival night.

'It is. Good morning, Doctors.' She gives them her brightest smile. Unfortunately, Andy didn't think to send her teeth with her, so the effect isn't as good as usual.

'So how are you feeling now? I gather from the staff that you had quite a bang on the head, and a bit of an issue with your heart.'

'I feel absolutely fine now,' May says, 'and if I could go home, I'd feel even better.'

The doctor draws the curtains around the cubicle and his two colleagues gather round the bed. The following examination doesn't bother May as far as being embarrassed goes but leaves her breathless. She does her best to conceal this, but it's no good.

'We'd like to keep you here at least another night, ideally. Because of your age, we want to be extra careful to be sure you're fit. I hear you live alone, May?'

'I do, but I've got very good neighbours. My . . . erm . . . bestie only lives across the road, and there are any amount of people on red alert for needy old people now

Ida Carnell's on the case. *Please* let me go back now, Doctor. I can't stand another night awake. I need to be in my own bed to set me right. I'll never get better if I can't sleep.'

The three doctors step outside the curtained area and May can hear them conferring. She crosses her fingers and almost prays. Eventually, the senior one comes back in. 'You win, May,' he says with a grin, 'but only if we can be sure there's somebody to take care of you, and you must promise to take it easy.'

May beams all over her face, giving him the benefit of a fine set of gums. 'Thank you,' she says, from the bottom of her heart.

Andy collects her later that afternoon, still in his work clothes and with her teeth in a plastic bag. 'I came as soon as I could,' he says. 'Emily's picking Tam up from school for me and then they're going to your house with some shopping. I'm making a shepherd's pie later and I'll bring yours round to you.'

His kindness almost finishes May off but she doesn't want the nurses to see her cry. They might class it as a sign of weakness and keep her here. A porter arrives with a wheelchair, to her disgust, but May knows better than to argue and gets into it without a murmur. She waves gaily to the other five patients, but only Dorothy is well enough to wave back. Lightweights, May thinks to herself, and then feels bad for being so critical. Dorothy is lovely, and none of them has May's gifts to keep them going. They're bound to be creaking gates, aren't they?

The outside world looks very bright as Andy drives her home, never exceeding forty miles an hour even on the straight bits of road. 'You can go faster than this if you want to, love,' she says. 'I'm not a piece of china.'

'And *I'm* not taking any chances with you,' Andy says, winking at her. 'Julia and Emily will be on my case in seconds if I don't bring you back in one piece.'

'Did you remember to feed Fossil?'

'Yes, Tamsin would never let me forget something like that. She's been nagging me about both cats non-stop. Stripey's settled herself in the bottom of my wardrobe so it looks likely there'll be a litter of kittens soon, and Fossil's been eating for both of them. He eats his food and then comes round to mine to see if there are any leftovers.'

May relaxes into the passenger seat and looks out of the window as the familiar landmarks flash by. The sun is warming her face, the birds are singing lustily and she's as happy as she can remember being for a long time. She's aware that this is largely because during the long, wakeful hours of the night, she made a serious decision. She's looked death in the face and hasn't flinched. There's no way of knowing what will happen to her if she lets go of the reins, but it's nearly time to find out. She's not going to tamper with other people's memories for much longer.

Hurting Julia has gone on long enough. Her new friend really cares about the people around her and she doesn't deserve to be treated like this. How many others has May unwittingly hurt in the past, she wonders? How many confused, worried villagers has she left in her wake as she selfishly syphoned off their precious memories?

The prospect of changing her way of life brings a wave of fear mingled with intense relief. May will leave the letters alone, particularly the poisonous ones, and never try to find any other sources. Never. This experience has left her bruised in more ways than one, right down to her bones, both mentally and physically, and hanging onto life regardless of the consequences suddenly doesn't seem so necessary. Maybe the alternative wouldn't be so bad after all? It's almost time to let nature take its course. But not quite yet.

# Chapter Twenty-Seven

That evening, May sits in her chair, knees covered with a patchwork rug and with her purring cat on her lap. She's surrounded by Julia, Andy, Emily and Tamsin. They've switched on the fire and she's eaten her dinner, or as much of it as she could manage.

Emily is shocked to see how changed May seems even in the short time she's been away. Her hair is as tidy as usual, if a bit flat, and she's wearing a clean dressing gown, but her face is drawn and looks more lined than usual.

'Are you ready for bed?' Emily asks, getting up to clear away the dinner pots. 'You must be shattered.'

'I am a bit tired, dear,' May says. 'It's been an interesting experience, but not one I want to repeat.'

Tamsin leans over and gives her a hug. 'We've got to go now, anyway,' she says, 'Stripey's nearly ready to have her kittens, Daddy says.'

'That's very exciting.'

'They'll come out of her bottom.'

'Yes, that's the usual way.' May shoots a glance at Andy but he's completely absorbed in watching Emily loading the tray with dishes.

Tamsin starts to giggle. 'It's a very silly way. Bottoms are rude.'

'Well, rude or not, sweetheart, Stripey doesn't have a choice.'

'She'll be very surprised. I would be.'

'So in that case you'd better be sure and not miss the great event. Emily will help me to bed, won't you?'

'I will, just as soon as I've washed up.'

'Don't worry, I'll do that,' says Julia. 'You two go on through.'

Emily regards her grandmother under her eyelids. Julia looks stronger today and she's losing that bewildered look. 'OK, thanks, Gran. The sooner May's tucked in, the better she'll be, I reckon. Those hospital beds are hard and there's no peace. Thank goodness there are no stairs to negotiate here.'

When May's been to the loo, put her teeth in a glass to soak and washed her face, Emily holds her elbow and guides her into the bedroom. She's surprised to be allowed to do this. From what she's seen of May up to now, she doesn't appear to be the sort of person who takes kindly to being propped up.

As if reading her thoughts, May says, 'Thank you for doing all this, dear. You can tell I need a bit more help than usual tonight, can't you?'

'I'm not surprised after what you've been through. I'd feel just the same.'

'Ah now, but would you? I've got to begin to remember my age, for a change.'

'But you'll soon be back to normal. This is just a blip.'

May's in bed now and Emily snuggles the duvet round her. 'Lean forward and let me plump your pillows,' she says.

May sighs happily. 'It's so nice to be fussed over,' she says. 'Oh, look, here's Fossil. He likes to sleep on my feet. Emily, you *are* staying around for a while, aren't you?'

'I was just thinking Gran looks a bit better and might not need me for long, but yes, for a little while. Why?'

'Oh, I just wondered. Have you ever thought of buying your own place here? As an investment, I mean?'

'I can't afford it, May. My apartment's only tiny but it costs a fortune in rent and I've got no prospect of promotion for a year or two. It's a lovely idea, though. Maybe one day.'

'One day's too far away. It'd be fun for you to have somewhere of your own now, wouldn't it? You could always rent it out until . . . well, for now.' May strokes the cat and waits. The room is very quiet apart from Fossil's loud purring.

Emily frowns. What's all this about? Has Gran had a hand in it? 'It's just not possible, though. Colin's agreed to me staying for an extra week on top of my holidays. After that I'll need to go back to New York to talk to him if I want to make any permanent changes.'

'I expect that'll depend on a lot of things, won't it?'

'How do you mean?'

May looks at Emily with her head on one side. 'Well, planning for the future isn't always as straightforward as it seems. In my experience, life has a habit of getting in the way.'

'Does it? I don't see how. I'll make my own decisions, Max or no Max.'

'Maybe I wasn't just thinking about him.'

'But who else were you expecting me to consider?'

Emily waits, but May seems to have run out of steam. The shadows under her eyes are getting deeper and her face is the colour of paper. 'We'll talk about this when you feel stronger. Now, get a good night's sleep and you'll feel sparkling again in the morning.'

'Will I?' May's almost asleep and Emily leans over to kiss her forehead, being careful to avoid the bruises.

'Course you will. And you've got the phone by your bed so you can ring us in the night if you need to, but I think you're going to sleep like a baby. I don't know why they say that, because the people I know with babies say they don't seem to sleep much.'

'Babies. No, they don't, do they? I think you'll . . .'

May stops talking and bites her lip. Then she sits up, suddenly wide awake again. 'Could you ask your gran to pop in here before she goes?' she asks.

'I will, but only for a couple of minutes. It's time you were asleep.'

Julia comes in as soon as Emily tells her she's needed. Emily hovers by the door, just out of sight, worried that May's going to want a long chat, and poised to step in. Julia perches on the end of the bed and smiles at May. 'Did you want me for something important?' she says, moving May's water glass a bit closer to the bed.

'I just wanted to say thank you for ringing the hospital to see how I was, and for your nice message,' May says.

Emily can just see her through the open door. May's cheeks are pink now and she's not looking at Julia.

'That's not a problem,' says Julia. She pats May's hand through the duvet. 'I realised as the ambulance pulled away that your little cottage was going to seem very empty without you in it. I always check to see if your lights are on and if you've drawn the curtains back as soon as I get out of bed. It's not the same without you.'

'I . . . I liked you sending your love,' May says shyly, snuggling down into her pillows and closing her eyes again.

Julia stands up to leave and Emily comes back in.

'I hope you're better soon, dear May,' Julia whispers, and heads for the kitchen, blinking hard.

Emily looks down and realises that May is already snoring gently. She straightens the covers and waits for a few moments to make sure May really is asleep. Her mouth drops open slightly and she lets out a ladylike snore. It seems very personal, watching someone when they don't know you're doing it, and Emily goes back to the kitchen before she can get any more worried about the frailty of this plucky old lady.

Julia is just finishing clearing up. Everything is gleaming and much tidier than usual. 'How is she really, do you think?'

'Just tired, I reckon, but it's been a shock to her, all this.'

'She'll bounce back soon. Nothing gets May down.'

'Hmm. I'm not so sure about that. May's a very old lady. She's not going to find it easy to get over a heart attack in a couple of days.'

They sit down either side of the electric fire, now safely turned off. The room is getting chilly. 'May's just been asking me why I don't buy a house in the village,' Emily says, watching her gran's face for any reaction.

'Really? Why would you want to do that?'

'I don't know. I thought you might have an idea why she said it?'

The look on Julia's face appears to be genuine astonishment. 'No, not at all. Buy a house in Pengelly and then never see it? That'd be silly.'

'Hmm. Oh, well, who knows why May had the idea then? It's a mystery.'

'You don't need the responsibility of a house when you've got a perfectly good room in my place.'

Emily leans over to squeeze Julia's hand and nods, fighting a sudden rush of nostalgia. If only her grandpa was still here. She misses him so much. Their home has been her sanctuary for years and the two of them her security when her parents were at constant war with each other. Somehow May has planted a thought in Emily's head that won't go away. What would a cosy nest of her own look like? Is there such a house here just waiting for her?

Julia's obviously been thinking along the same lines. 'Ignore May, darling,' she says, getting to her feet creakily. 'She's probably still a bit delirious.'

'Let's go home then. I'm shattered, and so must you be.'

There'll be time to dig a bit deeper in the morning. For now, Emily's own elderly lady needs to be tucked up in her bed. Emily feels the weight of worry and responsibility for these two very different but equally brave characters lying heavy on her shoulders but she still can't suppress the bubble of happiness that takes her by surprise. Being with Tamsin earlier was fun. The little girl had soon begun to chatter, overcoming her shyness in next to no time. It's Saturday tomorrow, and Emily's offered to look after her while Andy's at work. They're planning to build a den in Julia's garden and eat their lunch in it, after they've been for a paddle and maybe to see Tristram for coffee.

Emily pulls May's back door shut behind her and offers Julia an arm to go across the road. She glances back at Andy's house and sees a shadowy shape at an upstairs window. Has he been watching out for them? Suddenly, she hopes so. Wouldn't it be great to have someone who cares enough to see if you're safely home?

# Chapter Twenty-Eight

Julia listens to Emily padding around her bedroom getting dressed ready for her childminding duties and sighs with happiness. It's the farmers' market today and it'll be lovely to have Tamsin with them when she and Emily go up to the village.

She always adored the times she spent with Emily as a little girl and later when she was a somewhat edgy teen. As a mum, she'd found Felix hard work a lot of the time. He was prickly and prone to sulks. But even when Emily had been going through her moody phase at around fourteen, dressing all in black and painting streaks in her hair, she'd still been fun to be with most of the time. If she'd felt cross, she'd taken herself off to the beach to burn off her grumpiness.

'Is Tamsin coming over for breakfast, Em?' Julia shouts. 'Because if she is, I'd better get a move on.'

'No, we've got a little while yet,' Emily answers, sticking her head round Julia's door. 'Andy's bringing her when she's eaten. He says we won't have the right sort of disgustingly chocolatey cereal that she likes. I'm surprised he gives her stuff like that when he's so anxious about her health.'

Julia smiles. 'Oh, when you're a parent, you'll do anything to start the day off without tantrums,' she says.

'What are you saying, Gran? I can't remember kicking up a fuss about *my* breakfast.'

'No, but your dad did. He would only eat white toast with shop-bought strawberry jam. And me with a cupboard full of home-made preserves and your grandpa's wonderful wholemeal bread fresh out of the oven. Very irritating.'

Julia lets Emily help her out of bed. She doesn't really need her to do this, but it feels nice and she wants to promote the poor little old lady image as long as possible. All that talk of Emily buying a house, even though it's impossible, has made Julia long even more to have her granddaughter here permanently. It would be bliss. But Emily's career can't be ignored for much longer – she knows that – and she doesn't want to hold the girl back.

'Right, if you're ready to get organised up here, I'll go and make my preparations for the day,' says Emily, eyes sparkling.

'What do you need to do?'

'I want to find some clothes pegs, lots of old blankets or dust sheets, the two clothes horses from the outhouse and a couple of rugs.'

'You used to love den-making.'

'I've got a feeling I still do. There isn't much cause for rigging up a shelter inside a city apartment. This is going to be great. What time do you want to go to the market?'

'Oh, around eleven, do you think? We can get some

lovely cheese and so on for lunch, and there's going to be one of those artisan bread stalls. I might even *buy* a cake for a change. Tamsin can choose.'

'That sounds great. I'm glad I'm here to see it.'

'Yes, village life's got its good points,' says Julia, hoping there are enough stalls there today to impress her grand-daughter. This is just the kind of village PR that's needed to attract Emily for good.

Tamsin bursts into the kitchen half an hour later, just as Emily and Julia are clearing away the remains of their breakfast. 'Hooray!' she shouts. 'I'm here. Daddy wouldn't let me come any sooner. There's nothing come out of Stripey's bottom yet,' she adds, 'well, only a great big—'

'That's enough of that, thanks, Tam,' says Andy, following his daughter in. 'She wanted to come across to you at six o'clock, but I guessed that might be a tad early?'

Emily pulls a face. 'Well, maybe just a bit. I went over to see May at half-six, though. She's always awake by then.'

'We called on our way here. She's had her mountain of toast already. She was really sensible and took it back to bed with her. I'll go again after I pick the offspring up later.'

'And I can call mid-morning before we go up the hill,' Julia adds. 'Between us we can keep an eye on her. She's tough, is May. You'll be surprised.'

Emily still looks worried. 'So you said last night, but she's had a nasty setback with the heart problem. What do you think, Andy?'

He leans back against the worktop and folds his arms, accidentally providing an demonstration of rippling biceps, if anyone happens to be looking. 'I guess we'll just have to wait and see. Might be a good idea to get in touch with Ida to see if there are any more people we can rope in to call on May?'

'I'll probably see her at the market. Can you think of anybody?'

'There's always Pam at number eleven. Mind you, May says she smells of roll-ups and gin, and she can't stand cats. Or we could ask Frank at number forty. I'm surprised he hasn't already been collared by Ida for the scheme. He likes a game of whist, does Frank. That'd keep May busy while she's supposed to be taking it easy.'

Julia sees Emily checking Andy out, in what she must imagine is a subtle way, as he lounges there. Her granddaughter's eyes rest on his tanned legs, muscular and strong. He's wearing faded denim shorts and hefty boots. Julia thinks Andy might have noticed Emily observing him, too. Good. He's looking particularly handsome this morning. His curly brown hair is damp from the shower, as usual. He never has time to wait for it to dry before he leaves the house. He's newly shaven, though, and his checked shirt is clean, if well worn. The sleeves are rolled up revealing brown forearms. Julia can see why Emily's interest is piqued. If I were fifty years younger, she tells herself with a smile.

'What's so funny, Julia?' Andy asks.

'Oh . . . erm . . . I was just remembering how early Emily used to get up when she came to stay.'

'Emily goes on the beach before breakfast,' says Tamsin. 'I saw her with my special telescope.'

'Ah, it was you watching me, was it?' says Emily, and then looks at Andy and blushes.

He doesn't miss a trick. 'You didn't think *I'd* been spying on you, did you?' he asks, frowning.

'No, of course not.'

There's an awkward silence, luckily broken by Tamsin asking for some drawing paper. 'I want to do a picture of our den before we make it. It's going to be like a hobbit hole. Then I'll do another one when it's done. OK?' she asks Emily.

'Hobbits are very tidy people, you know,' says Emily. 'You'd have to keep it nice inside.'

'I'm tidy, aren't I, Daddy? Sometimes socks get lost on their own, though. Can we grow grass on the roof?'

As Emily settles their guest at the table and gets out the battle-scarred box of crayons that has been in the dresser since her own childhood, Julia marvels at how quickly her granddaughter has slipped into this role. As far as she knows, Emily's never had much to do with children, but she's sitting down with Tamsin now, and their heads are both bent over the paper, one dark and one fair. Andy's eyes are on them too, but his expression's unreadable.

'Give me a hug then, sweetheart. I'll see you about four o'clock,' he says, leaning down to Tamsin. She jumps up again and wraps herself around him and he lifts her up so he can kiss her.

'How much do you love me?' she asks.

'This much,' he says, putting her down and spreading his arms wide.

'I love you more. I love you THIS much.' Tamsin flings her arms open, narrowly avoiding demolishing a cut-glass vase on a nearby shelf.

'Tam, be careful. I want Julia's house to be all in one piece when I get back. I've got my phone with me, so call if there's a problem, Julia. Be good, little 'un? Please.'

He's not looked at Emily since the comments about the telescope, and Julia sighs. Why are the young so touchy?

He hesitates by the door. 'This is very good of you two ladies,' he says eventually.

Emily glances up and grins at him. 'Any excuse for a den-making session,' she says. 'We might even have a paddle first, if we're quick.'

He smiles back and Julia relaxes. She really will have to knock both their heads together if the pair of them carry on like this.

An hour later, Emily and Tamsin return from the beach with Tristram in tow.

'Tristram made us a yummy drink in his café,' says Tamsin happily. 'I had a fizzy milkshake with sprinkles. Do you know how to burp, Julia? Shall I show you?'

'No, not just now, dear. It sounds as if you've had a good time, though.'

'Shall I show you instead, Tristram?'

'Let's save that treat for another day, shall we, poppet?'

'Burping aside, I had the best cappuccino I've ever tasted,' Emily says. 'I'm definitely putting The Shack on my list of favourite places to eat. We had some gorgeous almond biscuits, too. Tamsin ate five.'

'They were very little, though. I would've had ten if you hadn't hidden them.'

'You won't want any lunch,' says Julia, laughing at Tamsin's scowl, 'and it's going to be posh nosh from the market today.'

'I bet I will.'

'Go and wash your hands ready to go out, sweetheart, while I talk to Tristram,' says Julia.

They sit down around the kitchen table and Emily tells Julia that she's already updated Tristram about May's sudden illness but that he was calling to see her anyway today.

'She rang me when she got home,' he says. 'She said to come as soon as possible. This is the first chance I've had. I've left the dogs behind because they always want to eat May's cat.'

'What could have been so urgent?' Julia wonders.

'Search me.'

'Didn't she even give you a hint?'

'Nope. I'll go and find out now – it'll save you two a trip – then you can pop over later. Oh . . . ah . . . Julia, I was wondering if you fancied coming out with me for dinner one night? It's just that I want to check out the competition, and George gets edgy if I go to Cockleshell Bay on my own.'

Julia's face is pink as she nods her agreement. 'That'd be lovely,' she says, not looking at Emily.

Tristram heads across the road, and Emily kicks off

her old trainers and finds sandals ready for the walk up the lane. 'It's odd, May phoning Tristram, isn't it?' she asks. 'You'd think she'd ask you or me if there was something she needed.'

Julia doesn't reply. She has a feeling there's a lot she doesn't know about May. Perhaps it's just as well.

Tamsin, chattering all the way, walks between Julia and Emily, holding each of them by the hand, as they wander up Memory Lane a little later.

'Please can we have a cake with chocolate icing on it, Aunty Jules?' she says. 'May likes chocolate. I can take her a piece later. I don't like May being poorly. She keeps going to sleep, doesn't she? Going to sleep's boring. Do you like going to bed, Em? I don't.'

By this time they're amongst the throng of visitors on The Level. The pub car park is full and cars line the pavement as people of all ages jostle their way to the village green.

'We've never had this many here before,' says Julia, feeling slightly dizzy as they make their way towards the bouncy castle.

Just as they reach the edge of the green, Julia hears Emily's name being called, very loudly. Her granddaughter freezes, rooted to the spot.

'Emileeeeee! Wait up, honey, I'm over here.'

She turns slowly, and Julia sees a look of horror on Emily's face.

'Hi, babe,' shouts Max, pushing his way through the crowd towards them. He's wearing a very loud Hawaiian shirt and baggy shorts. They don't suit him. Julia watches with plummeting spirits as a large, florid man follows Max. A very smart, excessively thin woman in spiky heels brings up the rear, with two sulky-looking teenage girls.

'I told Ned about this market of yours. He was mad keen to see some traditional village life, weren't you, dude?'

Ned nods to Emily, ignores Julia and Tamsin and makes his way to the loaded cheese stall, eyes shining. His family drift off after him.

'So, how the hell have you girls been?' asks Max, giving them all the benefit of his most charming smile. 'I've missed you, honey.' He gives Emily a hug and kisses her on both cheeks. 'Do you like the holiday gear? I borrowed it from Ned.'

'Can I go on the bouncy castle now?' asks Tamsin, pulling at Emily's shirt.

Emily looks down at the eager little face and to Julia's relief, nods. 'Of course. That's what we came for. Have a lovely day, Max. Enjoy the market and try not to patronise the locals.'

'But aren't you going to show me around?' asks Max. 'Grandmama can look after the kid, can't you?' he appeals to Julia.

Julia turns to Emily. 'Pass me my cardigan,' she says.

Max is totally lost now, as Emily starts to laugh.

'Silly, you're wearing your cardi,' says Tamsin, joining in.

'She means her fighting cardigan,' says Emily, between giggles. 'You've really upset her now, Max.'

'Huh?'

Julia smiles at him serenely. 'It's a bit of Olde English family folklore, passed down through the years, dear,' she explains. 'Apparently, so they tell me (although I think they're exaggerating), on a caravan holiday, years ago, Felix was ticked off for making a noise by some rather arrogant campers who'd chosen to pitch up near the play area. He came back in floods of tears and I set off to fight his corner, uttering the immortal lines as I left . . .'

'PASS ME MY CARDIGAN,' Julia and Emily chorus, in unison.

Max still looks puzzled.

'So whenever I got really cross, Don would say those words. It's good to air them again. Because, Max, you have seriously annoyed me. I suggest you get out of our way, leave my granddaughter alone and find someone else to take advantage of. I pity your poor wife and family.'

Tamsin's been listening to all this, wide-eyed. '*Now* can we please go to the bouncy castle?' she says loudly. 'I don't like this man, do you, Em?'

Emily's controlled her giggles now, and she looks Max straight in the eye.

'No, I don't, sweetie – not one bit. Let's go. Castles to bounce on, cakes to buy and dens to make. See you, Max. Have a nice life.'

Max's jaw drops as Emily leads the way to where small children are flinging themselves onto a brightly coloured creation with flags on the top. Julia gives Max a little wave as she goes. My work here is done, she thinks, rather smugly. He had it coming to him.

The rest of the morning passes peacefully. Max and Ned avoid them, and they buy an enormous crusty loaf and a whole basketful of delicious cakes, pasties, olives and cheeses. Julia even has time to spend a few minutes at Ida's information station, updating her about May and giving advice to a couple of new recruits for the Adopt-a-Granny scheme. They bump into Cassie with one set of very lively twin boys – the others are still at school – and Emily meets George and Cliff, shopping for unusually flavoured olives for Cockleshell Bay.

'Who's that lady with the orange fringe?' asks Tamsin, as they wend their way home for lunch. Julia looks round to see Angelina waving madly from the pub window. She raises a brimming glass to them and mimes 'chin-chin', but Julia shakes her head.

'If we go for drinks with Angelina, we won't be back in time for tea, let alone lunch and den-making,' she says. 'But I'd like you to meet her one day, Em. Tristram says he nearly married her once.'

'Well, I hope he's given up on that idea now,' says Emily. 'She looks as if she's a bit of party animal. He should find someone to keep him company at home, not drag him to the pub and get him legless. Can you think of anyone, Gran?' She widens her eyes as she looks across at Julia.

'Legless? I don't want nice Tristram's legs to drop off,' says Tamsin. 'Do you, Em? Hey, Aunty Jules, maybe Tristram needs a girlfriend to stop his legs falling off? I'm Robbie Partridge's girlfriend, did I tell you that? He asked me to play kiss-chase once but I said no. I wonder if Tristram knows how to play kiss-chase.'

'I think it's time we got ourselves home,' says Emily.

The den building is a great success. The garden looks like a bohemian festival site when they've finished. Julia prepares a jug of iced juice and a plate of assorted goodies.

'I'll take it out to the hobbit hole,' Emily says, hugging Julia. 'I'd forgotten how much fun it is making dens and then having picnics in them.'

After that, all is peaceful. When Julia goes out to look what's happening, peeping into the entrance of the den complex, she sees the two of them flat out on their backs with cushions under their heads and drowsing happily.

Emily sits up when she sees Julia, eyes wide. 'Oh, no, we fell asleep and I was supposed to go and check on Stripey,' she says, crawling out of the den. 'Andy left us a key so we could make sure she hadn't had her kittens.'

'Wait for me!' Tamsin's right behind her. 'I want to see.'

Julia watches them go across the road hand in hand, and her heart melts. This is just what Emily needs, Julia is sure, and Tamsin's blossomed this afternoon. She's lost her slightly anxious look for a little while. If only Emily and Andy weren't so prickly.

If Emily and Andy's friendship's ever going to get off the ground and be something more, Julia's going to have to take some serious action to make it happen. She goes inside again, thinking hard.

# Chapter Twenty-Nine

Tamsin rushes into her house and straight upstairs. 'Come on, Emily!' she yells. 'Stripey likes to be in Daddy's wardrobe usually.'

'Ssshhh, you'll scare her.' Emily follows more slowly, remembering when she was up here before and how uncomfortable she'd felt to be intruding on Andy and Tamsin's relationship. There are framed photographs hanging all the way up the stairs, of Tamsin at every stage of her development. Emily noticed them last time but didn't stop to look properly. At the top is one of a very frail-looking woman with dreadlocks tied back in a blue ribbon. She's cradling a tiny baby in her arms. The baby's face can't be seen because it's wrapped in a filmy woollen shawl but the look on the woman's face takes Emily's breath away.

Love, longing, joy and despair are all mingled together. Is Emily looking at the picture with hindsight and ima- gining these things? No, it's there for anyone to see. Allie must have only known her daughter for a short time but there can be no doubt that she was delighted to be a mum. Emily's heart aches for Allie, and for herself a little, too.

'I can't find Stripey, Em,' Tamsin calls. 'What are we going to do now?'

Emily goes into Andy's bedroom, feeling like some sort of Peeping Tom. Tamsin is kneeling by the wardrobe with the door open but there's no sign of the cat.

'Don't worry, sometimes mummy cats change their minds about where they want to have their babies,' Emily says soothingly. 'We'll look everywhere. She might even have gone round to see May. You search really carefully up here – check under all the beds and in all the corners and hidey-holes – and I'll go and search downstairs.'

Emily retraces her steps, averting her gaze from the picture of Allie and her baby. There's no sign of Stripey in any of the rooms. It's a cosy little house, and Emily feels as if she could settle down here quite happily. Stop it, she tells herself, you've got a perfectly good flat, and you wouldn't want to be surrounded by a dead woman's belongings, even if anything did happen with Andy.

Tamsin clatters into the kitchen just as Emily's trying to drag her gaze away from the collage of family photographs above the sink. 'I still can't see Stripey anywhere,' she says, her voice wobbling. 'What if she's run away?'

'Let's go and see May before we panic. Come on, you go first and I'll lock the door behind us.'

'Do you want to see Daddy's best picture first? I forgot to get it to show you. I'll go back.'

'But . . .'

Emily hears Tamsin bounding up the stairs again, singing as she goes. She's back in less than a minute, clutching an ornate, jewelled frame. The picture in it hurts Emily's heart even more than the one of Allie and her baby. This is Andy's wife on what must be their wedding day. Her hair is long and loose, backlit by the sunshine, and her smile is terrifyingly happy, with no shadow of what's to come. She's already pregnant, and one hand rests protectively on her rounded stomach.

'Me and Daddy kiss my mummy every night before he puts me to bed,' says Tamsin, sending another stiletto of pain right into Emily's soul. 'He says he likes her to watch him when he goes to sleep, that's why she lives by his bed. I'd better put her back.'

Emily wraps her arms around herself as Tamsin returns the precious photograph to its home, suddenly cold. May said that Emily might not be ready for Andy yet, but this proves Andy is in no way ready for any woman to take Allie's place. The thought is deeply depressing. She takes one last look around the bright, sunshiny kitchen, thinking of Allie in there, bustling around and preparing for her baby to be born, full of plans for the future. By the time Emily's pulled herself together and reached May's back door, Tamsin's inside.

May is in her favourite chair with Fossil on her knee. She's dozing, chin on her chest, and looks up with a start as Tamsin leans against her knee and wraps her arms around May's middle. Emily's startled to see that the old lady looks even more delicate than she did this morning, her cheeks slightly sunken and her hands on the rug more blue-veined than usual.

'How are you feeling?' she asks. 'Are you ready for a

cuppa? We're looking for the mum-to-be. Is Stripey here, by any chance?'

'Yes and yes,' says May, smiling. 'A cup of tea is just what my heart desires. And your cat has made a nest under the table on some old newspapers. I must have nodded off. I heard her come in through the cat flap but I haven't looked at her lately.'

Tamsin drops to her knees and crawls under the table. 'Emily,' she breathes, 'Stripey's got her babies. They must have fallen out of her bottom while we were making our den. They're here!'

Emily joins Tamsin on the floor. Sure enough, there is the happy little cat, purring proudly, and curled up next to her are three tiny kittens, two tabby and one black. As they watch, the biggest one wriggles blindly towards its mother and begins to suck enthusiastically. The black one stirs too and does the same.

'What are they doing?' whispers Tamsin. 'They're biting Stripey's tummy. Make them stop, Em.'

'It's fine, sweetie, they're having their dinner. Small kittens have to get milk from their mums. They can't have ordinary milk until they're a bit bigger.'

'Milk from their mums? Stripey isn't a cow!' Tamsin starts to giggle and soon she's rolling on the floor, holding her own tummy. May is chuckling too and Emily can't help joining in. The cat looks at them balefully and the two kittens carry on suckling. The other tabby isn't moving. Emily stops laughing and reaches out a finger to touch it.

'I think we need to help this one to find where the food is,' she says. 'It's very sleepy.'

Gently, she eases the kitten towards its mother's side, making room between the two other guzzling ones. To begin with it doesn't react but after a moment or two, Emily sees its nostrils twitch and it starts to search. She moves it forward further and it latches on, feebly at first but with growing gusto.

'So you're a vet and a midwife, as well as a childminder, a publisher and a housekeeper?' Andy's voice makes Emily jump and she looks up, stung by the words, but he's smiling down at her and his eyes are warm. She smiles back doubtfully, deciding he probably doesn't mean any harm even if there's a sort of challenge in what he says. Does he think she's setting herself up as some sort of superwoman, or what?

'Stripey's done it all herself,' Tamsin says. 'She's very clever. Emily didn't do anything.'

'Cheers, Tam,' says Emily. 'But she's right. Your cat has a mind of her own.'

May's frowning. 'You hadn't better move her yet, Andy. She'll only bring them back here if you do. Cats like to be in charge of where their babies live. I've seen it before. She might even hide them somewhere if you disturb her.'

'I can't leave them all night really. They might need help getting used to feeding. We'll put them back in the wardrobe – Stripey likes it there. I'll fetch them in an hour or so. We'd better go home for your tea, Tam.'

'But I was going to draw my hobbit hole. I want to go back with Emily,' Tamsin wails.

'No, Emily's worked hard enough today. We're going home now.'

'I don't mind, honestly,' Emily says. 'We were just . . .'

'It's tea time. Come on, Tamsin. See you in a little while, May. Oh, and thank Julia for me, Emily, would you?'

Tamsin sticks her bottom lip out but seems to realise she hasn't got a choice here and takes her dad's hand.

'Bye, Em,' she says. 'See you soon. Will you draw our den for me?'

'I'm rubbish at drawing, but I'll take some photos,' Emily says as they leave the room. She tries to glare at Andy but his back's turned.

After they've gone, it seems very quiet. Stripey's purring is the only sound to be heard. May looks sideways at Emily.

'He didn't mean to be rude, you know,' she says, 'it's just that Andy likes to stick to his rules. He thinks Tamsin needs keeping in check. He's probably right, too. She'd wrap him round her little finger if he didn't make a stand now and again.'

Emily shrugs. 'It's OK. I don't really mind if she goes home or comes back with me. It's up to him. He's her dad, after all. I'm just the temporary childminder.'

'Yes, you do mind. And I don't blame you, it's natural. You've enjoyed being with Tamsin, haven't you?'

Emily feels her face burning. Does she seem that needy to May? 'I'll make the tea,' she says.

'Isn't Julia coming over?' asks May, when they're halfway down the mugs that Emily likes to use.

'She said it might be too much for you if we both come over and keep you talking. Why, did you want her?'

'Oh, well, if she's too busy,' says May, sniffing and pursing her lips.

'Not at all. I'll text her.' Emily sends a quick message, and a couple of minutes later, hears her gran yoo-hooing from the back door. She leaves them alone together as she puts a load of washing in and checks that there's nothing out of date in the fridge. May's well known for keeping things long past their sell-by date.

As she throws away three suspect yoghurts and a rather furry piece of cheese, Emily can hear the reassuring murmur of the two older ladies deep in conversation. There are bursts of mirth every now and again and she can hear the tail end of a very familiar story. The friends are reliving a particularly awful drama presentation in the church hall, where not only did the curtain fall in the usual sense, but it also fell off the rails completely, knocking the vicar off his feet and demolishing half the scenery.

'And they had the nerve to say it was my fault because I pulled too hard,' Emily hears May say, 'but it was Charles who was to blame. He was supposed to check them before we started but he . . . was busy somewhere . . .'

Emily thinks that the two ladies would probably like more time to chat, so she takes a cloth and begins to wipe down the kitchen surfaces. A high shelf with a row of ancient containers on it catches her eye. There's a square Bovril tin, a Bisto drum and a tall canister that used to hold Cornish fairing biscuits. Intrigued, she takes the Bovril one down and gives it a shake. It rattles. Emily glances towards the living room but the others are still chortling away merrily. She knows she's being incredibly nosy but she can't resist lifting the lid.

Inside the tin is the most random collection of objects that Emily has ever seen. There's an empty green glass perfume bottle, a tiny china cat minus its tail, a Christmas bauble studded with fake rubies, a child's sock and three brass buttons, tarnished now but clearly once meant to grace a grand outfit of some sort. Mystified, Emily reaches for the next tin, but hears May calling to her. Overcome with guilt, she quickly refills and puts the lid back on the Bovril tin and heads back to the living room.

She's relieved to see that May looks much better now. There's colour in her cheeks and her eyes are sparkling, but Emily thinks it's time for a rest for both her charges, and with difficulty, extracts Julia and escorts her back across the road.

Later, still pondering the significance of the collection in the tin, Emily shoos her gran off to bed and clears away in their own kitchen, stretching tired shoulders. It's hard work being *in loco parentis*. Should she nip over to May's again before she turns in? Maybe she could ask her about the tins . . . or even have a peep in the other two? Andy must have fetched the kittens and Stripey by now – there might be some tidying up to do. She goes to the front door but sees Tristram disappearing into May's kitchen again. That's odd. He's been spending an awful lot of time there this week. Tristram sees her and waves. Emily waves back, putting the idea of further investigations firmly out of her mind. Tristram's a good man. May will be well looked after tonight.

# Chapter Thirty

May looks across at Tristram as he sits in the chair by her bed, one leg crossed elegantly over the other, for all the world as if he's lounging in a cocktail bar rather than the bedroom of an elderly lady.

'Have you finished your cocoa?' Tristram asks, leaning forward to take her mug.

'Yes, thanks, it was lovely. How do you make it so creamy?'

'Trade secret. If I told you, I'd have to kill you, as my son-in-law says.'

May settles herself more comfortably on her heap of pillows and sighs with relief. 'Thank you for sorting everything with Trevor for me.'

He sighs. 'That was no problem but I wish we didn't have to discuss dying, especially with a solicitor. It's so depressing, even at my young age. I hope you're not planning on going anywhere yet? You've got years left in you.'

'Everybody should make sure they've sorted out their finances. I hope you have?'

He nods. 'All neatly documented. It's very simple.'

She smiles at him. He's a very attractive man, she thinks, with his twinkling blue eyes and weathered skin. The short beard suits him. She can see why he's always been a magnet for women. As a teenager, he'd had to fight them off. He'd laughed them into bed, but he was never a good long-term prospect even then. She wonders how he feels about being alone now, although with Gina and Vince home, he can't really be lonely.

'Do you ever think of marrying again, Tris?' she asks him.

He eyes her warily. 'Why did you bring that up?'

'Oh, just wondering.'

'Not matchmaking, are you, by any chance? There's only one woman in this village that'd tempt me to have another try at matrimony.'

'Julia? Yes, I thought so. You could do a lot worse.'

'I'm almost afraid to try, May. I rather think that beautiful lady has it in her to be the love of my life.'

May feels a strange pain in the region of her heart. Why has she never inspired this kind of love? They sit quietly for a few minutes, but it's a comfortable sort of silence, the sort that old friends can have without worrying. Eventually, May's drooping eyelids tell Tristram that it's time to go.

'You've got a glass of water, some humbugs, a clean handkerchief and your phone handy,' he says. 'Anything else you need before I go home?'

'Yes. I want to ask you something.'

'Fire away.'

'Tris, would you take me to the beach tomorrow?'

'But you're not fit, love. You've been really poorly.'

'I know that as well as you do. We could take our time.

Just for a little while? You could even borrow a wheelchair, couldn't you? I'm sure there's someone in the village would have one knocking about.'

Tristram strokes his beard, his brow furrowed. 'I don't know . . . It seems a bit crazy. You should be resting.'

'There'll be plenty of time for that when we're both pushing up daisies.'

He laughs. 'I'll see what I can do. So long as you're on the mend tomorrow. If not, there's no way I'm taking you anywhere.'

May's face lights up. 'And one more thing.' She rummages under her pillow and pulls out an oblong case. She hands it to Tristram and he opens it, raising his eyebrows.

'But . . . this is Charles's gold fountain pen. Why on earth would you give that to *me*, of all people?'

May sighs. 'I just couldn't bring myself to throw it away. I bought it for him when we got engaged. Please take it off my hands, Tris, even if you never use it.'

They look at each other for a long moment and then without saying any more, he closes the box, puts it in his pocket and, leaning down, hugs May tightly before he leaves the room. She hears him whistling an Irish jig – he often does that to entertain her, and usually follows it with a little *River Dance* routine to make her laugh. His feet are tapping away on the kitchen tiles now. He's doing the dance even though he knows she can't see him from her bed.

How many men of eighty are still nimble enough to do that? she asks herself. There's life in the old dog yet, as they say. It'd be a shame if he ended his years without a woman to cuddle, although May's always thought the need for constant bouts of physical contact between men and women (or men and men, in her husband's case) is a bit overrated. Now and again can be great fun but not all the time, for pity's sake. She's aware that not everybody feels the same about it, though, and to be fair, she's had a few nice surprises in that area in her time.

Leaning back on her pillows again, May reviews the last couple of days. For someone who's normally fairly pragmatic, her emotions have been all over the place. Following the brush with death and short stay in the hospital, May has given the matter of her next steps considerable thought.

Without the letters or any other delightful objects to fill her life with their magic, she's aware that her body will wind down fairly quickly. All that's left is to decide whether to move everything along with more speed now. Perhaps this is a good time to make a dignified exit.

May feels as if she might at last have learned how to love. She's witnessed its power enough times, and seen so many men and women of all ages going head over heels for each other and making silly mistakes. Her susceptibility to the memories of everyone else have given her an insight into all kinds of second-hand love, but over the years there was only one man who really touched her heart, and that wasn't for long. Through their belongings, May has absorbed some of the deepest feelings of the Pengelly residents and many others. Now, after years of nothing more than friendly connections with the people around her, May's heart has been deeply touched by these last weeks surrounded by Julia, Andy, Tristram, Emily and Tamsin. They're more important than family to her, but she doesn't think they really need her. They'll mourn her in their own ways, but their lives will continue happily without May in them. Can she do it?

There are three choices. May could continue to read Don's more peaceful letters, which would mean she can go on as normal, just slowing down gradually, she supposes, and still collecting enough memories to keep her ticking over. That leaves her open to the vagaries of the whole thing, though; she has no point of reference because she doesn't know anyone else who's stretched this ability to its final limits. She won't be in control any more.

The second option is to go cold turkey with the memory harvesting, which could be dangerous, especially now the recent heavy influx of Don's more emotional family history has taken its toll on her health. She's finally plucked up her courage to dip into the vitriolic letters in very short bursts, reading snippets about the family feud that tore them apart. The effect of those letters has been drastic. With jangling nerves, she read of the anger and grief that rifts can cause, but worse was to come. Charles's death left many questions unanswered, and May has knowledge of it that lies heavy on her heart.

If she risks giving up her memory-gathering completely, May thinks her body will soon start to suffer quite badly. She imagines growing frailer and less steady on her legs and wonders how long it'll be before she loses her marbles or is crippled with arthritis. Not a tempting prospect.

On the other hand, the final choice of leaving this life *on purpose* isn't something to do lightly. Most people don't have any say in the matter of when they die unless they do something very drastic to hasten the Grim Reaper's visit, but May has power. She can go whenever she wants to. The problem is, how soon should she do it?

The only thing holding her back is Barbara. Not Aunt Barbara, but a much smaller version, named for the woman who bequeathed the necklace in a last generous rush of family feeling. May says the name in her head. She hasn't let herself think about small Barbara for a long time.

She was fifty-seven when she realised she was pregnant. Still nowhere near the menopause and feeling so young and fit, she didn't give much thought to the dangers of her occasional dalliances. Charles was preoccupied with his own affairs, and May was careless just once in the last year.

One of the lucky ones who don't pile on weight in pregnancy, May was able to disguise her condition for some months. By this time she wasn't socialising much anyway, spending a large part of the year travelling to far-flung places, so her disappearance for a while didn't cause a stir. She holed up in Yorkshire in a soul-destroying home for unmarried mothers and made the necessary arrangements as efficiently as she did everything else. When the time came, Barbara's birth was easy. Passing for forty was no problem – May didn't want any publicity as one of the oldest first-time mothers in Britain, although not having current medical details to produce caused some concern.

She put her baby up for adoption without a backward glance, or so she told herself, secure in the knowledge that a wonderful couple had been found to take Barbara and give her a loving upbringing. May made sure the new parents were aware that she would rather not be contacted in the near future but that her personal details must be made available if Barbara wanted them when she came of age.

As the years since Barbara's milestone birthday have gone by, May assumed her daughter had no interest in meeting her birth mother. Recently, though, with her own passing looming closer, May has wondered more and more about the girl, or woman as she is now. Surely the combination of genes that created her daughter must have resulted in a rather unusual human being? Barbara's father had been talented and intuitive, much like May's own Pa in character. Their brief physical relationship had been a joy to May. Passion, romance and fun in equal quantities. What amazing traits might have been passed down through the generations? Is Barbara out there feeling confused and troubled about her talents, if she has them? What should May do?

The thought of the appalling upheaval there will certainly be if she tries to find her daughter exhausts her. She can't face it, and it could be deeply unwelcome for Barbara. But she must do something.

May reaches for the writing set that lives in her bedside

cabinet. Bedtime has always been a good moment for attending to awkward correspondence. She's dealt with one addressed to Julia already and filed it. This letter doesn't take long to write and she doubts Barbara will ever read it, because she has no address to post it to. At least it's all there on paper, she thinks. Sealing the envelope, May writes 'For BARBARA – in case she ever comes searching. Please keep safe' in large letters on the front and then adds the only other information she has – her daughter's new name, Grace Clarke.

She kisses the letter for luck and pushes it right into the middle of the bundle in the brown envelope. She has a feeling they won't be disturbed again for a while. Julia will have no desire to read them, from what Andy has said, but she will never throw them away. If she eventually writes her book and uses the letters as a theme, she'll find Barbara's envelope. May has faith that she'll put it away safely, if so.

Soothed, she settles down to sleep. There are still a few jobs left. She longs to be on the beach just once more, and she wants to help celebrate Tristram's birthday. But most of all, May needs to talk to Emily again.

# Chapter Thirty-One

Andy's in his usual place slumped in front of the TV with a mug of tea and a slice of cold pizza when the doorbell bell rings. Through the frosted glass he can see a slim figure and his heart leaps. Is it Em? He flings the door open and beams at the sight of Emily standing on the front step clutching a carrier bag.

'Come in,' he says. 'You have no idea how much I was needing adult company. Tamsin's fast asleep and has been for ages.'

Emily hesitates, and Andy notices how pale she is. The shadows under her eyes are nearly as dark as May's.

'Are you sure you're not busy?' she says.

'Not in the slightest. Tea or coffee?'

'Oh . . . erm . . . have you got any peppermint tea? I've not been feeling great. My stomach's doing weird things.'

Andy rummages in the cupboard and digs out a battered tin. 'I don't know if this'll be any good. It's been there for ages. I don't drink fancy tea. Do you want to give it a go?'

'Yes, please. I guess it was Allie's?'

He looks down at her and sees that the blue eyes are desperately sad. 'Emily, what's up? I don't mind you having

249

one of Allie's mouldy teabags,' he says. 'They tasted of socks when they were new, so they probably won't be much different now.'

She sighs. 'You must miss her very much.'

'Well, the first years were hard, but now I . . . I've kind of got used to it.' As Andy says the words, meant to reassure Emily more than anything, he realises that they're true. The searing pain of life without Allie almost finished him off for a while, but gradually, gradually, his heart has begun to heal. Now her loss feels like an old scar – it hurts sometimes but mostly he's pretty much OK. He struggles to explain, not wanting Emily to think him unfeeling.

'They say grief's like stepping on a rake,' he says, pausing in his tea-making to try and get this right.

'A rake? As in a garden tool? You've lost me.'

'It's easy, imagine you're walking through a meadow of long grass, enjoying the sunshine and the flowers and the birdsong and so on, and then you step on a rake that someone's left there, prongs upwards, and it flips up and smacks you in the face. It bloody stings for a moment or two. Afterwards it aches for a bit and then the pain fades and you carry on walking.'

'Yes, I sort of see what you mean. But it's always there, isn't it?'

'It's there, but you learn to live with it and work around it. You have to.'

Emily looks down at the steaming mug he hands her. The teabag's floating around sadly, and the original scent of the mint seems to have disappeared completely.

'Come and sit down in the living room. You look shattered,' Andy says.

She follows him into the next room and puts her mug down on a coaster very carefully. Andy sees that her hands are shaking.

'Now are you going to tell me what's worrying you, or am I meant to guess?' he says, smiling.

Emily takes a deep breath. 'Tamsin showed me the photo by your bed,' she blurts out, 'and told me that you kiss it every night, and stuff.'

Andy scratches his head. 'Um . . . you've lost me. Why is that important now?'

'Well, it made me realise that you're still grieving so much that there's no room for . . . for me, I guess. Anyway, it doesn't matter. It's too late.'

'Doesn't matter? Of course it does! Look, Em, I keep the picture there to reassure Tamsin, that's all. Fair enough, I needed it just as much as she did to begin with, but now it's just one of those things you do at bedtime to make life easier. A kind of ritual.'

'You don't have to say that. I understand how you feel.'

'No, you really don't. Look, I've been thinking lately that I've been letting myself wallow. May has said as much, too. It's time to move on. I'll never forget Allie, but I'm sure she wouldn't want me to spend the rest of my life moping around wondering about what might have been.'

Emily looks up at him, incredulous. She heaves a sigh of relief and gets to her feet. 'Thank goodness you're not angry that she showed me the picture. I've been really worried. It seemed so private. I felt like a Peeping Tom.'

She's still ashen, and Andy puts his hands on her shoulders to reassure her, very conscious of her warmth and nearness. She feels fragile tonight, as if she's only just holding herself together, and her whole body is trembling slightly now. Surely the photo can't have made her feel this awful? 'There's no need to stress about it any more,' he says, 'and, as a matter of fact, if you want to make amends, I can think of a way.'

She looks up at him and he sees alarm in her eyes. 'I need to go home to Gran, she'll be wondering where I've got to.'

'Can't you just stay a few more minutes, Em? We've got unfinished business, haven't we? Remember?' He bends down and kisses her cheek very gently, feeling her instinctively move towards him.

In seconds, Andy has his arms around Emily so tightly that they feel like one person. The heat between them is intense and for a few moments they lean together in complete silence. Then, without warning, she breaks away, pushing him with both hands. Her cheeks are flushed now and her eyes are wide with alarm.

'Stop it. We can't do this,' she says huskily, pushing her hair back and stepping back a pace.

'But, Em,' Andy can hear the panic and confusion in his voice, 'don't go. I'm sorry if I freaked you out. I'll back off. We can just talk.' He takes a deep breath. Something's obviously rattled her, but what could it be? She was responding, he knows she was. What's gone wrong?

'I think I'm pregnant.'

The words are so unexpected that for a minute Andy can't take them in. When he realises what Emily's just said, he stares at her, his jaw dropping open like a cartoon character in shock. She waits for him to reply but he's speechless.

'Well, say something,' she mutters, biting her lip. 'I haven't told anyone else. I only let myself begin to consider it after something May said, but if this is the reaction I'm going to get I'll keep the news quiet.'

Andy blinks, and rubs his eyes. 'Ah . . . well . . . do I need to congratulate you?'

He feels a huge lump in his throat. He's never been the sort of person who says 'Why me?' when shit happens, but this is beyond a joke. To finally have the eureka moment that tells him it's time to move on and then to be told that the woman he so wants to be with is having another man's baby?

'No. If I'm not wrong – and I haven't done a test or anything, so I could be, I suppose – then it's one massive mistake.'

'Max?'

'Of course. And it's been over between us for a while, if I'm honest.'

'But, a baby? Were you not listening when they did family planning at school then?' The acid in his voice shocks Andy and brings tears to Emily's eyes again. He curses himself for his nastiness and tries to apologise, but she's leaving. It's too late to take the words back. There are so many questions he needs to ask but Emily's already in the hall.

'Em, stay and talk, please. Don't just drop a bombshell like that and leave me hanging.'

'Leave *you* hanging? How the hell do you think I feel?' She's gone, and he can't stop her.

# Chapter Thirty-Two

Emily sits on the rocks at the top of the beach, arms tightly round her bent knees. She's wearing an ancient pair of jogging pants, two T-shirts and a huge sweater, but she's still freezing. Her hair's in a tight plait because it's so greasy and she's got a purple knitted hat pulled down over her ears. Not a good look, but who cares? There's nobody to see her at half-past four in the morning. Even Tristram's not up yet.

The queasiness that's been plaguing her off and on is back today, big time, and she feels bloated and lethargic. If this really is what being pregnant's like, it's the pits already.

It must have happened that last evening they spent together. Max turned up unexpectedly at a book launch she was hosting, with flowers and chocolates and a million excuses why he'd been out of touch for a while. Emily knew she should have resisted. She'd pretty much decided to end it by then, but work had been gruelling that week and the thought of going out with Max after the party and being spoiled with champagne and delicious food that she didn't have to cook for herself was tempting.

They ended up in bed in Max's plush hotel room, and

of course he hadn't any condoms. He'd always left buying them to Emily, saying that he couldn't risk Marcia finding the evidence when she went through his pockets. It was a stupid risk to take, but by then Emily was exhausted and very tipsy. She fell asleep immediately afterwards and woke up in the morning feeling so hungover that it was all she could do to get herself home, ring in sick and go to bed for the day.

Emily presses her face against her raised knees and hides her eyes, like a child pretending to be somewhere else. An hour passes and the early morning chill bites deep into her bones, but she hardly notices.

'What am I going to do?' she whispers to a seagull that's edging closer to see if there's any chance of food. 'I'm not ready to be a mum. Max doesn't want me and I certainly don't want him.'

She gets to her feet as she hears Buster's morning greeting. The dog bounds up to her and jumps around madly, barking his joy at seeing Emily. Tristram follows more slowly with Bruno at his heels looking up at his master adoringly.

'I hoped you'd be here,' he says, as he approaches. 'Come back to my place with me and I'll make us some breakfast.'

Emily's stomach lurches at the thought of food, but she knows she ought to eat. Maybe she could manage some toast? They walk along the beach towards The Shellfish Shack. Emily isn't in the mood for polite conversation today but Tristram doesn't seem to mind. He skims the odd stone, and picks up a shell or two for Emily, but other than that he's in his own world. Emily briefly wonders what he wants to talk to her about but her mind is so full of baby worries that she doesn't give it much thought.

'Come on in, love,' says Tristram, switching on a couple of low lights. 'I'll just go and shut the dogs up round the back. Buster's in disgrace.'

'Really? What did he do?' She looks down at Buster, who's sitting on the step wearing his best angelic expression. He wags his tail and almost seems to smile.

'I was just watching the TV last night – Nigella, if you're interested – and the phone rang. It was Geoff from the pub saying Buster had called in.'

'Buster had gone to the pub all on his own? For a pint, presumably?'

'If only that was all he'd gone for. No, he managed to slip out of here while Gina was looking the other way, dashed up to The Level and sat outside the bar until someone opened the door.'

'I like his style.' This is just the distraction Emily needs. Buster looks up at her and wags his tail happily.

'Don't smile at him, Emily. He's a very bad dog. He dashed right through the bar and into the lounge, jumped up onto a chair and then a table and polished off a good dollop of three people's dinners.'

'He didn't!'

'He did. And not content with that, he then went upstairs to the kitchen and stole a couple of fillet steaks off the hot plate. I had to go and fetch him home in disgrace. This has cost me a slap-up meal for Geoff and his missus when they're next in here.'

Tristram takes the dogs round the back and Emily, still

giggling, goes inside. The restaurant feels like a warm cave and she gradually begins to relax for the first time since May was ill, as Tristram comes back and potters around preparing breakfast.

'Where are Gina and Vince?' she asks.

'They've gone to see Vince's mum for the day – they'll be back in time for dinner tonight. I can do a mean breakfast but I'm not up to whacking out thirty or so plates every evening these days. Toast? Brown or white?'

'Have you got any thick-sliced white bread?' says Emily, suddenly knowing that is the only thing in the world she wants to eat.

'Of course.' He pops four slices into the toaster and starts to grind beans for coffee. The rich scent of the beans as they release their fragrance sends Emily hurtling from the room to the toilet. When she comes back, Tristram's looking thoughtful.

'Are you not feeling so good, petal?' he says. 'Upset tummy? I've got camomile tea instead of coffee. It's nice with honey.'

She nods gratefully, and he passes her a plate of toast and the butter dish. They eat in silence for a while. Tristram's put the radio on and Emily can hear the soft sound of his favourite classical music station.

When only crumbs are left on the plate, Tristram reaches for Emily's hands. 'So, I brought you here to talk to you, but I reckon you've got something to say to me first. Yes?'

'You know what's up, don't you? I think I'm probably having a baby.'

'Max's, I'm assuming?'

'Of course. Unfortunately. And there's no future for us together. It was a huge mistake.'

'Have you made any plans yet?'

'I haven't had time. You probably think I'm really dim but I've only just started to figure out what was wrong. I must be about three weeks late, but I didn't really register it because life's been so chaotic lately. Surely you don't start throwing up that early? It might just be a tummy bug.'

Tristram pulls a wry face. 'Gina's mum was sick almost from the moment we did the deed and for the next nine months.'

'Thanks, that makes me feel so much better. Anyway, what did you want to say to me?'

'Oh, that. Well, I wanted to ask you if you'd go and see May as soon as possible. I've got the feeling she needs to talk to you, and soon.'

Half an hour later, Emily is opening the back door into May's cottage, still feeling awful. Her head's aching now and her heart is heavy. She doesn't want to tell May about her suspicions. Pregnancy isn't for idle chit-chat when you are in the depths of despair, but Tristram was adamant, so here she is.

'Hello, May,' she calls, trying her best to sound cheery. 'Are you up?'

May comes through from the bedroom. She's leaning on a silver-topped walking stick and is dressed for the outdoors. It's the first time Emily's seen May in trousers. They are smart, black ones, teamed with a chunky Arran jumper. A bright scarf is wrapped around her neck, and a puffy blue jacket is hanging over the back of a chair.

'Hello, my bird,' she says, smiling in delight. 'I was wanting to see you most particularly.'

'Why are you all wrapped up like that?' asks Emily, jolted out of her gloomy thoughts for a moment.

'Tristram's taking me for a walk along the beach soon. He's got his hands on a wheelchair. The sand's always firm when you get nearer to the sea and I can get out and walk a little way.'

'But . . . but why? Are you sure you're well enough?'

'Now don't you start fussing, too. I'm fine. It's something I need to do, that's all. Sit down, dear. It's time we had a proper chat.'

Emily flops into a chair, exhaustion sweeping over her.

'I was right, wasn't I? You're having a baby.'

May's words make Emily sit up straight, wide-eyed. 'What? How did you guess?'

'Ha! When you get to my age, you've seen enough girls in the family way to spot the signs. Now, what are we going to do about it, that's the question?'

For a moment, Emily is speechless, and May leans forward to pat her hand. 'Don't look so stricken, it's not the end of the world. I think the best thing all round would be for you to tell your boss what's going on. Colin, is it? And what did you say his surname was?'

'Dennis. Colin Dennis. Why?'

'Names are important, aren't they? I wanted to be able to visualise him. So, tell Mr Dennis and then settle down here for a while. What about that?'

'Hmm. I don't know if that'd work, May. I don't even know if I really am pregnant.'

May sniffs. She doesn't seem in any doubt about it.

'Go and talk to Julia first, that's my advice, and then ring Colin. He'll understand, won't he?'

'I'm not so sure about that.'

'At least give it a try. Emily, you're in danger of making mistakes here – big ones. I've been there so I know. When I married Charles, I let myself in for . . . certain things I wasn't expecting. I made my bed, as they say, and I was determined to lie on it, but he wasn't the man I thought he was. Not at all. It ended badly.'

'Really? Tell me more.'

A shadow passes over May's face. 'I can't. There are things that must never be discussed, for any reason. But what I'm saying is, follow your heart and make some strong decisions for yourself, before you miss the boat completely. Now, off you go. Tristram will be here any minute and I need to put some lipstick on and a dab of rouge and powder. No need to let myself go. Keep me posted.'

And with that, she kisses Emily and potters off to her bedroom again. Emily lets herself out, shaking her head in disbelief. She feels as if she's stepped right into Alice's Wonderland or Looking-Glass World. There are no white rabbits, but everything else is seriously odd.

# Chapter Thirty-Three

Julia is sitting at the dining-room table sorting letters when Emily comes back from May's cottage. She's pleased to see her granddaughter is looking better than she did earlier. Julia's been quite alarmed at how pasty Emily's been the past few days.

'You seem brighter, darling,' she says. 'Have you been to see Tristram?'

Emily nods, and sits down opposite Julia with a thump. 'Yes, we had breakfast at The Shack. Then I went across the road to Shangri-La.'

'Oh.' Julia pastes on a smile and tries to pretend she doesn't mind Emily being such good friends with May.

'Gran, can I tell you something?' As Emily begins to speak, the phone rings. Julia rolls her eyes and goes to answer it.

'Hello, Ida,' she says, pulling a face and mouthing 'Sorry' to Emily.

Her granddaughter shrugs and heads for the stairs. 'I'm going to have a bath. It can wait,' she whispers.

Before too long, Emily comes downstairs and sits down at the table again. She's wearing black trousers and a baggy white shirt. Her hair is loose and she's put some lipstick and eye shadow on.

'You look smart, darling,' Julia says.

'May reminded me about not letting myself go,' says Emily. 'I was feeling about a hundred and ten myself this morning.'

'Were you, darling? Why? Do you want a cup of tea?'

'Let's wait. I've got a bit of a stomach ache. I might go and lie on the bed for a little while.'

'Really? I hope you haven't caught a chill with all that wandering around on the beach. The summer's not really got going properly yet, and it's cold in the early mornings.'

'I'm fine, Gran – don't fret.' Emily seems about to say something and then changes the subject. 'You're still busy with the letters, then? What are you reading about today?'

Julia picks up the next letter. 'Oh, it's babies all the way at the moment. I'm in 1964. This one's talking about Kathryn having a bug, which turned out to be nothing of the kind.'

Emily doesn't respond, and Julia looks up from the pile of blue paper. She's alarmed to see that her granddaughter is clutching her stomach, face whiter than ever.

'Darling, whatever's the matter? You look dreadful. Do you feel sick?'

'Pains,' Emily murmurs, bending double over the table.

'In your tummy? Come on, let's get you up to bed. I'm going to ring Dr Clamp. You haven't been right for days.'

'I'm fine,' says Emily feebly, but she allows herself to be helped to her feet, and the two of them make their way slowly up the stairs. Once in Emily's bedroom, Julia undresses her like a child, slipping a giant-sized T-shirt over her head and turning back the covers.

'Now, into bed with you, and I'll go and make a hot drink,' she says, but Emily can't seem to move. She's holding her stomach again, and as Julia watches, horrified, blood begins to trickle down her legs, making a pool on the varnished boards.

# Chapter Thirty-Four

Lying in bed in the daytime isn't something Emily has made a habit of in recent years. She can hear clattering in the kitchen and the delicious smell of Gran's special chicken and vegetable soup floats up the stairs, as comforting as a warm bath. Emily doesn't feel sick any more, which is a great relief, but neither can she be pregnant, which is something she hardly dares to think about.

The last twenty-four hours have been a nightmare. She's gone from being stunned at the very idea of a possible baby, through seeing Andy's shock at the news, May and Tristram's calm acceptance, and then feeling wave upon wave of hideous cramps engulf her and knowing that her body has taken over and is forcibly expelling whatever was lodged in her womb.

Dr Clamp, when she came by yesterday afternoon, was very practical, saying that as there had been no pregnancy test she could only assume that this was an early miscarriage and if so, it probably would be no worse than an unusually heavy period. Gran wanted Emily to go to hospital to be on the safe side, but the doctor had said there was no need. Nature would deal with this and Emily would be right as rain in a couple of days, if a bit tender.

Now, Emily lets herself think about this almost-baby at last. She closes her eyes and lets the tears trickle down her cheeks unchecked. Why is she feeling so desolate? The last thing she'd wanted was to be a mum, and the timing was awful.

She hears Julia coming upstairs and tries to stop crying but she's unable to control the gasping sobs that are making her shake with grief.

'Oh, my love – I knew you were being too brave. Let it all out. A good cry's the best thing for you.' Julia sits on the bed, hands Emily a wad of tissues and hugs her hard.

Emily wails out her sadness and confusion on her grandmother's shoulder and after a while, the storm passes and she's able to sit up and dry her eyes. The soft summer breeze blowing through the open window revives her and the scent of honeysuckle is blissful. She can hear the sea: the tide is coming in and the waves have reached the shingle bank.

'I don't know why I'm making such a fuss,' she says. 'It's not as if I was planning a family with Max. He would have been horrified. And how would I have coped with a tiny baby, no husband to help out and me having to go out to work every day?'

'It isn't silly at all,' says Julia, patting her arm. 'Even if you were only just pregnant, your poor body would have been already flooded with hormones. Your brain isn't your own when you're having a baby. I used to howl at the least little thing.'

'Did you never want more than one child, Gran?'

Emily's never asked this before, but she's suddenly fascinated with the subject.

'After I had Felix, I was quite happy just to have the one,' Julia says. 'He wasn't an easy baby. Or toddler. Or grown-up, come to that.' She laughs. 'Actually, I had one more pregnancy when he was about two years old, but it ended very much like yours. And I'm ashamed to say I wasn't all that sorry. I've always said the Good Lord left out the maternal instinct when he made me.'

'But you love my dad, don't you?'

'Of course I do, and I was besotted with you when you came along, but I'm not the sort of woman who coos over random infants in pushchairs or goes all gooey over other people's tiny babies.'

'I'm the same. But I can't help being sad. I keep wondering what my baby would have looked like, if there really was one. What if I never have the chance to be a mum?' Emily can feel the tears coming again. She sits up straighter and blows her nose noisily.

'You're bound to have those thoughts. I did too, even though I wasn't keen on the idea of a second baby. Now, are you getting up for some soup and a nice cup of coffee or do you want it up here on a tray?'

Emily's tummy rumbles and she leans forward to hug Julia. 'It's me that's supposed to be here looking after you, not the other way round. Some of your stupendous soup is exactly what I need. It ought to be on prescription. Have I got time to freshen up a bit? I must look as if I've been run over by a truck.'

'No you don't, but there's all the time in the world. I've

got some crusty bread warming in the oven and an apple crumble with extra cinnamon and brown sugar for afterwards.'

'I'll be as quick as I can,' Emily says, heading for the shower.

When Emily comes downstairs she's still in her dressing gown. She flicks the switch on the kettle and gets the coffee beans and electric grinder out without much enthusiasm. Her grandfather always liked the performance of measuring out the fragrant beans, first taking a deep sniff of the tin to appreciate the full aroma and then tipping them into his ancient machine and noisily crushing them until they reached the exact texture he wanted. He had a silver and glass pot and a set of tiny coffee cups that he used regularly. Emily goes through the motions but her heart isn't in it today.

'You look how I feel, darling,' says Julia. 'Your great-grandmother would have said we need putting in a bag and shaking up.'

'Yeah, not a bad idea. Oh, the phone's ringing again – shall I get it?'

Julia's there first and raises her eyebrows as the caller speaks. 'It's *That Candice*,' she hisses, her hand over the mouthpiece. 'She says she wants to talk to you.'

Emily raises her eyebrows and reaches for the handset. The shrill tones carry even across the room. Emily's frown is deepening by the moment but when she answers, her voice is treacle-sweet.

'It's really good of you to call to see how I am, Candice,' she says, 'but I'm not sure how you know I've been ill?

Yes, a tummy upset. I must have picked it up from Tamsin the other night when I was over there.'

She listens for a minute or two longer. 'You saw the doctor, did you? Fancy that. You must have great eyesight . . . Hang on, say that again, I don't quite understand . . .'

Emily's face is bright red now and her knuckles are white on the handset. 'Well, thank you so much for filling me in, but whatever may or may not have happened between you and Andy in the past is none of my business. I suggest you find somewhere else to try and stir up trouble.'

She waits again, rolling her eyes in Julia's direction. 'Oh, really? Well, I hope you'll both be very happy in that case. Bye now. I've got to go and dig out my handy travelling suit of armour ready for when the next person tries to STAB ME IN THE BACK.'

She disconnects forcibly and folds her arms, eyes blazing. 'What a bitch,' she says.

'I'm guessing she was warning you off?'

'In a big way. The witch. She says she and *Andrew* have got history, and it would be better for everybody if I kept out of the way from now on because it won't be long before they announce that they're an item. Apparently they've been keeping it under wraps out of respect for Allie's memory. How long ago did you say it was that she died? Six years?'

'Yes, just after Tamsin was born. That's a load of rubbish, darling. Candice is very good at talking the talk. She's had her claws into Andy ever since he lost Allie and it's got her precisely nowhere so far.'

'But what if there *is* something in it? And why would she suddenly decide to ring me today? You don't suppose she knows about what's happened to me, do you?'

'Don't be silly, how could she?'

'I don't know. But she's always been very good at putting two and two together and making five. She's one of life's natural stirrers. Or then again, maybe she really *is* a witch.'

They grin at each other. Emily sits down at the table, coffee forgotten. Julia joins her and takes both her hands. They're cold, so she rubs them gently to warm her up. 'Look, you need to decide what YOU want before we go any further with this conversation. Has Andy said anything to you to make you think he's ready to let go of the feeling that he'd be betraying Allie if he met someone else?'

'Well, not in so many words. I thought he was pretty interested in me. Well, I know he is. But if he's been playing around with Candice . . .'

'Do you really think that's likely?'

Emily doesn't answer. Julia thinks her confidence must be at an all-time low.

'So, if Andy was to ask you to stay here with him and have a proper relationship, what would you say, Em?'

There's a loud knock on the back door and it opens to reveal the man himself clutching his daughter by the hand. Both look distraught but Tamsin has her lips clamped firmly together as if she's determined not to cry.

'What on earth's the matter, dear?' asks Julia, jumping to her feet.

'It's Stripey,' says Andy. 'She hardly ever goes out and leaves her kittens but she went into the lane early this morning and—'

'She's deaded!' shouts Tamsin, finally bursting into noisy tears. 'Her kittens have got no mummy now . . . like me . . .' Her sobs are getting louder, and Julia makes a move towards her but Emily is there first, scooping the little girl up and bringing her back to her chair by the table. She points to the kitchen roll on the worktop and Julia passes her a handful.

After a minute or two, she kisses the top of Tamsin's curly head. 'Hey, that's enough wailing, sweetheart,' she says. 'I'm not used to seeing you this upset. Who knows what could happen? My brain might explode.'

Tamsin stops crying for a moment to think about this. 'Might it?' she falters.

'Yup. You need to be very careful.' Emily makes a few Bang! Kerpow!-type noises.

Tamsin starts to giggle and the tears subside. She's still gulping and shaking, but Emily dries her eyes and cuddles her closer.

The look of relief on Andy's face is indescribable. He looks over at Julia and mimes, 'Think it was probably a fox.'

'Right . . .' says Emily. 'The main thing now is to make sure Stripey's kittens are looked after properly.'

'But they've got no mummy,' repeats Tamsin, beginning to sniffle again.

'No, but you haven't either, and you're fine, aren't you?'

Julia winces. Surely this is way too brutal for a small person. But Tamsin's head is on one side and she's obviously giving this idea some thought.

'I . . . s'pose.'

'And why are you fine? Who takes care of you?'

'My daddy.'

'Spot on. So you and me and Dad and Aunty Jules will all be the kittens' mummies and daddies, OK? We'll need to give them warm milk lots of times every day but soon they'll be big enough to drink from a saucer. And then they'll have some Weetabix. And after that we'll try them on some sloppy cat food.'

'Sounds like a plan to me,' says Andy huskily, smiling at Emily.

'Can we tell May? I want to phone her,' says Tamsin, looking at Julia hopefully.

'Of course you can. Here you go, I'll show you which buttons to press.'

'I know how. Daddy showed me.'

Tamsin waits for May to answer, still leaning on Emily so confidingly that her heart melts even more than it has already.

'Hello, May. I have got some very bad news,' says Tamsin gravely. 'Stripey is deaded . . . Yes, I know, it sucks. Sorry, I didn't mean to say that. Anyway, can I come over for a hug?'

She listens for a moment, and Emily can hear the distant murmur of May's voice.

'OK, I'll tell Dad,' she says, looking up at Andy. 'We can go now. May isn't busy. Come on, Daddy. Bye, Em.'

Julia peers at her granddaughter as Emily releases the little girl and gives her another kiss. She moves closer.

'Oh dear,' she says.

'What's the matter?' Emily looks up, and Andy gasps, seeing what Julia's just noticed.

'Em, I think you've got chickenpox,' he says.

# Chapter Thirty-Five

Emily lies in her bed yet again, too sticky and hot to be comfortable even in the cool of the night and so unbelievably itchy that the only way she can get any relief is to sit in a bath of salt water, and then get out and be daubed with calamine lotion by her patient grandmother. The days and nights creep slowly by, each one more boring and tortuous than the last.

Andy has wasted no time in going along to the next village to stock up on things that the invalid might appreciate. He brings ice cream, lemonade, a bag of ice, some throat sweets because the spots are even in her mouth and on the back of her tongue and a huge bar of chocolate for when she feels a bit better. There's also a thick, glossy magazine and some flowers from his garden.

'Don't look at me,' Emily moans, trying to cover her face with her pillow. 'I'm hideous.'

He laughs. 'Yep. But I've got quite used to the festering-boils look.'

'Don't joke. I'll be scarred for life.'

'No you won't. I had it when I was ten with loads of blisters, and I haven't got a single blemish now. Oh, except for the one on my bum. I'll show you sometime if you play your cards right.'

'Tempting.'

She closes her eyes and Andy leaves her to rest. It's time to feed the kittens again.

Emily drifts in and out of sleep, having nightmarish, fevered dreams. She hears the phone ring every now and again and Julia chatting away, but she's too ill to want to know who's been calling. Andy drops in regularly and brings Tamsin just for a few minutes whenever he can. She brings Emily something different each time she drops in. Sometimes it's a drawing, once she's clutching some rather wilted flowers from the garden, and one afternoon Andy lets her show Emily some photos of the kittens on his phone.

'I'm a good mummy,' Tamsin says proudly. 'The kittens drank all their milk up today. They got it in their ears and it was all stuck to their whiskers.'

'May's been asking after you constantly,' says Andy. 'She wants to come over but we don't think she should risk catching your germs. She can't remember if she's ever had chickenpox.'

It's a relief not to have to see May, much as she loves her. Emily doesn't want to talk about what's happened and May will be bound to mention it.

On the fourth day, Emily wakes up to sunshine pouring through her window. She lies very still, watching the dust motes dance and trying to decide how she feels. After a moment, she sits up gingerly. Her head isn't throbbing any more and the itching in her mouth and throat has almost gone.

Julia pops her head around the door. 'Oh, you look a lot brighter today, darling,' she says. 'How about some scrambled eggs on toast?'

Emily tests out this idea and finds she's ravenous. She nods enthusiastically and then lies listening as her grandmother potters around in the kitchen. It's strange how much better Julia seems now. She's more cheerful than she's been since before Gramps died. What's caused the shift in her mood, Emily wonders? And does this mean she should leave soon, to give Gran some space and let her begin to make a new life without Gramps? Every part of her wants to stay in Pengelly. These days and nights of tossing and turning have given Emily plenty of time to think.

At first, her thoughts go round and round in her head like furious wasps trying to get out. Gradually, though, she begins to get them into order. If Julia would actually benefit from Emily being close and not have her style cramped, Emily is seriously tempted to apply for a permanent transfer to the London office, with the condition that she works only part-time, but could they really live together on a permanent basis? The thought of going back to America is exhausting.

Glancing at her watch, Emily gets up quickly to save her gran bringing yet another tray upstairs. She shrugs on her dressing gown and goes downstairs barefoot before Julia can stop her. The shame of letting this much older lady wait on her washes over Emily but she couldn't have done much else, the state she was in. She realises now that she's been almost delirious for some of the time.

Maybe she was just so low after the almost-baby and the break up with Max that the chickenpox zapped her harder than if she'd been as fit as usual.

'What are you doing out of bed?' says Julia, tutting as Emily comes over to make coffee. 'You need at least another day of resting to set you right.'

Julia's cheeks are pink, and Emily thinks she heard her singing as she came down the stairs. She stopped abruptly when she was interrupted but her eyes are still sparkling. The back door is standing open and there's a faint breeze that brings in a fresh, seaside smell. There are a few old-fashioned roses from the garden in a jug on the table giving out their own subtle fragrance, and the equipment for jam-making is set out on the worktop – the old preserving kettle, battered but still as functional as ever, the giant wooden spoon, the labels and a new set of empty jars. Julia is wearing what she would probably call a day dress in chintzy cotton, with an open neck and short sleeves. It's bottle green, patterned with tiny sunflowers.

'You look amazing, Gran. What's put the smile on your face today?'

'Oh, I was just glad the sun was shining and that you're on the mend.'

Emily's not convinced. 'Are you sure that's all?' As she speaks, she hears footsteps coming down the side of the house and a familiar voice shouting, 'Hello?'

Julia stirs her saucepan of scrambled eggs vigorously, not looking towards the door. 'Come in, Tristram. Have you had breakfast already?'

He comes in, beaming when he sees Emily. 'At last! The patient is recovering. Fabulous news. As for breakfast, yes I have, but it was very early and those eggs smell so good I'm tempted to start again. That's if I'm not in the way?'

'Of course you're not, and Gran's made enough for a small army, as usual,' Emily says, her eyes on her gran. The older lady is still studiously not looking at their visitor, busying herself slicing more granary bread for toast and refilling the kettle. It seems much has happened while Emily's been out of action.

There's an almost tangible crackle of electricity between Tristram and Julia. Emily's heart aches when she thinks of her grandpa and how happy he'd been with Gran, but that's no reason to throw cold water on a new relationship, especially when he's such an old friend. But people will talk, and the talk won't all be positive. The village may sniff and say Julia's not taken long to replace Don. Is Julia strong enough to withstand the muttering?

'I'm here for the masterclass in jam-making,' says Tristram happily, sitting at the table. 'Julia was horrified when she found out that I'd never made any sort of pickle or preserve in my life.'

'Call yourself a chef?' says Julia. She dishes up soft, creamy eggs on toast and Tristram gets up to make tea. He seems very much at home here.

They eat in silence for a little while. Emily has to restrain herself from gobbling her breakfast down too quickly – it's so good to feel really hungry again.

Tristram finishes first, and sighs blissfully. 'I'm no mean shakes at scrambled eggs myself,' he says, 'but I've got to say those were the best I've ever had. So many people cook them for too long, and forget to add enough salt and black pepper. And you didn't stint on the butter either, petal.'

Julia blushes. Emily tries not to stare, but really, Julia's acting very oddly today. 'I'll load the dishwasher when everyone's finished,' she says, 'and then I'm going to take a really hot bubble bath with no salt in it, if you don't mind, Gran? My hair is in serious need of washing.'

'You go ahead now and enjoy it,' says Tristram. 'I'll clear away while Julia gets ready for my lesson. You need to rest today. It's tempting to do too much after you've been poorly, and this has been a nasty bout of the pox.'

Emily yawns hugely and doesn't argue. She feels somewhat in the way, and anyway she's more tired than she likes to admit. The much-delayed phone call to Colin can wait until tomorrow. She's still officially on leave, so they won't be expecting to hear from her yet.

'Are my spots going away at all, do you think?' she asks hopefully as she heads for the stairs.

The others both look at her and then at each other.

'I'm guessing that's a *no* then,' she says. 'Oh, well, I'm not intending to see anyone else but you lot for a while, am I?'

As she says this, the doorbell rings. 'Now who can that be?' asks Julia, pointlessly, as she always does.

Julia goes to find out and as her grandmother opens the front door Emily freezes with a mouthful of coffee ready to swallow as she hears the last voice she was expecting boom down the hallway.

'Hello! You must be Emily's glamorous grandma? I'm Colin Dennis, her boss. I thought as I was flying over to England to see my sick uncle it would be rude not to call and see how she's doing. I got the message about the chickenpox, so I knew we'd need to talk about how long she'd need to be convalescing. I've touched base in Devon at my parents' house, and hospital visiting isn't until later, so now . . . well, here I am.'

Julia's answer is lost in the coughing fit that overtakes Emily. Colin is in the kitchen before she can recover, his genial face, generous girth and shining bald head set off by a very smart grey business suit. Eyes streaming, and with Tristram patting her back helpfully, Emily doesn't present the picture of a calm, competent employee that she might have hoped for.

'Em, my goodness, you look even worse than I expected,' he cries, coming over and taking Emily by the shoulders. Her nose is running now and she can feel her spots beginning to glow and itch again. Colin drops his hands and takes a pace back.

'But . . . you said you'd had a message?' gasps Emily. 'I *was* going to ring you, but I hadn't got round to it. Who . . .?'

'A lovely old lady gave me a call and filled me in. She said her name was May. I'm not sure how she got my number, but she seemed very worried about you.'

Tristram hands Emily a tissue, putting out a hand to shake Colin's. 'That's our May for you. If she really wants to know something, she can find it out. She should've been a detective. I'm Tristram, by the way, it's good to meet you.'

'Oh, and you've got to be Emily's grandfather?'

There's an ominous silence. Emily wipes her eyes and nose and takes a deep breath to get her breathing under control. 'My grandpa died, Colin – remember?'

Colin slaps his forehead. 'So he did. I'm so sorry. I totally knew he passed away and of course that was why . . . oh hell, this is really crass of me. It's just that you look so . . . I mean you two look . . . I just forgot for a minute . . .'

'Quit while you're ahead, Colin,' says Emily through gritted teeth. Tristram and Julia are both avoiding her gaze now.

'I tell you what, let's start again,' says Colin. He goes out into the hall and comes back seconds later, smiling broadly. 'Hi there, everyone. I'm Emily's boss from New York City but I'm almost a local lad really because I'm originally from Plymouth and I have a great talent for opening my big mouth and putting my foot in it. I mean well and I'm quite harmless really. Even my mother says so.'

Tristram laughs, a great burst of amusement, and the others join in. Colin mimes huge relief and squares his shoulders. 'Right, now we can move on. I just wondered if I could have a chat with Emily, but even a goon like me can see that I've come at a bad time.'

'If you can stand looking at the spots and you don't mind waiting while I have a quick bath, now's a very good time,' says Emily. 'Is that OK with you, Gran?'

'Of course it is. Colin, sit down here at the table. Tristram will make you a pot of tea and I'll rustle up some breakfast while Emily gets ready. Then, if the sun's still shining, you can have coffee and some of my chocolate fudge cake outside later and enjoy the view while you chat.'

Colin opens his eyes wide. 'Emily Lovell, I can now entirely see why you love to come to this place. A beautiful lady to attend to your every whim, home-made cake to order and sunshine and a sea view on tap. Take your time in the bath, I'm in heaven.'

Emily goes upstairs to do her best with her appearance, carefully avoiding looking in any mirrors until she's plaited her clean, wet hair and dressed in her favourite jeans and a soft cotton shirt that doesn't irritate the spots.

When she re-enters the kitchen, Emily's confronted with the bizarre spectacle of the others absorbed in a production line of jam-making. Colin has taken off his jacket and rolled up the sleeves of his shirt. He's wearing Don's best navy and white striped pinafore, and Tristram has on an older, more faded version. Julia is bustling around organising her troops as they sterilise jam jars and top-and-tail gooseberries. Even more surprisingly, May is now sitting at the table too.

'It's nice to see you up and about, dear,' she says to Emily. 'I saw this gentleman coming to the door and I just wondered if it might be the nice Mr Dennis I spoke to on the telephone. And it was!' She beams at them all. 'I rang to see if Tristram might have time to fetch me over in the wheelchair we borrowed. It's really proving very useful.'

'I don't know why I didn't think of tackling jam-making this way before,' says Julia. 'It's so much easier with kitchen staff. They had the fruit picked in next to no time and now look at them. All they need is the promise of cake and they're happy.'

'Can I help?' asks Emily, rather feebly. She's suddenly feeling shattered and all this activity looks exhausting.

'Why don't you sit down with May at the table and design the labels for me? By the time that's done, Colin can have his coffee-break.'

Colin winks at Emily and carries on preparing the gooseberries as she settles down with a couple of felt tips and a strip of sticky labels to decorate. May is humming to herself happily, clearly delighted to be back in the midst of the action. Soon, Emily's into the swing of it, doing her best flowing script and drawing a tiny gooseberry complete with bristles in the corner of each one. She takes her time. It's a very satisfying job. The tangy scent of boiling gooseberries is like a blast from the past. Gramps always let her do the labels.

'Have you been a jam-maker in your time, May?' she asks.

'No, but I did have a reputation in the village for making very fine blackberry vinegar. I used to make it for the church fund-raisers.'

'Oh? What do you use that for? It'd be a bit odd on chips.'

May chuckles. 'You are silly. Blackberry vinegar is good to have on pancakes or sweet dumplings. It's also excellent mixed with hot water and sipped slowly as a remedy for coughs and asthma.'

'Your Charles suffered badly with asthma, didn't he?' says Tristram.

'Yes. He was addicted to my special vinegar. I never touch it myself. Gives me heartburn.'

May stares into space, as if looking right into her past. Her expression is unreadable.

'Are you OK?' asks Emily. May's plucking at the gingham tablecloth now, a deep furrow forming between her eyes.

'Yes, dear. Memories of old times can sometimes be painful, you know.'

'It must have been lovely to make something your husband enjoyed so much, though?'

'I . . . well, yes, of course. Lovely.' She bites her lip. Emily is intrigued. What's this all about? She's just about to take it further when Julia steps in, having completely missed the strange undercurrent.

'Right, off you go now, Colin, and take Em and May with you. Coffee will be served in five minutes,' she says. 'I've added the sugar so the jam needs to simmer for a while before I test it to see if it's ready to set. We can't do any more for the time being.'

Emily stands up stiffly and leads the way into the garden, with Colin pushing the wheelchair. The breeze has died down and it's pleasantly warm, but she shivers as she goes towards the swinging seat that has the best view of the cove.

'I'm getting the feeling that you'd rather be back in bed?' Colin says. 'I'm so sorry to put you on the spot like this.'

'Please don't mention spots,' Emily groans, scratching a hard-to-reach bit of her back.

They sit soaking up the sunshine and listening to the cry of the gulls.

'I can totally see why you love it here, Em,' Colin says, when Tristram has delivered steaming mugs of milky coffee and huge slices of fudge cake as promised.

May leans forward to reach her coffee. 'I think you two will probably want to talk in private,' she says. 'I'll drink this as quickly as possible and let Tristram take me home. Or . . . I tell you what, could one of you push me over to that other little table where I can look at the sea? Then you can say whatever you like and I won't hear you.'

Colin is too gentlemanly to agree to this without question, but Emily can see that May is determined not to get in the way so they reorganise themselves and May settles herself contentedly to watch a few holidaymakers making camp with windbreaks, deckchairs and numerous bags and baskets.

Emily sits back down again and takes a gulp of coffee. An unpleasant skin has formed on top of it, and she pulls a face. 'Why didn't you let me know you were coming, Colin?' she asks, playing for time.

'I like surprises, don't you? So, let's talk about your gran. She looks great to me, but you clearly didn't always think that.'

'She wasn't coping, or so we thought.'

'We?' This is through a mouthful of cake, but Emily gets his meaning.

'Erm . . . well, the other person who was worried was her neighbour across the road. His name's Andy. He's been very good about keeping me up to date.'

Colin raises his eyebrows but carries on eating.

'And also, May was worried, too. Gran was confused and very sad, and she'd almost become a recluse.'

Colin takes a large swig of coffee and burps contentedly. 'Whoops, sorry – that was so good I think I might just move in myself.' He turns to give Emily one of his more piercing stares. 'So, are you and this Andy together?'

'Why do you say that?'

'Come on, sweetie, I've learned to read your face.'

Emily pulls her mouth down. 'No, he's a single dad and he needs to focus on his daughter just now. Plus there's an overbearing ex around and I think there's more to that than he's letting on. But I'd like to get to know him better even if we only end up as mates. He makes me laugh . . . and stuff . . .'

'Hmm. And what happened to our old buddy Max?'

'You never liked Max, did you?'

'It wasn't a matter of liking him. I just knew he wasn't good enough for you. Any man who cheats on his wife, and twice over too . . .'

There's an ominous silence, and Colin slaps his forehead again.

'Twice?' she repeats.

'Oh, um . . .'

'You mean he wasn't just unfaithful to his wife, he was cheating on me as well? Colin, don't look so pathetic, just tell me.'

'I haven't got any proof.'

'*Just tell me, OK?*'

Colin leans forward and puts his elbows on his knees,

lacing his fingers together and resting his chin on his linked hands so that he doesn't need to look at Emily. The tweeting of the birds in the garden seems unusually loud as Emily waits for his answer. Her head is spinning slightly and the scent of honeysuckle is almost too powerful today.

'I'm pretty sure he was seeing Renata from accounts,' Colin eventually says. 'I saw them leave together a couple of times when you were away on business, and he's still hanging around her.'

Emily waits for the new pain of betrayal to hit her, but nothing happens. Can it be that she really doesn't care any more? She doesn't want Max for herself. Pint-sized, angry Renata is welcome to him. It doesn't matter. Relief floods her. She hoped she was over Max, but this proves it. The thought of Andy with Candice fills her with venom and jealousy, but Max can do whatever he likes, with her blessing.

She smiles reassuringly at Colin as he makes himself meet her eyes to check on the damage he's done. 'It's fine,' she says. 'Max is history. But I do need to talk to you about the future sometime. Not just now, but soon.'

'I was afraid of that,' says Colin. 'I'll take the tray back in now, shall I, and come back for May? We don't want either of you getting chilly.'

Emily stands up and goes over to where May appears to be dozing in the sunshine. May sits up straighter.

'Finished?' she says innocently.

'Were you listening, May?' asks Emily. 'You were, weren't you?'

'There's nothing wrong with my hearing, dear. I wasn't intending to eavesdrop but Colin has got such a nice clear voice. That American person does seem to be rather a snake in the grass, doesn't he? I don't want you to get lumbered with a time-waster. Life's too short. I can tell you that from experience.'

'Oh, May,' says Emily, laughing. 'You don't miss much, do you?'

'I like to keep my finger on the pulse, as they say. So, everything's falling into place. Now all you need to do is to deal with That Candice.'

# Chapter Thirty-Six

News travels fast in Pengelly. So far, Andy has never minded the way life in a small village means everybody knows everything about each other, but the bush telegraph really has been working overtime lately. He hears the gossip about Emily's possible miscarriage in the village shop the next day from Vera. How on earth has this news got out? Only the doctor, Julia, Tristram and Andy know about it, or so he thought, and none of them will have been shouting their mouths off.

'Of course, it's only a rumour,' says the rather poisonous shopkeeper, who has never, as long as Andy can remember, had a good word to say about anybody. 'I've always thought she was no better than she should be, swanning around with her fancy ways. She was a sulky one when she was a teenager and now she's got big ideas and bigger fish to fry.'

Ida is in the queue behind Andy, and even as he opens his mouth to speak, she's on the attack. 'And what makes you say that, Vera, if you don't mind me asking?' Her eyes are flashing, and Andy looks on admiringly, waiting for his turn.

Vera has the grace to blush. 'Well, it stands to reason.

That American . . . he wasn't just a friend, now, was he? And a famous author? I saw him on that morning programme on the telly last year. He won't be short of a bob or two, will he?'

'What exactly are you suggesting?'

'Oh, I'm not suggesting anything.'

Andy moves forward slightly and folds his arms across his chest. 'I don't agree.'

'What?'

'I think you're trying to insinuate that Emily's a gold-digger.'

'It's not for me to incinerate anything.' Vera's red-faced now, but from anger rather than shame at her accusation.

Hideous woman, thinks Andy. She's stuck her nose into my business ever since Allie was first ill, and she's not going to do the same with Emily. Incineration would be the best thing for her.

He puts his full basket down on the shop counter next to the till and looks across at Ida. She winks at him and does the same. 'It'll be a nuisance having to drive into Mengillan for my groceries, but it's a small price to pay for never having to see or speak to you again,' Andy says.

'Ditto, with knobs on,' shouts Ida.

They exit the shop together, trying not to giggle at the aghast faces of the other three people waiting to be served. 'Well, we showed 'em,' says Ida, giving Andy a hug before they set off up the street together. 'Shame I'll need to find someone else to adopt Marigold and her snappy little Pekinese, but it was worth it. So, is it true about Emily having lost a baby?'

'She's got chickenpox, you know that, Ida. And I'd be grateful if you'd pass the word around that there's nothing else going on.'

'Leave it with me, dear. I squash any nasty little stories that Vera's been spreading. But, while we're on the subject, May dropped a couple of hints the last time I saw her. She didn't mean to; I guess she was just thinking aloud. Very old people tend to do that sometimes.'

'I suppose they do, but I've never thought of May as very old, somehow.'

'Haven't you? My mother used to say all sorts of inappropriate things. She once asked the milkman how many times a week he thought married folks should have sex.'

Andy snorts. 'What was the answer? I'm asking for a friend, obviously.'

'He told her a little of what you fancy does you good, and then he went away quite quickly.'

Ida links arms with Andy. 'May's a wise old bird, you know. I realise now what she was getting at.'

'Yes, and I guess when you get to be a hundred and ten, you feel as if you can say what you like.'

'It'd be a shame to have all that life experience and not share it. She's seen and done so much. It's a pity she's so alone in the world.'

'May isn't alone. She's got Tamsin and me, and Julia, Tristram and Emily.'

Ida sighs. 'It's not the same as having a happy marriage and a family, though, I always say.'

'Not everyone would agree with you on that one, Ida.'

'Hmm. Andy, tell me not to be an interfering old

busybody if you like, but is there any chance of you and Emily . . .? I mean . . . could you . . .? It's been such a long time for you to be on your own.'

Andy tries not to mind the fact that this question is probably on a lot of the villagers' lips. It's good to live in a caring community in lots of ways, but this is just intrusive. He wonders how to answer. The truthful response would be that he can't get Emily out of his mind. Her wonderful hair, her provocative blue eyes, the way she fits into his arms as if she belongs there, the sheer fun of her. She haunts his dreams and his waking hours.

'I'm afraid Emily might still have other fish to fry,' he says eventually.

'You mean that smarmy American? Not likely. So do you want a lift to Sainsbury's? I'm going anyway.'

'Not sure if I've got time. Friday's my busiest day.'

'Come on, we'll be quick. My husband says I could have been a racing driver if I'd had the right wheels. And you can tell me more about Emily on the way.'

Andy laughs nervously and lets Ida lead him to her sporty little Mini. He's very much afraid this is going to be one of those lifts you never forget.

They bowl along the winding road to Mengillan, with Ida singing along to hits from the sixties on the radio.

'So have you had your invitation to Tristram's surprise party yet?' she yells, above the music.

Andy tries not to wince as Ida overtakes a tractor, nipping back in again just as another one trundles towards them. 'Yes, Gina rang me this morning.'

'Me, too. She's doing a few people at a time and swearing

them to secrecy. The only problem is that they can't fix a definite date until the last minute because of the weather. They want to be sure of being able to use the beach because there'll be too many guests to fit in The Shack. She gave me three possibilities.'

'Yeah. A beach party would probably sound dead glamorous if you didn't live here, but given the amount of rain we get sometimes, Gina needs to be able to rely on a good day to barbecue.'

'This is going to be a celebration to remember! It's a good job most of Tristram's buddies are as spontaneous as he is. A lot of people would moan if you couldn't give them a specific time and place for a party.'

'True. I suppose a few won't make if it clashes with other things but I bet they nearly all do.'

Ida nods enthusiastically and the car veers towards the hedge slightly. 'They've asked me to make the birthday cake. Gina's much better at decorating cakes than I am, but she won't be able to keep it secret with Tris around all the time. I'm going to make a huge chocolate sponge and freeze it when I get home. That's his favourite.'

'The only thing I'm not sure about is whether he'll be pleased.'

'Why wouldn't he be? He's one of the most sociable men I know.'

'Yes, which is why he might rather organise his own birthday bash. He's very particular about getting everything right when he's entertaining.'

'Oh. I see what you mean. But I don't think he'll be sniffy about details on his eightieth birthday when Gina and Vince have gone to so much trouble to get his friends together.'

'Let's hope you're right. Well, I'd better get a present sorted. Any ideas?'

'A new wife?' Ida cackles alarmingly, and swerves to avoid a sheep that's wandered into the lane.

'Really? Would he marry again, at his age?'

'You bet he would. He's not old yet – never let him hear you suggest he is. Tris always says there's no chance of him risking it a fifth time, but he's still full of beans. You just watch him.'

'But who'd be the right woman? You can't be putting yourself forward for the position, Ida?'

She takes her left hand off the wheel and swipes Andy round the ear. He closes his eyes as Ida's Mini lurches to the right and then straightens up again. Are groceries worth this? He's almost regretting his impulsive protest in the shop.

'Not me. I'm perfectly happy with my Harry, you know that. There'll never be anybody else for me. He's a one-off.'

'Julia always says that about Don.'

'Yes, she does, doesn't she?'

Ida turns the music up as an old Beatles song comes on, 'The Long and Winding Road'. You can say that again, thinks Andy.

# Chapter Thirty-Seven

Julia is still filled with restless energy even after May, Colin and Tristram have left and Emily has gone upstairs for a nap. Her granddaughter seems wiped out by her boss's surprise visit, but her expression when she gives in and heads upstairs to lie down is more peaceful than it's been since she arrived.

The jars of jam are lined up along the worktop. Sunlight bounces off their shiny surfaces, and the pale green of the fresh gooseberries has mellowed to a golden glow. Everywhere is tidy and clean – Colin and Tristram have made sure of that, vying with each other for the most sparkling side of the kitchen as they wiped and polished. Now firm friends, Colin has gone with Tristram for a tour of the village. He's accepted an impromptu invitation to stay for a couple of nights at The Shellfish Shack after he's visited the hospital because his parents now live in a tiny bungalow and he says their sofa bed is excruciatingly uncomfortable. He wastes no time in fetching a small suitcase out of his car so he can change into ancient jeans, loafers and a fisherman's sweater, his idea of what a Cornishman wears for relaxation purposes.

Julia sits down at the kitchen table, wondering how

to fill her time until they come back. The men have decided to cook dinner tonight and have challenged themselves to find as many different kinds of seafood as they can. Tristram has invited Andy, Tamsin and Vi, too, with Julia's permission, and she must start getting out the best crockery and cutlery soon and dig out her biggest embroidered tablecloth, but for now, she needs a distraction.

She picks out from the basket a pile of letters waiting to be sorted. Maybe reading a few of these will settle her jangling nerves, although when she tries to recall some of the ones she's already ploughed through, there's a terrifying blank. Waves of panic wash over Julia as she battles to remember something . . . anything. The ring . . . and Will. Those two are linked somehow. There's a mystery but it's as if she's wandering in fog. Where have those memories gone? Taking deep breaths, she spreads the heaps of letters out. As she begins to sift through them, she hears the doorbell.

May is standing on the doorstep, walking stick in hand and shoulders well back. She looks defiant but very pleased with herself.

'Good heavens,' Julia says, putting a hand on her heart. 'What are you doing back so soon, and out on your own? I thought Colin left you getting ready for a rest. And aren't you supposed to be using a wheelchair?'

May sways slightly. 'Are you going to ask me in or am I going to faint dead away on your step?'

Mortified, Julia ushers her in and goes to put the kettle on.

'Where's Emily?' May calls after a few moments.

'Ssshhh. She's having a nap,' Julia says, coming back with a tray of tea, 'and I don't want to wake her. You saw how she looked earlier. The chickenpox has taken a lot out of her.'

'And the baby, of course,' says May, staring Julia straight in the eye.

'How did you . . .? I mean . . .'

'Oh, I always know. I'm nearly a hundred and eleven, after all, dear. There's no mistaking that look, is there? Or hadn't you rumbled her?'

Julia is seething now, all amusement gone. Really, May is beyond a joke. She's crossed the line this time. How dare she interfere? It's as if she's trying to say she knows Emily better than her own grandmother does. The cheek of it.

May grins. 'Don't be cross, it doesn't suit you. Adds wrinkles,' she says.

Taking a deep breath, Julia tries to relax her tense shoulders. It's all been going so well with May. She mustn't spoil it now – the poor woman's been ill, after all.

'That's better,' says May. 'I've only come back over to tell you not to worry about Emily.'

'I beg your pardon?'

May drinks her tea in silence. She must have a gullet made of asbestos, thinks Julia. Presently, she puts her cup down carefully in her saucer. Julia is still biting her tongue and waiting for an explanation as to why she apparently mustn't worry about her own granddaughter.

May yawns. 'I'm getting old, dear,' she says finally.

Julia still says nothing.

'Everything is working out for the best, and anyway, I'll make sure all is well. That's what I wanted to say.'

May gets up to go, and Julia sees her out, mystified, but watching her carefully until the older lady is safely inside her own home again. Hopefully, this time she'll stay put. Julia comes back inside and tidies away the rest of the letters – it's no use trying to concentrate on any sorting now – but as she goes about her preparations for the evening, she thinks hard about what May has said.

When Emily gets up she finds the dining table already laid. A beautiful linen cloth patterned with embroidered wild flowers is the main feature, and Julia has kept everything else low-key so as not to cover it up too much. She's used straw mats and has fetched out the best cut-glass goblets, newly washed and gleaming. An arrangement of fresh flowers from the garden is the centre-piece.

'Why didn't you wait for me to help you, Gran? I could have done all this,' Emily says, folding her arms and frowning. She looks alarmingly like her father when she does that, Julia thinks.

'I enjoyed it. I needed something to do.'

'You should have had a rest like I did if we're entertaining in style later.'

'I couldn't settle. Anyway, you're the one who's been so off-colour. I'm fine.'

Emily doesn't seem totally convinced. 'Really? And if you're suddenly fine, what's changed? Because you weren't feeling so good when I arrived, were you? Far from it. And you're very pale tonight.'

Julia thinks quickly. 'I . . . I think I feel stronger because you've been around so much lately. It's helped me to feel as if life's still worth living,' she says, quashing her feelings of guilt about hindering Emily's working life. 'After your grandpa died, I was lost. Completely at sea. I still miss him all the time and think about him every day but gradually I'm starting to cope, and to live with that feeling instead of letting it take over. The time we had was precious but it isn't lost. Wherever I go and whatever I do, I take him with me.'

'Oh, Gran. It must be so hard to move on when you've had such a good life together.'

'Yes, love, it is. But we had our ups and downs, just like any couple. We didn't just sit around gazing into each other's eyes all day, you know – we had rows sometimes, too, quite fierce ones. And also, I keep thinking that there are some unfortunate people who've never had that sort of partnership.'

'How do you mean?'

'Well, like poor May, for instance. Her marriage wasn't much fun, and she hardly missed Charles at all when he'd gone, from what she said.'

'I don't think there's any way you should use the term "poor May". She was more than contented with her lot, as far as I could see.'

'So what are you saying?'

Emily thinks for a moment. Julia notices that she's looking a lot better for her sleep, even though she's still very spotty. Her eyes are less tired and she's left her newly washed hair loose so that it flows in bright waves over her shoulders. She's found another old favourite in her wardrobe by the look of it, a floor-length stretchy cotton dress in muted shades of blue. She was always one for leaving clothes behind 'ready for next time' as if she was making certain she'd be back soon. It has long flared sleeves that cover most of her gradually healing blisters.

'I guess all I meant was that everyone's different. Not all women need a man to make them happy.'

'And do you? Might Andy be the one you've been waiting for?'

The words hang between them. As Julia waits for this significant question to be answered, the kitchen door flies open and the two men come back in. Damn! What bad timing, Julia thinks, glaring at Tristram, who looks mortified at the lack of welcome.

'Are we interrupting something?' he asks.

'Not at all,' says Emily. 'We were just . . . erm . . .'

'. . . discussing what kind of jam to make next,' adds Julia, hastily. 'Have you seen your uncle already, Colin?'

'No, my mum rang to say they'd been to the hospital this afternoon and he was so sleepy he barely knew they were there. She's got the ward sister to agree to me having a visit in the morning just for half an hour, because that's when he usually feels like chatting. So, what shall I do first towards this spectacular feast?'

When Andy, Vi and Tamsin arrive, the kitchen is full of bustle.

'Will there be chicken nuggets and red sauce?' Tamsin asks hopefully.

'Only for special guests. We didn't have enough for everybody,' says Emily.

'Oh.'

'But you're the most special kind of person we know, so you'll be fine.'

Tamsin hugs Emily and rushes off to play outside, giving Julia and Emily the chance to escape to the comfort of the living room. Julia feels jittery and over-excited, as if something's going to happen but she's not sure if it's good or bad.

Vi comes in with Andy and settles herself next to Emily on the sofa. She's the sort of person who could be any age from fifty to sixty-five, strongly made, with broad shoulders and the sort of skin that ages well, with a healthy outdoor glow. Her grey hair is cropped short and her clothes look as if they've been the same style for ever – workman-like jeans, a checked shirt and trainers. Her only concessions to this night out are small diamond stud earrings and a slick of Vaseline on her lips.

'So who's the new man?' she asks Julia. 'Is he your toy boy or Emily's older bloke? And if he isn't either, please can I have him? He's cooking up a storm in there.'

'I didn't know you were on the lookout for a bloke, Vi,' says Andy, ruffling Vi's hair. 'You told me that men were an expensive luxury.'

'I know, but if I was to find one who could whip up fantastic dinners at the drop of a hat, and didn't mind my house being full of kids, there's just a chance I might reconsider. How about you, Emily? Has your hunky American given up and gone home?'

'Yes.'

The short answer doesn't put Vi off. 'Good. I didn't meet him but I saw him from the window and you can do better than that, girl. He looked a bit arrogant to me.'

Julia watches Andy and Emily studiously avoiding looking at each other and smiles to herself but Vi hasn't finished yet. 'And what about you, Julia?'

'What *about* me?'

'There are two of 'em in there. Tristram's too old for me but . . .'

Julia fixes Vi with her best mean stare and the other woman dries up at last. Luckily, Tamsin shouts at them all to watch her as she climbs up the compost heap, and Vi and Andy jump up to stop her covering her best dress with cabbage slime and worse.

Emily opens her eyes wide and puts her head on one side. 'Did Vi touch a nerve there, Gran?' she says.

'Don't be ridiculous,' Julia snaps back. 'How could anybody ever replace your grandpa?'

As she speaks, Tristram comes out of the house to call them for dinner. Julia looks up at him, and he returns her gaze without smiling. Has he overheard? And if he did catch Julia's drift, is she pleased that she's made her position clear . . . or not?

# Chapter Thirty-Eight

The final parts of the plan for Tristram's celebration come together at speed once Gina and Vince are sure the weather's taken a turn for the better and that it might last long enough for a barbecue. Andy, Vi and Emily all get text messages while Tristram is still with them for dinner. The pinging of the three phones almost in unison makes Tristram tut loudly.

'I should have confiscated those dratted machines before we started eating,' he says. 'Colin and I didn't slave in the kitchen for hours so that you could all distract yourselves with trivia.'

Fortunately, his disgust stops any of them looking at their messages while he's still around, and when Julia gets a call on the landline after Tristram's dragged Colin off for a nightcap at the pub on the way home she's able to confirm three of them will be there but that Emily's worried she's still contagious.

'Gina says you'll be fine. She's googled the chickenpox virus. You're OK if it's five days since the spots first appeared and you haven't got any new ones. The party's on Sunday evening so you've still got nearly two days to get better.'

'But I look hideous, Gran. I can't go to a party looking like this.'

'You'll be fine. Wear that dress again; it covers most of the spots. I'll put it in the wash tonight if you like so it'll be ready for then. It's a good job you were always leaving clothes here. You can slap a bit of make-up over the worst ones on your face.'

'Mmm. I suppose so.'

'You mustn't miss it if you feel well enough to go. It's not every day a man turns eighty and still has enough friends to have a crazy beach barbecue. She's a marvel, Tristram's girl,' says Julia. 'If I were organising a big do like this I'd need to have the time, date, menu and guest list sorted weeks before.'

'All the food that could be bought and made in advance is already in Gina's friends' freezers, and she's been baking at different people's houses all week,' says Vi. 'I saw her yesterday and she says the main problem's going to be getting Tristram out of the way for long enough to get the last bits done.'

Emily grins. 'Well, I reckon Colin's going to be hanging around for a few days. Were you listening to him raving about how much he loves it here? We'd better get him to ask Tristram to take him somewhere up the coast at the vital time.'

'Gina must have already thought of that, surely? She wouldn't risk him finding out too soon after all this secrecy.'

'She's relying on him doing his usual trip to town tomorrow to give her more time. She plans to give him a huge list of tricky things to buy. But if Colin steps in to help on the party day, they can do a sightseeing tour. I'll ring him when they've had a chance to get back to The Shack.'

'Does it seem weird having your boss hanging around, Em?' asks Andy. 'You weren't expecting him, were you?'

'No and no,' she says. 'It's good to see him away from the office. He's normally verging on the workaholic so it was a surprise to see him, but I think there might be more to this holiday than just wanting to talk to me and to visit his family. He's not looked well for a while. Maybe this is his way of giving himself permission to take a break.'

'He's carrying a lot of extra weight,' says Vi, sighing heavily, 'and he's got that flushed look that my Malcom had before he had his stroke. He was dead two weeks later.'

Andy sees the alarm on Emily's face and curses Vi inwardly. She never thinks before she speaks. 'I'm sure Colin's just ready for a good rest,' he says. 'A holiday down here with plenty of fresh air and exercise might be just what he needs to take stock. Vi, is there any chance you could take Tamsin back for me and get her in the bath? I'll be over soon but I promised Julia I'd hammer down the felt on the shed roof before I go home. The rain's been seeping in.'

'OK, the young 'un's going to need some scrubbing tonight. She's been making mud pies for the last half-hour. She's only in her vest and pants because I told her not to ruin her dress. Good job it's still warm outside.'

Vi heads outside and Andy rolls his eyes at Emily as he hears his daughter's fierce protests at being taken away from her sludgy cookery. 'But I haven't cooked the pies yet,' she howls. Vi doesn't stand for any nonsense and they're away over the road in the space of five minutes.

Andy gets the shed roof job done quickly and comes back into the kitchen to say good night to Julia. She's reading one of the letters and looking pensive.

'This one's about Kathryn's second baby. The poor little scrap had croup very badly all through every winter. I've sent Emily to bed, by the way. She looked shattered.'

'Try not to worry about her so much,' says Andy. 'She's loads better. Although I know what you're thinking; I'm a fine one to talk about not worrying.'

'You're getting more relaxed now, though – a bit, anyway,' Julia says.

Andy thinks about this and isn't sure if it's true. He still panics if Tamsin seems off-colour.

Julia seems to be guessing his train of thought because she adds, 'Everybody worries about their children, love. That feeling doesn't go away, even when they're fully grown and have long ago flown the nest.'

'I wonder if I'll ever have any more kids,' he blurts out.

Julia looks at him with her head on one side. 'Not unless you take some drastic action,' she says. 'Or not with Emily, anyway. She thinks you've still got a thing for Candice and she's worried about coming between you and Tam.'

'What? I've *never* had a thing for Candice!'

'Haven't you?'

He feels his face burning. 'Well, not a *thing* kind of thing.'

'That's not the impression she gave Emily when she rang her.'

'*Candice* rang Emily? But why would she do that?'

Julia stays silent. Andy turns to leave. 'I'm going to phone Candice right now,' he says.

'Good idea,' says Julia sweetly, raising a hand to wave goodbye. When Andy's safely out of the way, Julia rummages for the letter she was reading again. Something's niggling at her mind. Croup. Now why is the mention of that horrible childhood ailment ringing bells? She goes over to the bookshelf and pulls out her mother's old medical dictionary. It's well-thumbed and tatty. Julia's mother used it like a bible when anyone was even slightly off-colour.

She looks up croup and finds that the symptoms are often similar to those of asthma. That's it! She remembers a reference in one of Will's letters to Charles's chronic breathing difficulties. May used to make blackberry vinegar for Charles was addicted to it. Well, that's quite a sweet thing to do, and maybe suggests she was fonder of her husband than everyone thought.

There was something else much more significant in one of Will's other letters, but Julia's forgotten what it was. Something relating to that last voyage he'd planned with Charles. She reaches for the pile of letters she asked permission to bring over from May's to study more closely. She begins her search. She has to start somewhere.

# Chapter Thirty-Nine

The first thing Emily is aware of when she wakes on Sunday morning is the sunshine streaming through the gap in her bedroom curtains. It makes patterns on the wooden floor and warms her pillow. The birds are calling to each other and the sea is inching up the beach. Gina has been very careful to check the tides so that there will be enough sand for her guests to spread out on, and if the sun is this strong so early in the morning, there's a very good chance that it'll be a night to remember, with dancing in the moonlight and lots of ice-cold prosecco flowing.

Emily sighs. Why did she have to go and get chickenpox just when she needs to look and feel her best? Candice is bound to be at the party, wearing as little as possible, no doubt. Emily's blue cover-all dress is going to be disgustingly hot but she's too spotty to show any more flesh without putting people off their canapés.

She rolls out of bed and goes over to the wardrobe, flicking through the hangers to see if some wonderful, flimsy and yet decorously long-sleeved and high-necked frock might be lurking in there. It isn't, and she lets out a howl of frustration.

'What's wrong, darling?' Julia shouts from the landing.

'I'm like bloody Cinderella. I can't go to the ball because I've got nothing cool enough to wear.'

Julia comes in, her forehead creased with a frown. 'Cool, as in temperature . . . or the other sort?'

'Both. I need to talk to Andy properly tonight. And first I've got to convince Colin to let me work part-time from the London office. I've decided to stay in Pengelly, at least for the next few months, and see how it goes. But if I feel awful and I look a mess too, I'm not going to be able to do it very well.'

'That's wonderful news, darling! It doesn't matter how you look, though, does it? Surely it's what you're going to say to both of them that matters?'

'Well, yes, in a perfect world, but how confident would *you* feel covered in crusty blisters, Gran?'

'I see where you're coming from. Right, follow me. This situation calls for pushing the boat out.'

Julia goes back to her own room and when Emily catches her up, she's reaching up to get a huge suitcase that's sitting on the top of her wardrobe. Emily helps her to lower it to the floor. It's dusty but not very heavy. Julia blows the worst of the dust off and opens it carefully. Inside are several tissue-paper-wrapped parcels.

'I couldn't bear to get rid of these,' Julia says, reaching for the top one. 'Your grandpa and I used to go to quite a few parties when we were younger.'

She unfolds the paper and lifts out a strappy dress, long and flimsy, patterned with hazy, overlapping circles in shades of silver and pale lilac. The next one is shorter but equally delicate. There are three stunning dresses in all. One's clearly meant for winter parties, being deep red with sparkles. Another is knee length and very pink. The silver one is perfect.

'If this fits, could you wear your pale purple pashmina with it?' suggests Julia. 'It's thin and gauzy enough not to make you too hot and it matches perfectly.'

'Oh, yes! I'll go and try it on.'

Emily rushes back to her bedroom and slips into the dress as quickly as possible. It's a good fit, and almost reaches the floor. She rummages in a drawer for the pashmina and drapes it over her shoulders, undoing her plait and shaking her head. With her hair loose, there's not much spotty skin to be seen. A bit of foundation and some lipstick, May's elaborate necklace and some silver earrings – it could work . . .

Julia knocks on the door and pops her head round. 'Oh!' is all she says, but her eyes are shining.

'Thank you, lovely, lovely Gran,' says Emily, kissing her. 'You're my fairy godmother now too.'

'You *shall* go to the ball, Cinders.'

They hug warmly, and Emily has one more look at herself in the wardrobe mirror. She'll do.

'I just wish we had the ring. It'd be the finishing touch,' says Julia sadly. 'Still, we will, one day.'

'Will we? How?'

'There's got to be a clue in one of the letters. And I'll find it when I really get stuck into writing my book.'

Emily says nothing, but her shining eyes make Julia's heart sing.

'I'm just looking through a few of the ones I haven't

read yet,' she says. 'Sit on the bed with me and help for five minutes, would you? I want to find a particular date.'

'Why?' Emily sits down and reaches for a heap of envelopes.

'No, wait. I've looked at those. It's the time around when Will went away that I want to read.'

She names the date and both start to search. They work together in silence for a while, until Emily holds out a letter. 'Try this one,' she says.

Julia opens it. She reads aloud:

Dear Don,

Well, he's gone. I never thought our Will would actually leave us but it's all happened in a rush and he's in Ireland now, starting his new life. Don, I miss him so much. He was such fun. Mother is distraught.

Why do you think this has happened? It seemed to all stem from that last visit to you. Did something go on down there that I don't know about? I want to ask Julia about it but I know now isn't a good time. I wrote to her to say how sorry I was about her mother.

Don, should one of us go over to Ireland and try and persuade Will to come back? He didn't even say goodbye properly, just spent all his last days at the Catholic church praying.

Write soon, please,

Your loving sister,

Kathryn

'Is this what you were looking for?' Emily asks.

Julia frowns. 'Sort of. I really need something from

Elsie, because she was down here with Will. I've never seen the letters from that time; I was preoccupied with my mother.'

They hunt again. Emily's dying to go and get ready for the party but Julia's totally absorbed in the task. After a few minutes, Emily holds up another one. 'Bingo,' she says. 'Shall I read it out?'

Julia nods, very pale now.

I know you won't want to hear this, Don, because you said again in your last letter you just want us all to move on and stop talking about the ring, but I'm convinced Will knows a lot more than he's letting on, and it's somehow all tied up with that horrible husband of May Rosevere's. And yes, you shouldn't speak ill of the dead but that man was poisonous.

I've gone over and over in my mind what happened on our last visit when Charles drowned and I've come to the conclusion he was probably black-mailing our Will and got the ring out of him. Will isn't a bad lad but he's weak. He was under Charles's spell and that man was always on the lookout for ways to make money. May kept him short, I reckon; she was the one holding the purse strings and Charles had expensive tastes. It's my opinion he had Mother's ring and sold it. We'll never see it again.

Will isn't answering my letters or calls. I'm in two minds whether to go over to Ireland and confront him with this, to sort it out once and for all.

Julia looks up, dazed. 'I'm doing a lot of reading between the lines,' she says, 'but I have an awful feeling that Will was involved with May's husband's death.'

'You can't be serious? But Will's still alive, isn't he? Are you suggesting . . . murder?'

'I don't know. Maybe. Or it could still have been a tragic accident. Should I do anything, Em? Everyone assumed Charles did away with himself on that stormy night because he was convinced he was dying of cancer, like his father.'

Emily thinks hard. Gran's gradually getting back on an even keel, Uncle Will is in some far-flung village in Southern Ireland, allegedly crippled with gout and arthritis, which was the reason he gave for not coming to her grandfather's funeral. Would it serve any purpose to investigate more? She makes an impulsive decision.

'Leave it, Gran. Gramps must have worked this out too, and he didn't take any action. Neither should we. It's over. Perhaps he knew something about the ring as well, as he had the empty box?'

'I've already thought about that. But he would have given it to me if he had it.'

'But what if he didn't have it but he knew where it had gone and couldn't do anything?'

Julia frowns. 'It's all just guesswork. We might never know what happened.'

'It doesn't matter. Let's live life now, and not look over our shoulders.'

Julia smiles rather shakily and reaches out for a hug. 'Darling Em, I really think you might be right,' she says, 'but I would so love to have that ring.'

'Gran, I know you always thought the ring was lovely, but maybe it's time to let go of the idea of getting it back? It's making you anxious. Is it worth the worry?'

'Yes, it is. The ring would bring me peace of mind, I'm sure of it. I can't explain exactly, but my memory needs it. The stones are lucky.'

'Surely that's a bit of an old wives' tale?'

Emily sees Julia's mouth tighten into a hard line and wonders if she's said too much.

'I'm not in my dotage yet and I'm not dotty,' says Julia. 'I've researched opals. They're healing stones. Memory loss is one of the problems they can help with.'

'But you—'

'I don't want to discuss it any more. We're going to go out and enjoy ourselves now. If I'm meant to have the ring, I'll find it somehow.'

Tristram's party is in full swing when Emily, May and Julia arrive. Emily has fetched her car down the hill, brought May across the road and driven them all there, because she's still not enjoying wine much, even though she's otherwise better.

Julia has picked a cocktail frock with lacy sleeves for herself. It's midnight blue, with a sweetheart neckline and nipped in waist. She's wearing low heels and her very best filigree jewellery. May has gone for sparkly shoes and an ankle-length crimson silk dress that floats around her legs as she walks.

'Is that vintage?' Emily asks admiringly as she escorts May into The Shellfish Shack.

'Everything about me is vintage, dear,' May answers. 'You should know that by now.'

'Wow. You three look gorgeous,' Andy says, coming to meet them. He's in the navy jacket and trousers he wore for his date with Emily, with a white cotton shirt that shows off his healthy tan. Emily swallows hard. She wants to reach up and touch his stubbly chin, to slide her arms around his waist, to dance with him on the beach.

Steady, she tells herself. First things first.

Vince is making himself useful pouring drinks for anyone who doesn't want fizz. He smiles over at her and gives a loud wolf whistle and a thumbs-up.

'You scrub up well, Ms Lovell, even with the pox,' he shouts.

Emily pulls a face. Everyone in the room has turned to look now. She puts her shoulders back, holds her head high and makes for his impromptu bar.

'When does the man himself get here?' she asks, helping herself to a tall beaded glass of pink grapefruit juice and tonic from Vince's 'Virgin Mix' tray.

'He'll be making his big entrance soon. Gina says Colin's told him we're taking him over to George's for dinner. They've been out all day. Your boss has been a star.'

As he finishes speaking, there's a commotion at the door and Emily hears a familiar voice raised in surprise. 'What the hell's going on in my shack?' Tristram bellows, coming into the room and gazing around.

The guests surge forwards to surround him and Vince starts them off in a version of 'Happy Birthday' that might actually rattle the windows. Tristram's mouth is open in shock. His eyes are very bright as he looks from face to face, each one beaming with affection.

'Good God,' is all he says.

Colin is clearly very pleased with his efforts. He pats his new friend on the back enthusiastically and joins in the singing with gusto. When the first excitement has died down and Tristram has a flute of champagne in his hand, Emily slides up to Colin and whispers, 'I need to talk to you.'

'Pardon?'

She raises her voice and repeats herself.

'Oh. What, now?'

'Yes. It won't take long.'

Colin grabs a brimming glass and follows Emily out onto the terrace. It's empty of guests at the moment but it won't be for long because Vince will soon be barbecuing, so she begins as soon as they've sat at a table.

'I won't beat about the bush, Colin. Please will you consider letting me work just the first half of the week in London, basing myself the rest of the week here in Pengelly? I could travel to the London office, stay over Monday and Tuesday, come back here Wednesday evening and work from home for the rest. I've thought it through. It would be cheaper for you even with a hotel for two nights—'

He holds a hand up to stop the frantic flow of words and Emily's heart sinks. She's blown it. But when she looks at her boss to try again, she sees he's smiling.

'Stop right there, sweetheart,' he says. 'I've already

talked this through with Tristram. He's pointed out how useful you'd be to us over here and how much your gran needs you. I'm already convinced.'

'Really? Oh, he's such a sweet man, and so are you, that goes without saying. Colin, I appreciate this so much that I don't know what to say. I'll go and thank Tristram, too, as soon as I can reach him.'

They lean sideways to look through the door of the restaurant. Tristram's still in the centre of a group of his friends, regaling them with some sort of funny story, by the look of things.

'And the weird thing is, I never even knew I was allergic to mushrooms,' they hear him shout. Everyone guffaws.

Colin grins at Emily. 'Well, I reckon this surprise party idea's a success, don't you? Anyway, I'm more than happy for you to be onsite for fewer hours, starting from right now. In fact I've had a lecture from the birthday boy today about doing the same myself, before I kill myself with over-work. I've decided to employ an office manager, and he or she will take up the slack and cover some of the jobs that we've been doing. Obviously not as well as us, but we can live with that.'

Emily lets her breath out in a sigh and leans back in her chair. All this worrying about what she's going to say to convince him, and Colin's made his mind up already. She feels quite giddy with relief. Is her talk with Andy going to be as easy? She sees Candice heading for him, a glass of champagne in each hand, and thinks probably not.

Julia taps Emily on the shoulder as she mentally

rehearses what she'd like to say to Candice later. 'Do you think May's OK?' Julia says, glancing over to where May's emerging from the cloakroom, freshly lipsticked and powdered.

'In what way?'

'I'm not sure. She just seems a bit distant. She just asked me if I'd ever sell my cottage. Where does she think I'd go, for goodness' sake?'

Emily wrenches her mind back from planning vitriolic barbs that will reduce Candice to a snivelling wreck, and tries to focus on her grandmother. 'You don't want to move, do you?'

'Of course not. Unless . . .'

'Unless what?' Emily asks, when no more is forthcoming.

'Oh, nothing. I like my life how it is, and if I didn't, it's none of May's business. It seems as if the older she gets, the more she wants to keep an eye on us all. Now, who are you going to talk to first tonight?'

Emily glares at Candice's back and imagines pushing her off those heels and into one of the trifles on the trestle table.

'Watch this space,' she says.

# Chapter Forty

Emily is distracted from her mission to put Candice in her place by Ida, who wants to give her a hug and find out none too subtly what her future plans are. By the time Emily spots Andy again through the crowd, the canapés have been circulated and the barbecue is in full swing. May is holding court at the head of a long table, looking livelier than she's done since her attack. Her eyes are bright with laughter and her fabulous dress suits her very well. She could easily pass for seventy tonight, thinks Emily, admiringly. Andy beckons her to the bench and trestle table where he's just parked his wine glass.

'I saved you a seat,' he says, just as Candice shimmies over and sits down on his other side.

Emily freezes. To stalk off or to stay and do battle? No contest. She stays, taking the chair on Andy's left.

'So, are you over your spots, hun?' Candice asks Emily, leaning round Andy to see her better and narrowing her cat-like eyes. 'Oh, no, I can see you're not. I hope they don't scar. You'll need to be careful.'

'Thanks for the warning. I expect you know all about nasty diseases. Of childhood, I mean,' answers Emily, smiling at Candice.

'The second round of food's nearly ready, according to Gina, so we're going to have to eat again in a minute,' says Andy, sitting forward so the others can't see each other properly. He pours Emily a glass of merlot and tops up his own, ignoring Candice. Emily tries to tell him she's driving but it's too late. She'll just have to leave it.

Emily hears him mutter 'Play nicely' to Candice under his breath. She seethes. Does he think she needs protecting?

'Don't forget you've promised me the first dance, precious,' says Candice, taking a big slurp of her drink. 'The band will be starting up soon, while we finish eating.'

'I can't remember saying anything about dancing.'

Candice dimples at him. 'Must have been after the wine. You always forget things when you're tiddly.'

'But I didn't . . .'

Emily turns to her neighbour on the other side, who happens to be Vi, and begins to chat to her, giving Andy a view of her back. This is beyond a joke. Candice is a vulture. Emily has a feeling she won't let go without a tussle.

'Ignore her,' hisses Vi.

'What did you say?' The babble of conversation's very loud now and Emily's not sure if she heard correctly.

'The woman's an evil green-eyed witch. She's not even a true blonde. Summer takes after her dad and Candice just bleaches her own hair to match. She's got her claws into Andy good and proper. It's you he's got the hots for.'

All this is delivered in an undertone, but Emily gets every word this time, as Vi intends she should.

'Really? I'm not so sure any more.'

'Yes, really. Go get him, girl.'

'Oh, Vi . . . but . . .'

Just as Emily is about to question Vi further, the band begins to play a medley of gentle hits from the fifties, and conversation is difficult. Emily looks up as Gina starts to circulate with prawn kebabs and tiny fishcakes, but she's lost her appetite. She puts her hands in her lap and watches the singer, crooning about getting no kick from champagne. I know the feeling, she thinks sadly. At the end of the table May has started to laugh, for some reason.

Andy's not eating either. He seems to be as uninspired by the idea of food as Emily is, and yet it's all delicious, and piping hot. She glances down just as Andy reaches for her hand under the tablecloth. Their fingers link together and he leans slightly towards her.

'The only person I'm dancing with tonight is you,' he murmurs.

Emily turns to face him. His eyes are dark and full of longing. Candice is looking daggers at her from the other side.

'That's fine by me,' she answers, clearly, 'so long as it's not a fast one. I love slow dancing, especially in the moonlight.'

Candice opens her mouth to speak but seems to think better of it. She gets up from the table, picking her handbag up and slinging it over her shoulder. Afterwards, Emily still can't decide if the other woman did it on purpose but as Candice turns to leave, her bag swings in a wide arc and demolishes both Andy's and Emily's wine glasses, tipping red wine over the table. They jump to their feet but it's too late to stop the ruby-coloured river from flooding over onto their legs.

'Oh. My. God! I'm so sorry,' screeches Candice.

'Come on,' says Andy, grabbing Emily's hand, 'we need to get out of these clothes.'

'You sweet-talking devil. I told you he was keen,' says Vi. 'But you'd better be quick. That dress looks a bit delicate.'

They rush towards the cloakroom. Gina sees them coming and takes in the situation immediately. 'Follow me,' she says, and leads them to her own bathroom. 'Take that dress off, Em. And you,' she points to Andy, 'get out of those trousers.'

They do as they're told, giggling now, even though Emily's mortified at the thought that the wonderful dress could be ruined.

'Give it to me,' says Gina, reaching for the frock. She fills the bathroom sink with cold water and plunges the dress straight in, rinsing it very gently. As the wine turns the water pink, she lets the stained liquid out and adds fresh water. She does this five times, and in the end, Emily, wearing nothing but her best peach bra and pants set and the carefully draped pashmina, can see that the frock is at last clean.

'Do the same with the trousers, Andy,' Gina says, 'and the shirt – it's gone all over you. I'll have to dash now, though. I want to get Dad to cut the cake next. Help yourselves to mine and Vince's clothes, or whatever you else you need, although they'll probably swamp you both.'

'Thank you,' calls Emily, but Gina's already gone.

As Andy washes his clothes, standing at the sink in only his black boxers, Emily tries not to stare. His legs look longer even than she imagined, and his back is strong and well-muscled without being in any way beefy. She's painfully conscious of her spotty legs that are now on show, but Andy's too busy to notice. Finally, he's happy that he's got all the wine out.

'It's a good job I took my jacket off before we sat down,' he says. 'Are you OK?'

He takes Emily's dress and his own clothes and hangs them over the bath, using the shower rail as a washing line. Emily smiles up at him.

'Well, this is the first party I've been to where I've taken my clothes off in the bathroom with a man before I'd even had a drink.'

'Do you usually wait till you've downed your first six pints then?' he asks.

'It's well-known party etiquette. Stripping to your underwear when you're stone-cold sober and covered with pock marks is a bit unsavoury, don't you think? It smacks of desperation, somehow.'

'Shall we get dressed in borrowed clothes or shall we just stay like this? I don't mind the spots if you don't care about my bandy legs.'

'They're not bandy,' says Emily, unable to stop staring at his body.

Andy comes over to Emily and takes her very gently by the shoulders. 'Let's pretend there's nobody out there and carry on where we left off last time.'

He reaches round her and locks the bathroom door.

Emily slips her arms around his neck, accidentally letting the pashmina slip to the floor. She looks down at it, feeling very exposed.

'Leave it,' Andy says quietly. When he kisses her this time, the only distraction is the second loud rendition of 'Happy Birthday' from the other side of the building, but Emily is oblivious. When they surface for air, Andy strokes her face so tenderly that she wants to cry. She tries her best not to. A runny nose would really be the final touch.

'You're beautiful, Em,' Andy whispers, kissing the tip of her nose, which has somehow escaped the spots.

'Really?'

'Yep. Warts and all. Or blisters, anyhow.'

She pokes him with a finger. 'It's not funny being this hideous. Anyway, I'm glad you like me even though I'm spotty, because I'm sticking around. I need to talk to Colin more, but I think it's pretty much sorted for me to work here half the week.'

Andy's speechless. He hugs her so tightly that she thinks she might expire before she gets a chance to finish her sentence. Untangling herself, Emily leans back to look at him.

'This is all happening a bit too quickly for me,' she says. 'I don't want to be a wet blanket, but we've got a lot of talking to do.'

'Talking's overrated,' Andy says, moving in to kiss her again.

At that moment, there's a loud banging on the door. 'Come on out of there, Andy. You're missing the party, hun,' shouts Candice.

Emily pushes Andy away, and he sighs.

'Let's find something to wear and go and join the rest of them,' she says. 'I want to see May before she suddenly decides she's tired and has to leave. She told me she'd not stay late. And Tristram wants to talk to me too, or so Colin says.'

'You're in big demand tonight.' Resigned to his fate, Andy's rootling through Vince's wardrobe now. He tries on a pair of jeans but they hang off him so he finds some stretchy jogging pants and a T-shirt instead.

Emily has a similar problem with Gina's clothes but a long shirt with a belt round the waist makes a sort of dress, and they're ready to face the world again.

'I just want to say, before I go out there and get mobbed by all the women when they see my sexy new look, that I can't believe I've been lucky enough to meet you, Em. I promise I'll never let you down if you ever give me a chance to get to know you properly.'

Emily slips her sandals back on and fluffs up her hair. She smiles up at him. 'Just so long as you promise me one other thing too.'

'Anything.'

'Never, ever wear tracksuit bottoms like those again, OK? Right, let's go.'

# Chapter Forty-One

May drains her glass of bubbly and glances around the crowded room. She's not seen either Emily or Andy for a while, which might be a good sign, but just as she's feeling hopeful that romance could be in the air, she sees the two of them emerge through a door at the back of the room, looking flustered, and far less smart than usual. That Candice is hanging around outside. Does the woman never give up?

'Emily,' she calls, getting to her feet, 'have you got a moment?'

Fortunately, there's a break in the music just as May raises her voice, and Emily hears and responds immediately.

'Shall we go over and sit in one of the alcoves?' she says, taking May's arm.

May makes no protest at being supported across to the quietest corner. She's very tired now. There has been a chance to chat to all her favourite people and she's even managed to get a jibe in at That Candice, although the woman's so thick-skinned she probably didn't even realise she was being insulted.

'What's the problem, May? Did you need me?' Emily

asks, as they sit down side by side and both heave sighs of relief.

'I just wanted to say good night, dear,' says May. She leans on Emily and takes her hand. 'Colin says you're staying on in the village, is that right?'

'Yes, I'm so excited about it all. Living in Pengelly will be brilliant.'

'Near to your gran . . . and Andy and Tamsin?'

'Ah, that's the only part of this that bothers me. What if Gran and I drive each other crazy living under the same roof all the time?'

'I shouldn't waste too much time worrying about that,' says May, squeezing Emily's hand. 'Things can change.'

'What do you mean? Hey, you're not matchmaking too, are you? I've already had Vi on my case. I'm not about to move in with Andy. I hardly know him.'

May doesn't reply. The music seems to be getting louder and her head is beginning to spin. It might be the champagne, or it could be the power of her thoughts.

'Have you had enough partying?' asks Emily, after a few moments. 'I can run you home if you like? I'm about on my knees, too. The chickenpox . . . and everything . . . have made me really pathetic.'

'No, thank you, dear. You need to stay here and make sure that woman doesn't try anything else on with Andy. Men are so weak sometimes, even the best ones.'

'If you're sure. I've got to make sure Gran gets home safely, too.'

'Just call me a taxi, if you would. Here's the number.' May rummages in her bag. 'It's a friend of mine in

Mengillan. I warned him he might be needed. He'll be here in ten minutes and he'll see me inside safely.'

'Well, if you're sure?'

May nods, and Emily fishes for her phone and makes the arrangements.

'Just one more thing. I'm too exhausted to go all round saying goodbye to everyone and I've already had a good old chin wag with Tristram, but could you just send your gran over for a minute or two?'

Emily gets up to fetch Julia, then impulsively bends down to hug and kiss May. Neither of them says anything, but the warmth and affection between them is all May needs to keep her going for this last chat of the evening.

Julia is at May's side seconds later. She sits down and slips off her shoes.

'It's slippers for me all day tomorrow,' she says. 'These are crippling me. How have you managed to keep those sparkly numbers on all night, May?'

May laughs. 'I've always loved pretty shoes. Look, Julia, I haven't got much time left.'

'What?' There's alarm in Julia's voice and May curses her thoughtless words.

'I mean, my taxi's probably outside already. This is plenty late enough for me. I just wanted to say how much I've loved sharing the letters with you . . . and, well . . . just being your friend, I suppose.'

Julia frowns. 'You sound very serious. Why are you telling me this now?'

'Well, sometimes I think we miss our opportunities to

say what we feel. At a party when the fizz has been flowing, we've got an excuse.'

'That's true. And for what it's worth, I've loved it too, May. I wish we'd got our heads together earlier. There – I never thought I'd say that, but it's true. The misunderstandings we had are all water under the bridge now. I should have minded my own business. It wasn't your place to stop Charles getting his claws into poor Will. And if you've had a problem in the past with . . . appropriating things . . .'

'Stealing, you mean?' May's voice is sharp.

'It's nothing to be ashamed of, May. Kleptomania is an illness.'

May takes a deep breath and decides none of this is worth pursuing now. Let Julia think what she wants to. It's much too late for soul-searching. The warmth between them is real and the rest is over and done with. The two women look at each other, friends, neighbours, old adversaries . . . so many things. May gets to her feet and they kiss each other on the cheek.

'I'll walk you to your taxi,' says Julia, and May accepts gratefully.

'The side door, please,' she says. 'I'm slipping away quietly. No need for a fuss – it's Tristram's night, after all.'

Back at home and finally in bed, with some effort, May leans back on her pillows, supremely comfortable and completely content. It's been a great party and now is the perfect time to make her final exit. She has what she needs to end her life within easy reach.

May takes the bulky package in her hand, feeling an ominous tingle running through her fingers and up her left arm. They're bound to be strong stuff.

The distant crash of the cat flap heralds Fossil's arrival in the bedroom. He jumps onto the bed and settles down on May's feet, beginning to massage her toes. The gentle pressure gives her the courage to carry on with the job in hand. She digs deep in the envelope for the little leather ring box.

Placing it on the covers, May considers it. The ring that should be inside caused so much trouble for something so small. A lucky charm? Well, maybe, but not for Elsie, Kathryn and Will. If May could solve this final puzzle it would go some way towards easing her conscience, even if Julia's memories never fully return.

May takes the box and holds it in both hands, thinking hard and feeling the now-faint vibrations from the past. She casts her mind back to the time when Will and the girls were frequent visitors to Pengelly, picnicking on the sands, walking along the cliff path, swimming in the sea . . . and sailing.

Charles gave them all the chance to go for short voyages in his boat, May recalls, but Will was the one who came back for more, time and time again. He encouraged Charles in his plans for buying a bigger boat and even, to May's disgust at the time, offered to lend Charles his savings to further the scheme. May always kept a close guard on her own finances. She knew Charles much too well to agree to opening a joint bank account, which was something he'd wanted for years.

Did he think I was born yesterday? wonders May, as she remembers his impassioned pleas.

'But why ever not, darling?' he complained over and over again. 'We're married. We should share everything. Don't you trust me?'

The short answer would have been 'No'. Charles was expansive to a fault if he had money, always standing his round in the pub and contributing to church funds and the lifeboat support appeal, but it trickled through his fingers so quickly that May needed to bolster up his bank account to save him from crippling overdraft fees. What fun he'd have had if he'd had access to May's nest egg, too. She wasn't wealthy before she sold the big house, but her parents had left her with enough money to travel, within reason, and a small portfolio of stocks and shares that never failed to provide a modest but steady income.

May holds the box more tightly, focusing her thoughts on the ring. Somehow, she is sure Will was more involved in its disappearance than his sisters were. And Will was Charles's friend. An idea begins to form in her mind, a flickering candle at first, but burning into a strong flame. What if Charles heard about the opals and saw a way to cash in on Will's devotion? Even worse, could he have put pressure on the boy in other ways to bring him the ring to sell for his own ends?

She shivers as she remembers that Charles wasn't above blackmail to get what he believed was his due. He probably threatened to tell Will's family about their liaison. There was a very nasty incident with a young man from Truro early in their marriage when May still had some illusions about her husband, and it almost ended in a gaol sentence for Charles. May needed to step in with an alibi and a shining character reference for him that time. She found it hard to forgive and forget that episode. It was at that point she first had the shameful thought that if Charles were to die, it would be no loss to the world.

Thinking back to the mystery of the ring, May is sure that if Charles got hold of it from Will, he couldn't have sold it. If he did, the box would have gone with it, and there was no upturn in his fortunes, and no new boat. So what did he do with it if he did indeed manage to appropriate it? If it was secreted in the house, May would surely have found it when she cleared the place, even if it was tucked away safe from prying eyes. She did a very thorough job of sorting. It took weeks. Even more puzzling, how did the empty box get into Don's hands? If the ring was in it, Julia would have been wearing it long ago.

Defeated by the problem, May allows herself to think about Barbara for one last time as she prepares for her final task. The baby girl was so tiny and pretty, with her fuzz of blond hair and rosebud lips. Although May has tried hard over the years to fool herself that she was over all that motherhood nonsense, she finally acknowledges that the precious memories of her daughter have never left her heart.

Where is she now? Would she be interested after all these years to know that May did care about her after all, and only gave her away to provide her with a better life, with two parents who could give Barbara the love she needed? May has a sudden vision of her baby's father, as he was back then. He never knew she was pregnant and now he never will.

Their affair was fleeting but full of passion and laughter. There has never been any need to tell Tristram about Barbara. But now, as she nears the end of her long life, she thinks back to the hours of fun they've had. Tristram, thirty years her junior, seemed to be out of May's range for dalliances, but he made it clear that age was no barrier. She looked so young and Tristram has always seemed ageless. The memories of their times together are fresh in May's mind. The passion was brief but their friendship has grown stronger through the years. Still, all in all, she's glad she didn't tell him about Barbara.

Taking a deep breath, May gathers the scattered letters and the box together with a huge effort and pushes them into the envelope. Lying back on the pillows, she lets her mind wander through her happiest moments. Picnics on the beach, the warm breeze lifting her hair and scattering sand in the sandwiches. Paddling in the shallow waves, splashing and shrieking with her friends. Sitting on the harbour wall watching the gulls squabbling over crab claws, arms wrapped round her knees, deep in thought. Tristram . . .

The bedroom window is open and May can hear the waves on the shingle now. The tide is turning. She smiles faintly as she reaches for the package of letters, clutching it tightly to her chest as she did just before the heart attack. It's ironic that the very things that have been keeping her alive are going to be the death of her. The story of the vicious feud and the other darker secret hidden in the envelope will easily be enough to finish her off.

Pain lands like a sledgehammer, pushing the breath from her body and making sweat bead on her forehead. It hurts even more than she expected. Waves of nausea roll over May's rigid body, making her stomach lurch and her heart pound. She thinks vaguely about dropping the packet, maybe finding the one that's doing the worst of the damage and getting rid of it so nobody will ever know what she did, but her fingers can't let go now, clamped around the letters like a vice. There's a pulse throbbing in her thumbs. Her final heartbeats. The room darkens. Now everything is fading to black. The last sound May hears is the rhythmic purring of the cat, fast asleep on her feet. It's over.

# Chapter Forty-Two

The seagulls are awake long before Emily is ready to get up the next morning, wheeling and crying. It was a late night and she's still tired but she finally gives up on sleep and rolls out of bed at six, remembering that May will probably be gasping for her first cup of tea of the day by now. Slipping into the now familiar uniform of shorts and T-shirt, she peers at the world outside the window. It's overcast again, muggy and oppressive, although there's no mist today. The weather matches Emily's mood. Even the sea is a depressing slate grey. She grabs a warm sweater and heads for the stairs.

Across the road, the curtains are still shut and Fossil is waiting by the back door pretending he's forgotten how to use the cat flap, as he sometimes does. He winds himself around Emily's ankles as she goes into the kitchen. The silence doesn't alarm her to begin with, because May never has the radio on in her room and she might still be fast asleep, but as she enters the bedroom, she knows immediately that all is not well.

'Oh, May,' she whispers, bending over the bed to look more closely, 'I should have come sooner.'

She takes the lifeless hand in hers, desperately hoping

that the old lady is just deeply asleep, but the papery skin is cold. May's eyes are closed and her mouth is slightly open. She looks peaceful but very vulnerable lying there. It's the first time Emily's experienced death at first hand, and she begins to tremble, unsure of what to do next. Her heart skips a beat as she hears the back door open again and Tristram's voice shouting, 'Hello, May, I'm coming in.'

Emily turns to face May's old friend as he stands in the doorway, breathing deeply as he takes in the scene.

'I'm too late, aren't I?' he says. 'All of a sudden I was afraid I would be. Even though I ran the last bit, for some daft reason.'

'I think she's been gone for some time. She must have been worse than we realised. The heart attack really knocked her about, I guess.'

Tristram doesn't reply. His eyes are wet with tears. He approaches the bed and leans over May, gently touching her cheek.

'Precious May,' is all he says.

They stand quietly for a moment, each lost in their own thoughts, and then Emily stirs herself. 'We'd better phone somebody, hadn't we? There's no point in ringing an ambulance. What do we do, Tristram?'

'The doctor? Can you go down and get May's telephone book from next to her chair? She's got all the important numbers written in it.'

As Emily leaves the bedroom, she sees Tristram lean over to kiss May's forehead. Then he begins to smooth the covers around her. He picks up a big brown envelope that's fallen to the floor and pops it into the bedside cabinet. What a kind man, she thinks. He wants May to be as tidy in death as she was in life.

Downstairs, Emily tries to stop her hands from shaking as she finds the number and rings the out-of-hours doctor. Then she goes and puts the kettle on because she can't think what else to do. She gets out mugs, milk and teabags, adds a sugar bowl in case Tristram isn't as calm as he looks and goes into shock, and when there's nothing left to organise, Emily sits down at the table and begins to cry.

Much later, when the doctor has played his part and the undertaker has collected May to take her to the chapel of rest, Julia and Emily go across to Andy's house armed with May's trusty phone book.

He gives them both a hug and Emily wishes she could stay like this, leaning her head on his shoulder, feeling his strength and warmth and just letting somebody else take charge. She moves away, feeling the chill take over again. It's the first time she's felt warm all day, in that hug.

'You've got a lot of layers on for an almost-summer day,' says Andy. 'You're not coming down with something else, are you, Emily?'

It's lovely to be fussed over, even if it's only as a friend, but Emily hates to see the worried look on his face. 'No, it's just that I've felt so cold ever since I saw May this morning. I'll be fine when I've had a hot drink.'

'You've drunk gallons of tea today already,' says Julia.

Her eyes are red and she's looking her age. Emily feels a pang of worry and Andy seems to sense that Julia needs more than caffeine at this moment.

'How about a glass of wine then? It's after six and I'm not going anywhere.'

'Is Tamsin out?' Emily looks round as if she expects the little girl to pop out from under the table.

'Yes, erm . . . she's got a play date with Summer. They'll bring her back about seven, I hope. Any later than that and she gets so overtired there's no dealing with her.'

'Oh, yes, Summer's Candice's daughter, isn't she?' says Julia, looking across at Emily.

'I see. Well, we'd better not hang around drinking wine if you're expecting company,' Emily says.

'You're kidding, aren't you? All the more reason to stay and protect me.' Andy gets out a bottle of cabernet sauvignon and three glasses.

'Not much for me, thank you, dear,' says Julia.

'Oh, go on – just this once won't hurt.' Andy uncorks the wine and pours generously, handing Emily and Julia their drinks.

'Do you want to sit round the table or go into the living room while we make some of these calls?' he asks.

'Let's stay here.' Emily doesn't want to be reminded of the Dire-Straits-and-vomiting evening. She sits at the table and Julia flops down too.

The radio's playing softly in the background, some sort of easy-listening soft rock, and Emily finally begins to relax. 'It's been a bit of a day,' she says, as Julia raises her eyebrows at the already half-empty wine glass.

'I bet. I can hardly believe she's gone. It's as if we've lost our anchor.' Andy tops up Emily's glass.

The three of them sit in silence for a few minutes, listening to the music and letting the rich red wine do its magic. After a while, Emily begins to leaf through the phone book.

'Where do we start? The undertaker asked if there were family members to contact but I had no idea, and neither did Gran, did you?' she says, turning to Julia.

'I've been thinking since then – I could be wrong, darling, but I'm sure May said she was the last of her line. Is there anybody in the book who sounds hopeful?'

As they plough through the job of ringing the random people in May's book, the back door opens and Tamsin bounces in, followed by Candice and a small girl with white-blond hair, just like her mother's.

'Hi, sweetie,' Candice says to Andy, ignoring the rest of them and giving him a kiss on each cheek.

'Oh, hello there. Has Tam been good?'

'I always am, aren't I? Good as gold,' Candice says. 'Why is gold good, Daddy?' says Tamsin, crawling under the table before he can answer. Summer follows and the giggling begins.

Candice rolls her eyes at Andy and smiles. 'They've done a lot of laughing but they've been fine, as always,' she says.

Emily makes a valiant attempt to hide her instinctive loathing of this perfectly made-up woman but her mouth feels as pinched as if she's been sucking a lemon. How can Candice look so smart and tidy after having tea with these two hyperactive six-year-olds? They're out from under the table now and trying to escape into the garden.

'Hey, not so fast,' says Andy, catching Tamsin as she flies past. 'It's time for your bath.'

'Oh, noooooo.'

'Can't we just have five minutes' play outside?' says Summer, making big eyes at him.

Just like her bloody mother, thinks Emily. Now we're going to be stuck with them for ages and I bet Candice will manage to get some wine out of him before she goes.

But Andy's made of sterner stuff. He's soon dispatched Tamsin upstairs to find clean pyjamas and is easing the two blondes out of the door, saying good night as they go. Candice flings her arms around his neck for a hug and Summer does similar at waist level.

'I'll see you at the school gates, sweetie,' Candice says. 'We must do this again soon. Tamsin's a little treasure; she's welcome any time.'

As the door closes behind them, Andy heaves a sigh of relief.

'I'll try to make bath-time double quick and be down as soon as I can,' he calls over his shoulder as he heads for the stairs after Tamsin. 'Help yourself to more wine.'

Emily picks up the telephone book again. Exhaustion creeps over her as she ends yet another call to someone who is sad to hear of May's passing but not devastated.

'How does all this make you feel, Gran?' she says.

'In what way? I guess it's harder with it being the first death since we lost your grandpa. Did you mean how do I feel about May's death, or dealing with the aftermath?'

'Both, really. You were friends, weren't you?'

'In the end we were, but we hadn't been close over the years. I was only just beginning to understand what made her tick. Now she's gone I'm desperately sorry we didn't make the effort to smooth over our differences sooner. She was a complicated woman, but very interesting. There were so many of my own memories I wanted to share with her, but I left it too late. It was unfair of me to blame May for Charles's manipulative ways, but he was the sort of man who could and did cause a lot of damage and get away with it.'

'Was there something in particular that wound you up so much?'

Emily can just hear Andy reading a story to Tamsin now, his voice rising and falling as he does all the funny voices. She wants to creep closer and listen but Julia is speaking again now.

'Yes, there was, but I should have made time to talk to May more. She was so isolated when she came to live down here on Memory Lane.'

Julia's eyes are wet, and Emily reaches for her hand, still thinking about the long stand-off between the two charismatic older ladies.

'You shouldn't feel bad about it, Gran. Maybe you didn't have anything to say to each other at the time?'

'No, you could be right. But there are things I wish I'd discussed with her. She was so . . . instinctive. She understood a lot more than she let on. And I let what happened with Charles colour how I felt about May.'

Emily waits. Is Gran finally going to come clean about why she froze May out for so long?

'It was Will, you see. He was so fragile, both in body and mind. And when I caught Charles . . .'

'Go on, you might as well tell me now. I think you need to, don't you?'

Julia twists her hands together. 'Charles had got Will backed up against the graveyard wall. If Will hadn't cried out, I'd never have looked, but I saw them, and they saw me. Charles had his hands on Will's chest and he was just starting to unbutton his shirt.'

'But . . . what was Will doing about it? Was he pushing him away?'

'No, but he looked at me with such confusion on his face. His eyes were all glittery and excited but he seemed ashamed at the same time. I think Will had never dared to do anything like that before. He wanted it to happen, but he was disgusted with himself for how he felt, if you know what I mean? I was so angry with Charles for forcing his hand.'

'What did you do?'

'Well, you see – that's the thing, Emily. I did nothing. I was so shocked I just rushed away. When I got home, I planned to talk to Will when he got back for tea. But he never did.'

'What?'

'Oh, don't look so tragic. Nothing bad happened to him. He just left without a word. He sent a message with Elsie later to say he'd been invited to a party and he'd be very late. He came back after we'd gone to bed, packed, and we later found out that he hitch-hiked all the way back home. Don was horrified.'

'But didn't you say something the next time he visited?'

'I was going to, but I was away visiting my mother when Will came again. She was very ill . . . dying in fact. He didn't stay long, and it was soon after that he joined the priesthood and went to Ireland. It was around the time that Charles drowned, but I missed all that. I stayed with my mother for over a month until she passed away. Afterwards, I planned to have it out with Charles, but of course it was too late by then.'

Emily is stunned by all this. If only Gran had talked this over with May. And now even that's not possible.

'You'll miss May very much,' she says eventually.

'I will, and so will Tristram.' Julia's looking more like herself again now, and Emily thinks it must have been a huge relief to get those memories off her chest at last.

'It seems so awful that although everyone in the village seems to have quite liked May, nobody cares enough to weep and wail,' she says. 'There should be some of that after a death, surely? Howling and keening? Well, maybe not so extreme in this case but at least a few tears. Or are we just too buttoned up in Britain?'

Julia thinks about this, frowning slightly. 'I see your point,' she says, finally. 'But May was her own woman. She sometimes seemed a bit bored with her life but I don't think she was unhappy, even if she was sometimes lonely. Perhaps no one knew her well enough to feel the sort of raw grief that comes with close bereavements.'

'Like you felt after Grandpa died?' Emily doesn't

usually like to bring up those awful first days when her gran cried constantly and was unable to eat or sleep.

'Well, yes. Don and I were partners. We did pretty much everything together. We made each other laugh, argued about lots of things, but not seriously, and we talked all the time; it was such fun being married to him. Drinking tea in bed, with him reading snippets from the newspaper out to me, and me filling him in on the village gossip.'

'That sounds wonderful.'

'Yes, but the silence afterwards was hideous, especially in the mornings. I missed having someone to start the day with – to run through everything that was planned and so on. And the weekends seemed endless. May and Charles were never like that.'

Andy walks back into the long pause that follows Julia's words. Both women look sombre, clutching their now-empty glasses as if they're lifelines.

'I think I'd better open another bottle,' he says. 'It looks like it's going to be a long night.'

# Chapter Forty-Three

Later that night, when Julia and Emily are rather blearily making macaroni cheese to cancel out the wine, they hear footsteps coming down the side of the house and Tristram's voice calling, 'Are you at home, ladies?'

He comes into the kitchen, sniffing rapturously. 'That smells wonderful. We've been eating leftovers all day to make our hangovers better but I could use something hot.'

'There's plenty. I'm just going to put the dish in the oven to brown. It's good to see you,' says Julia. 'It's been a difficult day.'

They sit around the table and quietness descends. It's very peaceful, and Emily's eyelids begin to droop.

'Hey, don't fall asleep on me. I didn't just come round to cadge food, I'm here to tell you something important, Emily,' Tristram says, leaning forward.

'Do you want me to go somewhere else? Is this private?' Julia's half standing now, but Emily raises a hand.

'There can't be anything Tris wants to say that you can't hear, can there, Gran? We haven't got secrets from each other any more, have we?'

Tristram smiles. 'Right. Well, I don't know if I told you that May asked me to call in and see her, not so long ago?'

'Yes, I remember.'

'Well, amongst other things, May told me in confidence she'd decided to make a new will. She was planning to write it herself because it was very straightforward and she wanted me to post it to her solicitor, Trevor Marshall. He's in Mengillan. She'd written it all out ready.'

'Wow. This is like a mystery story. Carry on, I can't wait to hear what she wrote.'

'Well, at the last minute she changed her mind and rang Trevor to come to her to draft the will. She was worried it wasn't going to be legal, and he'd got the copy of her old one at his office so she was mad keen to let him know this one superseded it. She wanted me to be her executor and we asked Vi to be the second witness.'

'But what was it all about? Why did she need a new one so suddenly?'

'May was sometimes impulsive but she'd really mulled this idea over, and I think she had a feeling she hadn't got long left with us. Anyway, Trev's going to ring you soon to make an appointment but May said that if anything was to happen to her, I was to be the one to talk to you first to prepare you.'

'Talk to *me*? But why?'

Tristram smiles at Emily, his eyes very kind. 'Because, my lovely girl, May has left her cottage and a considerable lump sum of money to *you*.'

The silence following this bombshell seems to stretch indefinitely. Emily and Julia stare at Tristram. 'So that was what you were getting at when you dragged me out of the party to tell me about your future plans?' Emily finally blurts out.

'Yes. I couldn't give you details or tell you why you might be involved in them too because I had no idea how long May would be with us. I hoped it would be ages yet,' he says sadly.

'What's all this about?' Julia asks, but Tristram won't be drawn. 'It's not the time for that yet,' he says. 'Let's get the practicalities out of the way, and then we three are going to need to have a very big chat. Now, I'm starving. Did someone say macaroni cheese? We need to eat before Trevor gets on the case.'

Sure enough, only minutes after Tristram has eaten a hasty bowl of pasta and left them alone, Trevor rings.

'He's sorry to ring so late in the day but he wants to see you tomorrow morning, if possible,' whispers Julia with her hand over the receiver. 'What shall I say?'

'Tell him the earlier the better. This is so weird. I want to know all the details so that I might begin to believe it. Can May really have left me everything? Why ever would she?'

The next day, Trevor arrives almost before breakfast is cleared away, carrying a battered leather briefcase and a bunch of yellow roses.

'I brought these for both of you. They're from my garden,' he says shyly, handing them over. 'I always used to bring some for Mrs Rosevere. She liked them because they've got a proper scent. The yellow ones were her favourites.'

'May did love flowers that had a fragrance,' says Julia. 'And so do I. I'll need to organise something a bit special for the top of her coffin. I'll do them myself and we can all contribute something from our own places. The ferns and other foliage in May's garden will be good for filling it out, and there's some beautiful lavender.'

'Do we know when the funeral is yet?' asks Trevor.

'Monday of next week. It's all been sorted fairly quickly. The Methodist minister was free and there was a slot at the crematorium. May didn't mind if we used the church or the chapel, according to Tristram. There's nobody else to wait for – no family – so Tristram's helping us plan it. He's got the instructions that May left.'

Emily sits through all this small talk with growing impatience. When will he get to the point of his visit? Then she notices that he's casting sideways glances at Julia, who spots this at the same time.

'I'll leave you two alone to go over the paperwork,' she says. 'Call when you're ready for a cup of tea.'

Trevor smiles at her gratefully and sits down at the table, moving a heap of letters to one side. 'I see you brought all these back from across the road,' he says. 'Mrs Rosevere told me how interesting they were.'

'Oh, yes, they're interesting all right. Andy carried them over for us. I'm hoping we can use them in some constructive way. It'd be such a shame to waste them.' Julia's on her way out now and closes the kitchen door behind her.

Emily grins at the solicitor. 'I think she means she now wants *me* to write a book using the letters as a jumping-off point. Subtlety isn't Gran's strong point.'

'Will you do it?'

'I'm certainly going to consider the idea. There's a mystery hidden in there. A missing piece of jewellery. Gran would really love to have it.'

'Hmm. Intriguing.'

There's a silence as Trevor peers into his case. Then he pulls out two long envelopes. 'Both of these concern you, Miss Lovell,' he says, 'but I think I'll just give you the first one to read for yourself.'

'Could you call me Emily, do you think? Miss Lovell always sounds like an ancient spinster in tweeds.' She takes the envelope and looks down at the neat copperplate handwriting. Her name is on the front, but nothing else. She opens it and draws out the letter.

My dear Emily,

By the time you read this, I'll have found out if all that religious malarkey is true or not. If it is, I'll either be on a cloud wearing a nice pair of wings or down below, somewhere much hotter. If there's no truth in it, who knows what's happened to me? Anyway, that's not important.

What I want to talk about, Emily, is what happens next to YOU. Over the years when you've visited Pengelly I've watched you grow into a lovely young woman with a very kind heart and it's been my great pleasure to know you. These days, getting onto the property ladder is nigh on impossible, what with rising costs, shortage of suitable housing and all the rest of it, and I haven't got any family to pass my house to.

So my idea of giving you a leg up, as it were, is to give you a few more life choices.

I would love it if you decided to live in my little cottage, at least for a while, but I'm not making any silly conditions. You can do with it what you will. The building and its contents can be kept, sold or given away, as you wish.

Consider carefully who you share the house with, if anyone. You can be free now, hopefully much less tied down by mortgage and money worries (unless you've been silly enough to get yourself into debt already).

I wish you a very happy life, dear, and a lot of love, whichever way you choose to find it. Take care of my friend Julia – she has become very precious to me in a short time, although we've known each other for years. Also keep an eye on the lovely Andy and Tamsin, if you would. You could do worse . . . but I mustn't interfere.

Your gran's letters are going to be a very significant part of your life, I think. There's a book to be written in there somewhere. I know she's thought of tackling it herself but I think it makes more sense if you did it? A family feud, sisterly love, a sense of history . . . a missing link . . . do it, Emily.

Goodbye and good luck. Oh, and could you take charge of poor old Fossil for me, too? He's not long for this world and he smells a bit, but he's a good soul in his way.

Much love,
May Rosevere

Emily finishes reading May's letter and looks over at Trevor, who's got up to stand by the window overlooking the bay. His hands are in his pockets.

Emily clears her throat. 'What a random, generous thing to do, isn't it?' she says, blinking hard. She doesn't want to cry in front of the solicitor – he'd probably self-destruct with embarrassment.

'Generous, yes, but not random at all – Mrs Rosevere knew exactly what she was doing. And for the record, I think she was quite right.'

He blushes furiously and is suddenly very interested in a magpie perched on Julia's birdbath. Emily follows his gaze. One for sorrow, she thinks. Well, there's plenty of that at the moment. She takes a deep breath and gets herself under control. 'And the will?' she says.

Trevor turns round and comes back to the table. 'It's very simple. The cottage and the legacy of cash go to you. There's been money set aside for her funeral – that's already lodged with the undertaker at the top of the hill. She's added a separate sheet with her instructions for the service and cremation. She did consider burial but there were no plots available in the churchyard. I know Tristram has a copy of all this, too.'

'She's thought of everything. It seems incredible. And all her worldly goods to me?'

Trevor collects a few stray papers together busily and doesn't reply.

'And I can't even say thank you,' Emily continues.

'It's not for me to comment really, but I'd like to say

that the best way to thank Mrs Rosevere is to enjoy her gift to the full.'

'Oh, I will. I really will.'

'Do you think you'll want to live in the property? It's a fine little cottage, with some of the best views in the village.'

Emily leans back in her chair, more peaceful than she's felt for a very long time. To live in May's cottage and eventually produce a book? Can she do it? She'll have a place to call her own, where she can write to her heart's content, if she chooses to do so. If she decides that this is the right plan, she must make sure she lives like May lived: independent at heart, even if she does find a partner to share things with; brave and full of humour when things don't go to plan. Emily thinks of May and her wonderful legacy with a surge of gratitude that takes her breath away.

'It seems like an option, at least for now,' she says. 'And later . . . who can tell?'

# Chapter Forty-Four

The next few days seem to drag endlessly. The day before May's funeral, Emily asks Julia if she will come over to the cottage with her, just to help her to get a feel for the fact that it's Emily's now. They stand in the kitchen and look around, feeling like interlopers.

'There are so many treasures here,' says Julia. 'It'll be hard to know where to start when you begin to sort everything out. Look at those old tins on the shelf, for instance. They must be collectors' items now.'

Emily remembers the Bovril tin and its bizarre contents. She reaches for the canister that used to hold Cornish fairings, prises off the lid and tips out the contents onto the table. Julia gasps.

'What's all this rubbish?' she says, running her fingers through the small heap. There's a hairclip with a tattered flower attached, a pair of silver cufflinks, an ancient lipstick, a tiny photograph of the Queen in a gilt frame and some silver sugar tongs.

'I knew she'd taken those tongs,' exclaims Julia, picking them out and holding them up to the light, 'but why all these other things?'

'I have absolutely no idea, and actually, I don't want to know,' says Emily. 'Let's go home.'

The sun breaks through the clouds as the two of them go back across the lane and Emily takes that as a good omen for the next day's ordeal, but May's final goodbye takes place on the wettest day of the summer so far. The rain has been bucketing down since before dawn. Small rivulets of water are gaining strength as they pour down Memory Lane, joining forces as they go. Julia's conservatory has sprung a leak again and her begonias have all but been washed away. The clouds are low and heavy, and there's no way Julia and Emily will be able to walk up to the chapel without ending up looking like drowned rats.

The rain beats against the windows of the kitchen. The tide is out, but the dark grey of the sea and the overcast skies dominates the room. Julia has even had to put the light on. The fire is lit, but Emily still feels shivery. Tristram arrives, bringing a blast of cold air with him, dressed head to foot in ancient oilskins with his funeral-organising clipboard in a plastic bag. He drips on the doormat as he unpeels his outer clothing, shivering as stray droplets run down his exposed neck.

Emily goes over to give him a hug, flinching as his cold cheek touches hers. Tristram has been the mainstay of the funeral arrangements, with his checklist of May's requirements and a lot more of his own ideas of what would make a fitting send-off for his old friend. They couldn't have coped without him.

'Everything's going to plan. The Shack's all ready for the big event. Fancy – two big parties in quick succession.'

'This one's hardly a party,' says Julia, reproachfully.

'Oh, but it is. May wanted a good send-off and I'm making sure she gets it. The dogs have gone into kennels for the night, to their disgust. Buster can't be trusted near a kitchen any more and even Bruno was showing an interest in all the good smells. Gina and Vince have prepared all the pasties and mash for the wake,' he says. 'It was May's favourite dinner, and Vince has produced five different kinds, including two veggie options.'

'It sounds amazing.'

'Everyone can toast May in port and brandy or gin and tonic or peach spritzers or Virgin Bloody Marys. And there's champagne, obviously, and tea and coffee for those who want it, although personally, this sort of occasion always makes me want to get seriously drunk afterwards.'

'I'm with you on that one,' says Emily, dreading it already.

The phone rings and Julia pounces on it. She's been waiting for Andy to call to make arrangements to get to the service. 'Andy? Hello! . . . That's lovely. Come over here for half-past eleven and we'll have time for a quick coffee before we set off. The service is at half-past twelve. See you soon . . . No, there's no need to wear black. In fact, May said she'd like everyone to wear their favourite brightly coloured clothes. Bye.'

'That was Andy,' she says unnecessarily. Tristram and Emily exchange grins. 'Oh, and he says he'll run us up to the chapel if the rain doesn't stop, or even if it does. I'll be glad of a lift. There's no point in getting all dressed up if we're going to look as if we've just stepped out of the shower.'

Emily heads upstairs to try to find something to wear. She's left it very late because she still feels less than sparkling. Her hair is not as glossy as usual and her skin is dull and pallid.

After a search, Emily finds a purple dress at the back of the wardrobe that fits the bill. She hasn't worn it since she was eighteen but it's a classic style, ending just above knee length, with long sleeves, a Chinese-style collar and tiny silver buttons all down the front. She can dress it up with some glitzy accessories and her highest heels. Maybe her pale violet pashmina draped around her shoulders? She tries the whole lot on and it works.

Julia comes into Emily's bedroom just as she's about to look for a suitable necklace.

'You look absolutely beautiful, darling,' she says, standing back to admire the complete look. 'Have you looked at May's jewellery at all? It's yours now, of course. It might be a nice gesture to wear something that belonged to her.'

'Oh, that's a lovely idea,' Emily says. 'I'll put my comfy clothes on again and go over.'

'I can come with you if you like?'

'No, I think I need to do this on my own. As you say, it's mine now. It was bound to feel weird the first time I went there after May died, but I'm sure this time will be fine. Andy's been really good feeding Fossil for me, but I need to do what May would have done and just get on with it.'

Emily changes out of her funeral outfit quickly and heads across the road, wrapped in her grandfather's old wax jacket over leggings and a warm jumper. When she reaches the door, she falters for a minute but there's no point in hanging around. As she fumbles for the key in its not-so-secret hiding place, she thinks she might keep it with her from now on. Pengelly's not got much of a crime rate, if any, but an empty house is a bit too much of a sitting target.

A wave of musty air hits her as she enters the kitchen so she leaves the back door open. Stepping inside, Emily's heart sinks. The cottage feels so empty without May's lively presence, and sadness hits her all over again. Heavy footsteps on the garden path make her jump and she drops the key with a clatter. She turns, wondering what she'll do if it's someone after May's treasures. The sight of Andy in the doorway is both a relief and a worry. She'll have the chance to tell him what's happened now, but she's not looking forward to it. He must have a very low opinion of her.

'Oh, it's you. I heard a noise and I thought I'd better check,' says Andy. He grins. 'Vi's just come round to get her instructions for looking after Tam during the funeral; it's a school INSET day. I figured it was safe to nip out for a minute to make sure May wasn't being burgled.'

'That was sweet of you.' Emily looks at the yard brush he's clutching. 'Were you planning on sweeping them to death?'

He laughs. 'It was the first thing I grabbed. Think

yourself lucky; I could have gone into battle with the Hoover.'

'Well, it was a lovely thought, anyway. I was just going to see if I could find something of May's to wear later – a necklace or something. Gran thought it'd be a sort of tribute. Does that sound weird?'

'No, it sounds great. I think she'd be really touched.' He comes into the kitchen and leans on the table, looking at Emily properly for the first time. 'So, how have you been?'

Emily clasps her hands together. There's no easy way to say this, but she so wants him not to think too badly of her. 'I'm not doing too well, I guess. The chickenpox has gone but I'm just . . . so sad.'

The silence is deafening. He puts down his sweeping brush and shoves his hands into his pockets, as if he daren't let himself even think about touching her. When the moment has stretched way too long, he asks, 'I probably shouldn't ask this, but are you sorry not to be having Max's baby?'

'No. But I feel mixed up, somehow. I've never thought about being a mum before, or only in an abstract sort of way, but now, I keep wondering . . .'

Emily begins to cry, cursing herself for her weakness. Andy takes his hands out of his pockets and comes towards her. He looks down at her tear-streaked face and then tenderly puts his arms around her. She hesitates for barely a second before she moves closer and leans on him, revelling in the luxury of a man who doesn't seem to be demanding anything. She can tell he just wants to make her feel better. He holds her close, kissing the top of her head as she sobs wordlessly, letting out the regrets and the lost hopes, letting herself relax into this safe haven.

'Look, Em, you've made a mistake, but we've all done that,' he says. 'There's no harm done. A baby right now would have been difficult. Max is out of the picture, isn't he? You'll have other chances, if you want them.'

'Yes, he's gone. I don't know why I let it go on so long. But I feel so awful that I risked a child's future. What if a baby had actually been born? To a mum and dad who hadn't got much to say to each other any more and didn't even like each other very much?'

'It happens.'

'But it shouldn't. I know I've been totally irresponsible. If I ever think about doing the whole mum thing properly in the future, I'll make sure I pick someone who wants me and wants my children.'

'Hang on a minute.' Andy steps back to look at her, still holding her shoulders. 'This isn't all about you. Max has a role here, too. He must have had a hand in being reckless?'

'Max never admits responsibility for anything.'

'What a bastard. If he were here, he'd feel the might of my sweeping brush.'

Suddenly they're laughing, and it's so good not to feel guilty for a while. Emily glances at her watch and moves away from Andy, heading for the bedroom. 'We're running out of time. We can't be late for May's funeral. Come and help me choose something sparkly to wear?'

Andy follows her, and together they tip out the contents of May's meagre jewellery box onto the bed.

'That's the one,' says Andy, pointing to a glittering array of amethysts.

'That's May's Aunt Barbara's necklace, Andy. I've worn it before – May was really proud of it. And not only that, it matches the dress I'm going to wear. Brilliant.'

Emily picks up the necklace but Andy takes it from her hands and fastens it around her neck, turning her so that she can see them both in May's wardrobe mirror. He slips his arms round her waist and Emily leans back against him as they look at their reflections. The necklace clashes with Emily's sweater but her eyes are shining.

'It's perfect,' she says.

'At the risk of sounding as if I wrote this cheesy script earlier, so are you.'

Emily turns to face him and he bends to kiss her.

Eventually, Emily surfaces, head spinning. 'We've got to go; we'll be late,' she says. 'I need to get changed and Gran will be wondering what's happened to me.'

Andy takes her hand and leads her to the back door. 'We'll talk about all this after the funeral,' he says. 'But for now, you just have to know that this is the best thing that's happened to me for years.'

'Me, too.'

'And I want to say that even if you'd been pregnant with triplets, it still wouldn't have stopped me kissing you. Is that bad?'

Emily locks the door behind them as they leave May's

. . . no, not May's, her own house. She smiles at him. 'Not bad, just a bit . . . reckless?'

'Pot calling kettle?'

'You've got a point. Right, I'm going to go and try to make myself look presentable and there's not much time left to do it in. See you very soon.'

Andy kisses Emily again, but briefly this time. His lips are warm and she can feel the stubble on his chin. She reaches up to touch it. 'Are you shaving today, or going for the Poldark look?'

'Which do you prefer?'

She laughs. 'Either is fine by me. I'm not hard to please. So long as you bring a spare umbrella and make sure I don't disgrace myself by drinking too much fizz.'

'It's a deal. See you soon. I need to go and get into my suit and check there's no Weetabix or chocolate stuck to the sleeves.'

They part company in the lane and Emily goes back to prepare for May's last goodbye. As she crosses the road, she notices that the rain's stopped at last. A few rays of watery sunshine are trying to warm up the atmosphere, and there's a wonderful scent of wet earth mingling with the salty air. Today is definitely looking up.

# Chapter Forty-Five

The suit was expensive when it was new, and Andy is grateful for that, although wearing your wedding gear for a good friend's funeral is always going to be depressing. He stares at himself in the mirror and fixes his tie so that it doesn't look quite so much as if it's strangling him.

Vi nods approvingly as he comes downstairs. 'You've picked a very suitable tie,' she says. 'May liked bright colours. You can't go wrong with scarlet, can you?'

'I wish I could come,' says Tamsin sadly. 'Will you be long, Daddy?'

'I'll bring you a pasty and a piece of cake back from the buffet.'

'And for Vi. She likes cake.'

'For both of you. I'm going now. It's stopped raining but I'm taking the car so that I can give Julia and Emily a lift.'

He kisses the top of Tamsin's head and waves to Vi, mouthing 'Thank you' as he leaves the room.

Julia and Emily are just coming across the lane as he starts the engine, and they climb into the Land Rover, being careful not to snag their tights on the random pieces of garden equipment.

'I did mean to clean it out, but Tamsin's been a bit demanding today,' Andy says, pushing a strimmer onto the floor and brushing grass cuttings off the passenger seat. 'Sit on this bin bag, Julia. Then you won't get dirty.'

Julia does as she's told without comment. She's holding herself together fairly well at the moment, but Andy knows how hard this is for her. It's the first funeral she's been to since Don's, and it's in the same chapel and crematorium.

'The undertaker came and picked the flowers up this morning,' she says. 'Do you think May would have liked them, darling?'

'They're gorgeous, Gran. You're so clever. How do you know how to do that sort of fancy arrangement? I wouldn't have a clue where to start.'

'I went on a course at the village hall. Ida organised it. She's good like that. There's another one coming up soon for all of her Adopt-a-Granny gang. Then we're doing a gardening one.'

Julia burbles on for a couple of minutes about foliage and so on but falls silent as they pull into the chapel car park. The forbidding granite building is nowhere near as attractive as the mellow stone church further up the road, but Andy likes it better. It's solid and comfortable, with a beautifully polished wooden pulpit and long pews covered in faded flowery cushions, flattened by years of use.

'Oh, good, somebody's been in and done the rest of the flowers. Ida said it was all in hand,' whispers Julia, reaching for Emily's arm as they go up the aisle.

Andy looks around, amazed. On every pew end is a hanging display of yellow roses and that frothy white stuff. He can never remember its name – gypsy-something or other. Gardeners should have these names on the tip of their tongues, he tells himself. The stand in front of the pulpit holds a huge arrangement of more yellow and white flowers. Andy recognises chrysanthemums and tulips, plus delicate wild flowers and grasses in between. May would definitely approve – it's a riot of colour.

The organist is playing a random selection of background music. Snatches of songs from the shows blend with classical favourites, very un-Methodist but relaxing. They must be some of May's choices, from Tristram's list. Andy checks in his pocket for the reading that's his contribution. He hopes he'll be able to get through it without disgracing himself, but it won't be easy.

He wanted to say something at Allie's funeral – it would have been good to stand up and tell everyone about her love of children and how she'd longed for a baby and how excited she'd been when she knew she was having Tamsin – but he had to settle for writing it down and giving it to the minister. Some of the kids from the school where she was a teaching assistant were there and sang a song that she particularly liked. It was 'I Can See Clearly Now', and Andy remembers thinking how sweet but inappropriate it was when crippling grief meant he couldn't see anything clearly for his tears.

'They're here,' hisses someone in the row behind, and everyone shuffles to their feet. The minister starts to intone the familiar words as he leads the sad procession up the aisle.

As he struggles to hold it together, Andy feels Emily's hand slide into his and link fingers with him. Her warmth is comforting and reassuring. He looks across to see how Julia is doing and realises that Emily has her other arm around her grandmother's waist. Standing up straight, she's supporting them both with her presence, strong and steadfast. He breathes again. He can do this with Emily by his side.

'Please be seated,' says the minister, smiling down at them all from the pulpit. 'We are gathered here today to celebrate the life of May Frances Rosevere, a friend to all of us and much missed. We will be singing one of May's favourite hymns in a moment, which her neighbour, Andy, tells me she used to join in with at top volume during *Songs of Praise*, but first, a few words from Tristram to tell us how May arranged her service, and what we can expect.'

Tristram comes to the front of the church and Andy can't help being impressed by his outfit. He's wearing an old-fashioned frock coat in palest grey, charcoal-grey trousers with knife-edge pleats, the whitest shirt imaginable, a lemon-coloured brocade waistcoat and a yellow and white cravat. In his buttonhole is one perfect yellow rose.

'I'm not going to talk for long, folks – that's May's first instruction, and I quote: "You can be a bit of a windbag, Tristram, so wrap it up fast, understood?"'

There's a burst of laughter, and Andy begins to relax. This isn't like losing Allie. May had a good long life and she was probably ready to go in the end. He leans back and loosens his hold on Emily's hand, but she holds fast, settling herself so she's closer to him, near enough to distract him from what Tristram is saying. With an effort, he zones in again.

'. . . so all I want to say is that I was proud to have May as a friend for many years. Some of you children out there, and I mean the ones under sixty,' more laughter, 'will have thought of May and me as just two poor, lonely elderly folk keeping each other company in their declining years. May was thirty years older than I am, though – plenty old enough to act like a mum, but mothering wasn't May's style. She was an independent woman with forthright views. A few of you will have experienced the rough side of her tongue if you didn't come up to her standards.' The congregation are really with Tristram now. He'd make a great warm-up act, thinks Andy, smiling up at his friend proudly. 'But all of you will agree that we'll miss May in Pengelly. She was one of a kind. So today's all about celebrating her time with us, and you're all welcome back at The Shack after the cremation – which is going to be a very relaxed affair so if you want to go on ahead of us and open the bubbly to get you in the party mood, feel free. See you later to raise a glass – although I probably shouldn't be saying this in a Methodist Chapel – to our wonderful, feisty friend and companion, May Rosevere.'

A burst of clapping breaks out, and the minister looks thrown for a moment but he gets up and introduces the hymn quickly, before anybody else can make a speech.

They all stand to bellow out 'How Great Thou Art', and their combined voices shake the rafters.

Andy's poem is to come after the minister's review of May's life. He sits clutching his piece of paper as he listens to her story. The minister concludes, 'May was a hundred and ten years old when she died and starting to feel her age just towards the end, but she never lost her sense of humour or her kind heart. She was generous to the last.'

At this, a few heads turn to look at Emily, but she carries on staring straight ahead, and only a slight tightening of her fingers betray how much she must be hating the inmates of Pengelly knowing her business. Word has once again spread and everyone seems to know that she's the new owner of Shangri-La.

Andy squeezes Emily's hand and stands up to do his bit. His legs are shaking now, and he takes deep breaths as he walks to the pulpit. Luckily, May's not chosen the poem his mother had picked to read for Allie – the one about death being nothing at all. Death had felt like a bloody big something at that time. Now, though, with May's passing, it seems a lot less scary. He reads Joyce Grenfell's famous last lines:

> Weep if you must.
> Parting is hell.
> But life goes on.
> So sing as well.

There are a few tears now, and he sees the flutter of tissues in the congregation as they stand to sing another of May's favourites, the one about being in peril on the sea. It's a familiar one in a coastal village, and everyone knows the words.

After a short reading, which May has graciously allowed the vicar to choose, they stand for the next hymn. May's chosen well. 'Who Would True Valour See' is all about danger and giants and hobgoblins. It's Tamsin's favourite, too, because she thinks it's about hobbits. Then there are some prayers and a reminder about coming to The Shack and it's time for the final hymn, which is what May used to call 'a big screen belter'. Everyone stands to sing 'Guide Me, O Thou Great Jehovah', and if the rafters were shaken during the first hymn, this one nearly raises the roof. Afterwards they file out after the coffin, and Andy loads Emily, Tristram and Julia into his car to follow the hearse to the crematorium.

By the time they get back from the simple committal with just the four of them and the minister, the party at The Shack is in full swing. A cheer goes up as they walk in, and champagne glasses are thrust into their hands. Andy grins down at Emily. 'I might have to leave my car here. How do you feel about a walk back along the beach?'

'In these shoes?' She indicates her spindly heels and giggles. 'I'll take my tights off and go barefoot. Julia can get a lift with one of her buddies. No problem, this is a day for bubbly and gin.'

They stick together for a little while as Julia plunges into the crowd to greet old friends.

'It's so good to see Gran feeling sociable again,' says

Emily. 'I was beginning to think she'd had the best of her life and this last part wasn't going to be any fun at all.'

The pasties and mash come out soon after this, and everyone jostles for places at the tables. Some are left standing, trying to manage a glass, plate, fork and so on. Tristram can't have expected this many people to arrive, but the combination of flowing booze, great food and the genuine desire to pay tribute to Pengelly's oldest resident has filled The Shack to bursting point.

The party rolls on, gaining momentum as it goes. Andy spends a lot of his time trying to avoid Candice. She's wearing a dress that doesn't leave much to the imagination, as May would have said. Her eyes seem to be on him wherever he goes, and several times she nearly manages to squeeze in next to him at one or other of the tables, but he keeps on the move. He decides to slide off after a couple of hours so Vi can go home, remembering just in time that he'd promised to take a food parcel home for Tamsin and her faithful minder. He's lost sight of Emily, but when he goes to search for leftover pasties, he finds her sitting on a worktop in the kitchen chatting nineteen to the dozen with Gina.

'Is it OK if I make a doggy bag for Tam and Vi?' Andy asks Gina.

'Of course. Here, let me do it. What do they like?'

'Anything and everything. Are you ready to go, Emily?' Andy asks. 'I don't mind if you want to stay but Vi's going to be ready for a break by now.'

'Oh, stay a bit longer, Em,' says Gina. 'We've got things

to talk about. Vince will get you a cab home with your gran later. She's having way too much fun to tear her away yet.'

They look across and see Julia, nose to nose with Tristram, arguing about some long-ago detail involving who married whom in 1973.

'I'll hang on here, Andy, if you don't mind? I want to make sure she gets home safely. I'll see you tomorrow?'

Just as Emily says this, Candice rushes up. 'Are you going, sweetie? Can I have a lift? I've got to pick up Summer.'

Andy can feel the frost in Emily's gaze as she looks Candice up and down from the lofty height of her worktop. 'What a shame – he isn't driving,' she says, 'and you don't look as if you're dressed for a hike along the beach.'

Candice looks down at her strappy gold stilettos, which are even higher than Emily's. 'Oh, that's no problem,' she says, swaying slightly. 'I'm always happier barefoot. Come on, Andy, it'll be like old times.' She looks up at Emily. 'We used to play on the beach when we were kids, didn't we, sweetie? *And* when we were teenagers, come to think of it.' She snorts. Andy flinches.

Candice kicks off her shoes, picks them up and links arms with Andy. 'Right, I'm ready. We poor, hard-done-to parents have got to stick together, haven't we?'

Andy makes a non-committal noise, knowing Emily's icy glare is on him now. How is he going to wriggle out of this one?

'Our days of drinking all afternoon and into the night have long gone, haven't they, hun? Don't worry, though,

I've got a nice chilled bottle of prosecco waiting in my fridge – you can collect Tam and bring her over to mine,' says Candice, knocking another nail into Andy's fragile new relationship with Emily. 'The night is young, as they say. She can have a sleepover, like last time.'

She giggles again and puts her hand over her mouth as if suddenly realising she's said too much.

Emily jumps down from the worktop and makes to leave the room. 'Well, don't let me delay you,' she says. 'It sounds like you two have got a whole lot to catch up on. But I wouldn't hold your breath if you're waiting for a happy ending, Candice. Women like you were created to keep divorce lawyers in business.'

She stalks out of the kitchen. Gina follows, shooting a look at Andy that clearly says, *You haven't heard the last of this, mate.*

'Oh dear. Did I say something wrong?' Candice is all big worried eyes now.

'You know exactly what you did there, don't you? Look, if you need a lift home, here's a tenner for a taxi.' Andy gets out his wallet and throws a note at her. 'I'm off.'

He picks up his food parcel, which Gina has put in a cloth bag, slings it over his shoulder, and leaves as fast as he can, without even saying goodbye to Tristram. Emily's got her back to him, and she's talking animatedly to one of Vince's friends from up north. As he trudges back along the shore, Andy's heart is heavy. To have so nearly found his perfect woman and then have her snatched away from him, all because of one stupid night when he'd let his guard down? He can't let that happen.

But Emily's so on edge, after all that's happened to her lately. How is he ever going to win her back now?

The tide's coming in now and it's starting to rain again. Andy puts his hands in his pockets and speeds up. He'll get Tamsin to bed as early as possible, and then he can make a plan. It'd better be a good one, that's all, or the lovely warm feelings that have been growing between him and Emily will be over before they've even begun.

He's stomping along so forcefully that at first he doesn't hear Emily shouting his name, but as soon as he realises she's tearing after him, Andy turns, amazed. There she is, hair streaming behind her, carrying her shoes and almost breathless in her haste to reach him.

Instinctively, Andy opens his arms and she runs into them, wrapping herself around him and hugging him tightly. For a moment they stand quite still, as Emily's heartbeat slows to nearer normal and Andy's speeds up to match it.

'I'm sorry for being so grumpy,' says Emily, eventually. 'I had a sort of epiphany in there. It was as if I heard May telling me to stop being such a baby and take action. So I did.'

'You did what?' Andy still can't quite believe she's here.

'I went and got a fresh glass of red wine – the biggest one I could find – and then I threw it all over Candice.'

'You *didn't*?'

'I did. I feel a lot better now.'

They're both laughing so much that it's almost impossible for Andy to kiss her, but he manages it at last.

Some while later, when they can breathe again, they

link hands and begin to walk home. Whose home it will be isn't clear yet, but Andy finds he really doesn't care, just as long as Emily carries on holding his hand and smiling that smile at him.

# Chapter Forty-Six

Tristram and Julia sit on the porch swing watching the tide come in. Most of the funeral guests have gone home, and the last few are in the kitchen helping Gina and Vince with the tidying up. Julia's been flagging for a while, but a cup of coffee and a brandy are doing a lot to put the life back into her tired bones. Getting old isn't much fun on the whole, she thinks. Julia wants to feel the urge to go for a paddle, or dance till dawn, or even try skinny dipping. Instead, she leans back on the soft cushions and lets the brandy warm her.

'You look so beautiful, and I've hardly seen you today,' says Tristram, taking the hand that isn't clutching the brandy balloon glass. 'What a waste.'

'Well, you *have* been rather busy. What a wonderful goodbye you organised for May.'

'It's been nearly as good as the eightieth birthday bash. Talking of which, when I came in to my party that night, was my surprised look convincing enough?'

She laughs softly, squeezing his hand. 'It didn't fool me, but I think you got away with it. How did you guess?'

'I intercepted a phone call from one of our suppliers trying to arrange a delivery of champagne. Gina said it must have been a mistake but then I started to look for clues and I twigged what they were planning. Very sweet of them.'

'And nice of you to pretend you didn't know about it.'

'But you didn't fall for my act. You know me too well, don't you?'

Julia leans against his shoulder and wonders where this is heading. Is she ready for Tristram to take them on to the next logical step? There's nothing either logical or sensible about the way she feels tonight, though. The light breeze is faintly warm. It's been a sad day in many ways, as goodbyes always are, but Tristram has made May's funeral a joyous celebration of her life. He's a very special man, that's for sure. Julia's heart is racing now. What would Don say about all this? She changes the subject, playing for time.

'Are you going to tell me what you were talking to Emily about at your party now? I've been waiting patiently to find out. Come on, let's have it.'

'Ah. I wanted to run something past her.'

'Oh?'

'She'll tell you all about my plans tomorrow, I'm sure, but in a nutshell, I asked her to think about the future. I couldn't let on she was going to get May's cottage at that stage but I asked her if she'd consider joining me in my new project. I want to open a retreat.'

'You're kidding. Not some sort of bean sprouts and alfalfa place like that one up the coast?'

'No, my idea is more about starting something in May's honour.'

'I'm not with you.' Julia's exhausted mind is struggling with this. Why can't he just spell it out? She's too tired for guessing games.

'I asked Emily if she'd think about helping me set up a place where people who're suffering from short-term memory loss, or early-onset dementia and suchlike can come to get some peace. With a companion – someone who needs help learning how to help and to cope. I haven't really thought it all through yet; it's early days. I kind of hoped you'd help with the fine tuning.'

Julia lets this idea wash over her. She lets her mind drift back in time to all the occasions when she's been at the same functions as May over the years, sometimes circling each other like wary animals ready to pounce, but more often just ignoring each other. What a stupid waste of time and friendship. She remembers one occasion where an elderly gentleman from the sheltered housing in the next village was visiting Pengelly and was brought to a church social by his daughter. She plonked him down next to May, who was organising a tombola with her usual efficiency, and after a few moments, Julia noticed that as May was folding up tickets with the vital numbers on for the prize draw, the old man was taking them out and unwrapping them, dropping them on the floor with glee.

Julia was about to intervene, fearing an explosion of rage from May, when the older woman spotted what was going on and started to chuckle. She took the man gently by the elbow and led him away to find somewhere he could be more usefully occupied, finally finding him a bowl of soapy water to wash his hands and settling him in a corner with a blunt knife to butter some cobs.

May noticed Julia watching her as she returned to start her job all over again. 'What are *you* looking at?' she asked, rather sharply.

Julia felt wrong-footed and, trying to show sympathy for the muddle, muttered something about the old man being a nuisance, which wasn't what she meant to say at all. May frowned at her.

'It's good for the chap to have some company for a change,' she said. 'His daughter says he hardly sees a soul unless she visits. I don't mind a bit of mess. The old boy's a bit confused. It'll come to us all, I shouldn't wonder.'

May turned back to her task, effectively shutting Julia out when she was on the point of offering to help. Just one more occasion when they missed being friends.

She ponders on Tristram's plan. It's a good one, and worthy of May. But Julia is eighty-five. How long can she rely on her own grey matter?

'This is a subject very close to my heart at the moment,' she says slowly, wondering how much to divulge without scaring Tristram away. 'I've really been struggling since Don died; getting so forgetful it's quite terrified me at times. I . . . I could get much worse and end up needing help myself.'

'Let's hope it won't come to that, but if it does, we'll face it together. I've thought a lot about the effects of dementia, too. Both my dad and my grandmother ended up like that. I know it isn't genetic but I worry it'll get me one day.'

'Not necessarily, as you say.'

'But I feel very strongly that sometimes something can be done when the first signs are noticed, not when it's too late. Emily feels the same.'

'Because of me?'

'Probably. But it doesn't matter why. It turns out she's as passionate as I am about the whole project. We can make a difference. Not to many people, granted, but in our small way we'll be contributing.'

'It's a beautiful idea. I'll help all I can, Tris.'

He smiles at her. 'I hoped you'd say that. Of course, now the cottage might be available, I can move more quickly. It's the perfect place for a retreat.'

Julia frowns. 'But surely, Emily will want to live in it. Unless you're assuming she'll stay with me, and I don't see that as her plan somehow.'

'Well, it's not going to happen for a while. If she agrees, we can convert the loft as a flat for her anyway. And if everything goes as I expect it to with Andy, she'll move in with him and Tamsin at some point.'

Julia considers this. 'You're being a bit premature, aren't you?'

'This is a long-term scheme. If she does go to live with Andy, then the whole cottage will be vacant. If not, she could still live upstairs.'

'Are you saying you offered to buy 59 Memory Lane at some unknown time in the future?'

'Yes, sort of, but not just buy it – more like buy *into* it.'

'Well, you've left me a bit breathless and I'm not sure

if Emily will want to be pushed upstairs to live above the shop, as it were, but I've got to say it all sounds rather marvellous, Tris.'

'You're a darling. I talked to May about us, too, you know, not long before she died,' Tristram says, taking Julia's hand.

To her it feels comforting, and yet exciting at the same time. Hold on, girl, she tells herself, if you don't calm down, you'll not live to see the night out, let alone join in his schemes.

'Did you? What about us?'

'I told her I wasn't a very good bet when it came to women, but that I'd fallen for you in a big way and I wanted to end my days with you.'

'Not immediately, I hope?' Julia isn't ready to talk seriously about death.

'No. We've still got quite a bit of living to do, haven't we? I just wish I'd met you sooner.'

Julia thinks about the prospect of a future alone. To be with Tristram would be so much better, but she doesn't want him to think she's just using him to fill the gap that Don left. This man is far too good for that. The dreams Tristram has woven for them both whirl round in her head.

'If only we had more time together, my love,' Tristram says.

Julia reaches for his other hand and turns to look at him. 'It's not how much time you have, but what you do with it that matters,' she says. 'I learned that from May. I think she made every day count, don't you? And that's what we'll do.'

He smiles at her, and Julia's heart feels as if it might burst, even though the pang of grief at the thought of never seeing May again or being able to tell her about this moment with Tristram is leaving her breathless.

'I'd like to go down on one knee but I fear I might never get up. My legs are still a bit creaky after all that jiving I did at my party,' Tristram says. 'Julia, will you marry me? Please say yes. If you don't, I'll carry on asking you every day of my life until you give in.'

She laughs, and the pain of loss recedes for the moment as she gets to her feet, pulling him up with her. 'Then, let's save ourselves some time by getting engaged right now.'

Tristram starts to dance one of his famous jigs, creaky legs forgotten. 'Can I have that in writing?' he cries, reaching for the nearest paper to hand, which happens to be a party napkin. 'Have you got a pen?'

Julia shakes her head, giggling. 'Don't be silly, Tristram.'

'No, hang on. I've got the one May gave me. Charles's stupid swanky fountain pen. Here, open the box. It still works; I filled it with fresh ink.'

He leans on a nearby table and begins to write but the ink soaks straight into the napkin as if it were blotting paper. Julia examines the pen's case while she waits for him to calm down. The satin lining has started to come away at one side and she presses her thumb down on it, feeling a lump. She pushes her finger inside with mounting curiosity.

'Tristram, I think there's something in here,' she says, wriggling out a small tissue-wrapped package.

They stare at each other.

'Open it for me,' Julia whispers.

Tristram takes the tiny parcel and carefully removes the paper. There, shining in the glow from the fairy lights, is a beautiful ring. The opals gleam with all the colours of the rainbow and the diamonds twinkle in their ornate filigree setting.

Wordlessly, Tristram reached forward and slides the ring onto the third finger of Julia's left hand. It's a perfect fit, as she's always known it would be. She's shaking now, tears running down her cheeks.

'I can't even begin to explain how this wonderful treasure got in there. We'll work it out later. But for now, I'll marry you on one condition, Tris.'

'And that is?'

'Dance with me. It's a slow one, so your knees are quite safe.'

Soft music drifts from the restaurant as Tristram takes Julia in his arms for the very first time. They sway together in the moonlight as the tide flows in, the ring sparkles and the world carries on turning.

The method of making blackberry vinegar is so familiar that there's no need to open the recipe book. The proportions are easy to remember. A pound of ripe fruit to the same of sugar and a pint of vinegar. The big jam kettle is ready and the glass bottles are sterilised and lined up on the kitchen table, gleaming in the September sunshine. This year there's been a bumper crop in the sheltered spot at the bottom of the garden.

The blackberries are even plumper and juicier than usual. They've already been crushed, and then soaked in vinegar for five days. The smell is mouth-watering. Now it's time to boil the strained juice. After that there's just one small addition to be made.

Grinding up the sleeping tablets is a job that needs to be done carefully. None of the precious powder must be wasted and it must only be poured into four of the bottles. That should be enough to last Charles for quite a while. The labels have his name on. This always pleases him. Simple things.

When his asthma is really acute, Charles tends to use what he calls his elixir more quickly and it can make him a bit dopey, but with care, the scheme works well. It means that May can have a good night's sleep more often than not, without the need to worry about where her errant and somewhat dissolute husband is spending his night-time hours. The young men of the surrounding area are safe for a little while, too.

Finally, the vinegar is ready and the bottles can be sealed. All May needs to do now is to remind Charles not to drink the stuff before driving, and, of course, never to take it on the boat with him. The amount of rum he drinks when he's on board wouldn't mix well with the harmless sleeping tablets. That could be a recipe for disaster.

# Book Club Questions

- What would you do if you found you were distantly related to May Rosevere and suspected you had inherited her memory-harvesting powers?

- Was Julia right to throw herself into a new relationship so soon after Don's death?

- What difficulties might Emily experience in the next chapter of her life in Pengelly?

- Is May wrong to steal the memories of her friends and neighbours? Does the end justify the means?

- Is the loneliness of the older generation more of a problem in rural communities than towns/cities? Irrespective of this, how can it be tackled?

- If May was to visit your home, what would be the most promising source of memories she could plunder, and why?

- Is there more to Will's continued absence than meets the eye?

- How important was May's relationship with Charles, and would she have developed into a different character without it? Does the book's final chapter change the way you view their marriage?

- How important is it to hold on to our precious memories? Does the sort of memory loss that often comes with advanced age have to be a major problem?

- What is your own most treasured memory? What would you do if someone tried to 'harvest' it?

# A Q&A with
# Celia Anderson

---

**What was your inspiration for 59 Memory Lane?**

In the beginning when the idea for the book was just a small spark inside a bag of letters, I wanted to show that age is no barrier to adventures, and new love can sneak (or sometimes burst) into our lives at any time with no threat to the old. My family have a history of long, largely contented partnerships and it wasn't until my first husband David died suddenly that I had to face the fact that my own marriage wasn't going to get past the silver wedding mark. Everything changed at that time and I gradually developed a different way of prioritising which memories to hang on to and which to let go gracefully. This book began on what would have been David's 59th birthday, hence the title, and I was supported every step along the way by Ray, who had also suffered great loss and knew the score. The old memories merged with the new.

As for the letters, my aunt and uncle, Norman and Sheila (the original Don and Julia) moved to Cornwall at the end of WW2 and lived happily in a village near Falmouth all their own married life. After their deaths, when the amazing cache of memories they'd left behind was discovered, I began to wonder what secret powers and echoes might be waiting within those faded envelopes. Soon, May, Tamsin, Andy, Tristram and Emily popped into my head fully formed.

I also knew of a local lady who had lived a fine and active life until her death at one hundred and eleven, although I couldn't remember ever hearing her first name mentioned. It was only when I asked her daughter a few research questions when the book was well underway and the characters' names were already set in stone in my head that I found the lady in question was called Elsie May. I remember my mum telling me about this sparky person who, when her daughter Beryl worried that she was getting a bit too old to make her own mince pies at well over a hundred years old, said crossly that if Beryl wouldn't go out and buy the ingredients for her, she'd find someone else who would! That's what my May would have said too, I'm quite sure.

59 Memory Lane is a patchwork quilt of a book, with some truth and a whole heap fiction combined. We all miss Norman and Sheila very much – they were our family's shining stars; witty, good-looking and full of fun. There's a special magic about their part of Cornwall that only really happens for me out of season, so I'm aiming to spend more time there in the colder weather over the next few years. It's a great place to make stories happen.

**Have you always wanted to be a writer?**

It's been my dream from when I was a small child, writing stories and terrible doggerel, and when I won a fountain pen in a poetry competition for submitting a poem about a pet, my happiness was complete. Here's an extract:

*I have a little budgie, his name is Perkie-Joe*
*And when I go to talk to him he waggles to and fro.*
*He is so green and yellow with a bit of indigo,*
*And when it comes to night-time, to dreamland he will go.*

You can really see the potential for a career in literature…you can, can't you? I mean, be honest here.

**How do you find time to write? And where do you write when you do?**

I made the decision to retire early from my job as assistant head teacher in a primary school after years of teaching in KS2, so now my time is mostly my own. I loved working with the children, especially on their stories and plays, but it's total bliss to be able to get up very early in the morning and write whenever I like. I'm a big fan of afternoon naps, so on writing days I'm usually busy on the computer all morning and then come back to it for a couple of hours before dinner. I've inherited my dad's beautiful old desk but writing at the big table in the conservatory means I can spread out more (and also stare vacantly at the swans and ducks on the pond behind our house, pretending I'm thinking about the book).

**What would you like readers to take away from May's story?**

It would be wonderful if readers felt as if they knew May and the others so well by the end of the book that they wanted to know what happens next in Pengelly, because I'm dying to write a sequel!

**Who are your favourite authors and have they influenced your writing in any way?**

As a child I loved the imaginary world of C.S Lewis, and still do. Other firm favourites were Laura Ingalls Wilder (*Little House on the Prairie* etc) and Lucy M. Boston (*The Children of Green Knowe* series). The writer who influenced me most in writing about younger characters was an American author called Elizabeth Enright. Her series about the Melandy children was hugely inspiring and my set of her books are falling apart; Spiderweb For Two is the perfect children's mystery.

Mary Wesley, Rosamund Pilcher, D.E. Stevenson, Miss Read, Ruth Hogan and Elizabeth Goudge are all incredibly inspiring in the way they create a cast of characters who live on long after the book ends. Philip Pullman, Elizabeth George, Alexander McCall Smith (the Edinburgh books), Douglas Adams, Terry Pratchett and Nikki French are more favourites, and I'm enjoying the Robert Galbraith *Strike* series. I'm a hobbit fan too, still a little bit in love with Bilbo and his hairy toes.

Since joining the Romantic Novelists' Association, I've discovered a whole host of fabulous authors of romantic fiction and it's been wonderful to get to know many of them in person – too numerous to mention by name and especially my supportive and very funny Romaniac sisters. All the writers I've met in this way are so generous in the way they give their time to talk to less experienced writers and pass on helpful advice. They also understand the importance of cake.

**If a movie was made of your novel, who would you cast as your leading characters and why?**

The only easy answer to this question is that the two dogs would play themselves. Although they live in Brighton and Shropshire respectively, Buster and Bruno would probably be delighted to star for the price of a few decent bones. Otherwise, I have no idea, other than to grovel to Dame Judi or Maggie, preferably both.

**If you could run away to a paradise island, what or who would you take with you and why?**

I would be useless without my lovely family – husband, daughters and their blokes. Apart from them, I'd need the best cooking facilities a paradise island could offer, a laptop and internet access, lots and lots of food and wine and an endless supply of books. I'm not really paradise island material though – I get bored lying on a beach these days and my bikini body wouldn't pass muster unless swathed in yards of sarong. Oh, and I'd miss the rest of the family and my friends, so maybe they could tag along? And can I take my cat, Arthur?

## To hear more about 59 Memory Lane, follow Celia:

 @CeliaAnderson1

/CeliaJAndersonAuthor

# Recipe:
# Spicy Fish Pie

The two fish restaurants in Pengelly, Cockleshell Bay and Tristram's Shellfish Shack both have their own recipes for fish pie but sadly, neither will give their secrets away. This is Julia's own version, perfected over the years.

**Ingredients:** (Rough quantities to serve 4, can be adjusted to taste, and to size of appetites involved)

- 4 chunky salmon steaks
- A pack of large cooked prawns (250g, or more if you love them desperately)
- 4-6 parsnips, depending on size.
- 4-6 potatoes, ditto
- 1 tbsp cornflour
- 1 large cooking onion, finely chopped
- 1 400ml tin coconut milk (the lighter version works just as well)
- Chopped fresh coriander
- Curry powder of your choice, to taste (approx. 2 heaped teaspoons)
- 1 teaspoon Marigold Bouillon (optional)
- Lots of butter if you're not being sensible, less is OK if necessary
- Milk
- Salt & black pepper to taste

## Method:

1) Peel the potatoes and parsnips and put them on to boil.

2) Fry the salmon steaks on all sides in butter until not quite cooked through (or use Frylight spray if you want to keep the dish on the healthier side of lard-filled.) Take the skin off to give to the cat/dog/passing seagull and break the fish into large chunks, then scatter it into a deepish lasagne-type dish. Add the prawns.

   Note: *If you have bought plenty of prawns, you will probably eat a few at this point to go with the hefty slug of chilled white wine the cook should always have at their elbow.*

3) Mash the potatoes and parsnips with as much butter as you like and a dash of milk. Season as required.

4) Cook the chopped onion in butter until soft (or in something less indulgent if you must). Add the coconut milk, bouillon powder if used and curry powder. Simmer for ten minutes or so. Thicken with cornflour in a little milk. Pour this sauce over the salmon and prawns and sprinkle most of the chopped coriander over the top, saving some for a garnish if you remember.

5) Spread the mashed vegetables over the fishy mixture and smooth with a fork.

6) Cook for 20-30 mins in a hot oven until brown; about 180 in a fan, but you know your own oven.

7) Garnish with coriander and serve with lemon wedges to squeeze and a selection of vegetables. And more chilled white wine, obviously.

# Acknowledgements

Norman and Sheila Poynton, my charismatic aunt and uncle in Cornwall, were the inspiration for this book (and the real-life Don and Julia). They kept every letter written to them post-war and when they died, part of this treasure trove came my way. My mum and her siblings in the Midlands loved to write letters. Their lively correspondence sparked an idea that refused to go away, and so May Rosevere was born. This couldn't have happened without my beloved cousins: Jill, who was incredibly generous with her parents' precious memories, and Rosemary and David who shared our family's gossip and secrets. The extracts you've read are mainly fiction . . . but not all . . .

Another powerful catalyst was Ruth Hogan's amazing book *The Keeper of Lost Things*, which led me to meet my wonderful agent Laura Macdougall. That sentence doesn't in any way paint a picture of the cork-popping and joyful dancing that followed when Laura offered to represent me.

Working with Charlotte Ledger has also been a delight. Huge thanks to Charlotte and the team at HarperFiction for all their support, editing and advice as *59 Memory Lane* took shape and got ready to leave the nest.

Writing friends are priceless, and mine are all sparklers – The Romaniac girls; Catherine, Debbie, Jan, Laura, Lucy, Sue and Vanessa, and also the lovely Amanda James and Christine McPherson put the fun into the sometimes soul-destroying and often exhilarating process of making a book happen. I'm also hugely grateful to my feisty buddy Liz for her loan of the amazing Fighting Cardigan.

Finally, a resounding thank you to all my family and friends who've put up with far too much description of the world of Pengelly already, but especially to Laura, Hannah and Ray who provide the gin, cake and, best of all, the love.